WOLF BOY

EVAN KUHLMAN

A NOVEL

Illustrations by
BRENDON AND BRIAN FRAIM

Three Rivers Press
NEW YORK

This is a work of fiction. Names, characters, places, and incidents either are the product of the author's imagination or are used fictitiously. Any resemblance to actual persons, living or dead, events, or locales is entirely coincidental.

Illustrations by Brendon and Brian Fraim

Published in the United States by Three Rivers Press, an imprint of the Crown Publishing Group, a division of Random House, Inc., New York.
www.crownpublishing.com

Originally published in hardcover in the United States by Shaye Areheart Books, an imprint of the Crown Publishing Group, a division of Random House, Inc., New York, in 2006.

Library of Congress Cataloging-in-Publication Data

Kuhlman, Evan.
Wolf boy: a novel/Evan Kuhlman; illustrations by Brendon and Brian Fraim.—1st ed.
1. Traffic accident victims—Family relationships—Fiction. 2. Comic books, strips, etc.—Authorship—Fiction. 3. Brothers—Death—Fiction. 4. Loss (Psychology)—Fiction. 5. Teenage boys—Fiction. 6. Bereavement—Fiction.
I. Title.
PS3611.U368W65 2006
813'.6—dc22 2005018198

ISBN-13: 978-0-307-33798-6
ISBN-10: 0-307-33798-7

Printed in the United States of America

Design by Lynne Amft

10 9 8 7 6 5 4 3 2 1

First Paperback Edition

To Eric

PROLOGUE

THE PHONE CALL informing them of Francis's death came while Stephen was watching a Godzilla movie on TV and his sister was twirling her baton about ten feet away from him and his mother was in the kitchen making a carrot cake and his father was putzing around in the den, trying to think of something to do.

It was the second Saturday in January, 1993, a day Stephen's father would later describe as "unusually beautiful," but in truth it was a rather typical winter day for southern Illinois, where it would snow for a while, let up, and start snowing again. The sun did pop out here and there, causing the snow in their yard and on the tree branches to glitter, but despite the occasional blast of sunshine the temperature stayed quite chilly, high around fifteen degrees.

If that monstrous day held any beauty, perhaps it was when the family gathered for breakfast, Francis still alive and with them, talking and eating and gesturing and making plans, as the Harrelsons, five then not four, spent their last moments of innocence—at least for Stephen and his sister, who knew almost nothing of death and its apparent lifelong sting.

Breakfast began when Stephen appeared in the dining room, stretched the last molecules of sleep out of his bones, and took his seat next to Crispy, his sister, and across from Francis, his brother. His parents, Helen and Gene, were seated at opposite ends of the table like children who couldn't get along.

Stephen was in the habit of complimenting his mother on her

cooking skills, just to see the smile that would bloom on her face, so the first words he said that morning were, "Something sure smells good."

"It's my new strawberry lip gloss," Crispy said.

"Not you," he said. "You smell like a donkey."

"Dad!" she complained.

"Enough," Gene said.

Stephen spooned a small portion of scrambled eggs onto his plate from an iron skillet. Helen stood up and poured Minute Maid pulp-free orange juice into four glasses and a Tom and Jerry commemorative jelly jar (for Crispy) and distributed the juice around the table. Francis, who often had problems with congestion in the morning, held a paper napkin to his mouth and made sounds like an engine that wouldn't turn over, trying to clear his raw throat. Crispy started humming the song "Good Vibrations" by Marky Mark and the Funky Bunch. She bopped her head and danced in her chair, pretending that she was at least a few years older than ten. Sugar-loving Gene slopped blackberry jam on wheat toast that he had already buttered.

Gene was normally a grump in the morning, so it was smart not to say anything that he might take as an invitation to respond with grunts or with words made mean through exaggerated inflection, such as saying "oh, happy day!" to Helen needing the car. But Francis didn't always play it safe.

"I think it's going to be a good conference," he said, while chopping at his eggs with a spoon. "Dr. Albertson from Berkeley is the keynote lecturer. He's probably the top mycology guy in the country, though Dr. Fisher at Yale might disagree." Later that day, Francis and his fiancée, Jasmine, were driving to Chicago to attend the annual Midwest Mycology Conference at the Sheraton. Francis was one of five undergraduates selected to present a paper to fellow students.

Gene was glaring at the slow-drip coffeemaker, encouraging it to speed up. "Sounds like a barrel of laughs," he said in Francis's direction. Stephen grimaced and momentarily lost his appetite. Why was his father the kind of person you had to put up with instead of a great man?

"Drive carefully," Helen said, reaching for the saltshaker. "Arty's predicting occasional flurries for most of the day." Arty was Arthur Gifford, the Channel 7 meteorologist for the past nineteen years. He was a handsome man with a firm chin and a healthy Nordic glow, and he was Helen's imaginary lover. Helen required a rich fantasy life. Gene stopped paying attention to her sometime during the Iran-Contra hearings.

"I'll probably let Jasmine drive so I can prepare for my presentation," Francis said. "I'm going to be talking about fairy rings—you know, those mushrooms that pop up in our yard every spring. Fascinating little buggers. People once thought the rings were formed by dragons setting their butts on the ground."

Crispy giggled at the word *butts* and spat out a piece of egg. Stephen offered his sister a grossed-out look, then glanced at his brother and watched him sip his orange juice. While he never told Francis this, he believed that his brother was lucky to be so beautiful. Francis had long eyelashes, thin blond hair, and pale blue eyes, the watered-down blue of dyed Easter eggs. His appearance was that of something delicate and unprotected, in the rabbit and kitten class, and should someone or something ever attack Francis his only hope would be to outrun him, her, or it, which he likely could do. When Stephen and his brother used to run together through the neighborhood, Francis training for his high school cross-country meets, it was usually a dead heat or close to it, though Stephen often suspected that his brother would let up at the end so they'd finish neck and neck.

"So what are your plans for today, deadhead?" Francis asked Stephen. "Probe that girlfriend of yours?"

"Mind your language," Gene said, protecting Princess Crispy from the foul words that men sometimes speak.

"We'll probably go sledding later, if she's not grounded again," Stephen said.

"I'm going, too," Crispy said.

"I figured that already," said Stephen, sticking a finger into his mouth and pretending to gag himself.

What didn't happen next: the earth didn't rumble, and the house wasn't suddenly bathed in a purplish, heavenly light. No angels descended, the sun didn't weep, and a flaming golden chariot piloted by Apollo failed to appear at the front door. Even though Francis's life was winding down, none of them heard the ticking clock. So they all just sat there, eating their eggs and drinking their juice, when they should have been smothering Francis with kisses and telling him a thousand sweet things.

EPISODE 1

January

TWENTY MINUTES BEFORE breakfast had started, Stephen opened his eyes for the first time that day, having just cut short a dream where he was swimming though an underwater amusement park and was nearly out of air. He had an arrangement with his unconscious where he would wake up immediately should he run into serious trouble while dreaming. If he started falling from a dream-built skyscraper or was stuck in a pterodactyl's beak, he'd pull the plug, stop the show, and exit the theater.

He sat up in bed, scratched himself in several places, and watched snow fall quietly outside his bedroom window, prettily frosted at its edges. Stephen was usually charged with clearing snow from the stoop, sidewalks, and driveway, so quite likely later that morning he'd be shoveling the zillion snowflakes off the concrete and blacktop into piles that, had it been three or four years earlier, he and Francis would have played King of the Mountain on; but they didn't do that anymore and his brother was going to be gone all weekend anyway. Stephen despised winter and the entire history of human migration northward. Why didn't people stay put in tropical climates, where colorful toucans and hooting monkeys populated the trees, not just stupid robins and humdrum squirrels? Not to mention that the holidays were done and it was only Day Thirteen of the dreaded what's-a-boy-to-do period between the end of the Bears season and the start of the White Sox season. (He didn't much like watching Bulls basketball, where points came too easily, or Black Hawks hockey, where points were almost impossible to get.) Bears, the animals not the football players, were the smart ones, hibernating these months away.

His bedroom was filled with the things he loved. Posters of Sox stars Frank Thomas and Carlton Fisk were taped to his walls, as were pictures cut out of pro wrestling and baseball magazines. Above his bed a model of the space shuttle *Columbia* hung from the ceiling by a string. (The model helped spur his many dreams of space flight, he suspected.) Under his bed were two Teenage Mutant Ninja Turtle action figures, Leonardo and Raphael, which he secretly still played with, a well-thumbed-through 1991 *Sports Illustrated* swimsuit issue, and some long-missing underwear and socks. *The Amazing Spider-Man #372* rested on top of the bedcovers. Stephen was midway through a story where Spider-Man was battling arachnid robots, and even though the robots had the upper hand, surely good would prevail over evil once again and the robots would be destroyed. A school photo of Nicole, Stephen's girlfriend, was wedged between his pillows: he had kissed the picture so often it no longer tasted like chemicals. The bookcase was stuffed with *Mad* magazines and his comic book collection, and books about baseball, UFOs, ghosts, ESP, archaeology, and dinosaurs. On his desk he kept his ancient rocks and geodes, and some of his best baseball and football cards.

He was waiting to be called to breakfast for the third time before he responded, one of the many duties of a lazybones, when the sun found an opening in the clouds and illuminated the falling snowflakes, making them appear feathery and inner-lit. "Good job," he said to the universe. *This is the best we can do in January*, the universe said back.

As he often did when nature was putting on a show for him, Stephen started thinking about God, or at least the god of design. Even though the Bible, from what he knew of it, never spoke of this, Stephen believed that an artistic god existed—maybe not in heaven minding the store but somewhere—who insisted on things like patterns for each snowflake, despite the fact that plain old flaked ice would be simpler and more efficient. This same god drew unneeded yet dazzling designs on butterfly wings and turtle shells, painted stripes on tigers and zebras, and dabbed freckles on Nicole's face and arms. He went crazy on peacocks, could have done a little more with hippos. As Gene might have put it, God was cutting into his profits with all these bonuses and freebies.

While watching the snow and thinking about its maker, Stephen concluded that the "no two snowflakes are exactly the same" notion was a bunch of baloney, that there were, in fact, only 144 possible designs. To prove his theory he would need to build dozens of snow collection stations and place them across the globe, purchase several cameras fitted with close-up lenses, recruit an international staff of volunteers and make sure they are all hooked up to his computer database . . .

"Stephen, breakfast," his mother yelled up the stairs. "Sleepyheads never go far in life."

Although he was certain that hundreds, perhaps thousands, of sleepyheads had gone far in life, that greats like Einstein and "Shoeless Joe" Jackson spent considerable time dreaming up the formulas or home runs they would someday make happen, Stephen nevertheless kicked off his blanket and quilt, combed his hair with his fingers, wiped his sticky mouth on a pajama sleeve, went to the window and checked out the temporary diamonds piling up in the yard, ran into the bathroom and took a whiz, splashed water on his face and told that handsome boy in the mirror, "You have the heart of a champion," and sprinted downstairs and into the kitchen, joining his family.

THE HOUR BEFORE Francis left home to pick up his fiancée in Carbondale was mindlessly wasted. While Francis packed his overnight bag, Crispy and Stephen fought about which cartoons they would watch on television (Stephen's policy was to claim to like whatever shows Crispy hated), Helen emptied the dishwasher and got started on the dusting, and Gene drove to his furniture shop to make a quick check that his new apprentice, Todd Upshaw, wasn't raiding the cash register or smoking dope in the woodshop, this last offense being what led to the firing of Mel Griffiths, the apprentice before Todd.

Shortly after eleven, Crispy and Stephen were sitting near the TV and watching the *Land of the Lost* kids hide from a stegosaurus (Stephen thought that Holly, one of the lost kids, was a real cutie), when Francis came into the living room and set down his bag and squeezed Stephen's shoulder bones. Stephen smiled and peered up at his brother and said, "Bye." Just that single word, nothing poetic or saving. Crispy did a better job in her farewells. She jumped up on Francis, wrapped her arms around his neck, and gave him three pecks on his mouth. Francis carried her all of the way to the front door, Crispy dangling like a necklace, and then she dropped to the floor and scampered back to the television set.

"I'm heading out," Francis said loudly, pulling open the door. Stephen turned and looked at his brother and waved. Francis was always leaving and returning. It was no big deal.

"Say hello to Jasmine for us," said Helen, coming out of the den. "And drive safely." She was holding a feather duster in her right hand so she gave Francis a quick, one-armed hug.

"Will do. See everyone Monday," Francis said. He slung the strap of his bag onto his shoulder and left.

OUTSIDE, GENE HAD just returned home and was brushing snow off Francis's car, a maroon 1990 Plymouth. Gene started to reach for his wallet while asking his son if he needed a Jackson or two for snack money or parking fees, but Francis waved him off. "Okay then, have a good time at your mushroom shindig," Gene said. The snow had just stopped falling and a patch of blue sky hung above them. Perhaps that's where beauty showed itself, in the arrival of blueness on an otherwise gray day. Or in the way a chilly breeze moved Francis's hair or how the cold had pinkened his face and made his eyes wet as he stood, alive, just a few feet from his father.

"The conference might be a real ho-hummer," Francis said. "Have you ever been in a room with three hundred mycologists, most of them professors and grad students? I'm hoping to shake things up a little if I don't chicken out."

Gene shrugged. He couldn't imagine driving all the way to Chicago just to spend the weekend with three hundred anything, except maybe leggy supermodels. "You better get going," he said. "May the road rise up to meet you, and all of that happy Irish crap."

Francis smiled, then opened the car door with a gloved hand and tossed his bag in the backseat and slid inside. He wrapped a seat belt around his belly, glanced in the rearview mirror, pulled off his scarf and patted down his hair, started the car, pumped the accelerator, ran the windshield wipers twice, checked the mirror again, and backed down the driveway and headed north on Briarwood, waving spastically and honking the car horn three times.

As Francis and the Plymouth disappeared down the street, Gene waved the snowbrush at him. He had meant to make sure that Francis had his own brush, as well as flares, jumper cables, a bag of sand, a shovel, and a blanket, in case he got caught in a blizzard or had car trouble. But he had forgotten to ask.

Gene will soon think of himself as Francis's last chance. Had he embraced him, or said a few more words, or even tackled Francis and pinned him to the ground for a minute he would have altered fate by delaying his departure. But he failed to act and his boy paid for it. Helen, Crispy, and Stephen will adopt similar beliefs. If they had said or done one little thing Francis might have survived that day. One stupid little thing.

AFTER LUNCH, Stephen put on his coat and boots and grabbed the radio-controlled monster truck he had gotten for Christmas as his big present and ran outside. He set the truck down in the yard and pushed a lever on the control and the truck leapt forward, but soon its wheels were clogged with snow and all it wanted to do was whine and squeal and spin its wheels and not go anywhere. The truck's cries reminded Stephen of his sister, who seemed to have a complaint attached to every exhalation of breath: the ice cream she was eating didn't have enough chocolate chips or the buttons on her new blouse were too slippery. He let go of the lever and set the control in his coat pocket, then started kicking through the few inches of snow in the yard to make a path that the truck might follow, and for the pleasure of disturbing nature's plans for an even dusting, a joy similar to throwing a rock into a puddle or rumpling the covers of a freshly made-up bed. When Stephen stopped his kicking he looked back at the lane of grass. He had just done a good deed, he thought, freeing up some green in very un-green January.

"Shiver me timbers," he said, starting to feel the cold. It was one of Gene's winter lines, while Helen sometimes said, "It's as cold as a witch's disposition." The key to winter survival was to keep busy, Stephen remembered, so he bent and grabbed a glove full of snow and tried to form a snowball out of it, but the ball quickly crumbled. He was planning to make dozens of snowballs and then lure Crispy outside, or, if that failed, to build a snow fort, but it wasn't very good snow for packing (the formula was a little off), and fort-building was likely on that growing list of fun things he was pretty sure thirteen-year-old boys could no longer get away with.

Snow started to fall again, more energetically. He caught several snowflakes on his gloves and examined them before the flakes, under orders to not reveal the secret of limited number of designs, melted themselves. But it was too late: he had definitely seen these patterns before. Stephen peered at the eyeball-white sky and imagined God sitting on a wooden stool in his workshop and joyously cranking blocks of ice through some kind of snowflake maker, one with a rotating design wheel.

The wind picked up and chilled him, and since there was no one to play with Stephen decided to go back inside his warm house. He started trudging to the front door, and when he came upon the radio-controlled truck he walked right by it. In an hour or two his mother or father would see the truck and call him a nincompoop or something worse for leaving his best toy in the front yard, where one of the bad kids in the neighborhood might see it and steal it. Stephen periodically felt the need to remind Helen and Gene that he was part of the family. They'd never own up to it, but his mother clearly favored Francis while his father loved Crispy the most. He hated being the middle child.

Pulling open the front door, that first wave of heated air felt something like love. While he admired those thick-skinned souls who rode dogsleds across the Yukon or who manned science outposts in Antarctica, for now Stephen was happy to live a warm and cozy existence. He slammed the door shut, took off his coat and boots in the foyer, then went into the living room where he sat on the carpet and placed his socked feet against a heater vent, wiggling his toes. His parents were elsewhere in the house, so he wouldn't get busted for being a "heat hog." When his feet were toasty he scooted over to the TV and turned it on and saw that an old Godzilla movie was playing, so he stretched out on the floor and watched the film. In a scene where Japanese citizens were running like crazy to get away from Godzilla, he inserted himself in the movie. He was the little boy wearing a white baseball cap. His name might have been Terry. His hat went flying off, in the path of Godzilla, and for a second Terry thought about going back for his beloved hat, but he decided to keep running. He could get another cap but not another life.

Crispy danced into the living room and started twirling her silver baton. Stephen didn't understand why his parents allowed his sister to twirl the baton indoors since periodically the baton would escape her and bounce off walls, lamps, or his head. He stood up and was about to retreat to the safety of the couch when the phone, a green cordless with oversized numbers on the dial pad, which Gene had bought at the Kmart in Caswell a year earlier despite the fact that Helen had told him to get a beige or white phone so it would go with the wallpaper and carpeting (she also didn't much like the large numbers), chimed. Stephen was the closest to the phone so he answered it.

"Hello," he said, hoping that it was Nicole on the other end. She was a goofy girl, and sometimes she'd phone him and say, "I'm just saying hi," and he'd say hi back, and she'd say, "Okay, bye then," and he'd say bye, and she'd say, "Double bye," and so on, and ten minutes might pass before they became tired of the game and hung up their respective phones.

"Is this the Harrelson residence?" asked a woman's voice. Stephen thought that the caller was a saleswoman for *The Ledger.* Even though they were already subscribers their salespeople kept harassing them.

"Yes it is," he said.

"I'm calling from . . . is your mother or father at home?"

"Hold on." Stephen was about to yell for his dad—his mother hated talking to salespeople, whom she both despised and felt pity for, pity usually winning, so they were always changing long-distance carriers and buying lightbulbs to help support paralyzed veterans—but Gene walked in behind him so Stephen handed him the phone and returned to the living room and plopped down on the couch. Later, he'd wish that he had run upstairs or run away, because he could hear Gene talk to the woman, every awful word, and could see blood and even more important things drain from his father's face.

"This is Gene Harrelson. . . . Yes, I'm his father. . . ." The first sign of trouble. Gene was the father of two male children, and unless someone was phoning to complain that Stephen had been looking up her daughter's skirt or down her blouse, crimes he was likely guilty of, the call was about Francis. He glanced at his dad. Worry was narrowing Gene's eyes and flattening his half-smile of a minute ago.

"What, what are you saying?" Gene asked. "Prescott Memorial? I see. . . ." *Prescott Memorial sounds like a hospital,* Stephen thought. *What would Francis be doing at a hospital? Did Jasmine get sick?* Blood surged in Gene before leaving, reddening his face, and his mouth hung open when he wasn't talking, like he no longer had full control of its hinge.

"A car accident?" Gene said. "Oh shit!" *No no no no no,* Stephen thought. *Francis was in an accident? But he has to be okay, right? He's a safe driver, hardly ever goes fast. But sometimes he does.* Gene's eyes were now glistening, almost pretty, and his chest heaved, like the old man had just run a mile.

"So you're certain?" Gene asked. "Goddamn it! Yeah, well goody for Jasmine's family." *Was Francis badly hurt?* Stephen wondered. *Did he lose an arm? A leg? Not a leg. How will he run?* Gene's flesh was now ashen, almost bluish. He slumped against a wall while holding the phone to his ruined face and started shedding tears. The only other time Stephen had seen his father cry was a summer night a few years earlier when Gene got the news, also by phone, that his father, Marvin, had died suddenly. *But this couldn't mean . . .*

"No, we'll manage," Gene said to the caller. "What can you do from there anyway? But tell me one thing, was he . . . was he dead on arrival or did you, was there time to try . . ." *Dead on arrival.* Those three words tore dozens of holes in Stephen, like a flurry of gunfire. He collapsed onto the couch and felt parts of himself escaping through the many bullet holes. Francis, his smart, handsome, and fun brother, must be dead. But how? He was alive, just hours ago. He ate breakfast, smiled, touched Stephen's shoulders, said good-bye. *No. Please God. No.*

Gene was standing more upright now, though a tremble betrayed his new vigor, and it appeared that something other than blood was holding him up: his flesh was still lifeless. He hung up the phone, wiped his damp face with a shirtsleeve, and glanced at Stephen. It was a cold look that reached all the way to Stephen's bones, a look that said *how dare you still be alive when Francis isn't.* Gene took two steps toward the living room, then started to sink again. He backtracked and leaned into the wall and strained to recover a workable breathing pattern, then put a hand over his mouth. From behind that insufficient shield he said, "What the fuck? What the holy fuck?" Stephen was waiting for his father to then say terrible things to Crispy and him, but instead Gene turned and began a slow death row march toward the kitchen, hunched and pained like he was dragging a car behind him. "Helen, you in there?" Gene said, as he moved from the foyer and into the hallway that led to the kitchen. "I have some bad news." Helen had just put a carrot cake in the oven and was about to start on the frosting (the secret is to add a half cup of orange juice to the cream cheese base). Saturday dinners always featured a homemade dessert.

In the living room, Stephen glared at the television set. Godzilla was still on the rampage and was now hungrily eying the contents of a passenger train car. "Stop it," he said to the beast, but Godzilla paid him no mind, smashing the train car and continuing his destruction of Tokyo. Stephen then looked at his sister. No bullet holes in her yet. Crispy was twirling her baton, tapping a foot against the carpet, and singing a Whitney Houston song, "I Will Always Love You," making up her own words when she didn't know the real ones. She had sprinkled silver glitter on her face and in her hair and was wearing blue leggings and a bright red ruffled and spangled blouse, an outfit that a famous baton twirler might wear.

"Crisp," Stephen said, barely.

"Shut your trap, this is my favorite spot," she said, spinning the baton and seeming surprised that it stayed in her hand. But then she gazed at her brother and dropped the baton. It bounced one, two, three times and then settled on the floor near the fake fireplace. "What's up?" she asked.

"It's Francis," he said, firing the gun.

STEPHEN BOLTED UPSTAIRS to the bedroom he had once shared with Francis, and fell to his knees like those needing a big favor from God are supposed to do. He pressed his hands together in the proper way and cried ten thousand urgent prayers: "Oh God please save Francis, you have the power, please heal him fix him don't let him be dead, please God please raise him up and send him back to us you can undo all of this please please please I'll do anything you want, oh please take someone stupid and mean instead, please oh God don't let this be true, we need him here on earth, please God I will do anything, oh God please this is the last thing I will ever ask of you oh please God, please God don't let Francis be dead. Just send him back and I'll be good forever."

Prayer was the only possible remedy for something this big, but it didn't appear to be working: no second phone call came, saying it had all been a terrible mistake. It was understandable that God might not listen to Stephen's pleas that the White Sox win the World Series this year or for sudden wealth and two inches more height, but asking that he return his brother to him was the biggest prayer he would ever pray. The call should have gone straight through. Or perhaps God did respond by placing a holy hand on Stephen's skull and knocking him out for several hours.

Francis and Stephen are fishing at Shepherd's Lake. They sit on an old wooden dock, their legs dangling over the side and their fishing rods held outward, the lines cast into gray, still water. Francis is wearing black pants and dress shoes, and the collar of his white shirt is turned up like he's a tough guy. There are no clouds in the sky, but strangely it doesn't hurt Stephen's eyes to look at the sun. Perhaps he's wearing sunglasses, he's not sure.

Francis's line is tugged and he starts to reel in a fish. "Bet it's a beaut," he says, cranking the reel. This seems to take forever. Colors even arise for a minute, the sky and lake bursting blue and Francis's flesh turning pink before going white again. Finally, the fish is pulled out of the water, jerking and trying to break free. Francis grabs the line and lets the hooked fish fall to the dock where it continues its desperate flopping.

"Throw it back," Stephen says. "We aren't going to eat it."

"I just like watching it struggle," Francis says. "Hard to imagine, not belonging in this world of oxygen."

Francis takes hold of the fish, twists the hook free, and says, "Don't worry, he can't feel any pain," but blood begins spurting from the fish's mouth, gallons and gallons of it, splashing onto the dock and spilling into the water and making it a darker gray. Francis tells the fish to steer clear of worms on hooks from now on and drops it into the lake. The fish swims away, and when Stephen loses sight of it he turns toward his brother but Francis is gone. He sets down his fishing pole and stands up and peers back at the shore but doesn't see his brother anywhere. The dock, originally about ten feet long, is now at least fifty feet in length, and there are gaps in it, missing planks that have to be jumped over.

His fishing rod goes flying into the lake and skims atop the water. A really big fish, a marlin maybe, must have bitten down on the hook. But it's not a fish speeding away, it's Francis, more being tugged than swimming. "Hey, come back here," Stephen says, wanting both his brother and his fishing pole back.

Before he can dive into the water and swim after Francis the tide goes out, leaving behind a bed of sand littered with football helmets, broken bicycles, lumbering crabs, and strange luminous rocks that shoot silver light. Stephen jumps onto the sand, grabs one of the rocks, and feels around for a battery compartment but there aren't any seams. Where's its power source? The rock's light is almost too much so he closes his eyes.

In his bedroom Stephen opened his eyes. It was dark outside, meaning that he had been asleep for hours, maybe days. The house was quiet. Why had no one called for him? Come for him? His eyes and lungs ached from all of the crying he had done. A record cry, possibly, but he didn't want to call the people at *Guinness Book of World Records* and tell them about it.

"Francis, come home," Stephen said. Man or ghost, either one. Just come home.

Light from a streetlamp was creeping into his room and making shadows on the walls. Years ago, Francis used to create hand shadows with that light, rabbits mostly, or bugs with wiggly antennae. Or he would make the *doo doo doo doo* something-bad-is-about-to-happen sound from the movie *Jaws*, and soon Unsuspecting Hand, just out for a stroll, would be swallowed up by Shark Hand. Unsuspecting Hand would put up a valiant fight but in time his pinky and thumb would go limp. Shark Hand might then come after Stephen and he'd have to cover his mouth to keep from shrieking.

When Francis moved home from college, Stephen was certain that he would want to share the upstairs bedroom with him again, but it didn't happen. A man has to have his own space, Francis explained, as they carried his stuff to the basement. Stephen said that he understood but he really didn't. How could his brother prefer the basement, where every upstairs toilet flush sounded like a monsoon coming your way, to the funny jokes and fake farts offered in Stephen's bedroom? Those were the best times, when he and Francis lived in the same room and they'd wrestle and play and fall asleep on each other's bed. Even after Francis said that they had to pretend there was an invisible wall between their beds from now on so people wouldn't think they were gay boys, they still had fun. The fake wall wasn't soundproof so Stephen and his brother would talk to each other, sharing secrets, often made up, or tired ghost stories about the many one-armed child killers who lived in the neighborhood.

Fuck the world. If Stephen had owned anything deadlier than a squirt gun he would have shot out the streetlights on Briarwood, every last one of them. "Francis come home," he tried again, louder this time. "Stop screwing around."

It made no sense, Francis dying. While most kids may only think their older brothers are unstoppable, Stephen knew this to be true about Francis. As an infant, Francis swallowed a bottleful of St. Joseph's baby aspirin but survived. Helen must have told that story a hundred times. When he was fifteen, Francis was on a Science Club field trip when the school van lost its brakes and crashed into a mail truck. The van driver and all of the kids suffered broken bones or bad bumps and bruises, except for Francis, who walked away unhurt. And, two summers ago, Francis slipped on the high board at the city pool and hit his head on the board but suffered only a small cut. It was then that Stephen became convinced that his brother had an invisible protective shield around him, like the spaceships on *Star Trek.* Three times Death's dark ship had come for Francis and three times Starfleet forces repelled it. But it came a fourth time.

He stood up and stumbled into the bathroom and peed for what seemed to be a very long time—even emptied the reserve tank. He was all liquid now, tears and piss, and maybe throw-up soon if his stomach didn't settle. Flushing the toilet, he hoped that the rumbles would remind his family that he was upstairs all by himself.

Hearing noises downstairs, Stephen went to the stairwell and sat on the top step. His mother was speaking to a neighbor, Mrs. Borden, and two other women, probably from First Community Church, gathered in the living room.

"This is a terrible tragedy," said one of the churchwomen.

"Yes," said Helen.

"He was so young," said Mrs. Borden.

"Yes," said Helen.

"And so gifted, so full of promise," said a second churchwoman.

"I know," said Helen, her voice cracking.

Stephen hung his head and cried. He had thought he was all out of tears. "Please God, do something," he asked. "This is your last chance."

A minute later he gave God another final chance.

In time the visitors left and the lights were dimmed. Stephen, wanting something simple in his belly like a graham cracker, crept down the steps. Only the chandelier in the foyer was lit, turned low, so he twisted the knob a half turn, adding more light. The house smelled like burnt cake, and he was curious as to whether his parents and sister had eaten dinner. Did Mom make sandwiches? Were such things still possible? There was a tap at the front door so he opened it and saw a chubby man smiling one of those smiles where the edges of the mouth rose but the person didn't look the least bit happy. The man said he was a reporter for *The Ledger* named

Clifford Harper. "I'm sorry to bug you at a time like this but we need a picture of Francis Harrelson for the morning edition," he said.

Stephen wondered if the man was a government agent, disguised as a fat reporter. Francis wasn't really dead, that was just a cover story. His brother was working for the CIA, Mycology Division. *First fake the boy's death, say in a car accident, then hire some fatso to pose as a reporter . . .*

"We've been trying to call all night," Clifford said. "I was about to turn around but then I saw the light come on. So do you think you could get a picture for me? I'm afraid I'm bumping right up against deadline." The reporter reached into an inside jacket pocket, and Stephen expected him to pull out a gun or one of those glowing rocks, but instead it was a writing pad and a pen.

Stephen glanced at the phone and saw that the plug had been yanked from the outlet, then he hustled into the den and found the big box of family photos that Helen had been promising for years to put into albums. He pulled out a snapshot from the previous summer of Francis cheerfully holding a cat-sized mushroom he had picked in a Minnesota woods. He returned to the living room and handed the picture to the reporter.

"This should do it," the man said, examining the photo.

"You can't keep it. We need it back."

"I'll return it within forty-eight hours."

"Cross your heart and hope to die?"

Clifford reluctantly crossed his heart. "Hey, are your parents still awake? I'd like to get a few words from them for the article. A few words about the deceased."

"Just say that he was the best brother in the whole world."

"Sure, but could you please get your mom and dad? I'll only need them for a minute."

"They're dead," Stephen said, closing and locking the door. Through a side window he watched the reporter schlep to his car, a compact that he could barely squeeze into, and drive off. *Why Francis?* Stephen wondered for the hundredth time. Why did Francis have to leave this world while the dumb and (he suspected) smelly reporter was allowed to stay? *Why Francis?*

Still hungry for a graham cracker, Stephen started shuffling to the kitchen when he saw that Crispy was asleep on the couch. He wasn't normally the thoughtful, caring kind of brother, but this day was unlike any other he had ever lived through, so he went to his sister and pulled a wool blanket over her and tucked the sides under the cushions so she'd stay tightly wrapped. There was still glitter in her hair and on her damp face. He kissed her on the cheek and smelled strawberries.

"Francis?" she asked, opening her eyes.

"No, sorry," he said.

He looked at the phone and suddenly remembered that Francis owned a pager, so he dashed over to it and plugged it in and quickly punched in the number followed by 911. "Call back," Stephen begged his brother. The pager buzzed somewhere, at a hospital, or in a smashed car, or alongside a dangerous road, but Francis never called back.

EPISODE 2

The Burial

JASMINE ARRIVED AT the house shortly before the funeral. She had been driving Francis's Plymouth at the time of the accident but came away uninjured. The car had only one air bag and she was its beneficiary. She and Francis were traveling north on Highway 107 in central Illinois when an ice storm hit, glazing the roads and causing the Plymouth to slide into the path of an oncoming pickup truck. The driver of the truck, Michael Haynes, a thirty-one-year-old roofer, wasn't hurt but checked himself into a hospital due to shock.

She stood at the Harrelsons' front door, not sure whether to ring the buzzer, knock, or evaporate. She was leaning toward evaporation. Jasmine had been here just eighteen days earlier for Christmas Eve dinner: turkey, candied yams, mashed potatoes and gravy, green beans with sliced almonds, rolls, cranberry sauce, and a choice of pumpkin or apple pie. She had a sliver of apple. After dinner Francis announced that he and Jasmine were engaged and that the wedding would occur the following summer. Crispy and Stephen were ecstatic, and Helen and Gene seemed pleased to be gaining a daughter-in-law. To celebrate the engagement Gene brought out a bottle of champagne. The adults all got tipsy, especially Gene who sang, "I'm dreaming of a white Crispyness" to his daughter. Crispy giggled. Stephen smiled often at Jasmine and stole glances of her body, but it was harmless so she allowed it. Helen refused her offer of help with the dishes, but later when they found themselves alone in the living room, Helen told her, "I suppose you should call me 'Mom' from now on." "Sure, Mom," Jasmine said, feeling like she was living the right kind of life. She even saw a flash of herself and Francis at age thirty or so, on Christmas Eve, snuggled into each other on a couch and watching their children, two boys and a girl, tear open their many presents. Jasmine wasn't sure if she was ready for motherhood or even wifehood but wanted to give it all a try.

The night ended with Francis holding her on his bed in the cellar. A few kisses but no sex or horseplay, just cuddles and massages. The basement windows were frosted over and she felt safe, sealed inside with her honey boy, a man who loved to touch her not just in erotic ways. Having Francis wrapped around her was as normal as breathing. "I think we are going to have three children," she said, her head on his chest, rising and falling as his lungs moved. Francis said with a laugh, "I'm not sure about even one kid yet." "Because it's a rotten world to bring children into?" she asked. He took a few seconds to think about his answer. "No, it's not a rotten world, not really. I just don't want to be distracted from loving you." Her eyes filled with tears. "Corny, but sweet," she said, thinking that perhaps it wasn't a rotten world they were living in, at least not during Christmastime in southern Illinois in this snow-covered house, her fiancé breathing underneath her.

She wished for a blizzard that night, a nasty one, roads and airports closed, and ten-foot-high drifts. That way, she could cuddle with Francis for another week and spend more time with this imperfect but real family that she'd soon be married into, instead of heading to her parents' house in Naperville in the morning. There was love here, not much of the stuff between Helen and Gene but piles of it among the siblings and a fair amount bouncing between the parents and children. And she'd finally have a brother and sister, like she had always wanted, two younger earthlings to help shepherd through life. But it only snowed lightly in Hollis on Christmas Eve 1992, so the next day, after a cheerful and belly-warming breakfast, Jasmine drove by herself to Naperville.

Now Francis's death had returned her to 1178 Briarwood, Hollis, to the family she will never be a part of. *It can't be so.*

Since willed evaporation wasn't working, Jasmine chose to knock. Stephen opened the door and smiled at her, and she slipped inside and gave him a stuffing-squeezing hug. The beautiful little fucker looked just like Francis. A minute later she hugged Helen and Gene, who stood as statues to her affections, and when she tried to embrace Crispy the girl retreated behind her mother like a shy toddler.

"How was the drive?" Gene asked.

"Awful," Jasmine said. "I've never been so sad."

"I meant the weather," he said.

"Oh. Not bad."

Jasmine smiled at Stephen and he smiled back at her. *I'll take care of you now,* his look was saying to her. If only such a world existed.

GENE WANTED TO drive separately to the cemetery, but the muffler on his shop delivery van was shot, so Jasmine lent him her car, an old gray Honda with a faded bumper sticker that said "A woman needs a man like a fish needs a bicycle." Helen drove the Chevy, and Crispy also sat up front: she called it first. In the backseat, Jasmine and Stephen exchanged sad looks and peered out their respective windows at the bare trees and the fresh dusting of snow that had fallen on the town late morning.

It was a ten-minute ride through the streets of Hollis. When they arrived at the gates of Elmwood Grove cemetery, Stephen thought about a summer day two years ago when he and Francis had ridden their bikes here to hunt for mushrooms in a wooded area at the far end of the grounds. They didn't find any mushrooms and were eventually chased out of the woods by an irritated queen bee, but before leaving the cemetery they read several of the headstones in the old section and a few of the markers in the new section and guessed at the kind of lives the dead people had led before keeling over. One of the dead was a baseball player who never made it to the big leagues due to having no arms—he had to bat with his wiener. A baby who lived only a few days would have been the next Jesus.

Helen parked the Chevy at the end of a long line of cars and they all climbed out. The mortician, one of the Braverman brothers from Braverman's Funeral Chapel in downtown Hollis, walked up and said, "Hello folks, this way," and started leading them to the gravesite. Stephen had a sudden urge to run or to vomit all over Braverman's shiny black shoes but did neither.

They plodded their way past the already buried—a Wilma, a David, a Casper—and then were seated on cold metal folding chairs parallel to the copper and gray casket. The order from west to east was Jasmine, Stephen, Helen, Crispy, and Gene. The arrangement was influenced by Jasmine hanging back like she might not want to go through with it, and Stephen staying no more than a step ahead of her, keeping an eye out for her like his brother would have wanted him to, and by Gene already waiting for them in the east-most seat and Crispy plopping down next to him. About forty mourners, primarily Francis's friends and teachers from college and high school, including most of the Hollis Hurricanes 1991 cross-country team—Francis was their swiftest runner—stood in three lines on the other side of the casket. Aunt Tammy, Helen's sister, was among the mourners, but Uncle Tony and the four dumb-ass boy cousins weren't. It was just another workday or school day for most people, Stephen remembered. His eyes sought out Nicole and when he spotted her she started to sob. *This is going to be a huge mess,* he thought.

Reverend Gladstone from First Community Church stepped out of the crowd and stood in front of the casket. Oddly, Stephen expected him to juggle three tennis balls then pull a rabbit out of a hat. The reverend was wearing his white preaching robe, a wooden cross, and hiking boots. He glanced at the Harrelsons and shook his head like he was quite disappointed at the turn of events, then opened a bible—not the nice one with gold-edged leafing that he used at the church but something smaller and less ornate—to a marked page and started the eulogy. Francis might have wanted something like, "Ladies and germs and children of all ages," but Gladstone played it straight. Stephen couldn't hear all the words, there was a loud swarm-of-bees–like hum inside of him, but he caught the central themes: it's a tragedy when the young perish; God has a plan and wants Francis with him; we can question God's plan but ultimately we have to accept it.

"When we are feeling sad in our hearts about what happened to Francis," the reverend said, "let us take comfort in the fact that we do not have to suffer alone, that God will take on part of the burden."

"He can have all of it," Gene muttered.

As the eulogy continued, Jasmine took hold of Stephen's left hand and rubbed her thumb back and forth against it like she was trying to spark a fire. He gazed at her and watched tears skate down her face. She made no attempt to stop the tears or wipe away their trails. He then turned and looked at his father and sister, but not his mother. Helen was squeezing his right hand so tightly it had lost all feeling, and he knew that her face had to be showing something awful, something that would haunt him for years if he recorded it. Crispy looked like she wanted to tear the world apart. Gene was rapidly tapping his left shoe against the snowy earth, sending some kind of urgent message by Morse code.

Near the end of the services the sun came out from behind a cloud and caused many of the mourners to squint or shield their eyes. The light bouncing off the snow was so bright it stole the edges of things. "A reminder of His presence," Reverend Gladstone said, breaking from his script. *Shoo, go away,* Stephen told the sun with his mind, and a minute later it did.

"Ashes to ashes, dust to dust," said Gladstone. But Francis was not yet ashes or dust, damn it. *Love to love,* Stephen thought, making the correction. The reverend then closed the Bible, bowed his head, and prayed that Francis would find a peace in heaven that may have eluded him while on earth.

After everyone except Reverend Gladstone dropped a red rose on the casket, a hug line was formed. Most of the mourners shook Stephen's hand, though he suffered through a few kisses and face squeezes. Crispy had her arms folded in front of her and was not accepting hugs, handshakes, or kisses, but if someone she was fond of was standing in front of her, like Aunt Tammy, she'd stick out a pinky that the well-wisher was permitted to shake. When Nicole appeared in line, lovely and sad, Stephen couldn't decide whether to hug or kiss her and they ended up bumping noses and shaking hands. One of the last in line was a skinny old guy who said his name was Dr. Morris Cravens, from Southern Illinois University. "Your boy was brilliant, very brilliant," he said, first taking Gene's hand then Helen's. "Our field has suffered a big loss." The professor looked suddenly regretful, then kissed Jasmine on the cheek and shook Stephen's hand, but when he tried to give Crispy a hug she pushed him away.

Stephen and his family and Jasmine were now alone at the gravesite, though Stephen sensed that Braverman was lurking somewhere close by, perhaps behind a tree. Stephen glanced at the casket and concluded that it was far too plain. Francis deserved a customized burial box, one with secret compartments, racing stripes, and an emergency escape hatch. And everyone should have written sentiments on the casket like it was a giant cast. "Good luck in heaven," that kind of thing.

Braverman then materialized, asking Gene if he and the Mrs. would like one last look at Francis before the casket was lowered. "Not for the kids," Braverman said, in a quieter voice. There was no viewing of Francis's body due to his face being mangled in the crash. Helen said a firm "no" but Gene appeared distraught, like he wanted to return to the world of a few days ago when the biggest questions he had to face were whether to start carrying futons at his store, or if he should try some of those fancy lattes that everyone seemed to be enjoying instead of the Maxwell House mud he had been relying on all these years.

"Maybe for a quick second," Gene said, his unsure eyes not in full agreement with his words.

Helen shook her head and led Crispy and Stephen away from the gravesite. "Foolish men make foolish decisions," she said. Jasmine seemed torn by the choice but decided she didn't need a final look. She went to Stephen, elbowed him in the side, and whispered, "We should be getting stinking drunk right about now."

Braverman and Gene lumbered to the casket, then Braverman lifted the lid as thoughtlessly as one might open a freezer. Gene peered inside, and Stephen's biggest hope of all time, that the casket was empty, that Francis was on a secret mission for the government, died. The truth of whatever horror Gene was seeing was written all over his wrecked and ghost-white face and in the way he almost fell, Braverman having to steady him. Gene took a minute to gather himself, then turned and slogged by his family, saying only, "See you back at the ranch," his voice quavering. When he made it to the Honda he started it up and raced the engine, the pistons screaming on his behalf, and then drove away. Stephen wished later that he had ridden home with his father. That must have been the loneliest drive the old man ever took.

"We better get going," Helen said. "People are expecting us."

As they walked to the Chevy Stephen gazed at the sky and saw Francis, in his blue and white Hollis Hurricanes cross-country uniform, swimming between clouds. *There he is!* Stephen almost shouted, but since no one else was looking upward he suspected that he had a privileged view. He scanned the sky for a seam or a rip, some kind of opening that Francis could have slipped through, found none, then watched his brother swim like a turtle by pushing the air aside with his arms and kicking his legs. *Go,* Stephen said, or thought, his locked-down heart opening a little window. Francis took a break at each cloud, somersaulted, and swam to the next cloud. So this is what happens after death, Stephen thought, the sky becomes your swimming pool. *No wonder the sky is blue.* He wished for a jetpack so he could fly to Francis and swim alongside him, but rising on his tiptoes was as close as he could get. Stephen was hoping to watch his brother swim the entire length of the sky, but he was ordered into the car. "This isn't the day for dillydallying," Helen said.

Riding home, Stephen, when not checking the sky for Francis, stared at Jasmine's legs, all but hidden by dark hose. She smiled at him, though her smile was sad. He thought that if he disclosed that he had just seen Francis swimming above the cemetery she might cheer up, as would Crispy, but they could also become upset that they missed seeing Francis for perhaps the last time—who knows where he was swimming to. Plus, his mother would think that Stephen was telling tales, so he decided to lock the secret in a vault inside of himself that held all of the things he could never reveal to anyone—his shoplifting a cassette of Christmas songs from the Kmart in Caswell, seeing a *Penthouse* when he was eleven, his ever-changing thoughts about God—and not say anything about his brother's airborne ghost, which wasn't one of those miserable bawling ghosts you see in movies, but rather a happy spirit and thus appropriate for Francis who mostly walked the earth with a "shit-faced grin" on his face, as Gene might have put it.

DURING THE FIRST HOUR of the reception Stephen stationed himself next to Jasmine on the living room sofa, where he listened to her tell a group of mourners, including a pasty Dr. Cravens, that the crash was really the fault of the patriarchal world and its dangerous ozone layer-destroying automobiles. He stared at her intelligent face as she affirmed that in a more female world people would move in supportive circles instead of down lonely highways. There would be little need for cars, but if they existed they would be very safe.

That sparked within Stephen an image of spongy Nerf cars in pretty pastel colors, full-sized and functional. When the Nerf cars collided they'd gently bounce off each other and all of the passengers would laugh and then continue on their way. He committed himself at that moment to designing sponge cars for a living. There'd be problems to overcome, such as how well they would hold up in the rain, but he'd figure it all out.

"And of course we must also point a finger at Detroit and the oil cartel," Jasmine said. "If they didn't own most of Washington we'd be riding streetcars and trains everywhere. Our Francis is just another victim of their greed."

Professor Cravens appeared unconvinced, but the others nodded or offered "what can you do?" shrugs. Stephen now hated Detroit, and the Tigers and Lions, and the oil cartel, and Washington, and the Redskins, for their part in stealing his brother.

He stood up and wandered into the kitchen for a snack and saw that his father was attempting to tell a gathering of neighbors—Mrs. Borden; Don Alton and his new wife, Carla; the snippy and noise-sensitive Joe Koperdak; and Nicole's mother, Sally—about Francis's demise. It was high drama and no one could turn away. "It started out as an unusually beautiful day for January," Gene began, but then stopped. "It was a beautiful day for this time of year" he tried again. Gene's body began to quake and his face turned red with blood-born urgency. He was sweating into his shirt, and the veins that fed his workman's hands appeared monster-large, as if readying him for a do-or-die task. "It was . . . It was a . . ."

Stephen was stunned that his normally sedate father was attempting to burst through his casing. But Gene fell short. He gave up trying to tell the story and sucked in air while holding on to the stove for support. He wiped his damp face with a pot holder and retreated to his bedroom.

This scene would repeat itself many times over the next months, Gene trying to tell neighbors, customers at his shop, or his family about his firstborn's last day of life. Many were drawn to the performance: see Gene shake and break apart. He could always start the story of Francis's death but he could never finish it.

On his way back to the living room Stephen came upon his sister, standing at the window near the front door. She was in a velvety black dress and her normally all-over-the-place blond hair was held by a white butterfly bow. Crispy's face was more wounded and introspective than he had ever seen, so he briefly thought that he had discovered a different version of Crispy, one from a parallel universe, a sister that he could know and love at a more satisfying level and perhaps have a less-hostile relationship with. She had made an opening in the window blind by separating two of the vinyl strips with her fingers and was peering out at the world. "I want to be where the sky is blue," she said. Stephen tapped his sister on her shoulder and told her to come with him, which she did, and they hunted for Nicole and found her sitting alone in the den and eating a piece of cherry strudel that Mrs. Borden had brought over.

The three children bundled up and went outside and gazed at the sky, and saw that a patch of blue was evident to the south of them, above where Briarwood ended at Groveland, they guessed, so they began marching there. Stephen searched the sky for his brother but Francis was gone, swimming elsewhere. As they neared Groveland it became evident that the opening in the clouds was farther away than they had estimated, or it had moved, and was perhaps another half mile south, but they were tired, and cold, so when they reached Groveland they stopped and peered at the sky and soaked up some of the blueness that kids a half-mile to the south were reveling in, then Crispy said, "Okay." They trekked back home, Stephen's eyes hunting for Francis in vain.

When they arrived at the house, the driveway and the street were still overrun with cars. It appeared that not a single visitor had left the reception yet, even though it had been going on for nearly two hours. "I wish everyone would leave us alone," Crispy said, and Stephen said, "Me, too," and Nicole responded that if she guzzled a soda she could start belching like crazy, a good way to clear a room, but they both said thanks but no thanks.

As Stephen pushed open the door a wave of compressed sorrow hit them, and they no longer were three kids who went to look at a patch of blue sky, but were once again the sad boy who lost his brother and the sad girl who lost her brother and the sad girlfriend of the sad boy who lost his brother. While Crispy and Nicole went upstairs and tried to get through a game of Monopoly, Stephen roamed the house with heavy shoulders, listening in on various conversations about his brother and about life's injustices—some college kid said,

"Why couldn't it have been a worthless redneck?"—while others talked about the crazy up-and-down stock market, or how the Bulls had pummeled the Knicks the night before.

Stephen settled next to Jasmine. She handed him her can of Budweiser beer, about one-third full, and told him to finish it, which he did, apparently with his mother's blessing as Helen was sitting nearby and saw him with the beer and said nothing. This was the first time Stephen had drunk beer and it tore at his already upset stomach—he had to fight throwing up. But he downed it, and when Jasmine cracked open a second Budweiser he had a few sips of that one, too. He was hoping that the beer would smooth out the sharp edges of his distress but it failed to do that, not even by a little bit.

EVENTUALLY, ALL OF the guests had left except for Jasmine. She had put on her coat and said her good-byes, but when she opened the door and saw how thick the snow was falling she said that perhaps she had consumed too much alcohol to be driving. Gene told her she was welcome to spend the night.

A little after nine, Crispy and Stephen were huddled with Jasmine on the couch. Helen and Gene sat across from them, Helen in the uncomfortable chair she had ordered from the Penney's outlet store (it looked comfortable in the catalogue) and Gene in a cherrywood rocker he had built at his shop. The room was lit by a table lamp and by a flickering orange light from the fake fireplace, also obtained from Penney's (the fire looked more authentic in the catalogue). An electric candle, left over from Christmas, burned in the bay window.

Needing some noise, Stephen turned on the television with the remote. He flipped through several channels and decided to watch an episode of *Murphy Brown.* Stephen liked how Murphy didn't take anyone's crap. When it went to commercial, Jasmine asked Gene and Helen if they wanted to know anything about the accident or its aftermath.

"No, we're fine," said Helen.

"Let her talk," Gene said. "It's better to know these things."

Jasmine went on to disclose several horrific details about Francis's death, like that on the way to the hospital the ambulance had a hard time getting around traffic in the storm and twice it came to a stop for a precious minute. (Stephen wondered why a rescue helicopter wasn't dispatched.) And that Prescott Memorial was short-staffed and it took several minutes for a surgeon to answer his page. (What was the doctor doing instead of saving his brother? Stephen wanted to know.) And that Francis, who always wore his seat belt, wasn't wearing one this time. (Stephen decided that Nerf car engines wouldn't start unless all passengers were safely latched in.)

Stephen pretended he wasn't listening so he wouldn't be sent from the room: he wrestled with Crispy for the remote and fake-giggled at the sitcom when he felt like exploding into bits and never being put back together again. He learned that Francis flew from the car and landed on a grassy strip beside the highway. (Stephen imagined catching him.) And he learned that Jasmine tried CPR on Francis but he needed something other than air and heart pumps. (What was the exact thing his brother needed to stay alive? Stephen wondered.) And he learned the words the emergency room doctor said to Jasmine after declaring Francis dead: "Too much internal trauma, there wasn't much we could do. But we gave it a shot." (They certainly could have done more, Stephen suspected.)

"I didn't believe the doctor," Jasmine said, sniffling. "I smacked his shoulder, called him a liar. Nobody dies anymore, I told him, this is the nineties, damn it, we have all of this technology. Francis couldn't be dead."

"What else?" Gene asked. "What was the other driver like, that Michael Haynes?"

"Like a motherfucker," Jasmine said, anger tightening her face. "Sorry, but no other word fits. He sat in his truck while I tried to save Francis. Just sat there like a dumb fuck. I wanted to kill him, still do. Sorry."

"Sounds like he was in the wrong place at the wrong time," Gene said.

"We all were," Jasmine said.

Silence took control of the room for a minute, then Gene asked Jasmine if Francis said anything, while they were waiting for the rescue squad.

"Not then, but in the ambulance he started swearing, 'Fuck, oh fuck, oh fuck,' maybe a hundred times, like a mantra. When the swearing stopped, about a minute from the hospital, that's the first time I thought that maybe he wasn't going to make it. But I wouldn't let myself believe it."

"We never expect the worst to happen," Gene said. "What about the weather? When did the snow and ice get bad?"

"About an hour into the drive. The roads went from not too bad to awful in about a minute. The snow started while we were waiting for the paramedics. I had to brush it off Francis a few times." (Stephen imagined snow falling onto his dying brother in no more than 144 different designs.)

"Let's not be morbid," Helen said, rubbing at and taking interest in her left thumb.

AFTER GENE AND HELEN retired to their separate bedrooms the night turned more jovial. Jasmine, Crispy, and Stephen stayed up late watching overdue rented movies and eating cookies, brownies, and strudel that the neighbors had brought over. But in one of the movies a character named Francis was introduced, so Jasmine turned off the TV and said it's been a long day and they should all get some shut-eye.

Jasmine took Crispy's room as Crispy wanted to sleep on the couch again, closer to her mommy and daddy. Stephen went to say good night to Jasmine and found her sitting up in bed, reading a novel. He glanced at her eyes, dark and beautiful, and at her red nightshirt and the few inches he could see of her legs: a blanket and comforter were hiding the rest. She smiled and said, "You sure look a lot like your brother. Anyone ever tell you that?" (Many people had, but Stephen considered his appearance no more than 45 percent Francis-like. He had his brother's thin hair, bony frame, and power legs, but that was about it.) Jasmine then covered her face with the book and started whimpering in a pleading kind of way. Stephen returned to his room and cried himself to sleep.

At about 3 A.M. he awoke to the sound of someone making noise in the hallway. He rolled out of bed, opened the door, and saw Jasmine, dressed in day clothes and a coat, about to descend the stairs.

"Go back to bed. Everything's fine," she said from behind her hanging hair.

"What's wrong?"

She groaned, then said, "I just realized that your parents blame me for the accident, that they think it should have been me killed, not your brother. I can't stay here another minute."

"I don't think it should have been you," he said. "It shouldn't have been anybody."

Jasmine stepped to Stephen and bent down, her hair sweeping across his face. She kissed him on his forehead. "The highway was a sheet of ice," she said. "If I could trade places with Francis I would. I would."

"I know," he said, feeling the same way.

He followed her downstairs, to the foyer. She hadn't zipped her coat so he zipped it for her. "Tell Crispy good-bye for me," she said. "And tell your parents that I'm sorry." He offered her one of his winter hats but she said that she had a cap in the car.

She opened the door, said, "Oh, fuck," to the lightly falling snow, and walked to the Honda. Stephen stood in the doorway and counted the footprints Jasmine was leaving in the snow. It was cold and he was only in pajamas and was shivering but he didn't care. Jasmine waved to him, smiled, and slipped into her car and drove off. She was almost a block away before she turned on the headlights.

Watching the snow slowly hide his neighborhood, Stephen realized that Jasmine was right, that his mother and father did think that it should have been her killed, not Francis. And if given the chance they would trade Stephen's life for his brother's. He just didn't stack up in areas of intelligence, handsomeness, or a guaranteed bright future. Sure, it would be difficult for Mom and Dad, sending him to the gallows so that Francis's life could be restored. There would be tears, hugs, and apologies, and maybe even a brief change of heart as he wept at their feet. But ultimately they'd do it.

He closed the door and went and sat with his sister. Crispy was sleeping, her eyes moving behind their lids. He made sure that her blanket stayed close to her chin, and listened to the sounds of the furnace kicking on and off and his father sobbing in his bedroom. When he became sleepy, he climbed the stairs to his room and conked out as soon as he slipped under the covers.

In his dream, Stephen was walking in the woods behind Lincoln Elementary when a dozen wolves, their fur electric blue and eyes as blank as bone, started circling him. The wolves came closer, rubbing their snouts against his legs and inviting Stephen to join their pack. The wolves started to run and he ran with them, toward a throbbing purple light at the edge of the woods, where he hoped that Francis was waiting. But he woke up before reaching the light. "Dummy," he said to the "save me" part of his brain for pulling him prematurely out of the dream. Closing his eyes, Stephen was able to get back to the woods, but the wolves were gone and so was the light, and there was no sign of Francis anywhere. In this half dream that was slipping into a full dream, Stephen rested on a mossy log and waited and waited and waited.

EPISODE 3

Sledding

WHAT WENT WRONG, Nicole wondered, as she peered through a magnifying glass at a dead butterfly she had found in her mother's tomato garden the previous summer. It was a monarch or a viceroy, impossible to tell the difference, but the tip of one of its wings was an albino white and black instead of orange and black. Did the butterfly's chromosome in charge of coloring run out of orange just as it was finishing up, or did the white gobble up the color on the wingtip like a disease? Either way, she got a kick out of the fact that animal and insect chromosomes occasionally screwed up just like people chromosomes sometimes did, though not often enough. Where were the humans with five eyeballs or two noses? Perhaps they were hidden away in a government fortress in New Mexico. She'd love to meet all of those freaks, shake their seven-fingered hands and pull their ratlike tails.

The butterfly will be one of the feature items in Nicole's Museum of Fucked-up Things, which she planned to open someday in Memphis, not far from where she grew up. Nicole will be the curator and will travel the planet, searching for oddities of nature suitable for her museum. In the meantime she kept a small collection of fucked-up things at her house, including the butterfly, a Siamese banana (stored in the freezer), and a candy wrapper with the list of ingredients printed upside down. Private viewings of the fucked-up things were available for $1, or fifty cents for kids age seven or under, all money raised to be set aside for building the national museum and for acquiring rare items, such as one of those six-legged frogs born in rivers near nuclear power plants.

She heard a tap at the back door and recognized the sound as Stephen's apologetic, don't-notice-me knock from a few years ago when Nicole and her mother had just moved next door to the Harrelsons and Stephen was wondering if she wanted to come outside and play. He'd go to the trouble of asking, even though her answer was always yes. His knocks had grown more confident since that summer, until today.

"Damn it," she said, setting the magnifying glass on her desk. She had wished and wished for Stephen's brother to come back to life but it hadn't happened, so the whole death thing, a very dark cloud, was still lingering above her head four days after the funeral. She supposed that she could better accept death if it played fair, if it took only old people and mean people, but Francis was young and sweet. He had sometimes called her "Nicolette," and for a few crazy weeks she had suffered through a painful crush on Francis. This happened two years ago, when Stephen and Francis used to run up and down Briarwood, Nicole holding a stopwatch and awaiting their return. *Majestic* was the best word to describe how Francis ran, and she had an almost unbearable urge to run beside him, match his stride and run as far as they could go, hundreds of miles to Memphis or Chicago. Stephen didn't fit in this picture, even though she already liked him. And then one day her crush on Francis was gone. She watched Francis and Stephen dash down the street but this time Francis seemed too much like an animal, all leggy and floppy. "Ewww," she found herself saying. Stephen, more boy than animal, was the one for her. But part of her sadness about Francis dying had to do with the fact that any chance for a state-crossing majestic run with Francis was now gone for good, as was the girl who wished for such silly things.

She ran down the stairs to the back door, exhaled away some of her discomfort, then pulled the door open and saw a bundled-up Stephen, pink-faced due to cold weather and sad-faced due to Francis's death. "Hey," she said.

"Hey," he said, glancing at her eyes then looking down at his boots. "How's it going?"

"Good, good," she said, twisting at the doorknob and making the latch move in and out. "How are you? What's up?" *This isn't how we normally talk.*

"Not much. There's something I want to show you." He reached into the back pocket of his jeans and handed her a piece of paper. She unfolded it and saw a sketch of a sponge car, the Nerf logo printed on the door panel. Four smiling stick figure passengers were cushioned safely inside the blobby vehicle.

"It's a car made of sponge," he explained. "No glass, no metal, no gasoline that can blow up."

"Interesting," she said, though a part of her mind was thinking, *Sponge cars? What are you, nuttier than a nut roll or something?* "How's it powered?"

"Probably by solar panels."

"That would work." She handed him back the drawing. He refolded it and slipped it into his pants pocket.

"Do you want to go sledding?" he asked, not looking at Nicole.

Another question that he already knew the answer to. "Yeah, sure, but are you ready for that kind of thing?"

"Very ready." Stephen, with his parents' permission, had skipped school the entire week and mostly slept and worked on the Nerf car design, but he was now anxious, he said, to get out of the house and do something halfway normal.

She hurried to the living room coat closet and threw on her winter jacket and slipped boots on over her sneakers and ran back to Stephen and joined him outside. They found her plastic sled, leaning lazily against the back of the garage like it was enjoying a smoke. Stephen took hold of its rope and they began tramping through her yard and then down a snow-covered Briarwood.

"People asked about you," she said.

"Which people?"

"Teachers, I guess. And some kids."

"What did you tell them?"

"That you just fucking lost your brother and will be back when you're good and fucking ready."

"You really said that?"

"Yeah, but with my eyes, not words."

Nicole let out a visible breath. "Remember when my aunt died and it took me a few days before I wanted to go outside and do stuff? I guess it was the same with you. I think we played Wiffle ball that day."

"I won seven to zip," he said. "I never beat you in Wiffle ball before."

"Or since," she said, cracking a smile then quickly erasing it.

STATION HILL WAS owned by Illinois Power and Light, so "no trespassing" signs were posted and occasionally a guard would show up and chase everyone off the property. Stephen had sledded there dozens of times, including one night a few years earlier when Francis woke him shortly after midnight and announced that they were "hitting the hill." They got dressed, slinked through the house like cat burglars, made it outside, retrieved the wooden sled from the shed, and jogged all of the way to the power plant. The snow was perfect that night, not a single sled mark or footprint, save theirs, and was made sparkly and blue by the moonlight. As he and Francis rode together on the sled, Stephen imagined that they were brave explorers, blazing new trails while the rest of the world slept.

Sled riders had a choice of Scaredy-cat Hill or Danger Run. At thirteen, Stephen was expected to sled down only the jagged Danger Run, even though he preferred the lazy descent of Scaredy-cat Hill. Not to mention the stories that had been circulating since Stephen was little about a kid named Bo or Buford who hit such a bad bump on his way down Danger Run that he went flying over a security fence and landed on a transformer and was zapped to death while causing a major power outage. (Francis claimed to have witnessed the accident and said that Bo or Buford died grinning.)

Nicole and Stephen stood at the top of the hill and watched a boy and a girl, third or fourth graders, their bodies hidden behind thick coats, scarves, and caps, ride a toboggan down Scaredy-cat Hill, and then saw a man bump down Danger Run on a sled similar to theirs, only orange instead of blue. Danger Run offered moments when gravity lessened its grip and one was briefly airborne, a millisecond here, a nanosecond there. But barreling down a cliff on a ten-dollar slab of plastic now seemed foolish and dangerous to Stephen.

"I guess I'm not in the mood to sled," he said.

"Me neither, then," she said.

Nicole wrapped herself around Stephen and started to cry. He wanted to cry, too, but was all out of ammo. He let go of the sled rope and watched the children and the man drag their sled and toboggan up the side of the hill. Ten minutes of work for ten seconds of glory.

"Death sucks" was all he could think to say.

"I hate it," she said, into his jacket.

They were about to walk home when they saw Crispy coming toward them. She was wearing a pink coat with the fake-fur-lined hood and looked as fragile as a springtime snowflake.

"I thought you creeps might be here," Crispy said. "How's the sledding?"

"We decided we didn't want to sled today," he said.

"Dummies," she said. "We have to go at least once."

So they squeezed together on Nicole's sled, Stephen's arms wrapped tightly around his sister and Nicole's arms locked around him, and peacefully glided down Scaredy-cat Hill. Halfway down, Nicole turned the sled and they finished the run in a slow, spiraling loop.

EPISODE 4

The Birth of Wolf Boy

STEPHEN WAS HIKING through the snowy woods behind Lincoln Elementary, hoping to find his brother among the frozen, dead, and sleeping things. "Francis, are you here?" he asked, standing boot-deep in snow and looking up at clay-colored clouds and at a sun that was just a cold ball. "It's me, Stephen."

If his brother was planning to drop from the sky and rendezvous with him it would happen in these woods. He and Francis had owned this place. They used to hunt here for rocks, fossils, and arrowheads, and later mushrooms when Francis became interested in mycology. The brothers built forts and hideouts and ran from killers and hermits and crazed retarded men who Francis said were chasing after them with machetes and machine guns, though Stephen never saw them. During their final trip to the woods, the previous August, they sat on a log and talked about the possibility that their unhappy parents might get divorced, and about their girlfriends, Francis advising Stephen to spend the rest of the summer "boinking" Nicole. It was a sunny and breezy day, and Francis wore a white T-shirt with a screen print of a magic mushroom, new blue jeans, and black sneakers. He was full of smiles. The only horror of that day was that it ended.

Wind moved through the leafless trees, whistling a lonely song. Stephen whistled back, blew air through pursed lips. *Phewwwwwww, phewwwwwww.* A bird hidden high up in a pine tree chirped, but no answer came, so that sound was a lonely one, too. "Twip twip, twip twip," Stephen sang to the bird, but the bird didn't fall for it. A bear then roared. No, that was just a plane overhead. There weren't any bears in these woods, but there were deer. Stephen had seen a buck two days earlier, his antlers like frozen, misshapen hands and his eyes looking at the trees like he was imagining the hundred different ways he might weave through them. When the buck spotted Stephen it snorted then ran off, choosing one of the ways to go, two littler deer, the buck's kids he guessed, coming out of nowhere and following it, swishing snow off low pine branches they were dashing by.

He left the path and hiked through thistle, shrubs, and raspberry brushes. Besides hoping to find his brother, Stephen was searching the woods for something unabashedly green with life. Not a pine tree or any kind of evergreen—they had learned winter survival tricks eons ago—but a normally deciduous tree or shrub that still had its leaves, was maybe even flowering or putting out berries. While hunting for that trailblazing plant, Stephen heard a pop, turned quickly, and saw that a dry seedpod on a very dead weed had exploded and a teaspoonful of brown seeds were falling to the snow-damp earth. He didn't know what to make of the explosion, how such an event could take place months after the last day of life for that weed. He went to his knees and with gloved fingers pushed the seeds into the soil, as much as the frozen dirt would allow. He doubted that the seeds had a chance. They were probably dead duds.

The day was losing its light. Stephen found the trail and started looping back toward the school. About halfway there he stopped at a partially frozen creek where he bent and cleared a patch of snow on the creek bank, then took off his gloves and pried free an egg-sized stone, a "turtle rock" his brother would have called it, formed over a million years ago. He held the layered brown rock up to the sky, in case Francis was watching him through the clouds, then placed the ancient stone in the front pocket of his brown corduroys. He stepped onto the thin ice covering part of the creek, watched cracks form like lightning, then jumped to the other side and marched home.

* * *

STEPHEN REMOVED his coat, boots, and gloves in the mudroom, then went into the kitchen where his mother was setting Gene's dinner on the stove, keeping it warm for him. Smelled like pork chops, sweet potatoes, and green beans.

"Where have you been?" Helen said. "We never see you anymore. What are you doing all of this time? Are you sure you even live here anymore?"

"Nothing, just walking. It's exercise." Stephen couldn't tell his mother that the woods was the one place that Francis still felt alive and present to him, as if the woods, asleep for the winter, hadn't heard about the accident. He had power there, was king, could chase deer and squirrels and chipmunks, snap branches, pull out plants by their roots, curse the world, piss in the wild. No judgmental eyes ever fell upon him.

"It's too cold for exercise," his mother said. "You are going to catch pneumonia, out there for hours every day like this."

"No I won't. Is dinner ready? What's for dinner?"

"Dinner was almost an hour ago," she said, walking a pan over to the sink. "People who are never home and pretend they don't have families can fix their own meals. There's turkey for sandwiches, cans of spaghetti, whatever a world traveler would want."

Stephen shrugged. He didn't like pork chops, sweet potatoes, and green beans that much anyway, just a little. "I won't go out as much," he said, pulling open the refrigerator door. But his words were empty of truth. If anything, he needed to find a way to spend more time in the woods, maybe even skip school now and then. There could still be some woods-living Francis memories he hadn't found yet.

WORRIED ABOUT STEPHEN'S mental health, Helen decided that he needed to see a therapist. She phoned most of the psychologists and social workers listed in the GTE yellow pages, but they all charged at least $75 an hour, which was too much to pay someone to nod while you moaned and cried. Since Gene was self-employed they had a lousy insurance plan and it would all be out-of-pocket. Perhaps it was for the best. What if someone saw Helen walking with Stephen into a psychologist's office? They might mistakenly think that the appointment was for her, that she was the one coming apart.

Reluctantly, Helen called First Community Church and asked if they offered their members free counseling services. "Of course we do," said Kim, Reverend Gladstone's secretary. "What's your name again?"

"Helen Harrelson. But it's for my son, Stephen."

"And you say you are members?"

"Yes, since 1986, I believe." The Harrelsons did belong to the church but only attended three or four times a year: Christmas, Easter, and once or twice during the rest of the year so it wouldn't look like they were the kind of people who only attended on Christmas and Easter.

"I found you," Kim said. "You're at 1178 Briarwood, right? It says here that you are no longer getting the monthly newsletter. I'll have to fix that."

"Please do."

They scheduled a time, Wednesday at 4:30, and then Kim asked what the appointment was for.

"He lost his brother in a car accident." Sentences about Francis's death still felt like bricks falling out of her mouth.

"That's right, now I remember. The Harrelson funeral. I'm sorry, I should have put two and two together."

"Don't worry about it."

"How are you doing, Mrs. Harrelson? Would you like to schedule a session with Reverend Gladstone for yourself?"

"No, I'm good," she said.

DURING STEPHEN'S first meeting with Reverend Gladstone, the pastor talked about the Cubs' prospects for a winning season (God favored the meek so they had a chance) and asked questions like,

"Do you want to destroy something right now?" To the questions, Stephen shrugged or shook his head, but mostly he played with a red Hot Wheels car, opening and closing the doors and hood and rolling it on a glossy wooden table.

Midway through his second session, Reverend Gladstone said, "You are feeling guilty about Francis's death."

Stephen picked up the toy car, checked its underbelly, and turned the tiny front wheels with a finger.

"You are feeling guilty," Reverend Gladstone repeated.

He set the car down and said, "Nope." But Stephen knew that he was guilty, that he had killed his brother. Before the crash Stephen had secret psychic powers. At least one out of every ten times he could correctly predict who was on the phone or at the door before the phone was answered or the door opened. And just two months before White Sox rookie prospect Jessie Garrett died in a boating accident, Stephen had a flash that someone on the team might be in trouble. But what was he doing while his brother was busy dying? Watching a Godzilla movie. Had he been paying attention, he could have used his powers and warned Francis to stay home that day, or to at least fasten his seat belt. Appropriately, his psychic abilities died when Francis died.

He went back to playing with the car. Reverend Gladstone, confident that he was on the right track, encouraged Stephen to express his feelings of guilt and powerlessness. "If you don't want to talk, that's fine, but please find some way of communicating what you're going through. Write a poem, or a symphony. Draw your feelings, or paint them."

Stephen pushed the car back and forth on the shiny table. "I'm kind of busy," he said.

HE WASN'T REALLY very busy, so that night Stephen took a pen and notebook down to the basement, plopped onto his brother's bed—still unmade, like Francis had left it—and began doodling. He turned one of the doodles, of a bunny rabbit, into a superhero called Rabbit Man. Rabbit Man carried a bow and shot carrot arrows, could hop higher than the tallest skyscraper, and his favorite expression was, "I'm so *fur*ious." Romaine lettuce was his kryptonite. But there was one big problem with Rabbit Man, Stephen realized, after spending an hour drawing the superhero and thinking up ways he could spend the millions of dollars coming his way from Rabbit Man comic book sales: rabbits were wimpy and easily frightened. Too much like Stephen. What he needed, what the whole world needed, was a superhero with fangs.

He kept doodling and eventually came up with Wolf Boy, a teenage superhero with nearly limitless powers. Over the next few days he wrote stories and drew stick figure art for a comic book titled *The Adventures of Wolf Boy*, then he asked Nicole to do the final drawings—he had seen her draw gargoyles and other freakish creatures on school desks and library carrels and knew she'd be perfect for the job. Nicole was eager to help out.

Stephen presented the comic book to Reverend Gladstone at the start of their third appointment.

The opening tale, "A Moonlit Night," was about the origins of Wolf Boy. On the night of the full moon, Kip Laredo, boy reporter for *The Daily Uh-Oh*, was hiking through a woods at the outskirts of Forgotten City when a white wolf leapt out of the trees and bit him on the neck. Kip, in a daze, watched brown fur sprout from his flesh, felt his teeth morphing into fangs, and saw steely claws form on his fingertips. "W-what is happening to me?" Kip asked.

"You are now among the chosen," said the white wolf, scratching at a flea with a hind leg. "Each month during the full moon you will transform into a wolf and have the power of a hundred boys. A hundred strong boys I mean, not wimpy kids like you."

"I can do almost twenty push-ups," Kip pointed out.

"Impressive. Anyway, you are to use this power to—"

"Save the world?"

"Save smave. Just try to keep the world going."

The white wolf bounded off, and Kip got up and leapt toward home. But before arriving there Kip used his new powers to chase away a gang of ruffians that were harassing an orphan girl, and to catch a purse-snatching robot before it could motor away.

"VERY NICE," Reverend Gladstone said. "I always like it when good triumphs over evil."

"Me, too. I wish real life was like that," Stephen said.

"I think that world is coming. We just need to be patient."

The second *Wolf Boy* story, "God's Accident," excited Reverend Gladstone from the start of it. In that story, Forgotten City was at war with neighboring Edenville, space aliens were invading, and many of Forgotten City's best and brightest were being killed in shuttle crashes caused by terrorists. It was too much for Wolf Boy to handle, so he leapt up to heaven to ask God for help. While looking for God, Wolf Boy came across an old man in a wheelchair, staring at a display of a thousand video monitors.

WHAT ABOUT YOU ANGELS? YOU CAN STILL DO GOOD WORKS, RIGHT?
SURE, BUT WITH THE BIG GUY OUT OF IT MANY OF THE ANGELS WENT TO WORK FOR SATAN: THE PAY IS BETTER AND THE SNACK ROOM IN HELL IS OUT OF THIS WORLD.
HE WAS IN A TERRIBLE ACCIDENT A FEW MONTHS AGO. GOD CAN'T BE KILLED BUT HE IS NOW LAME, ALMOST MUTE.
SOME OF THE OTHER ANGELS JUST SIT AROUND HEAVEN SMOKING CRACK COCAINE ALL DAY. IT'S QUITE DEPRESSING.
?
IT MUST BE SOMETHING ON ONE OF THE EARTH MONITORS.
WHAT IS IT, GOD?
TH-THAT P-P-POOR G-GRASS-HOPPER.

DON'T WORRY, I'LL SAVE HIM!
WHOOOOOOSH
SECONDS LATER, IN FORGOTTEN CITY.
LOOK OUT, LITTLE GUY!
WHAM!
OUCH.

"Awesome, totally awesome," said Reverend Gladstone in his I-know-how-to-talk-to-teens voice. "Of course your presentation of God isn't exactly biblical, but most folks question God from time to time. You do know that he cares about us, right?"

Stephen shrugged. "Do you think I have enough talent to be a professional comic book writer, if I practice?"

"Why not, if that's where your heart is," said Gladstone.

"It's many places," Stephen said, picking up the toy car.

* * *

WHEN HELEN ARRIVED at the church, Reverend Gladstone told her that there had been a breakthrough, that Stephen was finally dealing with his sense of powerlessness, but his case may even be more complex than he, a pastoral counselor, was trained to deal with. "You might consider professional psychotherapy for Stephen, or better yet art therapy. Naturally, we'll still be here if you need us."

"There's a bit of an insurance problem," she said. "You mentioned something about art therapy?"

"Yes, the comic book, *The Adventures of Wolf Boy*. You haven't seen it? Amazing stuff. It seems to be the way he's dealing with his brother's death, through stories and drawings. Encourage Stephen to keep at it. He could be the next R. Crumb."

"Who?"

"Mr. Natural? Those trippy comic books from the sixties? Never mind."

"Thank you, Reverend. We'll consider all of the options."

"See you on Sunday?"

"For what? Oh, services. Yes. If not this Sunday, then the next one."

On the way home, Helen said nothing about the comic book, even though Stephen was flipping its pages noisily. Instead, she talked about Reverend Gladstone's days as a pothead and a minor criminal, before he found the Lord and met the woman who would become Mrs. Gladstone, in that order. "Faith can be a powerful thing," she said. "If you have any of that stuff."

EPISODE 5

Dining Alone

IT WAS SPRING NOW, temperatures were rising and sunshine was more abundant, and the crocuses that Helen had planted in the front gardens the previous autumn were pushing through the soil. But when Helen saw the purple and yellow crocus heads she wanted to poke them back into the dirt. She didn't, but she wanted to.

Helen was ever trying to lose herself in household duties and soap operas, but her shows ended at four o'clock and there were never enough dishes to wash or tables to dust to fill an entire day. Time, more than ever, really needed to be killed, even the passing of a single minute was sometimes a drawn-out, impossible process, each second trying to nudge Helen into letting go, releasing her grip, and dissolving into a trillion sad atoms. Free, but too much. What's an atom to do?

When *The Ledger* arrived on their doorstep each afternoon (except on weekends when it was delivered in the mornings), she would stop whatever she was doing and flip through the local news and obituary pages, to see if any area mothers had just lost a child to a car crash, disease, or other intrusion. If she found one, she would write a letter to the woman about Francis and the accident, saying how, as a mother, she had to find a way to keep going, even when she felt like laying down her cards and never returning to the table. She felt a little bit better being part of a club, but what a terrible club it was: Mothers of Dead Children, southern Illinois branch.

* * *

HELEN STOOD AT the kitchen sink, bleeding into sudsy dishwater and staring at her two wounded fingers. She had cut them on a broken wine goblet while doing the dishes and was more interested in watching the blood flow than stopping it with a rag. She didn't normally do well with blood, and had it been a few months earlier she would have been cursing the vile red stuff while speed walking to the medicine cabinet in the bathroom. But Francis was dead and flowing blood was nothing more than flowing blood. Stephen, sitting at the dining table with his father and reading a book about the history of comic books, saw the mess and told his mom she had better put Band-Aids on her fingers. "And antiseptic," Gene added. Helen nodded and walked slowly to the bathroom, drops of blood speckling the cream-colored carpeting in the hallway and marking her route.

Before long Helen was scuttling back into the kitchen where she snagged her set of car keys from a key hook. "Be back in a quick sec," she said.

Gene, sawing through a turkey and tomato on rye sandwich with a steak knife, asked her if she should be driving.

"I'm fine," Helen said, wiggling her two gauzed fingers in front of his face to prove they weren't dead on the vine.

"I'll need to head back to work in a bit," Gene said, his forehead creased with worry. Helen said nothing more and hustled outside to the car and started it up.

GENE TOOK A few bites of his sandwich, then pushed his plate aside. "Where the hell is your mother going?" he asked. "How am I supposed to get back to work?"

"You can borrow my bike," Stephen said. He was reading about Jerry Siegel and Joe Shuster, the two teenagers from Cleveland who had come up with the idea for Superman, and wondering if someday a kid somewhere would be reading about Stephen Harrelson, creator of Wolf Boy. *Stephen Harrelson was a remarkable teenager and is even a more remarkable adult. Besides creating the greatest comic books of all time and eventually acquiring Marvel and DC Comics, Stephen is the CEO of Nerf Automotive, a company that manufactures safe cars out of sponge material, and he has recently proven that snowflakes come in only 144 designs . . .*

"I haven't ridden a bicycle in years," Gene said. "I'd probably crash, go down in flames." He frowned, tapped a finger against the table. "Your mother worries me. She's running from this thing. I can't blame her for that, but she needs to find a way to stop running."

"She'll be home soon," said Stephen, looking at panels from *Action Comics #1,* where Superman debuted. But he wasn't certain his mother would be returning, that night or ever. While Gene was venting his sadness every few days, getting halfway drunk and spewing terrible words about Francis's last day on earth, his mother had *androided* herself since the crash, shut down her feelings. Rarely did her mouth rise into a smile or fall into a frown, even when watching her favorite sitcoms or Arty Gifford's segment on the Channel 7 newscast. Stephen figured that, like all androids, she'd have to blow a circuit eventually. Melt down, run away, or beat the crap out of Gene.

HELEN DROVE TO Dominic's Italian Eatery in neighboring Caswell and took the table by the window and ordered linguini and a side salad with oil and vinegar dressing. But when her food arrived she could eat only a few strands of pasta and a bite or two of the garlic bread but none of the salad: it was too green and zesty, she didn't deserve it. She had squandered her life. Helen had taught fifth grade at Lincoln Elementary for two years when Francis was a toddler, but soon Gene was making good money at the store and she didn't need to work. But she had loved teaching, not always the day to day of it but the fact that she was encouraging young lives, helping them get going. And she knew that many of her students would someday tell a wife or husband or their graduating class that Helen Harrelson, their perky fifth-grade teacher, made all the difference, kept them from a life of dumbness and despair.

Before long her leave of absence from teaching became a permanent resignation. She had her kids, her TV programs, and Gene. It seemed to be enough of a life, but then Gene turned cold and the children grew older and started to push away from her skirt. The happiness leaving her was a slow, persistent leak.

Then something beautiful happened: she and Francis became friends and confidants. After Francis bought the Plymouth (with financial help from Gene), he started taking her shopping, and to restaurants, and for drives. Their favorite lunch spot was here, at Dominic's. Nobody knew them so they were free to act crazy, sometimes even holding hands while they waited for their food. Helen did so enjoy how Francis gripped her hands delicately like they were something precious, the way Gene used to a billion years ago.

They'd eat linguini or vegetable lasagna and talk about their lives: Francis mostly about school and his plans for the future, while Helen would complain about the monotony of motherhood. Or she might bitch about the lack of sex just to see him blush. A few words like "I still have needs" would send a pint of blood gushing to his face. Francis didn't like to talk about Jasmine or his girlfriends before her, but Helen could tell he had some kind of sex life: his blushing seemed more due to habit than innocence.

She had killed her own son. Francis had been living in a dorm room at Southern Illinois University, but toward the end of his freshman year he got in trouble: a party he was attending was broken up by campus security. The officers smelled marijuana so Francis was written up and Helen and Gene were sent a warning letter. One more alcohol and drug policy violation and Francis would be kicked out.

So she suggested that Francis live at home for his sophomore year, where it would be easier to avoid parties. It was only a forty-minute commute to the university. Gene seconded the idea, adding that they'd save a pile of money. Francis moved into the basement. That's what killed him. Had he been living on campus he would have left for the conference from Carbondale, not Hollis. He might have completely missed the ice storm.

Truth was, Helen wanted Francis at home. He was handsome, fun, and smart, and she had played some small role in making him handsome, fun, and smart. She even enjoyed washing his clothes and dishes and picking up after him. Just walking by the cellar door, knowing he was down there, gave her chills of happiness. She had invested twenty years of love in that boy and finally he was starting to love her back. Ultimately, though, he didn't love her enough. When Francis announced his engagement to Jasmine, Helen suddenly felt old and gray and done with her life. How could Francis abandon her like that?

"I'm a terrible mother," Helen confessed, to the salad.

She ordered two glasses of burgundy and guzzled them down. When the waitress, age nineteen or twenty with dark features—Indian? Pakistani?—brought the check, Helen handed her $20 for the $13.38 bill, told her to keep the change, then advised the woman to never have kids. "They'll break your heart," she said.

"Too late," said the waitress, patting her belly and smiling. Sentimentality took root in Helen and she wanted to ask the future mother how far along she was, whether she hoped for a boy or a girl, and if she had any questions about teething and potty training. Helen scooted out of the restaurant, not allowing any of it.

She sat in the Chevy in the restaurant parking lot and thought about her options. She didn't want to go home, to that oversized doghouse with central heating, perhaps ever again. But where was happiness waiting for her, checking its watch? Possibly on quiet Poe Street in Toledo, Ohio, where she had grown up, or outside Atlanta where her sister, Tammy, and her husband, Tony, and their four spirited boys lived. More likely, happiness was waiting in a town she had never heard of, one with brick streets, a bandstand, and frequent parades. Feeling tipsy and tired, Helen decided to postpone her dramatic escape from Hollis to a day when she needed it even more than now, this miserable starless night in Caswell, Illinois, dark side of the earth.

She started the car and pulled out of the lot, drove down the alley, and turned onto Water Street and stopped the Chevy in front of Dominic's. She peered inside the restaurant and for a sweet, gasping second she thought she saw Francis and herself seated at the window booth, talking and holding hands. But then those happy apparitions were gone. The candle on the table was still lit, as Helen had left it, but the knocked-up waitress blew it out and cleaned up the plates and silverware. She didn't need any more symbolism in her life right now, Helen reminded the universe, but the candle didn't magically relight itself.

Before going home she drove by Lincoln Elementary—her classroom was in the far eastern part of the building, close to the kindergarteners' playground—and then by Gene's store. The lights were on, so her long-ago teddy bear must have gotten a ride to the shop. He was probably just sitting in the office, feeling sorry for himself. *Gene, you dumb turkey, wake up.* She thought about driving the Chevy through the shop's front window, then crawling out of the debris and telling her husband, "Let's kill each other or love each other, none of this in-between shit." But that would mess up the Chevy, her future escape vehicle, and probably hurt like hell. She drove on.

Ten minutes later she pulled into her driveway, smoothly applied the brakes, set the car in park, cut the engine, turned off the headlamps. The double-decker doghouse was dark, except for the stove light in the kitchen and the light in Stephen's bedroom, where three or four bulbs appeared to be burning. What was he doing up there, trying to catch a tan from the sixty-watt Sylvanias? Perhaps in five or six years Stephen will love me like Francis did, Helen thought, trying to place an older face over Stephen's current boyish looks in her mind, but he kept pushing away the mask.

Stephen was sitting at his desk writing a comic book story when he heard his mother come home. "Thanks," he said to God, not knowing if he was just talking to the air. He closed his notebook, turned off the desk lamp, stood up and kicked off his sneakers, killed the overhead light, then went to his bed and hid under the covers. In total darkness, until his eyes adjusted, Stephen activated his sonic Wolf Boy hearing and listened to his mother walk through the house, do something with a pot or pan in the kitchen, and pad through the living room and start up the stairs. Wolf Boy stilled himself, directed his tail not to tap, and pretended to be asleep.

HELEN BEGAN CLIMBING the stairs to check on her babies, but then stopped on the fifth step and retreated to the landing. There were things up there she'd love to see just about every night of her life, but not tonight. Crispy will be too damn beautiful, with her unblemished face, sleeping that angel's sleep of hers, while the biochemical mechanisms of her eventual blossoming and ruin—domestic servitude, motherhood, and a jellyfish for a husband (if she followed the family tradition)—continued their unholy work. Stephen, her surviving boy, will be handsomely faking sleep as a way of avoiding kissing his dear mother good night. There wasn't a male on earth who wanted her kisses, apparently. She thought about dashing up the stairs and forcing a kiss on Stephen *for his own good*, but it was just the wine making her crazy, she suspected. "Good night little ones," she said, probably out of earshot.

Before going to bed, Helen cleaned the bloodstains off the carpeting in the hallway. As Heloise in her *Ledger* household hints column had said it would, a splash of peroxide and a wet rag did the trick.

EPISODE 6

The Partnership

NICOLE AGREED TO do all of the sketches for future issues of *The Adventures of Wolf Boy* in return for half interest in the comic book company, which they named Supernova Comics, Inc. Nicole was the president, treasurer, chief artist, advertising director, sandwich maker, and copy girl, and Stephen was the publisher, vice president, chief storywriter, distributor, and pencil sharpener. Their goal was to publish a new *Wolf Boy* title every other month, and to introduce two new superheroes with their own line of comic books each year.

They worked on the comics in Nicole's bedroom when her mother was at work or on a date. As they sat on her bed or the floor, he'd read part of a *Wolf Boy* episode and she'd begin to sketch it. Occasionally they'd argue over matters such as whether Wolf Boy should have a tail, but always in the smiley, nonthreatening way that children who like each other argue.

When the sketches for *Wolf Boy #1* were ready they marched downtown to Hollis Public Library and Xeroxed twenty copies of the issue, assembled the pages in the proper order (in all but two cases), and stapled them together. They set the price at $2 and put aside five copies of the historic first edition, to be sold for $10,000 each once *Wolf Boy* and the Supernova comic book line took off. The fifteen remaining copies they tried to peddle at school and door-to-door in their neighborhood, but after a week had passed they had sold only six comic books, one of those to Crispy who paid only seventy cents.

Unappreciated and twenty dollars in the hole, the business partners considered dissolving Supernova Comics, Inc., but decided to press on. "I'm sure the big comic book companies started off just as slowly," Nicole said to a dejected Stephen as they sat across from each other on her bedroom floor. She was sketching the cover for *The Adventures of Wolf Boy #2* and he was writing one of the stories.

"The first issue of *Captain America* sold a million copies," he pointed out.

"And Wolf Boy could kick Captain America's ass!" she said. "We'll get there."

IN THE OPENING STORY of *Wolf Boy #2*, "Wolves in the Family Tree," Kip Laredo learned of his secret heritage, that going back to great-great-great-great-great-grandpa Horace, all of the Laredo males had been bitten by a white wolf during their adolescence, and, except for a bad wolf here and there, all of them had become superheroes. Kip's brother, Johnny, was a superhero named Wolf Brother, and his father, Buddy, was a do-gooder called Wolf Daddy. Kip had wondered why his brother and father disappeared for a few days each month, and why Buddy bought plastic shavers and shaving cream by the truckload.

Now that he had come of age, Kip, as Wolf Boy, joined forces with his brother and father. Wolf Boy, Wolf Brother, and Wolf Daddy would send tornadoes back into the sky, catch plummeting airplanes, and nab terrorists before they could launch their atomic itching powder bombs. On slow days the trio would chase liquor store bandits and those lowlifes who tried to ride the solar trains without paying.

In the second episode, "Death of a Dream," Johnny Laredo was killed in a shuttle explosion while on his way to a superhero's conference on the ice planet Zambobia. Nicole protested this story element, saying that it was way too early to kill off Johnny, that readers had barely gotten to know him. "That's my point," Stephen said. "He just started out. That's why it's so tragic."

SUPERNOVA
COMICS
INC.
$2.00
The
ADVENTURES of
WOLFBOY
#2
DEATH
OF A
DREAM!
STORIES BY
STEPHEN HARRELSON
ART BY
NICOLE STRUSSMAN

"But superheroes aren't supposed to die," she said. "That's what makes them so super."

"Maybe in Metropolis, but in Forgotten City superheroes die all the time," he said.

"I think I like Metropolis better," she said.

The partners compromised by inserting a short story between the two main pieces, where Wolf Boy and Wolf Brother forced the evil Dr. Strangebrain to come up with a potion called Lunar Juice, so they and their father could transform into their wolf personas at any time and not have to wait for the full moon. But they didn't know that Dr. Strangebrain had slipped essence of banana peel into the Lunar Juice, making the superheroes vulnerable to all kinds of accidents, from falling safes landing on their heads to deadly shuttle explosions.

EPISODE 7

Father and Son

GENE STOOD AT his office window, looking for signs that spring had locked in, that the worst winter of his life was finally done. It probably was. Trees were greening, and across the street Abe was selling pansies, daffodils, and hyacinths in front of his hardware store. Gene then tracked a young lady in skimpy pink shorts crossing the street and stopping in front of Abe's to sniff the perfume being offered by the hyacinths. A meeting of spring flowers! He imagined following the woman as she meandered from store to store, just to be within reach of a not-yet-trampled life.

He sat down at his desk and fiddled with a catalogue from Barnard Building Supply, shaping it into a telescope and looking through it like he was a sea captain searching for land, then opening it and reading product descriptions. It was hell, spending so much time alone at his shop, but being at home was even worse. No matter what room he was in, a voice in his head would say, Look at the section of carpet that Francis used to stretch out on to watch TV, or the window he broke twice in the same summer fouling off baseballs, or the table he sat at for ten thousand meals, or the rag he used to wash his sweet face with. If Gene went outside for some relief, he'd be asked to look at the sugar maple Francis used to climb or the street he skinned his knees on falling off bicycles, scooters, and skateboards. But he didn't want to look.

Despite all of the time he was spending at the store, Gene wasn't selling much furniture. The shades were usually drawn and the front door sign was often flipped to the "Sorry, We're Closed" side during business hours. When his sadness became too much for him he'd lock up the shop and hit City News, two doors west of his store, where he'd glance at the covers of magazines with titles like *Spread* or *Butt Thrasher* while pretending to read a hot rod magazine. Or he'd head to Sweet Surrender, across the street and one block east, where he'd order a hot fudge sundae or a double-dip ice cream cone, heavy on the sprinkles.

Gene flipped through the catalogue. He could order four dozen brass doorknobs from Barnard's for only $77.90, plus shipping and handling. That was exactly what he needed in his life, forty-eight brass doorknobs. He didn't make or sell doors but at least he'd have a box full of shiny things to throw at customers stupid enough to waddle into his little shop of horrors.

"Ah, damn," he said, watching a gush of tears fall out of him and plunk onto the catalogue. He never knew when these flash storms were coming: he could go from dry to weepy in a heartbeat. *What kind of man am I,* Gene wondered. He didn't kiss Francis good-bye before he left for the conference, or even hug him or shake his hand. Besides possibly sticking it to fate by delaying Francis's departure, kissing or embracing his son would have been the *human* thing to do. January 9, the one day he needed to live right, he just stood there and watched Francis get into his car and drive away, Gene some sort of frozen freak, incapable of showing affection. In Russia and Egypt and a hundred other places men kiss their grown sons good-bye, so why not in the goddamn United States of America, the greatest country on earth? *Unfuckingacceptable.*

BACK HOME, Stephen decided it was time to go see his father at his shop. Before Francis's death, he would visit the store two or three times a week. He enjoyed watching his father and the apprentice turn raw wood into beautiful furniture and was pleased when Gene would let him apply the first coat of stain to a desk, or sand a drawer front. He occasionally even tried his hand at sales, asking a customer about his or her furniture needs and showing what they had in stock, mentioning, if the customer appeared unsatisfied with the selection, that his daddy would be happy to custom build anything he or she wanted. If price was a concern, he would point out that their furniture was sturdier than anything to be had at department stores or at the Oak Expressions store in Caswell, Gene's biggest competitor. When Stephen was successful, Gene would pay him between $1 and $10 commission, depending on how much the customer had spent.

Stephen hadn't been to the shop since Francis died. Nor had his mother or sister, as far as he knew. Gene had told his family that business was terribly slow and that he even had to lay off the bookkeeper and the apprentice. Stephen got the message, which was to let his father stew in his own juices. But it was April now, normally a busy time at the shop as people awakening from winter doldrums might suddenly realize that they needed new furniture in their lives or would seek Gene's help in restoring the old stuff. Gene would also start selling seasonal items in April, such as birdhouses and window planters. There should be plenty of work for Stephen.

He hopped on his twelve-speed and started pedaling. It was a sunlit day, the sky was bluer than it had been in a while, and most of the trees were well into budding, some offering brilliant pink flowers or white flowers with thin red lines, the lines seeming like an afterthought. Stephen passed by two boys tossing a baseball to each other, and by a roaming pack of high school girls, some of them in shorts and halter tops even though it couldn't be more than sixty degrees out. He whistled at the girls, but not until he was safely two blocks past them.

Stephen parked his bike, then pushed open the door of the shop and stepped inside. He almost didn't recognize the place. Half the sales floor lights were turned off or had burned out, the furniture was arranged more haphazardly than usual, and some items still had tags from Gene's annual Presidents' Day Sale attached to them.

He went into the office. "Surprise," Stephen said to his dad. Gene was sitting at his desk and had an absent, nobody's home look.

"There he is," Gene said, coming to life. "Aren't you supposed to be in school?"

"It's Saturday."

"That's right." Gene picked up a sales receipt and appeared to be diligently studying it, like it contained a hidden code or a watermark.

"What can I help with today?" Stephen asked.

"Nothing. As you can see, it's pretty slow here."

"We could build birdhouses."

"No, I'm afraid there won't be any birds this year. Birds have been canceled."

Stephen didn't know how to respond. In actuality Hollis was now loaded with birds again. He had seen a cardinal on the way to the store, and a songbird that was mostly yellow and black.

"I think I'll go back to the shop," Stephen said.

"Whatever floats your boat," Gene said.

In the woodshop, Stephen was expecting to inhale the pleasant odors of freshly planed wood and sawdust, but there was only a musty smell from some water-damaged furniture not yet restored. He almost gagged. What had his father been doing all of this time? He had hoped that Gene was building furniture as a way of keeping himself from thinking about Francis, which would account for the crazy hours he had been putting in at the store, but there was no evidence that he had done any woodworking since January. There were several half-finished projects in the shop that had been started before the crash—a partially stained bookcase, a desk missing two drawers—but nothing appeared ready to ship or sell.

Stephen looked around the shop, and it suddenly seemed like the most dangerous place in the world. There were saws with angry teeth and machines with terrible blades that could rip your arm off or shred your fingers before you knew it, drills that could enter your body without first asking for an invitation, and chisels, wood picks, and hammers that could tear you up if you weren't careful. There were evil staple and nail guns that might pierce you of their own volition, and stacks of hardwood boards that could fall and crush you.

Stephen thought of his father, sitting frozen in the office and avoiding all of the blades, nails, and saws, and he understood that it might be a very long time before Gene started building furniture again.

He went back to the office and asked his dad if he had thought of something he needed help with.

Gene shook his head. "Not today, old bean," he said. "See you back at the nut farm."

Stephen felt something drop inside of him, a bird shot out of the sky. The world of just a few years ago, when Gene would swing Stephen in his arms and tell him how precious and gifted he was now seemed like some other kid's life. It wasn't that way with Francis: Gene had loved and praised Francis his full span.

Stephen frowned and trudged to the front door, giving his father plenty of time to say, "I love you! Don't go! Stay with me the whole damn day. We'll have lots of fun." But Gene stayed silent, almost motionless.

At the door Stephen flipped the "Sorry, We're Closed" sign so it said, "Yes, We Are Open," left the shop, and climbed onto his bicycle and started pedaling home. *My poor dumb dad,* he thought, as a semitruck rumbled by and pulled him along in its wake.

EPISODE 8

Jasmine and the Swimmer

JASMINE DROPPED OUT of school after the accident and moved back to her childhood home in Naperville. Besides needing a place to live that was nowhere near Carbondale, she was happy to be reminded by her parents, Fay and Myles, of her faults and bad choices. Perhaps she wasn't as good and smart and self-actualized as she thought she was. Francis, who sometimes kissed her skull and said, "I love your brain," who told her she was kindhearted, who said he could only marry a woman who knew her worth, well, he was a rare bird.

One night in late April she said good night to her parents and retreated to her bedroom. Gail had garage-saled all of her stuffed animals, but Jasmine recently repopulated the room with a teddy bear, a giraffe, and an alligator. They were charged with protecting her from nightmares but were doing a crappy job.

She sat on the bed and wondered why her bed always seemed to be waiting for her. Was that also true with chairs? Toilets? She was attempting to distract herself with small thoughts as the nightly dilemma had returned: if she stayed awake she'd think about Francis and if she went to sleep she'd dream about him. So she repeated a nonsense phrase in her mind—*the purple rhinoceros drinks banana daiquiris*—hoping to think and dream only of purple rhinos drinking daiquiris that night. It didn't work.

Jasmine awoke at about 3 A.M. and stumbled into the bathroom and saw Francis. He was sitting in the bathtub and moving his arms like he was swimming, but there was no water in the tub. His eyes were colorless and his wounds had healed, and dressed in torn black pants he looked like an afterlife castaway. "What do you want?" she asked, trying to stay calm. Francis silently mouthed an answer, so she studied his mouth. But that scared her. His mouth was a dark cave, full of a hundred-legged slithering things, no doubt. She ran from the bathroom and into her bedroom where she hid in the closet, pulling the door closed and shaking. As a child she would take shelter here during storms or when her mother and father were fighting, the sleeves of blouses and sweaters becoming fifty loving, protecting arms. But now it was just a dark, lonely place. She kicked open the door and let in some light.

Her dead fiancé was in the bathtub. Fuck.

She rechecked the bathroom. Francis was still swimming in the bathtub air, still trying to tell her something. *Speak, damn it.* His dark mouth remained horrifying. That was the mouth she used to kiss, the mouth that used to say all of those poetic things to her—it had been full of light. "Be right back, hon," Jasmine said, posting a smile. She hurriedly used the downstairs bathroom, then retreated to her room. She sat on her bed and squeezed her stuffed giraffe, Nexus, and tried to figure out what to do about the ghost in the bathroom. She had petitioned heaven to return her honey boy to her a hundred times, but now that Francis was here she wanted nothing to do with him. "Go to the light, babe," she said through the wall.

Minutes passed and added up to hours. It was starting to become light out. She returned to the bathroom. He was still there. "I'm sorry, but you have to leave," she said. "My folks will be getting up soon." He mouthed one more thing—it looked like "oh aaa, oh aaa"—and his arms kept going like crazy, like he was paddling through an ocean somewhere. "Where are you swimming to?" she asked. He didn't answer. Jasmine looked at the 5 percent that was left of the man she had loved, said, "Good-bye, sweets," and then retreated to the hallway and pulled the bathroom door closed. She counted to thirty, then opened the door. He was gone. Thank God. She stumbled back to her room, collapsed onto the bed, and sobbed. The dead should really stay in their own world.

EPISODE 9

The Crush

FOR A FEW WEEKS following Francis's death, Crispy had adopted her brother's morning throat-clearing ritual, hacking away during breakfast and her first hours at school, but an examination by the family physician, Dr. Samuels, failed to find a physical cause. "You have nothing more serious than a frog in your throat," he told the girl. Crispy knew that Dr. Samuels was joking, that there was no actual frog in her throat, which, when she thought about it, was a disappointment. The malady cleared up when she simply forgot to clear her throat for two days in a row. When, on the third day, Stephen said how nice it was to have quiet breakfasts again, Crispy remembered that she was supposed to be clearing her throat, but her heart wasn't into it: as diseases went, it was too noisy. "The frog jumped out," she said, expecting roaring laughter, at least from her father, who always chuckled at even her dumb jokes, but nothing, not even a smile from any of them.

Marky Mark would have laughed at the frog joke, slapped his knee and said, "Good one, girl." Crispy had fallen in true love with Marky. She was constantly listening to her two Marky Mark and the Funky Bunch cassettes, clipping Marky's pictures out of *Tiger Beat* and *Teen* and reading articles about what a dream date would be like for him, and scribbling Marky's name on school book covers. She'd watch MTV from after dinner until her bedtime, hoping to see one of Marky's videos, and even tried to start a local Marky Mark fan club, but Erin and her other friends weren't interested in joining.

There were nights when Crispy, about to fall asleep, would see Marky, shirtless and in Calvin Klein jeans, sitting on her bed. Marky and the band were headed to New York or Paris for a major concert but he just had to stop in to say hello. Marky would plant his lips on hers before leaving, the kiss tasting like cherry pie. When Marky was out of town, Crispy had the flat Marky in her poster to stare at for hours and hours. He stared back at her, too, never once blinked.

Imaginary Marky, poster Marky, TV Marky, musical Marky, and magazine Marky weren't doing quite enough to end her sadness over Francis leaving, so one day Crispy wrote a letter to the real Marky Mark and asked him to come fetch her.

Marky Mark
Marky Mark and the Funky Bunch
Hollywood, California

Dear Marky:

I am writing to you because Marky Mark and the Funky Bunch is my favorite band in the world and you are my favorite singer in the world! I also think that your brother Donnie of New Kids on the Block is hot, but you have even more talent than he does. You are so great! I have your records and one of your posters. My favorite songs are "Good Vibrations" and that song you do with Daddy Screechie called "Move On."

I'm a normal girl who lives in Hollis, Illinois. It's a dumb town. I'm sending you a picture of me from fourth grade. I don't know if I'm pretty. Some people say yes and some people say no. My life is terrible. I'm hoping you will come save me. I saw in Teen *magazine that you own a red Ferrari. It's really hot! You can come pick me up in your red Ferrari or any car will do. I want to move because my brother died. It was a car crash that did it. He was my favorite person. He would take me for rides in his car and go fast. I loved him every day. Since he died everything stinks. My parents are weird and don't talk to each other. My brother who is still alive smells but he is okay. I hate my house.*

Please come and get me. I am only ten so we can't get married yet, but you can kiss me if you think I'm pretty. I won't tell. I can help with the band. I can clean and cook and even make spaghetti with meatballs. You will find that having me around is lots of fun. I can twirl a baton in case you want a baton-twirling girl on stage for any of your shows. I don't play any instruments but I am willing to learn. I can also sing okay. In third grade I sang a solo at the spring festival and everyone clapped. It was to "If I Had a Hammer."

Write back and let me know when you are able to make it. Don't call or I will get in so much trouble. I will be waiting for you. Remember I am your biggest fan ever!

I love you.

Christine Harrelson
1178 Briarwood
Hollis, Illinois 62945

P.S. I can't wait until your new album comes out!

Crispy mailed the letter and began imagining the sights and sounds of a red Ferrari pulling into her driveway. She wondered if Marky would just honk the horn or if he'd come to the door, wanting to meet his future bride's family before spiriting her away.

EPISODE 10

The Official Record

"It's your turn to do one of the messy things," Gene had said to Helen, before leaving for work that morning. He wanted her to call Braverman and request two copies of Francis's death certificate so they could get payment on a small, $3,000 life insurance policy they had taken out on each of the kids years ago, never believing they'd have reason to collect.

Helen hated the coldness of Gene's words, but she supposed that there was some truthfulness to them, that it was indeed her turn. It was Gene, after all, who had made the funeral arrangements, including ordering a $4,500 top-of-the-line casket for Francis, even though it was a closed-casket ceremony and no one would see the luxurious powder-blue satin lining. And Gene was the one who chose and paid for the marker, going with the model with a golden eagle on it, while Helen would have chosen a softer, more Francis-like emblem, such as roses. Gene also took on the burden of deciding what to do with the wrecked Plymouth, first dumbly suggesting that they get it repaired so that Helen would have her own car. "I'd rather die than drive that thing," she said to him, immediately regretting those words as Stephen and Crispy were close by and certainly their developing skulls already held enough worrisome thoughts about mortality. Gene ended up selling the car to a junkman for $50. And it was Gene who answered the phone call from Gillian, Francis's girlfriend through most of high school. She had moved to California after graduating but was going to be in Hollis for spring break and hoped to see Francis, maybe get a pizza with him and catch a movie, unless he was married or otherwise unavailable. "He's no longer with us," Helen heard Gene say to the girl. Apparently Gillian thought that he meant that Francis had moved out, as Gene's next words were, "Sorry, I meant to say that he's gone from everyone. A car accident, back in January." The call lasted another ten minutes, Gene sometimes holding the phone a good foot away from his ear. Helen was sitting in the living room in the uncomfortable chair and couldn't hear what Gillian was saying, but she imagined that when Gene pushed the phone away the girl was crying too loudly.

"That was Gilly, she didn't know," Gene said, making his way to his chair and then sitting down. He sighed and tapped a hand rapidly against his breastbone like he was trying to put out a fire. "I guess I should have lied, told her that Francis was married and living in Australia, or some such. That way, he'd—"

"Still be alive to someone," Helen said, finishing his sentence like she used to do when they were first dating and he allowed such things.

"Exactly." Gene sniffled, then picked up his mechanical pencil and went back to work on *The Ledger* crossword puzzle. He had been about halfway through the puzzle when Gillian called.

"I really liked that girl," Helen said, but Gene didn't respond. Helen had figured that Gillian and Francis would eventually be married, but halfway through their senior year in high school he broke up with her, later explaining to Helen that Gillian was too old-fashioned for his tastes, that he wanted to date an independent woman who would not only expect to be treated as an equal but would demand it. That was another Could Have Been World that never happened, Francis and Gillian married and living in Hollis.

"What's the name of a city in Greece that starts with an *A* and is six letters long?" Gene asked. "The fourth letter might be a *t*. Or an *e*."

"I don't know Gene, I just don't know anymore," Helen said, tired of trying to make sense of Francis's short life and horrendous death, or how any given life plays out this way instead of that way, destiny and free will and a hundred other forces and inclinations tugging and pushing and making a big mess of things.

"That's more than six letters," Gene said. "Won't fit."

HELEN WAITED UNTIL her soap operas ended at four before calling the funeral home. One of the Braverman brothers answered—she wasn't sure which one. "We would have provided you with one copy of the certificate shortly after the funeral," Braverman said, after Helen explained why she was calling. "It's part of our award-winning customer service package."

"I don't think you did or Gene would have mentioned it," Helen said. "And besides he wants two copies, one for the insurance company and one just in case anything else comes up."

"I'm pretty sure we did give you that one copy," Braverman said, then offering to get the two "additional" copies of the certificate, but there'd be a small processing charge. Or, he said, Helen could contact the state Division of Vital Records in Springfield directly or go through the County Clerk's Office in the county where the death occurred. "Let us know if you need anything else," he said, apparently eager to ditch Helen.

"I won't," she said, but a minute after she hung up she wasn't sure if she said that to Braverman or to the dial tone.

State or county, county or state? Helen debated. She imagined at the state level death certificates were stored in ratty cardboard boxes in warehouses as long as football fields. Probably millions of Illinoisans had died since they started keeping records. In Fayette County, she imagined, the death certificates were reverently kept in some sort of gold-plated hope chest that could be opened only with a skeleton key—Helen smiled at the appropriateness of this—the key held by the county clerk, a gentle, bow tie–wearing man who looked a lot like Henry Fonda. The other workers were all chubby ladies who had knitted curtains for the office at their own expense and who sometimes brought in homemade cakes and muffins for visitors to enjoy. And whenever a new death certificate arrived in the office the ladies and Henry became a little sad. Death was such a terrible, terrible thing, they all agreed.

After getting the number from information, Helen phoned the Fayette County Clerk's Office and was soon speaking to a woman named Dotty, who had a slight Southern twang to her voice and who did sound, to Helen, like she was overweight and fully capable of sewing curtains and giving away homemade baked goods to strangers.

Dotty told Helen what she needed to do—send in a letter with information on the "decedent's" name and age, and the date and location of death—and $7 for the first copy and $3 for each additional copy, in the form of a check or money order made out to the Fayette County Clerk. The certificates should arrive within four weeks.

"Thanks for all of your help," Helen said. "This isn't the easiest thing."

"That's what we're here for," said Dotty. "Who, may I ask, did you lose?"

None of your big fat muffin-making business. "My son Francis," Helen said, her voice slipping a little. "In a car accident. On one of your highways up there. January."

"Huh. I don't remember that one. How old was he?"

"Twenty."

"Oh dear me. I have a boy seventeen and another one fifteen. Sometimes I want to lock them up, not let them out in the world."

"Enjoy your living boys," Helen said, hanging up.

THE CERTIFICATES ARRIVED just six days after Helen sent in the check. Her plan had been to set the sealed envelope on Gene's dresser and to let him deal with it, but with Helen's morbid side running around unleashed these days she just couldn't resist taking a peek.

It was midafternoon. A Tuesday. The kids would be arriving home from school soon. Helen didn't want Stephen and Crispy to see the certificates, or even know that such things existed in the world, so she took the envelope into her room and closed the door and locked it.

This is what life has come to, Helen thought, holding the glassine envelope containing the official record of Francis's death between a thumb and index finger, her hand quivering. "God help me, please," she said, tearing open the envelope quickly, as one might tear off a Band-Aid to cut down on the pain. She pulled out the two certificates and set one copy on the bed, facedown.

The certificate she held was smudgy, cheap. No gold edging or wax seal, and no lovely calligraphic writing: the data was typed, and the typewriter used had a jumpy lowercase *r,* making the *r*'s in Francis and Harrelson look like they were ascending, leaving the other letters behind.

Francis's exact time of death had been 2:12 P.M., the certificate said. The accident had happened at 1:30, according to *The Ledger,* so her child held on for about forty-two minutes. Not very long at all. At 2:11 still some hope maybe, the doctors working feverishly, injecting this or that and applying the heart paddles one more time, or whatever they tried. Hopefully everything. What *exactly* had Helen been doing at 2:12 P.M. on January 9? Probably gathering the ingredients for the carrot cake, she guessed. How could she have not sensed that her child was dead, like those mothers on television? What was wrong with her?

It only got worse. "Multiple blunt force trauma chest/head" was listed as the cause of death. Not just one trauma but many, to Francis's beautiful face and his lovely, almost birdlike chest. "Oh, Francis!" Helen said, gasping. "I'm so sorry. I'm so completely and totally sorry." Sorry that he had to suffer. Sorry that she couldn't protect him from the things in this world capable of causing blunt force trauma like concrete roads and cars made of steel. Sorry for any harsh words spoken to him over the years. Sorry for that time when he was five and picked dandelions for Helen, and she said, "Why are you bringing me weeds?" Sorry for not letting Francis—when he was eight—into her and Gene's bed after he had a nightmare, because it was only a dream and he was a big boy now. Sorry for not loving Jasmine as much as Francis had wanted her to.

Helen rubbed her eyes and was surprised to find them dry. It had felt like she had been weeping, yet no tears. She hadn't cried much since the accident, but blamed this on having too many tears, not too few. Those millions of teardrops were jammed together, trying to squeeze through two little ducts, and the result was that very few made it through. But surely she has been crying on the inside, night and day.

There was a bit more to read yet, and Helen wanted to get it over with so she continued. The contributing factors to Francis's death were, according to the certificate, "Was passenger in a car that collided with a second vehicle" and "winter storm." Mercifully, they didn't list Helen as a contributing factor, even though she should have been so listed. Helen apologized again to Francis for being a needy mother, one who had wanted only a bit of companionship with a beautiful and bright young man. Someone to talk with, hold her hand now and then. It didn't sound like the worst crime in the world but the punishment had been severe. Francis getting death, Helen life.

THE FURNITURE STORE closed at six on Tuesdays, but Gene didn't arrive home until 8:30. While he was eating his dinner—warmed-up baked spaghetti and cucumber slices—Helen informed him that the "paperwork" from Fayette County had arrived and that she had set it on his dresser.

Gene wiped his mouth with a napkin, then looked around to make sure that the children were not within earshot. "Did you . . ." he asked.

"I did," she said, feeling a gush of tears gather at the ducts. "It's pretty bad."

"Gotcha," he said.

ON THE NIGHTS Gene was at home he normally did the crossword puzzle after dinner, then retired to his room—he had his own TV in there—but that night, after completing the puzzle, he stayed in the living room and watched television with Helen and the kids.

He finally went to his bedroom a little after eleven. He closed the door, but the light stayed on for another hour.

Helen stealthily walked by his room a dozen times, listening for any sobs or curses. There was none of that, but during her third pass she did hear Gene say, "It's only a piece of paper, Gene. Just a stupid piece of paper. Deal with it." Some kind of pep talk, Helen figured, that had no chance of working.

EPISODE 11

Mushroom Hunting

"MORELS, MORELS, EVERYWHERE," sang Nicole, gazing at the selection of mushrooms in the part of the school woods that she and Stephen were exploring. "I'm getting tired of seeing morels."

Stephen was glancing at pictures of morels in *Morrison's Pocket Guide to Common Mushrooms,* one of his brother's guidebooks. "Some of them could be poisonous false morels," he warned.

"Imposters!" Nicole said angrily, to any false morels out there.

They continued hiking through the damp woods and soon crossed paths with an old woman who was picking mushrooms like berries and stuffing them into a plastic grocery bag. They helped her to fill it. "I usually don't meet children interested in mushrooms," the woman said, slipping her hand into a patch of morels and plucking five at a time. "What's your story?"

Stephen wanted to tell her about Francis and his love of mushrooms but he couldn't say the words. There was no way to mention his brother without the conversation leading to the fact that Francis was dead. "We were bored and needed a hobby," he said.

"This is a good one," the woman said. "Just be careful, and don't eat any mushrooms unless you're one hundred percent certain they're safe. I've never known anyone who died from mushroom poisoning but it happens."

"Which mushroom do you think is the most messed up?" Nicole asked.

"Honey, they're all a little funny if you ask me," she said. "But the strangest mushroom I've ever seen was Dead Man's Fingers. They look just like their name, like blue and gray fingers sticking out of the earth. I saw them in a preserve in Missouri. I wanted to turn tail and run."

Stephen looked up "Dead Man's Fingers" in the index of his guidebook. "Is that them?" he asked, pointing to a picture.

"Eck," the woman said. "It doesn't get much creepier than that."

"*Xylaria polymorpha,*" he said, showing Nicole the photo. She jumped back and said they definitely belonged in her museum.

AFTER THE WOMAN LEFT, Nicole stooped and picked a morel and stuck it in a pocket of her rain poncho. The mushroom wasn't suitable for her museum of fucked-up things—just about everyone had seen morels before—but she did enjoy the fact that their caps looked like miniature brains.

"So why was your brother so into mushrooms anyway?" she asked, trying to nudge Stephen into talking about Francis, to say a few sentences that were made up of more than three words.

"Because he thought that mushrooms were the most mysterious things ever," Stephen said, closing the guidebook. "For instance, they can appear overnight, they grow out of dead stuff, and they don't do the sunshine-photosynthesis thing so they could care less about the sun. And he said there are fungi in the Northwest bigger than small cities—I'm not kidding, there are mushrooms as big as Hollis, even bigger. And Francis said some mushrooms are good for your health, some can kill you, and others help you meet up with God."

"That's crazy talk," she said. "Why would God be inside a mushroom instead of a palace or castle?"

Stephen shrugged. Why *would* God live in a mushroom of all possible places? It was a question he'd like to ask his brother but he hadn't seen Francis since the funeral, when he was swimming in the sky.

After hiking a bit farther they decided to take a rest on a fallen ash tree, a clump of ruffled turkey tail mushrooms between them. They talked about school ending in three weeks and their plans for the summer—a period of goofing off followed by a period of more advanced goofing off—and the stories that were slated for *The Adventures of Wolf Boy #3.* The first episode was going to be about Kip Laredo's mother, Sarro, but Stephen was keeping a tight lid on the details until he had finished writing it, only telling Nicole that she might want to start sketching androids. The issue would also include an advertising flyer for Nicole's Museum of Fucked-up Things.

"Tell me a memory," Nicole said, strumming a few of the turkey tails like she was expecting them to produce mushroom music. Tell Me a Memory was a game they sometimes played, where they each would share an early memory and whoever had the more interesting memory would get a kiss.

"Here's one," Stephen said, after searching his brain. "One time when I was six or seven, Francis and I were digging in the back yard for diamonds and pirate treasure. We found the skeleton of a small animal, and Francis said it was a miniature dinosaur, Tyrannosaurus Tiny—I know, don't laugh—and that the skeleton would be worth millions. We were going to use the money to buy dune buggies and a mansion that only we would live in, and maybe a candy factory. But then Dad came outside and said the skeleton belonged to a squirrel. Francis just laughed and stuck out his tongue. I felt like an idiot. Miniature dinosaurs! Geez."

"Too funny."

"Yeah, but I really hated it when Francis teased me like that. Sometimes I felt so small around him."

Nicole nodded and leaned closer to Stephen. "I don't have any good memories today. Which means you won." She kissed him softly on his chin. Her kisses often landed there.

As Nicole pulled back he gazed into her eyes, those magical blue gumballs. Life buckled, briefly lost its way. The wet, electric air shimmered, some kind of bird cawed, and the enormous, unmanageable world became small again. There was only Stephen and Nicole, in the woods, on a rainy spring day. Stephen was trying to think of a few poetic words to capture the moment, when Nicole slid off of the tree and said, "Come on, let's go find some of those God mushrooms."

Minutes later, on a narrow, winding deer trail, they came upon three mushrooms the size of dinner plates attached to an elm tree. While Stephen paged through the guidebook Nicole tore off a small piece of mushroom and stuck it into her mouth, even though Stephen hadn't determined yet that it was nonpoisonous. "Weird, it tastes like watermelon," she said.

"Dryad's Saddle," he said, looking at a picture in the book and then at the actual mushrooms. "*Polyporus squamosus.* I never thought we'd find one of these suckers. It won't kill you."

"Are these God mushrooms? I'm starting to see God."

"You are?" Stephen tore off a chunk of mushroom, closed his eyes, winced in advance, and dropped it into his mouth. He opened his eyes and saw Nicole running around the woods, her arms outstretched. "Look!" she said. "Everything is God! The trees, the sky, you!"

He glanced at the trees, at the sky, and at his hands, but everything appeared rather ordinary. "Liar! I know you are faking."

"Busted," she said, grinning.

He reread the passage on Dryad's Saddle. "The book says that it got its name from the fact that it's big enough for sprites and fairies to hide under."

"I knew it! Come, let's do a little fairy dance." Nicole flapped her arms and danced among the trees and bushes. Stephen shook his head then ran after her, flailing his arms.

"I feel silly," he said.

"Then my work is done," she said.

On the way to their bicycles Nicole grabbed her stomach and moaned. "I don't feel so good. I musta ate a bad mushroom." She collapsed to her knees, then fell back onto leaf litter and blue ferns. "This is it, I'm dying," she said. She flopped her body, stuck out her tongue, and kept her eyes open and tried not to blink.

"I knew I should have brought a shovel," he said.

"Hah! You really should try to save me. That's what boyfriends are for." She opened her mouth wide. Stephen crouched, then inhaled deeply and put his mouth against her mouth and slowly blew all of his air into her. He sat back and poked her in the side. "Are you alive now?" he asked.

"Nope, sorry, it didn't take. So you want to be dead with me?"

"My clothes will get wet."

"It's only rain. Us mushrooms love it!"

He pushed a stick aside and stretched out next to her, then gazed up at the trees, the many branches and pine needles all looking like they were permanently stretching for something just out of reach. With the return of green life, Francis was disappearing from these woods, a little more each day. Stephen didn't know how to stop his brother from leaving for good, or even how to slow him down.

"Here, my pretty," Nicole said in a witchy voice, handing him an invisible Death Cap mushroom, which he pretended to eat.

"Are you dead yet?" she asked, a few seconds later.

"Not quite."

"Dead yet?"

"Dead!"

She took his hand and placed it on her belly, then said in a stodgy, masculine voice, "Here lie the bodies of Nicole Strussman and Stephen Harrelson. Two of the best kids ever. Turns out they were made mostly of funny bones, with a few sad bones. May they rest in pieces. Amen."

"Amen," Stephen said, remembering that his girlfriend was, quite wonderfully, a nutcase.

* * *

THEY MIGHT HAVE stayed dead longer, but flying bugs and creepy-crawlies were starting to vie for their remains. After dusting themselves off they ran down the muddy trail to the main path and to their bicycles, catching their breaths before riding home. "Do you have to die every time we go mushroom hunting?" he asked, kicking up his kickstand.

"I didn't die that one time," she said, climbing onto her bicycle.

"You mean the day you pretended that you turned into a toad."

"Yeah, and being dead and being a toad aren't the same thing. Unless you're a dead toad."

As they rode their bicycles rain began to fall in oversized droplets. "Last one home is a rotten mushroom," Nicole said as they picked up speed and pedaled their bikes through widening puddles. Stephen won the race just as the rain ended, by half the length of his bike. He told the rotten mushroom he hoped to see her later that day.

IN HIS BEDROOM, Stephen listened to pea-sized hail pelt the roof while he changed into dry clothes. He loved the idea of hail, how snow had found a way to sneak into the warm months and check out all of the living things. He considered running outside and packing a hail ball and getting in one good toss, but decided he needed to write the last few paragraphs of "Mother's Secret," the story about Sarro Laredo.

When the storm cleared, he took his notebook over to Nicole's house to show her the finished story. Her mother was grocery shopping so they had the run of the place. They ended up in Sally's bedroom, a room forbidden for them to be in, sitting knee to knee on her bed.

Nicole opened her sketchbook, picked up a pencil, and said she was ready to start drawing. Feeling a little embarrassed, Stephen fell back onto the bed and began reading the episode aloud. "Three weeks after Johnny Laredo's death . . ."

THREE WEEKS AFTER JOHNNY LAREDO'S DEATH.
ARE YOU OKAY?
I...
I THINK SO...
ZZZT
ZZT
ZZZT
ZZT
MOMMY!
I'M RUSHING HER TO THE HOSPITAL!
NO NEED FOR THAT...
ON
OFF
ALL WE NEED IS A GOOD REPAIRMAN.

Nicole tapped the eraser end of the pencil against her lips. "Let me guess—Sarro's an android. That's why you had me sketching androids, right?"

"Bingo," said Stephen, taking a peek at Nicole's sketch pad. She had started drawing Sarro and Kip's faces, and part of a couch. He thought that Kip and Sarro didn't look broken enough.

"Does Sarro run on batteries, or does she have a charger unit?" Nicole asked.

"She's solar powered. That's why if it's cloudy or smoggy for a few days she starts to wilt."

"I'm the same way. So what happens next?"

"They rush Sarro to Ralph's Android and Robot Fixit shop. That's when Buddy tells the kids that their mom's an android."

"What a shocker!" she said. "Go on."

"Poor Crystal," said Nicole, sympathetically shaking her head.

"It's even worse for Sarro," Stephen said. "If she does live forever she'll end up attending Buddy's funeral, Crystal's funeral, Kip's funeral . . ."

"Maybe Sarro could write a book called *It's Not Easy Being an Android.*"

"I'll have to think about that one."

"Do it! So what happens at the repair shop?"

"Ralph removes one of Sarro's panels and finds that her sadness filter is totally shot and her joy sprocket is fused shut."

"A joy sprocket? Interesting."

"So Kip tells Ralph about Johnny's shuttle accident, and Ralph says he can put in new parts but Sarro will keep suffering blowouts until her central processor processes Johnny's death, but they could speed things up if they talked about the accident with her—and Buddy says there has to be some other way, besides talking."

"That sounds like something a man would say," Nicole said. "Go on, read some more."

Nicole had been straining to hold in her laughter, but then she finally let a few giggles fly.

"This isn't supposed to be a funny comic book," Stephen scolded.

"I know. I was just wondering if you have a joy sprocket somewhere." Her eyes went hunting. "If I could see one it might help with the sketching."

"Shaddup!" Stephen said, fighting back a smile.

"Shaddup yourself," she said. "Okay, Wolfy, where were we?"

"Well . . . are you paying attention? After suffering several more breakdowns, Sarro banishes herself to the Where Dreams Come to Die Trailer Park, high in the mountains. When Kip wants to visit her, he—"

"Jumps from an airplane?"

"Nope."

"Takes a helicopter?"

"Not likely."

"Turns himself into Wolf Boy and leaps up the mountain?"

"That's it!"

Nicole smiled broadly. "We are like two halves of the same colossal brain. Go on left half, tell me more."

"Sure. During one of his visits . . ."

ONE DAY...
WHERE DREAMS COME TO DIE TRAILER PARK

KNOCK KNOCK
COME IN.

MOM?!
I HAVE TO BE WHO I AM, NO MORE MASKS OR LIES.

MAYBE WE SHOULD TALK ABOUT JOHNNY.

THE DAY JOHNNY WAS BORN WAS THE HAPPIEST DAY OF MY LIFE.
AND THE DAY HE DIED WAS THE WORST DAY.
FOR THE NEXT SEVERAL HOURS WOLF BOY AND SARRO TALKED ABOUT JOHNNY'S LIFE...
...AND THE HORROR OF HIS DEATH.
I STILL FEEL THIS BIG HOLE IN THE PIT OF MY NUTRITION CHAMBER.

I HATED THE WORLD FOR NOT PROTECTING JOHNNY.

AND I'M MAD AT GOD.

LATER.
GOOD-BYE. I'LL BE BACK SOON.

WAIT.

I FEEL MY SADNESS FILTER WILL FLUCTUATE PAST THE POINT OF TOLERANCE IF I WATCH YOU LEAVE.

WELL C'MON THEN, IT'S TIME TO GO HOME.

WHERE DREAMS COME TO DIE TRAILER PARK
THE END

"Oh goody, a happy ending," Nicole said.

"It's more like a happy-for-now ending," Stephen said. "Anything could still happen."

Nicole had sketched only a few panels, but the sun had come out so Stephen suggested that they take a break and go outside. The air was still electric from the lightning charges and seemed, to Stephen, to be newly made. Nicole searched the sky for rainbows, but the only rainbows were in the oil splashes on her blacktopped driveway. They were beautiful, Nicole said, like God had dropped balloons filled with rainbow water from the sky. To Stephen, the thought of God tossing water balloons at them was a bit unsettling.

EPISODE 12

Children of Time

HE FELT A LITTLE drugged by the too-many fragrances and colors and sounds all around him, his ears taking in bird chirps and insect buzz-buzzes and child squeals down the block, his eyes soaking up all of the watercolors out there and his brain naming them—lazy orange, dried-mud brown—and his nose aware of smelly flowers and freshly cut grass and his own slightly sweet sweat. Life was on parade and Stephen, sitting on his front stoop, was enjoying the extravaganza. Many of the lilies in the flower gardens were burst open now, pollen-laced pistils inviting bees to come on in, other buds shyly awaiting their cue. Large black ants and smaller brown ants crawled across the bumpy sidewalk, and sometimes onto Stephen's sneakers and socks. The yews on either side of the stoop were quietly growing, bright green branches shooting out of the dark green, the shrubs badly in need of a haircut. Birds drifted across the sky or were settled in the oak and the sugar maple and on the power lines. A squirrel pounced by in the lawn, hunting for edible things, and then back the other way. Humans drove past, a red car followed by a white car followed by a black truck. Above him, the sky was a deep seawater blue, perfect for swimming in if his brother was still up there, and the sun was curling light into everything living, including Stephen. It was late June, and even though his brother was still very dead at least life was starting to cook.

"Hey, doofus," said Francis, perched on a lower limb of the

maple tree. Stephen looked up and was instantly flushed with joy. It was the thirteen-year-old version of his brother in that tree, a version Stephen barely remembered. Francis's hair was a lighter blond and hung in bangs, and he was wearing cutoffs and a muscle shirt with a picture of a dinosaur on it. This was the kid who taught Stephen how to ride a bike without safety wheels on it, letting go of the bike seat before Stephen wanted him to. It was also the boy who pushed his face into the snow during "smear the queer" and who often pulled down Stephen's pants or shorts when a girl was nearby, but you had to take the good with the bad.

Tears were pooling in his eyes, but Stephen didn't want his brother to laugh at him for being a crybaby so he wiped his eyes with his shirt, stood up, and dashed over to the maple and climbed it, settling next to his brother. Before Francis became too mature for such silliness, he and Stephen had spent considerable time in this tree, including several failed attempts at building a decent tree house, one they could sleep out in and sneak girls up to.

"I've been looking for you in the woods," Stephen said to his brother.

"I've been looking for you in the woods," said Francis, falling backward and dangling from the branch by his legs.

Stephen dropped backward and gazed at the upside-down houses across the street. He had long suspected that this was the real world, skies made of grass and lawns made of sky. He glanced at his brother. "You're my imagination, right?"

"You're my imagination, right?" Francis said, sticking out his tongue.

Stephen pulled himself up to the branch, let his blood drop, then offered a hand to his brother and yanked him back to Right-side-up World. "Don't say everything I say."

"Don't say everything I say," Francis said.

"I mean it."

"I mean it."

He gazed at Francis. His brother was flawless, except for a little divot in the skin near his left eye, from a pebble shot out of Don Alton's lawn mower when Francis was twelve, the divot never to be filled in. *I had a brother, damn it.* "What year is it?" he asked Francis.

"It's 1986, dummy. Why are you asking me dumb questions?"

"No reason." Stephen peered down and saw the summer of 1986. Their house was white with dark green shutters instead of blue with white shutters. The walk and stoop were fresh concrete, no cracks or raised stones, and there was the old silver mailbox with a black iron eagle on it. The shrubs on either side of the stoop were babies and still had their nursery tags attached. There were no lilies, or even the curvy flower gardens. A pedal go-cart was in the side yard, as was a sprinkler, not running, attached to a winding hose. In the driveway sat the white Ford convertible they had owned for only a few weeks that summer. Helen was worried that strong winds would pluck her babies out of the car if they drove with the top down, and Gene said there was no point in having a convertible if you have to keep the top up, so he sold it, almost crying when the car's new owner drove it away. In the front yard there was an overturned tricycle (Crispy's) and a blue kickball (Stephen's).

"Earth to Steve-o," said Francis.

"What's it like being dead?" he asked.

"Are you crazy?"

"I meant to ask what it's like being alive."

"You've gone ape shit! You should know what it's like being alive 'cause you're alive. It means you get to do stuff, mess with girls, and eat and play and fart around and do it all again the next day. Geesh!"

Stephen took hold of his brother's hand, but Francis pulled it back. "I don't know about you, Stevie," said Francis. "Ross said you might be a gaywad. You're not a gaywad are you?" Ross was Francis's best friend from fourth grade through most of tenth grade. He showed up late for both the funeral and the reception and mussed Stephen's hair at both locations.

"Not a gaywad," Stephen insisted.

"Just a regular dork then," Francis said.

The brothers smiled at each other, and Stephen wondered how long this kid would stick around. Time was probably already out hunting for thirteen-year-old Francis, calling for him. "It's cool being alive, don't you think?" Stephen said.

"Yeah, it's cool, but stop saying weird things, weirdo."

Stephen spotted a black and orange caterpillar slithering on a narrow branch and pointed it out to his brother. They watched it inch along, then Francis welcomed it onto his hand. "It's going to turn into a butterfly or a moth," Francis said.

"I know that already," Stephen said.

"No you don't."

"Yes I do."

"No you don't."

A younger and happier, still-stands-on-the-balls-of-her-feet Helen appeared on the front stoop. Her hair was a mess of curls, like how she wore it that summer. She was in a white dress with tiny blue flowers and was holding open the screen door, the old wooden door that would snap against your rump if you weren't fast enough getting inside. "Francis, come home," she called. "It's lunch time. Francis. Lunch."

Francis set the caterpillar onto a leaf and nudged it with a finger to get it crawling again. He slid to the edge of the branch and said to Stephen, "See you later, masturbator."

"Don't go," Stephen pleaded. "Stay the whole summer."

"I wish." Francis hang-dropped from the branch and landed awkwardly on the lawn, tumbling onto his knees. After he picked himself up he glanced at Stephen. "Just so you know, it's not too bad being dead. Kind of like a forever June day."

Stephen puckered his lips and blew a kiss to his brother, just to see Francis screw up his face, and watched him run to their mother.

"Up in the tree again, I see," said Helen, rubbing Francis's shoulder. "You are going to worry your mother to death." Francis slipped into the house, but Helen stayed standing on the stoop for a few seconds, peering out at the neighborhood. Did she sense that these days of happiness wouldn't last forever? "I'm over here," Stephen shouted, but his mother didn't look at him. She retreated and the door smacked shut loudly.

Stephen wanted to run inside the house and be six years old again. Besides Francis and his mother, he'd get to see the toddler version of Crispy and a livelier, hairier Gene. But before he could scamper down the tree a robin fluttered onto a branch above him and brought with it seven years of time. His house was blue again with white shutters. The mailbox was white and had a painting of a cardinal on it. The hardtop Chevy was parked in the driveway. There were no go-carts, tricycles, or kickballs in the yard, but there were gardens and the lilies were in bloom.

A few branches above him, the robin that brought back time was furiously building a nest out of twigs, netting from an onion bag, and other materials. Stephen looked for the caterpillar that he and Francis saw but couldn't find it. It must have been from 1986. It probably built a cocoon and turned into a butterfly, but then what? Did it migrate two thousand miles or was it eaten by a bird, right out of the starting gate? There ought to be records, somewhere, of how every butterfly fared.

Stephen panicked, felt too far away from his own life. He climbed down quickly and ran into the house. "I'm home," he said loudly.

"I didn't know you were not home," Helen said from the kitchen. She was returning a bottle of Windex to the cabinet below the sink.

"Need help with anything?" he asked, walking to his mother.

"No, I'm beat. I think I'm going to read in my room for a while. Try your father."

"What are you reading?"

"Just a book. Check with your father. He finally takes a day off from work but has been fidgeting around all day. He could use a playmate."

Stephen found Gene in the den, folding a map of Illinois. "What's up?" he asked him.

"Oh, nothing much. I have to deliver a chair to a customer in Delfield next Thursday. I haven't been out that way in a year or two."

"Do you want to do something? Play catch?"

"I'm kind of busy." He unfolded the map and studied it, or pretended to.

"What about later?"

"The future is unknowable."

"I know the future. You'll be busy."

Gene gave him a hurt look, then returned his eyes to the map. "We'll see," he said.

Stephen then ran upstairs and knocked on Crispy's door. She was playing records and apparently couldn't hear him, so he opened the door and saw his sister slow dancing with a red throw pillow. Crispy scowled, dropped the pillow, and pushed him out of her room and closed her door.

He started down the stairs, but then the music stopped and Crispy opened her door and hung halfway out of it. "Why are you being a pest?" she asked.

"Just wondering if you wanted to do anything."

"Like what?"

"Doesn't matter to me."

"Even Life?"

"Sure. Even Life."

She dashed to her closet and retrieved Life, the game no one will ever play with her even though it was her favorite, and started setting it up on her floor. Stephen sat across from her. Crispy handed him a pile of money, then spun the wheel and got a two. "Lowest number goes first," she said. Stephen shook his head then spun an eleven.

Crispy decided on the college route while Stephen ventured straight into the business world, a move he would regret as his sister was earning twice what he was. He also tried the stock market too often and lost his shirt. Crispy reached Millionaire Acres first and won by almost $200,000.

"Want to play again?" she asked, after kissing her stack of money.

"Why not," he said.

Crispy grinned then spun the number wheel and got a ten. "High number goes first," she said.

EPISODE 13

The Museum of Fucked-up Things

COME ONE, COME ALL,
TO NICOLE'S MUSEUM OF FUCKED-UP THINGS!

Nicole's Museum of Fucked-up Things is an actual museum located in my bedroom, which is in a house, which is in Hollis (Go Hurricanes!), which is in Illinois. Currently there are no regular visitation hours, but I will be happy to arrange a private showing for only $1 (fifty cents for children seven and younger). Mention this flyer for half off the admission price.

While our inventory changes all of the time, here's a partial list of the many bizarre items you will find at Nicole's Museum of Fucked-up Things:

A conjoined (Siamese) banana. Purchased at the Kroger store on May 3, 1992, and stored in my freezer. *I can't believe they let me buy it! I'm still afraid one of my mom's dumb boyfriends will make a banana split out of it.*

A dead monarch or viceroy butterfly, with the upper tip of its right wing colored white instead of orange and black. Found in our garden in August 1992. *No, I didn't kill the poor thing. I think my mom sprayed too much pesticide like she always does. RARE item.*

A peanut shell (empty) with room enough for four peanuts. Replaces three-pod peanut shell, which is apparently not that uncommon. *I will pay $10 for a five-pod shell in good condition. Contact me at 933-5908, between 7 and 10 P.M. Monday-Friday. If an adult answers hang up!*

Article from *The Tri-County Times* dated June 11, 1986, and titled "Fire Destroys 9th Street House." A child playing with a lighter is believed to have caused a fire last night that destroyed a home on Ninth Street in Huntington, officials reported. No one was injured.

Firefighters responded to the blaze at 841 Ninth Street at 10:03 P.M. and had the fire under control by about 10:40 P.M., Fire Chief Nick Cotton said. But by then the first floor of the house was nearly completely destroyed. "Flames were shooting out of the kitchen windows when we got there," Cotton said. "We did what we could, but it looks like it will have to be torn down. That little girl is very fortunate."

Cotton said that when they arrived on the scene, Nicole Strussman, 6, who lives in the house with her parents, was standing in the front yard while holding a cigarette lighter and watching the flames. "As far as causes go it doesn't get much easier than this," Cotton said. "Parents really need to talk to their children about the dangers of lighters and matches and keep them well-hidden or locked up. The lighters and matches, not the kids."

According to reports, Nicole's mother, Sally Strussman, 34, was at work when the fire started, but the whereabouts of her father, James Strussman, 40, was unknown. Outside her burning house Ms. Strussman was heard saying, "I'm going to kill the (expletive)," apparently referring to her husband.

Police Captain Jeremiah Langfeld said that James Strussman could face a charge of child endangerment if he left Nicole unattended. Cases like this "prove the value" of the Tennessee law that forbids children under twelve years of age from being left at home alone, Langfeld said. Mr. Strussman could not be reached for comment.

The damage to the house and its contents was estimated at $78,000, reports said. "The house and just about all of their belongings are gone, but it could have been a lot worse," Cotton said. "You can build a new house and buy new stuff, but you can't replace a child."

Okay, I fucked up, but so did my dad by leaving me home alone and going out drinking. If you are a little kid reading this, do not play with lighters and matches! The pretty flames just aren't worth it.

Reese's peanut butter cup wrapper with the list of ingredients printed upside down. Purchased at Dairy Land, December 1991. *Those dumb crackheads at the Reese's factory!*

Topps 1991 baseball card with the picture of Yankees outfielder Milt Longfellow on the front, and the stats for David Gilbert, pitcher for the Pirates, on the back. *Donated by my boyfriend Stephen. I love him! He said it's worth at least $30. It would be worth a lot more but Gilbert and Longfellow both suck.*

Nicole Strussman's first box of Playtex tampons (empty). Purchased at Kroger, June 1992. *Ewww! Periods are the most fucked-up thing ever. They really should be optional. Boys have it so easy.*

Dryad's Saddle mushroom. Picked in the woods behind Lincoln Elementary School, May 1993. *FOR SALE: BIDDING STARTS AT $10. Warning: may contain fairy DNA or traces of God.*

Collins-Strussman divorce notice. From *The Tri-County Times*, August 29, 1986. Sally Collins-Strussman and James Strussman of Huntington were divorced on August 27 in Holmes County Family Court. *I haven't seen my dad since I was six. My mom's boyfriends have all been circus freaks!*

Three photos of a neighborhood cat, Alfonso, who has one blue eye and one gold eye, and a stub for a tail. *He's mean. I wonder if it's because his eyes and tail are screwy. Once he kicks the bucket I hope to have him stuffed and featured in the museum, if his owners, the Bordens, don't mind.*

Nicole Strussman's baby teeth (2) from when she was eight years old. Preserved due to the miracle of lamination. *Sometimes I freak out when I realize I have things like teeth. I don't want to be an animal! Since these teeth are nearly identical I am willing to sell you one of them. BIDDING STARTS AT $20.*

A snakeskin without the snake inside. Found at Horseshoe Lake State Park, July 1990. *Where did the snake go?*

More bizarre things coming soon!

Museum Visitors: rare autographed copies of The Adventures of Wolf Boy *comic books are now available at the museum and soon we will be selling "I Visited Nicole's Museum of Fucked-up Things and Will Never Be Normal Again" T-shirts and bumper stickers. Please consider buying these fine items or making a donation to the museum. All money raised will be used to acquire rare items (shrunken heads, etc.) and for our national museum. For now, there is still plenty of room in the current museum, so please contact me at 933-5908 about lending or donating your many fucked-up things. I'm especially interested in freakish things of nature, such as bees with an extra set of wings, two-headed rats and frogs, albino animals (small), conjoined fruits and vegetables, etc. Do not send anything living through the mail.*

If the fucked-up thing is you, please send me a testimonial and a picture.

Sincerely fucked up,
Nicole Strussman, Curator
Nicole's Museum of Fucked-up Things
1176 Briarwood Ave.
Hollis, IL 62945

EPISODE 14

In Today's Mail

CRISPY WAS MARCHING home from her friend Erin's house, twirling her baton when she felt like it and not twirling it when she didn't feel like it, when she came upon Cameron Dunfee playing in a muddy ditch. Cam had been goofy for Crispy for a long time, picking dandelions for her and offering to carry her books after school and so on, but Crispy didn't go for the mud-loving boys. She wanted her first boyfriend to be clean and sophisticated, a kid who would never even consider dropping a daddy longlegs down her blouse.

"What are you doing?" she asked Cam, watching him drag a stick through a few inches of mud.

"Looking for toad eggs."

"Oh. Find any yet?"

"Not yet. It might not be the right time of the year."

"Then why are you looking?"

"Because I am."

"What will you do with the toad eggs if you find some?"

"Take them inside and try to hatch them with my mom's sunlamp."

"Don't you think the toads can hatch them better than you can?"

"It's an experiment," he said.

Crispy knelt across from Cam and found a twig and used it to help search, doubtful that toad eggs could be found in muddy ditches.

"I wonder if you want to go out with me," Cam said, staring at the mud.

"Do you ask every girl who stops by to go out with you?"

"No. Just three so far."

"I can't. I already have a boyfriend."

"Who's your boyfriend?"

"It's a secret. But his initials are M.M."

"Mickey Mouse?"

"Not Mickey Mouse."

"What about Mighty Mouse?"

"Not funny!" Crispy said, standing up and scampering home.

When Crispy stepped inside her house she nearly bumped into her mother, who was sorting through the mail. "This one's for you," Helen said, handing Crispy a thick brown envelope sent to her from Interscope Records. "Ooh," said Crispy, smiling brightly. She ran upstairs to her room, threw the baton onto her bed, slammed the door shut, and tore the envelope open.

Crispy was hoping to find a pile of love poems Marky had written just for her, an advance copy of the band's new CD, and an airplane ticket to Hollywood, but the envelope contained only a letter from someone named Deb McMullen and a catalogue of Marky Mark and New Kids on the Block merchandise.

Dear Devoted Fan:

Thank you for your recent letter, telegram, or other form of communication. Rest assured that Marky and the members of the Funky Bunch very much appreciate your loyalty and interest in their groundbreaking music. Unfortunately, due to their busy schedules personal replies are impossible, and autographed photos cannot be sent until the reasonable fees detailed in the enclosed catalogue are paid.

We hope you will continue to support Marky Mark and the Funky

Bunch by buying their records, attending their concerts, and by purchasing several items from the catalogue. Marky has vowed to donate 5 percent of the profits from catalogue sales to environmental organizations that work to stop the destruction of the rain forest and to end the brutal practice where cute baby seals are clubbed to death for their pelts. (Please obtain your parents' permission before ordering with their credit card.)

Thanks again for your interest in Marky Mark and the Funky Bunch. Marky and the band members truly enjoyed your letter, telegram, or other form of communication.

Sincerely yours,
Deb McMullen, publicist

Crispy sneered at Deb McMullen, then balled up the letter and tossed it at her Rainbow Ponies collection set atop the dresser, wobbling but not flattening one of the ponies. She was getting tired of their constant cheeriness, anyway. Didn't Rainbow Ponies ever have bad, rainbowless days?

She looked over at the Marky in her poster, but something was disturbingly different about his smile: it was a dopey, money-grabbing grin, like the kind found on salespeople at the Fairchild Mall. *We are so happy to see you! Please spend all of your cash in our dumb store!* Crispy liked the old Marky better, the one who didn't care that she was a kid with hardly any money.

But who knows, maybe you had to buy a few items before the real Marky noticed you, before your name was placed on a list of available girls. She begrudgingly opened the catalogue and flipped slowly through its colorful pages. There were several New Kids on the Block items that made her pause, such as a board game where you had to help the New Kids find their way around the block, but the Marky Mark merchandise was what really drew her interest. A pink baby doll shirt that said "I Love Marky Mark" in gold lettering, $24 for kids' sizes, was a must, and even though she already owned one of the three posters in the poster set, on sale for $19.95, she had to have the other two, a concert picture of a shirtless Marky performing on stage, and one where Marky was sprawled on the hood of his red Ferrari. She also wanted to buy three autographed photos at $15 each, Crispy choosing two shots of Marky by himself and one where he was clowning around with his brother Donnie. She'd pass on the photo of Marky and Deborah Harry presenting an award at the 1992 Grammy's, Marky's eyes locked on Deborah's sunken boobs.

Crispy ran the figures in her head and determined she'd need about $90, plus postage and handling. Since there was only about $20 in her gorilla bank, mostly in coins waiting to be rolled into paper sheaths, she'd have to hit up her father for a raise in her allowance and volunteer to do extra chores for money.

She glanced at the Marky Mark poster. "You have to come for me," she said, shaking a finger at Marky. "Or else." She'd give him until the end of summer to rescue her, and not one day more.

DOWNSTAIRS, Helen was in a tizzy. A *third* set of Francis's death certificates had arrived in today's mail.

The second set of certificates had come about a month after the first two copies. At the time, Helen was only slightly troubled by this error—Dotty or one of the other ladies in the clerk's office must have forgotten that she had sent the first set. She placed the envelope in the top drawer of Gene's dresser, in case they might need the extra certificates later.

Now, just ten days after the second set had arrived, the Harrelsons owned two more copies of what had to be the worst official document that existed anywhere. "What kind of sick joke is this?" Helen asked, shaking the envelope that held the certificates, hoping they'd somehow shatter.

She went to the phone and angrily dialed the Fayette County Clerk's Office, got Dotty again, and told her about the extra certificates. "If I see any more of these things I'll die, I'll blow up," Helen said. "Completely disintegrate. Then there will be another death certificate. Mine."

"Just throw away the unwanted copies," Dotty said. "That's what the others do."

"The others? What others?"

Dotty explained that they were having trouble with their computer software, that for a small number of customers the computer kept saying that the request for records was still active when it really wasn't, so the staff continued sending the paperwork out. "This one lady in Taylorville got eight copies of her birth certificate. Imagine that."

"I'd love to have eight copies of Francis's birth record," Helen said. "Even a thousand copies. I'd wallpaper the walls. But this, this is death. We already know he's dead. Please stop telling us."

"Not to worry," Dotty said, in a soothing, motherly voice. "Our computer guy is going to be here tomorrow and he should be able to fix the problem."

"Goody." But Helen didn't have much faith in the Fayette County computer guy. She saw him as Emmett, the fix-it shop man in the later episodes of *The Andy Griffith Show.* Emmett will scratch his head a few times, then whack the side of the computer with a monkey wrench and say, "That should do it."

"But if you do get any more copies just tear them up," Dotty said. "That's what everyone else does."

Oh God.

AFTER SAYING GOOD-BYE to Dotty, Helen retreated to the kitchen, where she pulled a box of chocolate cake mix from a cabinet. She needed something to occupy her mind and her hands, and won't Gene and the kids be surprised to see a homemade cake? Saturday Dessert Night hadn't returned yet and Helen was doubtful that it ever would.

As she was pouring the mix into the bowl she heard Crispy gallop down the steps. "I'm in the kitchen making a cake," she yelled to her daughter, but there was no immediate response. It was then that Helen remembered she had left the two copies of Francis's death certificate on the phone stand in the foyer.

Crispy came into the kitchen, reading one of the certificates. She was dressed in red soccer shorts and a white long-sleeve T-shirt with a print of a toucan and the words "Save the Planet." A blue butterfly bow was in her hair and summer freckles dotted her face. "What does 'multiple blunt force trauma' mean?" she asked.

EPISODE 15

Bluebells

GENE SLEPT SOLIDLY until about 4 A.M., but after that he wasn't able to find a wink of the precious stuff. Worried about what might happen later that morning, his thoughts were behaving like Indy race cars zipping around an oval track. All he could do was watch from the stands and hope there weren't going to be any horrible wrecks.

He was scheduled to deliver a grandmother's rocker to a longtime customer up in Delfield, the town where Francis died, somewhere between State Route 107 just south of County Road 38 and Prescott Memorial Hospital, home of incompetent doctors and bumbling nurses. Did they just leave his dead boy alone in a room until Braverman could get a car up there? Gene wondered. They should have bathed Francis, brushed his hair, rubbed ceremonial oils into his skin, said prayers over him. But they probably just left him alone in a room somewhere.

He had mapped out a route that would allow him to avoid that stretch of 107 by at least a mile. In none of the scenarios Gene had imagined did that part of the highway treat him kindly: the road might buck him off, or worse. He had driven 107 a dozen times in the past, never knowing it would one day gobble up his oldest son. What idiot decided to put a two-lane highway there? Gene wanted to know. Make it a divided highway with four lanes instead of two and Francis would probably still be alive today, on a mushroom hunt or getting fitted for his wedding tux.

That's what Gene's mind was working on while the rest of him was sitting up in bed and watching daylight gather steam. At 7:15 the alarm clock buzzed, telling him it was time to wake up. "We are not amused," he said, flicking the alarm button off.

After he finished showering, shaving, and getting dressed, he wandered into the kitchen and found Stephen at the breakfast table, working his way through a triangle of peanut butter toast. "You do know it's morning, right, like 7:30 or a little after," Gene said.

Stephen chewed through the wad of bread in his mouth. "I thought I might help with the delivery today," he said.

Gene gazed at Stephen skeptically, wondered what was going on in that blond-haired skull of his. "That's okay, I'm sure I'll be fine," he said.

"I really don't have anything else to do," Stephen said.

Gene poured a cup of coffee and let the feisty vapors rise into his nose and loosen his sinuses. He pulled open a kitchen cabinet door, stuck his tongue out at the box of Raisin Bran, and then poured a bowl of it. He dearly missed Tony the Tiger and Cap'n Crunch, but after age thirty those kid cereals will kill you.

"What about your little girlfriend?" Gene asked. "You don't want to spend all of that time away from her, do you?"

"She's grounded again."

"Ah," he said, and by saying no more he was agreeing to the come-along plan.

RIDING WITH HIS father to the shop, Stephen thought about some of the deliveries he had helped with over the years. His brother and father would do the heavy lifting and he would carry in drawers or hold open doors. It was usually a big pain and the pay was minimal, but he now saw those deliveries as magnificent events, the Harrelson men carrying tables, dressers, and chairs into houses and apartment buildings, often up several flights of stairs, the customers almost always happy to see them. There was that man who started rocking as soon as they set down a rocker, saying the best days of his life were spent rocking on his grandparents' porch. There was that little girl who pulled open dresser drawers, planning how she'd arrange her dolls, and that family who invited them to stay for the first meal at the new dining table. It was important work they were doing, helping people live their lives.

He glanced at his dad. Gene showed a tense, worried look. "The Sox have won three games in a row," Stephen said.

"Maybe it's their year," Gene said.

"Last night they were down four to one against the Angels but they scored three in the eighth and two in the ninth. Were they any good when you were a kid?"

"The White Sox? I guess they were okay. I was more of a Tigers fan. Al Kaline, Mickey Lolich, Gates Brown—now they could play baseball. I've told you the formula for getting to the World Series, right? You need pitching, pitching, and what else?"

"More pitching," Stephen said, earning a smile from his father.

As they pulled into the lot behind the store, Stephen considered asking Gene to take him to a Sox game later this summer, but it would be such a beautiful, happy thing that he already knew the answer: "We'll see." Stephen suspected that he might be the only thirteen-year-old boy in Illinois who had lived his entire life in this state without seeing a White Sox game in person.

Gene unlocked the store's back door and Stephen slipped in ahead of him and turned on the lights. But his father told him not to pull up the shades as the store wouldn't be opening until they returned. Gene had neglected to phone Suresh, his new part-time assistant, and ask him to come in for the morning.

After Gene checked his phone messages, he and Stephen carried a grandmother rocker out to the van and tied it down. A grandmother rocker is designed so that a grandparent and grandchild of average size can sit side by side on it. Lying on its back, an unnatural position for a rocker, it filled most of the van's rear space. "This is going to take the better part of the morning," Gene said, arranging a blanket over the chair. "You sure you're up for this?"

"It might be fun," Stephen said.

"Fun it won't be," Gene said. "Survivable, maybe."

ON THE WAY to Delfield, Stephen gazed at his father and wondered what he was thinking about at that moment, driving with his second son to the town where his first son had died. He studied Gene's face and thought, *Who is that stranger driving this van?* His father didn't look anything like him, a fact Stephen always found odd. Stephen shouldn't look much like his mom, she's a female after all, but why wasn't he more or less a carbon copy of Gene? His dad had raisin-colored hair, not Stephen's blond-brown mix, a rounder face and a flatter nose, and a bit of a belly, while Stephen was skin and bones. But more importantly they *were* different. Stephen suspected that his father preferred the Cubs to the White Sox, though he was smart enough not to admit it, and Gene could be mean-spirited at times, while Stephen believed in peace, love, and kindness. What was most astonishing was that his father had abandoned the world of boy-girl love, the hand-holding, valentines, and unexpected kisses, while Stephen couldn't imagine living without it. But despite all of Gene's shortcomings and periodic meanness, Stephen loved him. He loved his old man.

Stephen needed to think of new *Wolf Boy* stories, so in his imagination he took a pencil to his father and transformed him into Wolf Daddy, father of Wolf Boy and the late Wolf Brother. Wolf Daddy sprouted a beard, his teeth sharpened into fangs, claws sprung out of his hairy hands, a bushy brown tail pushed through his overalls, and his shirt started spitting buttons as it could no longer contain his expanding chest. Wolf Daddy howled and howled while piloting the missile-proof van down the dangerous streets of Forgotten City, bombs tearing up the asphalt all around them, as he and Wolf Boy attempted to deliver a lifesaving fusion gun to the beleaguered forces of the Forgotten City Police Department and Donut Works. Despite all of the bloodshed and chaos, Wolf Daddy and Wolf Boy mostly talked about the Forgotten City Fugitives baseball team and their amazing four-armed mutant pitcher, Elmer "The Squid" Henderson.

IN DELFIELD, they carried the rocker into Mrs. Walters's house and placed it in the living room, near the fireplace. Stephen was hoping that the elderly Mrs. Walters would start behaving grandmotherly and offer them cookies and milk, but that didn't happen. She just handed Gene a check and said, "Looks like it was worth the long wait." Gene apologized for the delay and said things had been crazy at the shop ever since the apprentice quit.

When they were back on the road, Stephen suggested that they stop for an early lunch somewhere, but his father shrugged off the idea. "Let's get the hell out of this awful place," he said.

Minutes later, as Gene was telling Stephen the secrets of running a successful business, such as the importance of building a loyal client base, he turned onto 107 and headed south, passing County Road 39, County Road 38 . . .

"Oh crap oh crap oh crap," Gene cried. He jerked the van's steering wheel and turned off the road and stomped on the brakes, and then fell against the steering wheel and held on to it like it was a life ring. "I didn't mean to come this way. Goddamn it!"

Stephen wasn't used to seeing his father fall apart during daylight hours. Sometimes at night when he had been drinking, sure, but during the day he was normally as solid as stone. "What's wrong?" he asked.

"This is the place, the place . . ."

"Where Francis crashed?"

"Where he crashed," Gene gasped. "Where he died."

Stephen looked around. It was strange being here, on this one little patch of earth where everything changed, but finally he was seeing what his brother would have seen at the end: the light poles and wires, the slight rise of the road toward the horizon, a handful of houses, most of them white and with chimneys. A few road signs, too, and a blue water tower that said "Delfield" on it, far off, beyond the trees. Green now, naked then.

"Is this the exact spot where it happened?" Stephen asked.

"What? I don't know. Maybe a little farther down the road."

"We should find the exact spot."

"Hell's bells. What we should do is get away from this horrible town and never come back."

"I'd like to find the exact spot," Stephen said more quietly.

"This whole damn county should be obliterated, wiped off the map," Gene said, sweeping out an arm. "Ka-boom! Replace it with a forest—hand it back to God. No roads, anywhere."

"Please?"

Gene's face was sopped with sweat and tears. He dragged a shirt-sleeve across his face, then cut the ignition. "Five minutes. We'll give it five minutes and then we're gone."

Stephen nodded in agreement to the terms, then he and Gene climbed out of the van and started walking down the highway, on the grassy berm. After they marched about twenty feet, Stephen stopped, turned to his father, and asked him if this was the spot.

Gene peered back down the road and scratched his scalp. According to *The Ledger* article, the two vehicles collided about an eighth of a mile south of County Road 38, and Jasmine had said that the Plymouth slid into the southbound lane. "I think we're pretty close," he said.

They began walking again, and soon came upon three red lines that had been spray-painted on the highway, possibly by a patrolman marking the accident. "We might be here," Gene said.

Stephen nodded, then looked at the grass near his feet. He could almost see a wounded Francis lying there, breathing deeply and desperately while Jasmine gently brushed snow off his face. How did his brother spend his last minutes of life, he wondered. Was he still himself enough to catch a snowflake on his tongue and consider its design? Did the snow trip memories of days spent diving into snow piles and playing King of the Hill? Or did the snowflakes seem like visitors from the next world, coming for him? Stephen wished that he had been there, to help Jasmine brush the snow off his brother's face, to kiss him, and to tell him a happy memory story, one that Francis could take with him to the sky.

"Let's put up a marker," Stephen said, sniffling. "So people will know that Francis was here."

"Now you're using your noggin," Gene said.

In a ditch populated by tall weeds and reeds, Stephen searched for sticks that he could fashion into a cross. Meanwhile, Gene stayed standing next to the highway, trucks and cars screaming by him. "Slow down," he pleaded, but the cars and trucks didn't slow down.

Stephen returned with two thin sticks that he was attempting to tie together with a weed stem, but the stem kept breaking. "Hold on," Gene said, scooting to the van and returning with a piece of twine. He tied the sticks together, then pulled out his pocketknife and sharpened the one end of the vertical stick so it would be easier to set it into the earth. Stephen took the cross from his father, crouched, and pushed it into the ground.

"Good job," Gene said. "Maybe people will see this thing and ease up a little."

Stephen rose and gazed at the simple marker. Ten or twenty years from now when he's filthy rich due to his Nerf car business he'll return and put up a hundred-foot-tall neon-lit cross in honor of his brother. "I sure miss you, Francis," he said. "Over and out."

Over and out. Those words reminded Stephen of the holiday season three years ago when he and Francis played with walkie-talkies, the kind with a reception range of a few hundred yards, a gift to Stephen from his parents. The brothers would tramp through the neighborhood or inside the house talking to each other, but there usually wasn't much to say other than "roger," "ten four," or "over and out." Sometimes at night they would do space missions in their bedroom. One of the beds was always Mission Control, while the closet or bathroom was outer space. Stephen's missions were always mundane, but when Francis traveled into the galaxy things would get hairy. He would crash his spaceship onto a planet of monsters or cannibalistic cheerleaders, or, while working outside the ship, the tether would break and Francis would start drifting into space. Back at Mission Control Stephen would try and save his brother, but it was touch and go. Francis's voice would start to weaken—"I'm . . . all . . . out . . . of . . . air," or "I'mmm flooooooatingggg passssst Pluuuto"—and Stephen would tell Commander Francis to hold on, that help was on its way. Francis's radio might go dead for a minute while Stephen repeated, "Mission Control to Commander Francis, come in Commander Francis." In time Francis, or an android or shape-shifter disguised as Francis, would return safely to earth, even if the cause of it was Helen yelling up the stairs that it was way past Stephen's bedtime.

"We better go open the store and do some business," Gene said. "You ready?"

"No, not quite."

While Stephen peered at the cross and thought about Francis's last minutes of life, Gene went to the ditch and twisted three blue flowers off at their roots. He walked to the van where he found a roll of duct tape in back and tore off a three-inch piece, then returned to the cross, stooped, and taped the flowers to it. "It was missing something," he said, straightening up. "I think they're bluebells."

Stephen wanted to ask his dad why the flowers weren't bell-shaped if they were bluebells but he held his tongue. "They're pretty," he said.

MEANWHILE, IN DOWN-TOWN FORGOTTEN CITY...
TH-WAKK!
KER-POW!
THE DAILY UH-OH
IT'S OVER, IGUANA MAN!
POW!
YOU WON'T ESCAPE THIS TIME!
I'LL FLIP YA FOR IT, WOLF DADDY!
ACK!
HEADS! I WIN!
THUD!
K-POW!
NOW TO CLAIM MY PRIZE!
HISSSS!

AAAAH!!!
HERE WE ARE AGAIN, HERO.
SEEMS LIKE YOU'RE ALWAYS SAVING ME.
GO ON, PULL ME UP.
NOT THIS TIME, OLD CHUM.

THE DAILY UH-OH
LOOK!
UP THERE!
A MAN JUMPED!
I'VE ONLY GOT SECONDS --
--TO SAVE THAT GUY!
IGUANA MAN!?
OOF!!
DAD?!

THE NEXT DAY, ON THE ICE PLANET ZAMBOBIA.

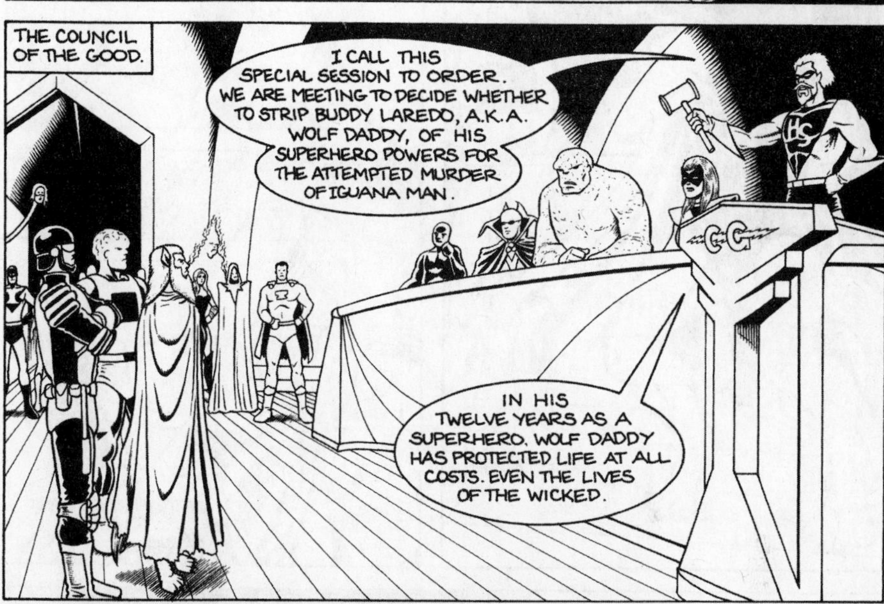
THE COUNCIL OF THE GOOD.
I CALL THIS SPECIAL SESSION TO ORDER. WE ARE MEETING TO DECIDE WHETHER TO STRIP BUDDY LAREDO, A.K.A. WOLF DADDY, OF HIS SUPERHERO POWERS FOR THE ATTEMPTED MURDER OF IGUANA MAN.
IN HIS TWELVE YEARS AS A SUPERHERO, WOLF DADDY HAS PROTECTED LIFE AT ALL COSTS. EVEN THE LIVES OF THE WICKED.

BUT IT IS THIS COUNCIL'S CONCLUSION THAT SINCE THE DEATH OF HIS SON JOHNNY, OUR BELOVED WOLF BROTHER, WOLF DADDY NO LONGER BELIEVES IN A JUST WORLD.

WOLF DADDY, YOU HAVE NO RIGHT TO DECIDE WHO LIVES AND WHO DIES.
WHAT DO YOU HAVE TO SAY FOR YOURSELF?

I JUST WANT TO SAY MY RECORD SPEAKS FOR ITSELF: 482,287 PEOPLE SAVED AT LAST COUNT. WHAT'S MORE...
I...

OH HELL. WHAT DOES ANY OF THIS MATTER, WHEN THE GOOD DIE ANYWAY?
DO WHATEVER YOU WANT TO ME.

SO YOU PLEAD GUILTY?
AS CHARGED.

SO BE IT. AFTER CAREFUL CONSIDERATION, THE COUNCIL HAS VOTED UNANIMOUSLY TO TAKE AWAY WOLF DADDY'S POWERS.
HS
CG

SLAM

ZZZZZ-
-ZAP!

LATER... NO LONGER ABLE TO LEAP HOME, BUDDY LAREDO WAITS TO BOARD THE SPACE TRAIN BOUND FOR VELAROS 7, MARS, EARTH AND CUCAMONGA.

EPISODE 16

The Ghost Channel

TIRED AND LEGALLY drunk from three beers, Jasmine sat at her desk and stared at a stack of mail, mostly letters and sympathy cards that had been piling up since January. *Screw them all,* she thought. If her friends and professors really cared about her they could phone or stop by.

She rummaged through the pile and decided to read one of the three letters from Stephen. Mercifully, it turned out to be a short note.

Dear Jasmine:

Guess what? Nicole and I went mushroom hunting and found three gigantic mushrooms stuck to a tree. They taste like watermelon and fairies used to hide under them.

Please write back one of these days because I need to know if you've seen Francis since the accident. I think I saw him swimming in the sky at the cemetery. Could heaven be an ocean? Could he be thirsty and trying to find water? Let me know your ideas right away!

Your friend,

Stephen Harrelson

P.S. Nicole wants to know if you have any messed-up stuff for her museum.

She set the letter down and thought about the night she saw Francis swimming in the bathtub. The memory of his dark, moving mouth still haunted her. She had written off the experience as an extended hallucination, but apparently, there had been another sighting of Francis's ghost. *Coincidence,* her rational self piped in. Even if a hundred people hallucinated the same thing it didn't make the hallucination real.

On the other hand, her emotional-intuitive self said, it would be just like Francis to jump off the escalator to the afterlife so he could stay close to those he loved. Her rational and emotional sides grappled, and her rational mind, a strong believer in calisthenics and healthy living, easily clobbered her slothful, chocolate-loving emotional-intuitive side.

Jasmine finished the last sudsy inch of a Miller Lite, then found a pen and a sheet of typing paper in her desk and wrote Stephen a letter.

Handsome:

I'm sorry that I haven't been in touch sooner. I've wanted the outside world to leave me alone, but that world includes sweet people like you so I suppose I should let some of it back in.

As a matter of fact I did "see" Francis once. It was very strange. He was in my bathtub and moving his arms like he was swimming, and he was trying to say something. This lasted several hours, BUT I do not believe that he was actually there, in the tub. I think the same thing happened to you at the cemetery. We miss him so much that our minds are playing tricks on us, imagining that his ghost has returned. He was stolen from us so we stole him back for a little while, or rather we thought we did.

I don't believe in ghosts. Do you? I do believe in spirits and/or souls, but I don't think they would retain the image of the body after death, just like a crab looks nothing like its shell. So take comfort in the fact that something of Francis is still out there. And his love will always be with us.

Tell Nicole I'll keep my eye out for messed-up stuff. Love her, and your sister, and your parents. As far as love goes it really should be an open tap.

Write back to me you sweet, sweet boy.

xoxo

—Jazzy

Only half-believing her argument against ghosts, Jasmine set the letter aside to mail in the morning, shed a few thick tears, then went to her bed. She stretched her arms and faked a yawn, signaling her body that it was sleepy-by time. *Francis thirsty? How awful.* But she better not think about that right now or it would darken her dreams.

She slept for a few hours but then was suddenly wide-awake, like someone had injected her with methamphetamine. She considered downing another beer or waking her mother and asking to borrow a Valium, but decided instead to roam downstairs and watch a little television, let some old *Bonanza* or *Dick Van Dyke Show* episode calm her racing heart.

She stretched out on the couch and turned on the TV. Whatever channel she had on was showing a swimmer working his way across a lake or ocean. Perhaps it was a surfer who just lost his board, she thought, or one of those dolts who periodically tried to swim across the English Channel. Jasmine hit the info button on the remote and learned that she was watching Channel 24, CNN, which couldn't be right, so she flipped to the next channel, C-SPAN, and saw the same image of the swimmer, and then on to USA, where the swimmer was waiting for her. The damn cable company had really screwed up this time. She pressed the remote's forward arrow and flew through the channels, all of them showing the same video. It was a bit like watching a cartoon made from rapidly flipped static images: on

Channel 52 the swimmer's right arm was just coming out of the water, on 53 it was perpendicular to the water, and on 54 it was scooping back into the lake or ocean. (Reversing the channels, however, did not reverse the swimmer.) She kept flipping through the normally dead channels, but the swimmer owned the airwaves all the way to Channel 999.

The camera moved closer and she recognized the swimmer as Francis. *Of course.* The torn pair of black pants was the big clue. Francis did not look at her or the camera and kept swimming. *Where is this lake or ocean?* she wondered. *Where is he swimming to?*

Jasmine pressed the power button and Francis disappeared. She looked around the living room, searching for clues that she was stuck in a dream, but everything looked rather normal. "Wake up, you're dreaming," she said, but her lucid self failed to show up and pluck her out of the scene. She hit the power button again. Channel 999 was snow, like it should be. She flipped forward through the stations and settled on a Scooby-Doo cartoon, but then the screen flickered and the video of the swimmer returned. She tried a few more stations, but Francis was swimming on them as well. She decided to watch the show.

It was beautiful, seeing her honey boy moving again, even though he was dead. She slid from the couch to the Oriental rug and scooted closer to the television. "Where are you going, sweetie?" she asked. At least the water was calm. But there was no sign of land, or a reef, or a rescue chopper, any obvious chances for him to rest. She kissed the screen where Francis was. A jolt of static electricity tingled her lips.

Jasmine stayed huddled on the floor and watched Francis swim. Finally there was something on television worth staying up for. Francis kept making the same smooth motions with his arms, legs, and head: no variations or letups. If the swimmer was someone other than her former fiancé it would be a boring film: there would need to be a shark or a storm, some element of danger to keep her interest. She sang, "I see London I see France, I see Francis pulling off my underpants." She had sung that to him once in real life. She always felt more creative around Francis, like there were jokes, poems, all sorts of great and funny things lining up in her mouth, ready to tumble out. Francis wasn't distracted by her words or by what she did next, lifting her shirt and rubbing a tit against the screen. He kept swimming, so she dropped her shirt. She couldn't even seduce the hard-up dead these days. But he was getting to her. The way his synchronized arms and legs thrashed and kicked through the water was arousing. She wanted to be kicked through, thrashed through by Francis.

If Francis was in a timeless place he could swim forever, love forever, screw forever. There was only a glass screen that separated them, that kept her from an eternal swim beside her beloved. She could smash the glass with her hands, bleed out, and join him. But Jasmine believed there was still a minuscule chance that a decent life was waiting for her here on earth.

"Come to me if you need to," she told the swimmer. "Take shelter here."

Francis turned and started swimming toward Jasmine. Just as it looked like he was about to swim through the screen, Jasmine freaked and punched the power button. But then she quickly turned the TV back on. It now showed a Flintstones cartoon. She waited for the cartoon to switch to the live (or dead) feed of Francis swimming, but the cartoon ended and another one started. She tried each of the sixty-two stations but could find a swimmer only in an old episode of *Flipper*, but he wasn't Francis. Where had the Ghost Channel gone? Jasmine turned off the Zenith and hurried up the stairs, expecting to find her honey boy swimming in the bathtub, but he wasn't there. "Come to me," she said. "Tell me what you need to tell me."

She moved to the edge of the tub and imagined trying to hold down Francis's swimming arms. She would do that, hold his arms, let him rest. Shortly after the accident she began to imagine scenarios where Francis survived the crash and she tended to him, massaging his legs back to life or changing his bandages. Life not only stole Francis but also her chance to heal him.

She sat in the tub and lay back. The iron was cold against her skin. She pulled up her shirt, unzipped her jeans. "Come to me," Jasmine said. "I am your woman, your love, your life. Come to me, you beautiful, beautiful man. Come."

Francis didn't come.

EPISODE 17

A Visitor

HE HAD SPENT much of the day with Nicole doing next to nothing, watching TV and helping her search for a lost necklace and talking about her dumb dad who didn't even call or send a card for her fourteenth birthday. Now, returning home, he hoped to shoot baskets in his driveway and sweat a little, pretending that there were only three seconds left in game seven of the NBA championship and the Bulls, down by a point, were smartly relying on Stephen Harrelson instead of Michael Jordan to win it. He could shoot a thirty-footer from the street or dribble for two seconds, then take the game-winning jump shot. But his father's Chevy was parked on the driveway near the hoop, as was a red truck, rusty at its edges, that had the words "Baron Roofing," along with an out of town phone number, on its door. Stephen walked the length of the truck and peered into its cab—messy with tools, nails, an overflowing pile of coins in a tray between the seats, and empty McDonald's french fry boxes and plastic Mountain Dew bottles—then gazed at the house: it didn't look like they needed any roofing work done, but what did he know about roofs?

He went inside, kicked off his sneakers in the mudroom, then proceeded into the kitchen but came to a stop when he heard the visitor in the living room, talking to his parents. "This whole thing is still messing with me," the man said. "It couldn't have just been a random event. I refuse to believe that."

"It better have been random," Gene responded.

The stranger sounded about thirty years old, Stephen guessed, perhaps an uncle or a distant cousin he hadn't met yet. With more curiosity than caution he padded though the kitchen and down the short hallway and into the living room, where the visitor was sitting in the middle of the couch like he owned it. Stephen's parents were in their assigned seats, Gene in the rocker and Helen in the uncomfortable chair. Gene was holding an empty bottle of Michelob by its neck and swaying it back and forth, keeping time. Helen had a focused but worried look like she was being forced to take a test she hadn't had time to study for.

Gene glanced at Stephen and addressed him. "Uh, that there is the one and only Michael Haynes, from the accident," he said. "The other driver."

Floor it in reverse! Stephen wished at that moment for the power of invisibility like Professor Nobody, one of his Wolf Boy villains, possessed, or the ability to freeze time until he could figure out what to do. He glanced at his mother, smiling feebly, then at Michael Haynes, who motioned for him to come closer. Stephen took five steps forward instead of backward, a malfunction of will. Michael grinned and reached out his hand: four fingers and a thumb, what you'd expect. Stephen shook the man's hand weakly, then firmed up his grip, a test of strength here in the center of the wrestling ring, fans cheering for good-guy Stephen Justice to shatter the fingers of the evil Michael the Marauder and bring him to his knees, begging for mercy.

"Good to meet you, partner," said Michael, pulling back his hand but not shaking it or showing any signs of pain. "Ever since I saw your name in the paper, the obituary, I was wondering what you looked like. I guessed wrong, figured you were a redhead."

"Yeah." Michael was dressed in jeans, work boots, and a tucked-in white dress shirt that looked to be freshly ironed. He was muscular and tanned and had thick and wavy brown hair. It was going to be difficult for Stephen to hate someone this good-looking, though it was a different kind of handsome. Michael was pretty in the slightly dangerous way hawks were pretty. Francis had been pretty in a harmless blue jay way.

"Don't be rude, take a seat," Helen said. There are mothers and fathers who would shuttle their children away from encounters with brother-killers, but Stephen didn't have those parents. He sat down on the carpet, wished he could get away with turning on the TV, even one of his mom's soap operas.

"I was just telling your mom and dad how freaked out I've been since the accident," Michael said. "I'm not getting much sleep, lost my girlfriend . . . everything's haywire. I even started going to church on Sundays. It doesn't make a lick of sense to me how your brother—a good guy, I could tell, just from his picture in the newspaper—ended up getting killed in the accident and I wasn't even scratched. It has me wondering if I was spared for a reason, if God has a special plan for me. Now I'm not saying that God didn't spare Francis on purpose, or anything—"

"We heard you weren't much help after the accident," Gene said.

Go, Dad, go, Stephen thought. *Kick the crap out of him.*

"Sorry about that," Michael said. "I was frozen by shock, and when that takes over, forget it, you have no free will at all. I wanted to go help Francis, I really did, but I couldn't convince my hands to open the truck door so I could get out. That isn't my nature. Hell, when I was twelve I saved a kid from drowning, Robbie Peshek. He's still out there, thanks to me, and has two kids, who should also be thanking me."

Stephen tallied Michael's score: three lives saved to one life taken.

"What do you think your special plan is?" Helen said, shifting in the uncomfortable chair. "The one God might have spared you for?"

"That's what I've been trying to figure out these past months. I'm sure it's not putting on roofs. I've been thinking of starting classes in social work or even becoming a priest, if they'd take me. I wasn't the best person, before the accident." Michael steepled his hands, then bounced the pads of his fingers against one another. "Here's the other thing. I probably shouldn't be admitting this, but since the accident, when I'm out driving, I have this urge to mess with the other drivers, tailgate the guy in front of me, pull into the lane of an oncoming car, just for a second or two. Not to cause any real trouble, but it was like the crash with Francis interrupted my life, interrupted all of our lives, and reminded me that life is very short. Now I want to return the favor to others, to strangers, interrupt them somehow and shake them and say 'wake up, man, this game doesn't go on forever.' I haven't done that yet, but I've only got a hold of this thing by the tail—it could break free any day."

"I'd be careful," Gene cautioned. "You don't want to hurt anyone else."

"Right, right, right," Michael said. "I'm hoping my calling is something less risky, like counseling. Of course it will take years of study and a cartload of money to get my degree and license. Interrupting I could start today."

"I'd go with counseling," Helen said. "Just make sure that regular people can afford your fees."

Michael bobbed his head, then looked at Stephen, "Hey, partner," he said. "I suppose you want to take me outside and clobber me with your baseball bat until I'm crying for my mama."

"A little," Stephen admitted. It would be sweet, taking a swing at Michael's head with his Louisville Slugger, knocking that pretty thing all of the way to Louisville.

"Stephen!" Helen scolded.

"If I were in his shoes I'd want to do the same," Michael said. "But the crash wasn't my fault, it was due to the bad weather. Have you folks seen the accident report? There's a category called 'act of God.' "

"Why are you here?" Stephen blurted. He could feel his mother's Eyes of Correction on him, but he hungered to know the answer.

"Since the accident I've been wanting to come up to Hollis to meet you folks and see the town where Francis had lived, the house he grew up in, get some sense of him," Michael said. "Did he live in this house all of his life?"

Gene nodded. "Except for one year in Carbondale, at the school."

"Good, good. And the other reason . . . I want to ask your forgiveness. The accident wasn't my fault, the report says that, but I was wondering if you could forgive me for being where I was on that particular Saturday, and for the shock, for not helping out." He scanned their faces. "Can you folks forgive me? I'd understand if you can't."

Helen glanced at Gene, who was peering out the window at the front garden, looking at the lilies with some disdain. "We forgive you," she said. Gene sighed. In his mind Stephen told Michael, *Go hump a donkey.*

"Thank you, kind people." Michael dabbed his wet eyes with the palms of his thick hands. "I'm usually not like this. This whole thing is turning me into someone else."

Crispy came in the front door a few seconds later, carrying her baton. Michael turned toward her. "You must be Christine," he said.

"Who are you?" she asked, pushing the door closed. *Run,* Stephen was telepathically telling her.

"My name's Michael. I was, unfortunately, involved in that accident with your brother."

Crispy let out a shriek and bolted up the stairs.

Michael grimaced. "She must think I'm the bogeyman."

"That girl has a good head on her shoulders," Gene said. He stretched his arms back, did a half-assed yawn. "I have to get back to the store. You're not planning to stay for dinner or anything, are you?"

"He can stay for dinner if he wants to," Helen snapped.

"I'm just asking," Gene said.

"No, but thanks for the offer," Michael said. "It's a long drive so I should be going. But first, is there anything you folks need?"

"We don't need anything," said Gene.

"I'm only asking because I got a small settlement from the accident. If you need a new washer and dryer, or would like me to make a mortgage payment for you, whatever you want, just say the word."

Helen and Gene spoke at the same time, Helen saying, "We can't take your money," and Gene saying, "We didn't see a penny." Gene had more to say. "How were you able to get money? The accident wasn't anyone's fault."

"True, it wasn't, but my cousin is an attorney, a real greaseball. He made a few threatening calls, started taking depositions. The insurance company for that young lady who was driving—"

"Jasmine Chambliss," Helen said. "Francis's fiancée."

"They were going to be married? Oh Jesus. Anyway, her insurance company panicked and cut a check for $20,000. Apparently they don't like taking their chances in court. Jack, that's my cousin, took $4,000 and I got the rest. So if there's anything you need . . ."

"No," Gene said, firmly.

"Okay, I was just trying to be helpful. It's only insurance company money, no skin off anyone's nose."

"How many times do I have to say no?" Gene asked.

"Sorry," Michael said.

Stephen thought about the offer and figured that Francis wouldn't mind if Michael Haynes gave him enough to pay for two tickets to a Sox game and a limo ride to Chicago and back for him and Nicole. But he couldn't ask for the money.

"Back in a sec," Stephen said. He rose and walked quickly through the house and outside to Michael's truck. He pulled open the passenger side door, slipped into the cab and grabbed a handful of coins—pennies, nickels, and dimes, a quarter or two, some kind of token—and put the money in his shorts pocket. It wasn't enough to buy White Sox tickets, but he was going to get something out of this deal, say three or four packs of baseball cards and a Milky Way bar. He then stole about a dozen roofing nails, in case he wanted to build something this summer, and snagged a Stanley retractable tape measure, which would come in handy when he constructed his Nerf car prototype.

He slid out of the truck, closed the door, and was about to head into the house when he heard someone moving around in the mudroom. The measuring tape was still in his hand so he stuffed it in a back pocket of his shorts.

Michael Haynes came out of the house and smiled at Stephen. He wasn't as pretty in sunlight, Stephen observed: his skin was pocked and his eyes were slightly recessed in their sockets like they were a little afraid of the world. "It was nice to spend some time with you, partner," the killer said. "Sorry about what happened to your brother. It's a terrible shame."

"Do you have any brothers?"

"Yes, two younger ones, always getting into trouble. I've been a piss-poor role model."

"Maybe that's your calling. Helping your brothers instead of running people off of the road."

"That could very well be. You're a pretty smart kid."

"Not really. I can't handle algebra."

Michael patted Stephen on the head, then walked to his truck and climbed inside. He smiled, started the truck's ignition, backed up, and applied squeaky brakes before heading out, north on Briarwood, in the direction of the highway. Stephen told Michael Haynes to go hump that donkey again, then went inside.

His parents were actually talking to each other.

"He drove a hundred miles to kick us all in the head," Gene said, shaking his kicked head. "That's what this was all about."

"He wasn't as awful as I thought he would be," Helen said.

"Awful enough," said Gene.

"I liked his tan," Stephen said, wanting to be part of the conversation.

"He should be using sunscreen when he's working on roofs," Helen said.

"Let him burn up," Gene said.

Helen nodded. She'd let Michael Haynes burn. "What about the insurance money? Should we make some inquiries, or whatever you have to do?"

"No," Gene said. "That's not what Francis was all about. What would money do for us?"

So much for the Sox game, thought Stephen.

* * *

AFTER HIS FATHER left for work, Stephen hustled upstairs and checked on his sister. Crispy didn't respond to his knock so he opened her door and saw her lying on her bed, clutching a stuffed panda bear, an old friend.

"That man is gone," Stephen said.

"He's not allowed in our house," Crispy said, scowling.

"I know. He's gone and he'll never be back."

"He's dumb and ugly."

"Very dumb and very ugly."

Stephen couldn't think of anything else bad to say about Michael Haynes, so he offered to measure Crispy with his new Stanley retractable tape measure. Crispy held the silver tab to the top of her head while Stephen pulled the metal tape across her body and to her sneakers. "Four foot seven and three-sixteenths," he announced.

"I think I'm growing," she said.

"I think you are, too. We'll have to measure you every week to see how fast."

Crispy let go of the tab and the tape zipped into its housing, which caused her to giggle. She wanted to measure Stephen, so she got up from the bed and Stephen stepped on the tab with a socked foot and started pulling the tape up and handed it to his sister. Crispy rose on her tiptoes and extended the tape to the top of Stephen's head.

"Almost five foot four," she said.

"I'm shrinking, I'm shrinking," he said, trying to mimic the voice of the wicked witch in *The Wizard of Oz* but missing by a mile. "Help me! Soon I'll only be one inch tall."

"I will squash you like a bug!" Crispy said. "Or keep you like a pet."

"The second one, please." He slid his foot back and the tape *zlim zlim zlimmed* into the base. "I love that part," Crispy said.

Stephen lent his sister the Stanley retractable tape measure so she could measure everything in her bedroom, then went into his room, closed the door, and sat on his toy chest and peered out the window. Michael Haynes was long gone, so Stephen had to use Super Wolf Vision to see him, driving the Baron Roofing truck on the highway now, passing an ice cream truck, then a yellow Beetle, scouting for unhappy drivers who needed to be interrupted.

Michael wasn't the worst person on earth, a grade C to Francis's A+, but if someone had to die in that crash it should have been him, not Francis, or Jasmine, another A+. That's how it would play out in a fair world, Stephen thought, the A+ people would get to stay and the C people were always at risk—and the D's and F's could forget about making it to old age. Bummed out by the fact that Michael Haynes still existed in the world when his brother did not, Stephen found his writing pad and a pencil and banished Michael to Forgotten City.

SUPERNOVA COMICS PRESENTS:
GET TO KNOW YOUR VILLAINS AND EVILDOERS

THE INTERRUPTER

NAME: MIKE "JUMBO" HAYNES

ALIASES: "THE INTERRUPTER," "PEA-BRAIN MIKE"

AGE: UNKNOWN -- HE STOPPED COUNTING WHEN HE RAN OUT OF FINGERS AND TOES.

LIKES: CHEWING CHEWY THINGS -- JERKY, TAFFY, SHOE LEATHER, ETC.

DISLIKES: EVERYTHING THAT ISN'T CHEWY.

WEAPONS: NONE (UNLESS LETHAL BAD BREATH COUNTS.)

SLOGAN: "I AM THE INTERRUPTER AND YOU HAVE BEEN INTERRUPTED AND SAVED."

ONE NIGHT MIKE WAS DRIVING TO A GROCERY STORE TO BUY CHEWY THINGS WHEN HIS TRUCK AND A CAR BEING DRIVEN BY A BRILLIANT SCIENTIST, DR. GALILEO NEWTON, COLLIDED.

AS IS NORMALLY THE CASE WHEN MORONS CRASH INTO GENIUSES, DR. NEWTON WAS KILLED INSTANTLY WHILE MIKE WAS NOT INJURED. MIKE CLIMBED OUT OF THE TRUCK AND WAS WALKING HOME...

...WHEN A BOLT OF LIGHTNING STRUCK HIM AND BURNED A BIG LETTER "I" INTO HIS CHEST.

MIKE APPEARED EVEN MORE DUMBFOUNDED THAN USUAL, SO GOD SENT DOWN AN ANGEL TO STRAIGHTEN HIM OUT.

"IT'S AN 'I', AS IN INTERRUPTER," THE ANGEL SAID. "YOU WERE JUST INTERRUPTED AND SAVED BY GOD, AND NOW YOU MUST SERVE GOD BY INTERRUPTING AND SAVING OTHERS. REPEAT AFTER ME: I AM THE INTERRUPTER."

MIKE SCRATCHED HIS BIG MELON HEAD. "IF YOU'RE THE INTERRUPTER, THEN WHO AM I?"

MAJOR CRIME #1: INTERRUPTING A SOLAR BUS BY STEPPING IN FRONT OF IT AND YELLING HIS SLOGAN, CAUSING THE DRIVER TO CRASH INTO THE FORGOTTEN CITY ACADEMY FOR SQUEAMISH BOYS.
KRA-BOOM

MAJOR CRIME #2: INTERRUPTING THE ANNUAL ORPHAN SCOUTS FUND-RAISING COOKIE SALE DRIVE BY STEALING ALL OF THEIR COOKIES.
COOKIE SALE TOD

CURRENT STATUS: BANISHED TO THE MUSHROOM PLANET MYCOVIA BY WOLF BOY.

FUTURE THREAT LEVEL: SLIM TO NONE. WE DID HEAR THAT THE INTERRUPTER IS TRYING TO BUILD A RAFT OUT OF MUSHROOMS SO HE CAN FLOAT BACK TO EARTH. GOOD LUCK WITH THAT, MIKE!

LESSON TO BE LEARNED:
"HE WHO INTERRUPTS MUST BE WILLING TO BE INTERRUPTED, AND HE WHO IS... WHAT WAS THE QUESTION AGAIN?"
- CONFUSEDIOUS
FORGOTTEN CITY'S GREAT CRACKHEAD PROPHET.

COMING ATTRACTIONS:
IN THE NEXT EXCITING ISSUE OF *THE ADVENTURES OF WOLF BOY* YOU'LL GET TO KNOW THE INVISIBLE DR. NOBODY.
HERE'S A PREVIEW:
SOMETIMES I FEEL SO VULNERABLE, LIKE PEOPLE CAN SEE RIGHT THROUGH ME.

EPISODE 18

Floating

HELEN STOOD ON the front stoop, shaking. A gentle breeze ruffled her yellow dress, and the July sun was high in the sky, shining down. Birds chirped their little brains out. Cars passed blurrily on Briarwood. Near Helen, on the stoop and sidewalk, was a scattering of mail, mostly bills and catalogues, that she had dropped. In her hands she held two envelopes from the Fayette County Clerk's Office containing death certificates seven and eight and nine and ten.

God is really messing with me, Helen thought, or maybe it's the devil. What was next, a carpet-bombing of certificates dropped by planes, Helen and Gene and the kids drowning in a sea of death records?

"Stop it," she said to God, the devil, the mailman, and the Fayette County Clerk's Office. "Have mercy."

Helen suddenly wasn't feeling right. Too airy, almost weightless, like the forces holding her earthbound had taken a hit. She tried to breathe in deeply, to center herself, but her rhythm was screwy: she could inhale okay, but as soon as she tried to exhale she'd be inhaling again, as if her body was trying to puff itself up with air, aiding buoyancy.

She went back inside, would pick up the mail later. Moving toward the living room, where she hoped to lose herself in a soap opera, Helen felt like she was walking an inch above the carpet. *Oh dear.* Her deck shoes *were* touching the carpet as she walked, but it seemed like she was trying to rise out of those shoes and float upward, thin white shoestrings the only thing preventing Helen from bumping up against the ceiling. Were such things even possible in this Newtonian world of natural laws?

"Help!" Helen said. "Help me." She considered calling 911 but what would she say to the operator? That oxygen was now helium and she was in danger of floating away, so could they please send someone with a net? Might she ask Mrs. Borden or one of the other neighbors for help? *No, no.* If Helen somehow survived this day she'd become the laughingstock of the neighborhood. *Floated to the clouds lately, Helen?*

Viv Davis might be the only one who could help her, Helen thought, while holding on to the stairwell banister. Viv was a sad mother Helen had sent a sympathy card to in May after seeing in *The Ledger* that she had lost a daughter and two grandchildren in a car crash. They exchanged a few letters and phone calls, Viv sometimes remarking that she felt like she was halfway out of her body, like she couldn't decide whether to stay or go. The only thing Viv had found helpful were the grief support group meetings at St. Vincent's Hospital. She urged Helen to come with her to the meetings, but Helen had no interest in watching a bunch of blubbering women spew sadness, so she kept saying no. She'd only join the support group, Helen had decided, if things went from bad to awful.

She was now at awful. *What day is it, Wednesday? Does the support group meet on Wednesdays or on Thursdays?* Maybe Viv and the blubbering ninnies would be willing to hold Helen down, keep her from dissipating into the atmosphere, and share some antifloating secrets they had learned from their own experiences: gravity pills you could order from a pharmacy in Brazil, or an iron suit Helen could wear to keep her grounded.

She tossed the envelopes from Fayette County into Gene's room, found her purse, then went to the door and looked worriedly at the Chevy parked in the driveway. About a thirty-foot walk, Helen estimated, but there were no ceilings out there to keep her from floating only so high. "I am bound by the nonnegotiable forces of gravity," she said, taking that first step.

HELEN SAT IN the Chevy in the St. Vincent's parking lot, feeling like a failure. She had tried going into the hospital a few minutes earlier but the automatic doors seemed threatening, so she retreated to the safety of her car. Damn. She couldn't even ask for help right.

She was about to start the car and head back home when she saw the spare key to Francis's Plymouth dangling from the ring. She had forgotten that it was still there. "In case you ever need to run away," Francis said when he handed her the key. What a trouper.

Helen couldn't turn the ignition. What if the Chevy started floating? It could be the day for all leaden things to sprout wings. She saw her car rising and then floating around the planet. The Red Cross would periodically drop supplies to her from a helicopter, or maybe it would be Arty Gifford in the Channel 7 Sky-watch chopper, bullhorning forecasts for endless sunny days. In many of the towns she visited people would hold signs that said, "Welcome, Floating Lady." Other signs would say, "Why Didn't You Do More with Your Life?" She was going to be a teacher, nurture a thousand young lives. Instead, she became a breeder and a kept woman, and failed at both. Francis was dead. Gene no longer wanted her.

There was a tap at the car window so Helen rolled it down. It was a woman, dressed in a nurse's uniform of all things. Her name tag said "Millie."

"Are you okay?" Millie asked.

"I'm fine," Helen said, smiling.

"Are you sure?"

"I'm not sure. Maybe I better get to a hospital."

"You're already at a hospital."

"I think I knew that."

Millie talked Helen out of the car, took her by the elbow, and led her into the hospital. Helen feared that the automatic doors would crush them but they made it safely inside. That happened once, in Belgium or someplace. A family of five was wiped out by automatic doors.

HELEN SAT ON a gurney in the emergency room, behind a blue curtain. *What's the emergency?* she wondered. Or perhaps she was one of the prizes on *Let's Make a Deal.* Behind curtain number three it's your very own crazy lady! She laughed at the thought, but almost expected Carol Merrill to pull open the curtain.

I better figure out what went wrong. I was looking forward to watching Doogie Howser, M.D. *tonight, and now I'm in a hospital. How ironic. Has irony, that normally rare monkey, taken control? Too weird to think about. Irony World! Holy shit. Maybe Doogie is roaming the E.R. I'm here, Doogie! That show is always unpredictable, just like real life, which is pretty much a tossed salad, wherein tomatoes and radishes must learn to exist side by side, and a worm might be hiding under a spinach leaf, you just never know.* Helen realized that she liked using the word *wherein*, even in her thoughts. It made her think of herself as an important legal scholar. *Shit. I should have done more with my life. I graduated cum laude, which is Latin for "smart as a whip." I could have studied Latin, Portuguese, Swahili, all of the languages of the world. And seen the world. Paddled through Venice, ridden a yak somewhere, wherever there are yaks. Hollis is just a pimple on God's body. Why am I living on a pimple? I want to see all of it, this amazing blue planet. There's still time, right? I'm only forty-two. There better still be time, buckets and acres and decades of it.*

When a nurse, not Millie, pulled back the curtain, Helen asked, "Where are my parents?" The nurse shrugged, and Helen remembered that her mother and father, Lillian and Carl, were dead. But for a few seconds, thirty-five years had slipped away and Helen was seven again, and her mother had just rushed her to a hospital in

Toledo. Helen had tripped over a doll that Tammy had left on the cellar stairs and broken her right arm. She didn't know that pain could be that big or that her arm could bend that way. The doctor awarded Helen three suckers for her bravery, all of them grape. The kids in her second-grade class signed her cast and drew pictures on it. Linda Payton, her best friend, wrote, "Next time break your head!" She was a strange one. Five weeks later the cast was cut off and her arm was whole again. It was an absolute miracle.

"We need to ask you a few questions," the nurse said. "Are you allergic to any medications?"

"Penicillin. Wait, that's Gene."

"Are you currently taking any prescription or over-the-counter medications?"

"Ginkgo. It's for something. Memory."

"Are you under the influence of alcohol or narcotics?"

"I lost my son."

"What's that?"

"Nothing."

"Are your parents still living?"

"No."

"What did your mother die of?"

"Heart sadness."

"You mean heart disease?"

"Okay."

"And your father?"

"Bad luck."

"Ma'am?"

"He was killed in Florida during a robbery. The first time he had any decent money in his pockets someone took it from him."

"Siblings?"

"These horrible people keep sending me mail I don't want to see."

"Do you have any siblings?"

"Yes. Tammy. Healthy, happy."

"Children?"

"Stephen, and the girl. Christine. Healthy, not happy. I just lost my son, Francis."

"I'm sorry. Your primary complaint is . . ."

"Floating, as in not wanting to. 'Unmoored' might be the medical term."

"Do you want to hurt yourself?"

"I lost my son. During an ice storm."

"Have you ever . . ."

"Of course not. I'm a mother. I have responsibilities."

The nurse wrote a few notes on a clipboard, offered a flat smile to Helen, and said that Dr. Phillips would be down shortly for a quickie evaluation. "Standard procedure in cases like this," she said.

"What kind of case am I?" Helen wondered aloud.

"Ask the doctor. Good luck, Mrs. Harrelson."

Helen was trying to remember the path back to the front entrance so she could retrace her steps and free herself, when Dr. Phillips came in.

"Did you hear the one about the young doctor who was so stressed out that he had to admit himself to his own psych ward?" Dr. Phillips said, picking up her chart. "Sorry."

She wanted to leave. This was silly.

"So we're feeling a little off today?" he asked.

"Just having a few, you know, nonsense thoughts."

"Like you might float away?"

"Among others."

"Do you know what day it is?"

"Wednesday."

"Who's the president?"

"Clinton. I like his wife."

"Are you hearing voices?"

"Only yours."

"Good. Have you ever hurt yourself?"

"I fell down the stairs once. But it was an accident."

"Not all accidents are accidents."

"I was only seven."

"It was probably an accident. What's the story then? Problems at home?"

"I lost my boy, Francis. He was twenty. Your age."

"I'm twenty-eight. When did he die?"

"January. A Saturday."

"So we have a delayed grieving reaction here, do we? It's not that uncommon. 'Problems related to bereavement' it's called."

Helen folded her hands together and felt a throb in one of her palms. *The heart so easily relocates itself.*

"Have you been actively grieving your son's death?" he asked, some kindness in his voice.

"I don't know. The days keep passing. I was planning to go to a grieving support group today. Right here."

"It's a good group. Give it a try." Dr. Phillips scribbled something in her chart. "Let's get you started on Xanax, and an antidepressant, probably Zoloft. Follow up with your family doctor within a week. Any questions?"

"No one has ever really floated away, right?"

"Nope, never. It's quite impossible."

She stood up and gazed at Dr. Phillips, and even though his hair was darker and wavier than Francis's hair, and he was taller and his ears weren't close to right, he became Francis for a moment, and a wave of sorrow released in Helen, finally let go after all of this time. She fell into Dr. Phillips and sobbed on his shoulder, cried and cried, the teardrops painful like she was crying glass. "I'm sorry, I'm so sorry," she said.

Dr. Phillips patted her on the back. "We better get you started on the Xanax. Wait here."

The doctor left for a minute and then returned with a Xanax tablet and a paper cup full of water. Helen looked at the white, chalky wonder pill, placed it on her tongue, and downed it with the help of the water. She imagined levies being built, sandbag by sandbag.

"I'm sorry about my outburst," she said as Dr. Phillips led her toward the waiting area.

"Did you hear the one about the medical student who decided to go into psychiatry even though he's uncomfortable with human emotions?" he said, with a sad smile. "That's me. I'm the joke."

AT THE FRONT desk Helen was handed back her insurance card and prescriptions for Xanax and Zoloft. The nurse offered no love or encouraging words. Helen glanced at the automatic doors and told herself, *You can do this.* She clutched her purse, hoping that it would divine her the way home.

She started meekly toward the doors, but then a man coming into the hospital opened them for her and she scurried through. You can't trust those sensor eyes. People have been crushed to death.

The Chevy was waiting for her in the visitor's lot, where she had left it. Thank God for small favors. But was God capable of big favors? That was the burning question. Helen climbed in, wiggled into a position of comfort, and let the automatic shoulder harness tie her down. She put the key in the ignition and . . . and . . . and no, she couldn't turn the key. A bomb could be wired to the engine. She had seen movies where the innocent wife got into the car, started it up, and *kabam!*—she was blown up. Helen wasn't ready to be confetti.

She removed the ring of keys from the ignition and pulled off the Plymouth key. *Why only one air bag, Plymouth? Was it a model meant for loners?* She and Gene should have helped Francis buy a nicer car, something lined with air bags. She kissed the key and dropped it into the tray between the seats. *Thernk.*

She put the Chevy key back into the ignition, but she still couldn't turn it. It was too nice of a day to die. *Oh hell.* She collapsed into the steering wheel and her nose—was her nose really that humongous?—set off the horn. Beeping the car horn with her nose was something new so she tried it again. *Beep. Beeeeeep. Beep.* She was like a bird that somehow knew how to drive, honking the horn with her beak, she reasoned. There was a tap at the car window. It was Millie again. Helen rolled down the window.

"I saw you going to your car," Millie said. "Are you okay yet?"

Helen nodded, smiled, and said, "Nope."

Millie led her back into the hospital. The automatic doors opened wide then lurched mad-dog-like, startling Helen, but they stopped before crushing her.

It was déjà vu, almost. This time they had taken her purse. What did they think she's going to do, eat it?

"Back for more, I see," said Dr. Phillips, coming into the examination room. "The Xanax isn't helping?"

"No, I don't think it is."

"Let's double it up and start you on the Zoloft, the one-two punch," Dr. Phillips said, punching at the air and smiling.

"I can't go home. I can't let my children see me like this."

He gazed at Helen. "I really don't think your case is that serious, but if you need a break we can house you for a day or two here at the St. Vincent's Hilton. No more than three days or your insurance company will scream bloody murder. I'm afraid that's the best I can do."

"Three days? That's all I need."

"I should tell you that there are some very disturbed individuals up there, every one of them worse off than you. Schizophrenics, manic-depressives—it can get pretty loud. If it's too much, just sign out. This isn't forced."

"Thank you for the three days," she said.

HELEN WAS STANDING at the window and gazing at the parking garage when Gene came into her room. "Oh, hi," she said, turning to him.

"Hey," he said. "I brought you a robe like you asked. I hope the white one is okay." He set the folded robe on her bed.

"It will be fine."

"So how long you in for?"

"Three days max. They didn't want to admit me but I insisted. I need a little rest."

"Is the car okay?"

"Did you know that 'problems related to bereavement' is a medical diagnosis? I just learned that."

"The car?"

"It's locked."

"I'll probably have someone come for it. This isn't the best neighborhood."

"It's safe, Gene."

"All right. So what should I tell the kids?"

"Tell them that I'm visiting Tammy in Atlanta for a few days."

Gene glanced at Helen's feet, covered by yellow footsies. "Is there anything else you need? Money? A transfusion? A cake with a file in it?"

Helen smiled. "I'll be fine. It's just . . . I couldn't deal with those damn certificates. It's like he died ten times on us, not just once."

Gene groaned, letting out a day's worth of steam. "I'll call those idiots in Fayette County tomorrow. Read them the riot act."

"Thanks. I just want it to stop."

He bobbed his head, then turned and started for the door. "I better get going. I'll need to fix the kids their supper."

"Gene?"

"Yes?" he said, not looking back at her.

"So many things need to change."

"Right-o. Make a list. I'll look it over."

Gene left, and a few minutes later Helen peered out the window and saw him walking to the Chevy and testing the doors to make sure they were locked.

What an idiot, she thought, but she wanted to amend that

thought when Gene leaned into the car and put a hand over his face. He stayed like that for a minute, gathering his strength.

"Oh, Gene," she said, pressing her face against the glass.

As a green-banded patient Helen was free to come and go, but she spent the night in the ward meeting her fellow inmates and playing Ping-Pong with a seventeen-year-old patient named Allie. Helen had to fight staring at the bandage on the girl's left wrist and at the scars on her arms and legs. "Don't worry, it's only bloodletting," Allie said, during a break between matches. "I never go too deep. I couldn't do that to my mother. My dad, shit yeah, but not my mother."

"Yes, don't do that to your mother," Helen advised.

The next morning, Helen attended a leatherworking class where she made a nifty change purse for Crispy, and then had a half-hour session with a hyper Lisa Fesko, licensed social worker. Lisa lectured Helen on the five stages of grief and concluded that the reason she ran into trouble was that she tried to breeze through the early stages. Helen raised her hand, then realized she wasn't in a classroom. "What if there are really ten thousand stages of grief and this is just the start of it?" she asked.

"Trust me, there are only five: denial, anger, bargaining, depression, and acceptance, in that order."

"Acceptance? Of my child being dead? Never."

"Ultimately it's the only way. If you cheat on any of the stages you'll only be cheating yourself."

"I think I can live with that," she said.

After her appointment ended, Helen strolled to the nurse's station where she showed Nurse Bea her green band, was buzzed free, and took the elevator to the first floor where she roamed the halls, smiling at sick people and at nurses and doctors and even a priest. When she came upon the maternity ward, Helen gazed for a minute at the lone baby on display, a little girl with coal-colored hair, asleep but moving her fingers.

A vein of sadness opened in Helen. Francis had been born *here,* in this antiseptic place, spending more time with doctors and nurses than his dear old mom. It didn't seem right, giving birth in a hospital, where the sick and dying come hoping to be fixed. If Helen could jump back twenty years she would have given birth to Francis at home, with a midwife helping out, her baby boy spending his first days of life only at her milk-heavy breasts, comforted by the sound of her heartbeat.

She studied the baby girl, wondered about her future. In contrast to the girl's dark, thick locks, Francis was born with hair so lightly blond it was white, Helen worrying that she had just spat out a tiny old man. But he was a real baby, soon one minute old, and then an hour old, and then a day old. One of the nurses told Helen that according to an old Romanian folktale children born with white hair have been touched by God. "He's going to have a very special life, make his mark in the world," the nurse had assured her. But Francis's marks had been only small ones, made with chalk, too easy to erase.

Helen wished the baby girl well, then strode down the hall to the pediatric ward, where she stood at a window and watched two girls, sisters probably, one in a hospital gown and one in street clothes, play catch with a stuffed animal, a wiry brown monkey.

The girl in the gown suddenly stiffened and fell backward, hitting her head on a plastic desk chair and slinking to the carpet. She was having a seizure. Helen attempted to reach for the girl but the glass was in the way. The child's mother ran to the girl and tried to hold her down but she kept convulsing. Nurses swooped in, and the mother and sister were sent from the room.

They came and stood next to Helen. The girl sobbed and tapped at the glass and said, "Come on, Brandy, you can do it." The woman shook her head. "God, this is so awful," she said. "We were planning to take her home tomorrow. I was hoping the new meds would do the trick. How many more of these can her little body take?" She dabbed at her eyes with a tissue, then glanced at Helen. "I'm sorry for sharing my burdens. I don't even know you."

"I'm just a mother," Helen said.

A doctor injected something into the shaking girl's hip while two nurses strained to hook up an IV. To Helen, the sick kid looked like a rocket, breaking apart. She was so little, so fragile. How could anything inside that child cause such a violent storm? *Fix the kid with the seizures already*, she said to God.

"I have to go to her," the sister said.

"Soon angel, soon," the woman said, putting her arm around the girl and pulling her closer.

After the seizures abated and the woman and girl were allowed back in the room, Helen marched to the stairs: she didn't want to stay one more minute in this hotel of horrors. But on the second floor landing she sat down on the cold concrete and started crying, for Francis and for his bright future now gone, and for sick children who wanted to keep playing Catch the Monkey but their bodies wouldn't let them, and for stupid too-vulnerable life so easily wiped out, whether you are a boy mycologist headed to a conference or an armadillo trying to cross the road.

She stood up and sighed, then wiped her eyes with a robe sleeve. Apparently her cure was crying, and this was likely just the start of it. She climbed the stairs to the psych ward, reassured Nurse Bea that yes she was fine, that weeping was a normal part of human life, and went into her room where she changed into regular clothes and flushed the Xanax and Zoloft samples down the toilet. She trotted to the desk and signed out, took the elevator to the first floor, scurried through the harmless automatic doors and went to her car, put the key in the ignition, and turned it. She drove home on roads, not through the air.

LATER, AFTER THE children had said good night, Helen sat at the kitchen table and thought about her marriage. She and Gene once had a fevered love, but it died long before Francis did. They had fallen for each other at Western Michigan University: she was studying to be a teacher and he was taking business classes. On a Saturday when they should have been cramming for spring finals they instead drove to the dunes along Lake Michigan. It was a surreal place at night: white sands, dark water, a star-filled sky, and a steel plant that belched orange smoke. The beach was empty so they made love in a recess between two dunes. She let it all inside her: Gene, the stars, the whole damn galaxy. Afterward, as they sat at the edge of the water and dug their toes into the sand, Gene crooned the old song "(I've Got a Gal in) Kalamazoo," including the line, "what a gal, a real pipperoo." Helen trembled with happiness and wondered why love was always so hokey. "That's by Glenn Miller & His Orchestra," he said. "It was one of my mother's favorites. Though I'm not sure what a pipperoo is." She shrugged. "I'm happy to be one," she said. They didn't know yet that they had just conceived Francis.

Where did it all go? Passion and love, those crazy kids, must have run off together, she thought. "Come back, you liars," she asked of them. Or maybe it was the waves that night at the dunes, wetting the sand again and again, that whispered lies to Helen about continuance, that Gene's love would stay, that the children she would someday bear would grow up and grow old. Or it was Gene who said, and sang, those lies.

"Come back here, you sweeties," she tried again.

GENE CAME HOME shortly before midnight. "Glad you're back," he said to his wife. No flowers, no candy, no kisses.

"Thanks. Want to snuggle?" she asked.

"I better not. I think I pulled something at work lifting a hutch." He rubbed at his lower spine.

"How about fucking. Do you want to fuck me?"

"Helen!" he said, frowning. "What's got into you?"

"Not you, lately. Is that a yes or a no?"

"I guess it's a no. Not tonight."

She stood up and threw the salt and pepper shakers at Gene. She was aiming for his head but the salt missed badly, and Gene caught the pepper before it could strike him and set it atop the microwave. "I'm married to a meat loaf," Helen complained, before stamping to her room.

EPISODE 19

Wonder World

IT WAS TERRIBLY HOT in the world and even steamier in her room, but a box fan was hurling air at Nicole as she lay stretched out on bed, a living five-pointed star, and while the air coming from the fan was not exactly cool and refreshing, at least the squealing fan engine was trying really, really hard to comfort her and make her happy, which was more than she could say about most people she knew. She smiled at the Arctic-Air 1000 appreciatively and offered it a queenly wave.

Summer was about half spent, and Nicole was thinking about the passing of days and about her future—if she'd even have a future. That elusive future, should it show up, ought to look something like this: she and Stephen will be married and she'll work as curator of Nicole's Museum of Fucked-up Things while he'll be a snowflake researcher or Nerf car designer or whatever the hell he wanted to do; the money from museum ticket and gift shop sales would make both of them stinking rich. The kids she'd have with Stephen—tentatively named Zack and Zelda—would be mutants, Nicole certain that anything born out of her womb would be at least half messed up. Zack could be an aqua boy, with fins instead of arms and gills instead of lungs, and Zelda a kangaroo girl with a pouch on her stomach to keep toys in. She wouldn't put the freaks on display at her museum, that wouldn't be good parenting, but picture postcards of the kids would be for sale at the museum gift shop.

"A beautiful life," Nicole said, seeing that beautiful life.

Somehow, in this world of bombs and bad guys, and fires and disease and car accidents and other god-awful future stoppers, she and Stephen had to find a way to make it to that beautiful life. But who knew if there'd even be a world waiting for them in five or ten years? Fifty-fifty, at best. One unhappy dude with access to an arsenal of nuclear bombs and that would be the end of humanity. (Except for that race of human beings that secretly live one mile below the earth's surface, and maybe a few hardy Australians and Icelanders.) She and Stephen, and Zack and Zelda, better not count on that untrustworthy future to come looking for them, Nicole decided.

"The future starts today," she said to her new friend, the box fan. Nicole leapt up from the bed and ran downstairs and outside to Stephen's house, but heard from his mother that he had gone to the store or someplace, he was never around anymore, so she dashed home and hopped on her bicycle and rode to Dairy Land.

STEPHEN WAS AT the store, feeling packs of baseball cards, when Nicole came inside.

"What are you doing?" she asked.

"Trying to figure out which packs have Sox cards and which ones have Cubs cards so I can just buy the Sox ones," he said.

"You can tell just by feeling? That works?"

"Not very often. What are you doing here?"

"Umm, buying licorice," she said, snagging a box of Good & Plentys from a candy rack.

They paid for their candy and baseball cards, then went outside and sat on a short brick wall in front of the store. Stephen peeled open the pack and was happy to discover that there was a White Sox card inside. That it was a mug shot of Tim Landon, a square-headed rookie who was so far spending the year in Charlotte, was a bit of a disappointment.

"Let's get married and make a baby," Nicole said, tearing open the box of Good & Plentys.

He glanced at her. "Are you high?"

"High on love!"

"We're not old enough to be married."

"Probably true. So let's make a baby first and get married later."

"You're too young to have a baby."

"Not technically. Plus in India if you aren't pregnant by fourteen you're like yesterday's news."

"This isn't India."

"Then why are the first Americans called Indians?"

"You're driving me crazy!"

"Crazy in love?"

"Just normal crazy."

Nicole poured several candies into her hand and offered them to Stephen. "Since you're being bad you can have Plentys but not Goods," she said.

"I'm not in the mood," he said.

"What are you mad about? I'm the one who has to carry the creature for nine months. I mean our perfectly normal boy or girl. Besides, we're going to make babies someday, right?"

"That's too far away to think about."

"Not that far, I hope." Nicole formed a fist around the candy, shook her fist, and reached into the ball of candy and yanked out a pink piece. "Oh good, a Good," she said.

Stephen started sorting through the baseball cards, hoping that Nicole didn't really want to have a kid. It would be another five to eight years, he figured, before he'd be ready for his part of the task, inserting Tab A into Slot B. Just catching a glimpse of Nicole's panties when she was wearing shorts made him feel so weird and spacey that he wondered how he could ever survive going all the way.

A car pulled noisily into the lot and stopped a few feet short of them. A hunched-over old man got out of the car, shuffled toward the store, and pulled open the door so slowly the bell didn't ding.

"Poor guy," she said. "Let's stay young forever."

"Good plan," he said.

She opened her hand and saw that the candies had melted together. "Oh crap," she said, stuffing the Good & Plentys back in the box in fused twos and threes. She offered her candy-stained palm to Stephen: "Have a taste." He took hold of her wrist and licked her hand, enjoying the salt of her flesh as much as the sugar of the candy. Nicole wiped the rest of the pink and white mess onto her soccer shorts.

The old man came out of the store, carrying a bottle of something wrapped in a brown paper bag. "You two cooking up a storm?" he asked, and Nicole and Stephen smiled and nodded. They watched him drive off in a pale green Ford Fairlane, its muffler scraping the road and sparking.

"What's his life like?" Stephen asked.

"Easy. He has a wife named Mindy who hates him, and three boys named Larry, Harry, and Jerry, who hate him, and a cat named Stinky who hates him, but it's okay because the booze loves him like a crush."

"My dad sometimes drinks because of what happened to Francis. It puts him to sleep."

"I know. So, back to making a baby. I'll give you all of my baseball and football cards. Even the rookies."

"Not until we're married and together for good."

"Or maybe sooner, who knows. Do you think of the future much?"

"Every day." What Stephen imagined: he and Nicole will have an apartment, a cheap but cozy place with steam heat and peeling wallpaper and a claw bathtub. Nicole will attend art school and Stephen will write comic book stories and take engineering classes and work on designs for ultrasafe cars that may or may not involve sponge material. He wanted to take Nicole's hand and leap into that wonder world of the future where they were free to do the many things that adults take for granted, like falling asleep in each other's arms and going through the night that way, undisturbed. This wonder world would never happen if some pretty boy or jock stole Nicole away from him. A 68.2 percent chance of that happening, he had calculated.

"But if we have a baby now it will make you happy again," Nicole said. "You'll have a little kid to play with."

"Is that why you want to do it? To make me happy?"

"That's one of the reasons. You're always moping around."

"So? Don't do things to make me happy, just do things because you want to do them."

"I'm only trying to help," Nicole said, her smile gone.

"I don't need any help."

"Pardon me, but you need lots of help. You're fucked up, but in a bad way. Someone has to say it. You can't be sad about your brother forever."

"Watch me." The quarrel seemed to be its own thing, dragging them along in its net.

"Stop being so mean," she said, folding her arms over her chest.

"You're the one being mean."

"Shut up."

"I don't have to shut up."

"You do if I say you do."

Something jagged was turning in Stephen's gut. He wanted to pull Nicole's hair, and tell her that he hated her and that she was dumb and ugly. But none of that was true. He loved Nicole, and she was smart and beautiful.

"Let's not fight anymore, okay?" he said. "That's what adults do."

Nicole exhaled noisily. "You're right. I don't want to fight with you, ever."

"Me neither. And I'll try not to mope around so much."

"Be as mopey as you want." She shook the box of candy—*chi chi chi.* "I don't really want to have a baby, not yet. I'm just worried like crazy about the future, that it might never happen."

"It will happen. It has to."

"Maybe. But look at your brother. He should be right here, bullshitting with us and drinking a Coke."

"True, but most kids make it to their future. At least eight out of every ten."

"Let's hope like hell we're among those lucky eight," she said.

LATER, AFTER DINNER, Nicole, Stephen, and Crispy played Freeze Tag, Three Square, and Run for Your Life. Crispy protested if no one chased her, tried to get her out, or threw the kickball at her, or if they did those things too often. While trying to elude Nicole during Freeze Tag, Stephen thought about how difficult Francis was to tag, how his brother would juke his wiry body this way or that way at the last second, or name a new place home base right before Stephen was about to touch him. So many summer nights, just like this one, spent playing with Francis in the yard, running in and out of shadows, shrieks and squeals and "ha ha, you missed me."

A puffed-up sun set as they played, the western sky splashed with blood orange and peach. Venus arose and twinkled. Streetlamps buzzed on. Three tired children called it a night.

EPISODE 20

Ashes to Ashes

ON A NIGHT when Gene was at work and the kids were up in their rooms, Helen went outside and dumped old charcoal out of the grill, then filled it with sticks and dried grass. Atop the kindling she set the stack of death certificates, all of the copies Fayette County had sent her minus the one Gene had mailed to the insurance company.

She squirted the papers and sticks with a quarter can of lighter fluid, then set the can a safe distance from the grill, on a picnic table. This was going to be a big old fire, but one Helen and the house and the children inside that house needed to survive.

She took a book of matches out of her pocket and tore off a match. It looked puny, not up for the job, but when she struck the match it formed a pretty flame. "For Francis," she said, tossing it at the wet certificates.

Tongues of fire leapt from the grill. Helen jumped back. Then the fire calmed and got to work, erasing all of those awful words like *trauma* and *accident* and the good words, too: Francis's name, his date of birth. Fire was a great equalizer, she thought. A breeze lifted sparks and ash from the fire and sent them heavenward. Helen's eyes followed the rising sparks and soon she was looking at the sky, mostly clouded over, though a few dozen throbbing stars could be seen.

"You only get to die once," she said to Francis.

* * *

In his bedroom, Stephen saw sparks move past his window and feared that the house was on fire. He quickly went to the window and looked out but couldn't see flames or any evidence of danger. Someone in the neighborhood had just set off fireworks, he guessed. He went back to his desk and got back to work on a Wolf Boy story titled "Time, Thy Enemy."

In her room, Crispy was writing in her diary when she saw some flashes move past her window. She figured the light was from a few fireflies sending out their signals. Maybe tomorrow she'd try to catch some lightning bugs and keep them in a jar, she thought, and give them funny names like Sparky and Lightning Rod.

"TIME, THY ENEMY"

GASP! THE SHUTTLE EXPLOSION THAT KILLED JOHNNY!

AND HIS FUNERAL AT SUMMER'S END CEMETERY!

JOHNNY LAREDO WAS YOUR BROTHER, YES?
L8R
B4
TELL THE TRUTH, WOLFY. DON'T *TICK* ME OFF.

SORRY, CLOCK MAN. I DON'T KNOW ANY LAREDOS.
IT'S A BIG CITY.

JOHNNY...
DON'T LIE TO ME. YOUR TIME IS WINDING DOWN.

JUST THEN...

HOWWWWL!
THE MOONLIGHT--! HE'S FREE! GET HIM, YOU FOOLS!
B4
TICK TOCK!
TICK TOCK!
11:59
FIRST THINGS FIRST...
I'M PUTTING YOUR BOMB OUT OF COMMISSION!
TNT
TNT
KER-WHACK!
FFZZZZZZZZZ

GAH! MY DETONATION TIMER! YOU LITTLE--
SORRY, CLOCKIE!

TAKE A TIME-OUT, GUYS!
WHACK!

KER-CRUNCH!
I'LL ESCAPE USING THE SUPER SECRET TRAP DOOR!

BONK!

THE SECRET DOOR'S TOO SMALL! I'LL HAVE TO--

DON'T HURT ME! I'M JUST A SIMPLE TIME-KEEPER WHO WENT ASTRAY. PLEASE, I'LL DO ANYTHING YOU ASK.
YOU CAN TURN BACK TIME SO I CAN SAVE JOHNNY LAREDO AND KEEP HIS FAMILY FROM A LIFETIME OF SORROW?
Y-YE-YES, I CAN TURN BACK TIME.
THEN START TURNING.
SO BE IT, WOLFY.
ENJOY YOUR TRIP.

HUH?

BACK IN CLOCK MAN'S HIDEOUT...
TIME-ASONIC

WHAT'S FOR DINNER?
THE USUAL: MINUTE RICE WITH A PINCH OF THYME, NO SECONDS.
WOLF BOY, THAT FOOL...
L8R
Time to KISS the COOK

I'VE SENT HIM BACK TO THAT DAY IN JANUARY, BUT HE'LL HAVE NO MEMORY OF HIS TIME HERE, AND NO IDEA THAT JOHNNY LAREDO IS ABOUT TO BE IN AN ACCIDENT. HE WON'T BE ABLE TO CHANGE ANY OF IT!

AND NOW I HAVE MORE TIME TO FORMULATE A NEW PLAN, ONE THAT WILL TAKE CARE OF WOLF BOY FOREVER!!
HAHAHA
HAHAHAH
Time to KISS the COOK
THE END?

EPISODE 21

Mother and Daughter

By the end of July, the annuals available at Dunnigan's Garden Center were overgrown spindly things with tangles of roots busting through their plastic containers, in search of someplace to call home. As Helen assembled two flats, it was as much out of sympathy for the homeless flowers as it was a desire to brighten up the front gardens.

She carried the mess inside to the register. The teenaged cashier shook her head when she saw the flowers, as if mixed flats were proof of some sort of tragic human flaw. Helen reminded Miss Priss that the flats were on sale for $6.99, and the girl said, "Yeah, I know, I work here. Need anything else?"

Since Francis's death questions like "need anything else" gave Helen pause. What she needed was for these clerks and phone operators to restore Francis, turn back time.

"Two bags of topsoil, and one peat moss," Helen said.

"The dark peat or, you know, the other kind."

"Let's go with the 'you know, the other kind.' "

Helen paid for the flowers and dirt, and the cashier handed her a receipt. "Pull around back and Jason will help you with the soil," she said.

"You have a nice day," Helen said.

"Right," the cashier said, blankly.

Jason turned out to be a delight—smiley, attentive, and cute (long sideburns worked for him)—and when Helen got out of the car to open the trunk he looked her up and down. *God love this boy.*

"Thanks so much for your help," Helen said, after Jason had loaded the soil and peat. "So is this your career or what?"

"Nah, I'm studying computer science. I'm going to make millions." Jason was now addressing Helen's breasts directly. "I better get back to work. Stop again real soon."

"I'll do that," she said, grinning. It had been many months, perhaps years, since anyone had seriously lusted after her. She must not be getting out enough. Jason ogled Helen one last time before he walked away and disappeared inside a greenhouse.

She climbed into the Chevy. *He will take me in his arms and kiss me like he means it, and his sideburns will tickle my skin. He will pull off my clothes, shred them really, and do me all night, but afterward he will still love me, he will come up with some goofy nickname—Helena, Helen of Joy, something like that—and pick flowers for me. I will kiss his nose and we will go jogging together, and I will lose ten pounds, not that I need to, Jason says my body is perfect, absolutely perfect.*

Helen slammed the brakes on her fantasy right there. Who was she kidding? Jason didn't really have any interest in her ancient, unhappy bones. Even if he did want her that way, love and romance, what Helen truly needed from a man—she could handle the sex issue herself—were the last things on his Precambrian brain. "Oh pooh," she said, pulling out of the lot.

HELEN'S FIRST TASK was to cut back the flowers so they'd be able to support themselves without having to rely on sticks and wires. She was curing their disabilities. The next challenge was to untangle all of the roots. Most of the flowers had wrapped their roots tightly around their small allotment of soil, then sent the roots on a dirt-seeking mission through the small openings in the bottom of the plastic packs. The roots were now twisted together in some kind of root orgy.

As she was separating the flowers, Crispy bounded out the front door and asked her mother if she needed any help.

"This is a surprise," Helen said. "I thought you didn't like playing in the dirt anymore."

"Sure I do. Plus, I'm raising money for some very important causes. Do you think you could pay me two dollars for helping?"

"What are the causes?"

"Saving rain forests and cute baby seals."

"In that case I'll pay you three bucks." Helen told Crispy to run into the kitchen and grab the biggest spoon she could find. Minutes later she returned carrying a wooden spoon, a sauce spoon, and a soupspoon. "Will any of these work?" she asked.

"I'd use the sauce spoon if I were you," Helen said. "That's the bigger metal one."

Crispy tossed two of the spoons aside, then crouched next to her mother and asked if she could plant all of the "snapping dragons" by herself.

"You sure can. Here's the plan: dig the holes two to three inches deep and six to eight inches apart. After you set the flower in the hole, pack fresh topsoil, the dark stuff, all around it, and then sprinkle peat moss, the light stuff, on the soil. Got it?"

Crispy nodded and began digging the first hole. She was straining with the spoon, so Helen handed her a trowel and said, "Let's trade." But it was still a struggle to dig those two inches, as evidenced by Crispy's scrunched face and stuck-out tongue. Despite Helen's soil improvement efforts over the years the gardens were still substantially clay.

"If you need any help . . ." Helen offered.

"I got it, Mom," Crispy said.

When the hole was ready, Crispy grabbed a snapdragon and dropped it into its new home. She started squeezing dirt around it, then remembered her mother's instructions and scooped a trowel full of dark soil from the bag and poured it around the flower and packed it down, then topped it off with peat moss. She smelled her hand and winced, then looked at the remaining flowers and said, "Let's plant all of them for Francis."

"That's a sweet idea," said Helen. "You miss your brother, don't you?"

"Yes," Crispy said.

"Me, too," Helen said.

As Crispy pondered which snapdragon she wanted to plant next, Helen gazed at her and wondered what it was like for a ten-year-old girl to lose her brother. Helen had lost both of her parents when she was in her twenties, but that was different, she was more or less an adult and parents are expected to die eventually: the mind fights the idea but also prepares for it, starts imagining a post–Mom and Dad world. But siblings are expected to still be around when one is thirty, forty, fifty, sixty, seventy, eighty.

"Sorry," Helen said.

"For what?" Crispy said, packing peat moss around a snapdragon.

"That Francis is gone."

Crispy flickered her eyelids, like she was kicking out dirt that had gotten into her eyes. "We have to keep planting before it gets dark," she said. It was a little after seven. Plenty of light was left.

While Helen dug at the soil with the sauce spoon she kept an eye on Crispy. The more she looked at her, the more beautiful her daughter appeared to be. Her blond hair seemed to be jewel-specked when it caught the sun, and there was something extraordinarily holy in the way she'd tuck strands of that jeweled hair behind her ears and how the hair kept leaping back in front of her face, a face that still held some kid pinkness. "You are beautiful," Helen told her.

"Thanks, but I'm just average," Crispy said.

The world stopped turning. How was it possible that Crispy didn't know how beautiful she was? Helen wondered. Was it her fault? Gene's? She couldn't think of a remedy, other than complimenting Crispy again. "You're really very beautiful," she said.

Crispy glanced at her mother. "Don't be a do-nothing," she said.

Helen, not wanting to be a do-nothing, grabbed the stem of a half-dead pink dahlia and planted it. She didn't have the heart to tell the flower that it was an annual, and that the first frost might be only two months away.

EPISODE 22

Gene the Cheater

GENE WAS TIRED of the daily sameness of the world. Why couldn't he look out of his office window and see mountains and pine trees instead of shops and offices? Or one of those gorgeous cathedrals with spires that shoot into the clouds? Instead of Fords and Hondas, why not flying cars from the future? Replace the people with baboons or dress them in Wild West clothing. Gene would be their brave sheriff, willing to look danger in the eye without blinking. Though he'd probably need to blink eventually.

Feeling bored, sad, and horny, a dangerous brew, he opened the top drawer of his desk and pulled out the business card of his former bookkeeper, Marjorie Reed. What a sex kitten she was. Marjorie had long, muscular legs—two halves of a nutcracker ready to snap him open—and cascading dirty blond hair. Firm breasts, too. Helen's had been droopy since forever. To do the books Marjorie needed to stop in only once a month, but after electricity started arcing between them she'd come by two or three times weekly. This was their routine: as she'd pretend to reexamine the already balanced ledger and receipts, Gene would slowly edge closer to her, and eventually their bodies would touch and stay glued for up to an hour or more. She'd point to some numbers and he would bend over her and smell her flowery smells and look down her blouse. He liked when she wore lacy bras where he couldn't quite tell if he was seeing something nipply or not. Marjorie might reach for a paper clip or a pen and her arm would brush up against his pants while she talked about her youngest's day at school or the latest shenanigans of her idiot husband, Jeffy.

Francis's death didn't immediately slow things down with Marjorie. In the sympathy card she mailed to the house she wrote to Gene, "If there is anything I can do, get ahold of me." When he thanked her for the card she said that she licked the envelope with the entire length of her tongue.

The seductions became Gene's medicine for grief. He'd phone Marjorie and ask her to stop by the office, saying he thought that there might be an imbalance in the books somewhere. She'd say something like, "You just caught me coming out of the shower and I'm dripping *www*wet." During their last night together at the office, in early February, she said that women and men have similar needs and if they didn't act on those needs they might go crazy. "If you don't want to mess around here, there's that new Motel 6 out by the interstate. You seen it? What do you say, Gene? I'll even pay for the room."

Damn if that didn't ruin it all. Gene owned a hundred Marjorie fantasies, but a new one appeared at that moment. He and Marjorie will run away to someplace warm and sunny and bang like crazy. That was the good part. But then one Sunday he'll be watching a football game and Marjorie will want to get frisky then and there, not willing to wait until halftime. He'll say something like "maybe after the game," and she'll say fine but return ten minutes later wearing something depressingly see-through and block the TV. The Bears are actually putting together a sustained drive and he's going to miss it. So he tries to look around her to the TV and she freaks out, saying he's just like every other man. That's Gene's point. He is like any other man so occasionally he needs to watch men in uniforms kick the shit out of one another. Marjorie will leave in a huff but return the next day, and when she sets her bag down Gene will wonder why he let that smelly oversexed goat back in the house.

That was the life that waited for Gene at the Motel 6. "I'll have to think it over," he said, backing away from Marjorie. The next day he phoned her at home and dismissed her. Strictly for financial reasons, he said.

I should rehire her tonight, Gene thought, rubbing the lettering of Marjorie's business card. Take a risk, sin like there's no tomorrow, because maybe there isn't. "Forget it, you can't do that to Helen," he said, putting the card back in the drawer.

Normally when he was feeling weak like this he'd go for an ice cream cone, but Gene had become bored by the twenty-one flavors offered at Sweet Surrender, even vanilla, chocolate, and strawberry, the standbys. Nester, the storeowner, said the next new flavor wasn't due out until the fall and it would be pumpkin. Pumpkin! Gene couldn't imagine enjoying a vegetable-based ice cream, even though he had always liked pumpkin pie, especially with a dollop of cream on it.

Visiting the newsstand had also been a huge disappointment lately. The ladies on the covers of *Cheeky* and *Beaver Patrol* were as hot as ever, but Gene realized one day recently that the airbrushed mamas weren't undressing for him, but for the cameraman and for a fat paycheck. The sweat on their brows had been spritzed on, and conditions of *nipple erectus* had been induced by air-conditioning. Fakers! Gene wanted a woman to either desire him or not, full throttle or dead engine, either was fine. But none of this faking business.

He stood up and wandered through the showroom and into the woodshop and started hammering nails into a block of pine. Abe sold three-inch wood nails at his hardware store for almost nothing a pound so it was dirt-cheap therapy. And he loved the *whoomp* sound of a nail being struck and going in deeper. *Whoomp, whoomp.*

Gene was behaving more like a businessman these days, answering phone calls and turning on the store lights at the correct time, more often than not, so sales were about 60 percent of what they should be. Which was still not enough to justify rehiring the naughty bookkeeper, but he was on the edge of doing that anyway. He whacked three more nails into a wood block, then returned to the office and made a deal with God: if a customer came in the store in the next two minutes he would forget about messing around with Marjorie, forever. Not trusting the office clock, he counted to one hundred and twenty on his own. *One eighteen, one nineteen, one twenty.* Not a customer in sight. God, in his infinite wisdom, had given him the go-ahead.

He fished Marjorie's business card out of the drawer and thought about the day two years ago when she walked into the shop and confidently handed him that card. She was hitting all of the downtown stores, trying to drum up business. She wore a green dress that fit her nicely, but Gene mostly noticed her hair, a shaggy, feathered-back configuration that would have looked out of style on most women, but on Marjorie it made her appear sleek, aerodynamic, zero to sixty in whatever. And he liked how her business card was plain, blue lettering on white card stock, yet stylish, especially how she presented her phone number the old-fashioned way: WEbster-3-8036.

Not to mention the fact that she only wanted $18 an hour to do the books, half of what he had been paying an old geezer named Bert who smelled like cherry cigar smoke and still called black people "the coloreds." It was time to modernize, he decided, so he "released" Bert like he was a draft choice that didn't work out, and hired Marjorie. The rest of it fell on the horny side of history.

He picked up the phone, then set it back down. He tried to stop himself from calling Marjorie by imagining what Helen, the woman he vowed to love, honor, and protect, was doing now—maybe setting his dinner on low on a burner, or folding laundry. But no matter what he saw her doing she had her back turned to him. It was like she knew that he was about to mess up and didn't want to see it.

"God forgive me," he said, picking up the receiver and dialing WEbster-3-8036, intending to hire back Marjorie and tickle her fancy and everything else.

"Gene Harrelson! I was just thinking about you," Marjorie said in a peppy voice.

"You were thinking about me?" he said. "That's funny, I was just thinking about you."

"How cosmic. We need a new dresser, Gene. The one in the boys' bedroom is shot, the screws holding the little handle jobbies are all stripped, so Jeffy is like why don't you call Gene to see if you still qualify for an employee discount, even though I'm not an employee anymore, and I'm like, even though Gene has a great big heart that isn't going to work, but he said to call you anyway, so I said okay, I will when I get around to it, but you called first. I'm right, right? About the discount?"

"Yes, but I plan to rectify the situation by giving you your job back. Hell, you can start today if you like."

"Oh shoot. Shoot!"

"What is it?"

"After you let me go I took on a lot of new business. Too much really. I'm probably going to have to drop one or two of my accounts. I hardly have any time with the kids anymore. I'm sorry, Gene. I'm just too busy."

"I can pay you more. Even double."

"I'd love to, but I really have to put the children first. I'm sure you understand, being a family man."

"I could go $45 an hour."

"Christ, you can't afford that and I know your books. I tell you what, though. If you still need a bookkeeper a year from now, when my littlest is off to school, I'm all yours. I'll charge you $28 an hour, which is what all my new customers are paying."

"A year is a long time to wait. Do you think you might stop in now and then, not to do the books, just to talk?"

"Is that why you called me?" she asked. "Because you're lonely?"

"That's half of it," he said. "I just want to go back to the old days, how it was between us."

"Yes, well, that's a bit of a problem for me."

"Why's that?"

"Because of what we did, how we were. We didn't commit the cardinal sin but we committed lots of baby cardinal sins."

"I don't think we did anything, other than a little sparking and wishing."

"In the Bible it says lusting for someone else's spouse is as big a sin as adultery."

"No it doesn't. Does it?"

"I think so. Adultery is only a couple commandments away from murder. Do you know the Lord's Prayer, 'Lead me not into temptation,' that one? I'm saying it every day and it's starting to help. Maybe you could do that, too."

"I could probably go fifty an hour."

"Look, I have to hang up, Jeffy is due back. Let me know about the discount."

"I'll hold the job, but I hope you can start sooner."

"You still working late, all sorts of crazy hours?"

"More or less."

"Try not to work so much. Go home to your family."

"All right."

"Good-bye, Gene. May the Lord be with you."

"Bye. Please come back to work soon."

"You are supposed to say 'and also with you.' "

"Oh. And also with you."

"Thanks, that's sweet. Bye, dear."

"Bye, honey," he said.

Gene set the phone down and sighed. No way could he wait another year for a piece of ass, even a prime piece. Besides, by next fall Marjorie will probably be even more bibled up. Those kinds of things tended to get worse before they got better.

Of course there was Helen, who by contractual obligation owed him occasional conjugal bliss. But he had done wrong by her so many times that even if she allowed sex it would feel like he was cheating on his exams, the big ones. If their marriage could be saved the process would not start with sex. In fact, sex would need to be far down the road for it to work. He and Helen would have to pretend it was a hundred years ago and they were courting. Only hand-holding would be allowed for the first three months, and then maybe one quick peck on her cheek. In the good old days no one came standard with genitals. They didn't bloom until the wedding night.

It was only seven o'clock, but Gene decided to close the store early and put a buzz on, just a little one. Not being more than half of a drunk was one of the few things Gene was proud of. Even during his reckless college days he had stuck to these rules: never drink during the day and never drink two days in a row. His dad, Marvin, had been an alcoholic, and he wouldn't allow that kind of life for himself no matter how sad and lonely he was feeling. The booze had probably chopped ten years off Marvin's life, but even worse than that was having to watch his normally eloquent and animated father slowly erase himself every night, each glass of high-powered wine subtracting bits of Marvin. He didn't curse, didn't beat Gene or Gene's mother, he'd just drink until he was about gone, then stumble into his room and sleep it off.

Gene walked the three blocks to Spanky's Tavern and ordered a quart of anything from Spanky. Gene was only half-banned at Spanky's, his gin-soaked sob stories about Francis were scaring away customers and depressing a normally chipper Spanky, but he was allowed to sit and drink a soda or get his booze to go.

The bartender handed him a quart of Old Milwaukee wrapped in a bag and asked for two dollars. He paid the man, and Spanky started walking to the other end of the bar but stopped when Gene said he had a crucial question to ask. Gene looked around to make sure there was no one close by except for some young guy bumping a pinball machine, then said, "Do you happen to know any ladies of the evening, as they say?"

Spanky held up an empty beer glass and looked to be examining it for water spots. "Trouble at home?" he asked.

Long before Francis died, Gene used to come in here once or twice a week to drink a single beer, watch the game if the Sox, Bears, or Bulls were on, and complain to Spanky about Helen. Apparently Spanky didn't record any of those bitchings. "Let's just say I'm getting desperate," he said.

"I see. I've met a few but they aren't welcome here. The girls I know I wouldn't send my worst enemies to. Walking petri dishes, I hear."

"Oh, well. Thanks anyway."

"There might be one lady. She comes in here Tuesday nights. I've probably seen her leave with a dozen different guys. I don't know if she charges, she might just be easy."

"Even better. Tuesday nights you say?"

"Get here early. First guy who buys her a drink seems to hit the jackpot. You can't miss her. She has bright orange hair. Like Raggedy Ann."

"Raggedy Ann? That's kind of sick."

Spanky lifted his arms in the air and raised his shoulders in a "whatever" pose and then walked away.

BACK AT THE STORE, Gene sat at his desk and sipped the beer. By now he had thought of screwing a forty-year-old Raggedy Ann in every manner he knew of. Tuesday was only five days away. He'd dress nice, put on some cologne. Tell Raggedy Ann he loved her button eyes.

The alcohol made Gene almost cheery. If there were people around he might have said "hidey-ho" to them. After he finished the beer he was trying to decide what to do with the empty bottle—throw it in the trash, recycle it, or try to build a tiny ship inside it—when he heard a tap at the front door. A chill ran up his spine and made his mouth say, "Shit!" Who knocks at the front door of a closed business?

He walked cautiously out of the office and to the door. "Who is it?" he asked.

"It's Marjorie. Let me in."

Gene pulled back the shade and saw that sure enough it was Marjorie, standing outside his shop. He unlocked the door and let her inside.

"We only have ten minutes," she said, letting her purse drop to the floor. "I told Jeffy I had to go to the store for some feminine products. That always shuts him up."

He looked her over. "You're as beautiful as ever."

"Thanks, but there isn't a lot of time for talking. Where do you want to do it? On your desk?"

"Are you serious?"

"Too much talking, but yes. After you called I started thinking how you and me are naturals this way. It's wrong, and a sin, but maybe we have to hit rock bottom before we'll be ready to welcome the Lord into our hearts. I'm not at rock bottom yet. Are you at rock bottom?"

"I'm at least two tiers from rock bottom."

"Good. Now where do you want to do it? We're down to eight minutes."

"How about on that table right there?"

Still not believing his good fortune, he watched Marjorie kick off her tennis shoes, pull off her shorts (white) and panties (pink), but leave on her socks and a blue polo, and probably a bra. She sat on the table and leaned back. This particular table Gene would have to stop calling "Amish-style."

"Come here," she said.

He moved closer to her. As he started to undress he wasn't sure if he was going to be ready for instant sex, he usually liked a little foreplay, a few dirty words, but as he shed his boxers he was good to go.

"How about from behind, if you don't mind," he said, not sure why he didn't want to see her face.

"Okay, Gene, whatever you want," she said, getting on all fours on the table. "All I ask is one little favor. Don't say my name, okay?"

Gene climbed onto the dining room table. He was pretty sure that the four oak legs would support their weight, though his knees were already complaining that they would have preferred the carpeted floor.

He paused before entering Marjorie. He knew that he was at some kind of threshold, that he was about to enter a forest that would forever change him: Gene the Cheater he was about to become. There should be a dragon he had to fight first, or a gnome with trick questions that he had to answer before he could pass through the gate. This was too damn easy.

"Everything okay?" she asked. "This is what you want, right?"

"I do," he said, going inside her.

He closed his eyes and the usual sex films started to play, clips of females he had wanted dating back all the way to his high school days where Donna Closterman, leggy basketball star and class president, was his obsession, but then Helen suddenly appeared in the film, shaking her head and looking disgusted. This couldn't be good for his erection, which was flagging, so he opened his eyes and watched himself push into Marjorie and heard her moan "yes," meaning that she must be liking it, that he was finally making someone happy. This strengthened Gene but also saddened him a little: it really was heartless doggy-style sex they were having.

A few seconds after he was done, Marjorie asked if he was finished yet and he said yes, but he'd still be happy to do whatever she wanted. She pulled away from him, the dreadful uncoupling, and slid to the edge of the table and started getting dressed. "Next time we can worry about me," she said. "I wanted to get this first one over with. Sorry, but I have to get back."

"There's going to be a next time?" Gene asked, covering his sex with his hands. His boxers had fled the scene of the crime.

"I think so. I still need to shake some of this devil out of me."

Marjorie left him with a quick kiss and advice that he go home and spend some time with his family, and consider keeping "a box or two" of rubbers at the store.

HE STAYED ANOTHER two and a half hours at the shop, waiting for guilt to kick his ass, but all it did was tug at his earlobes and give him disappointed looks. Hell, he had waited twenty years before he cheated on his wife, which was longer than most men went, not that he was expecting a trophy. Plus, Helen was partly to blame for all of this, if only 5 percent. It takes two to implode a marriage.

Gene was twiddling his thumbs and thinking about nothing when the phone rang. He answered it right away, sidestepping the usual debate.

"I knew you'd still be there," Marjorie said. "Sorry for calling so late. I had to wait until the kids were settled."

"It's all right. What's on your mind?"

"I'm feeling bad about what we did, Gene. I'm not blaming you, I came to you, after all, but it's like I'm ashamed for both of us, how we didn't even try to say no to ourselves. We have families, kids. Is that how we should be behaving?"

"What do you want me to say here?"

"I want you to say that we'll never do that again. That even if I have a weak moment and come to you, you'll turn me away."

"I could say that, but it wouldn't be true."

"Fair enough. I have to be strong in my own right. But if I'm not, please remember what I said, to never say my name during it, okay?"

"I promise," he said.

Marjorie asked him to recite the Lord's Prayer with her and Gene agreed to, but he couldn't remember all of the lines so he just echoed what she said.

"I better go," she said. "Be good."

"Good night, dear," he said, hanging up.

Gene leaned back in his chair and scratched his neck. All he had wanted was a freebie, something without any complications. Maybe if he was a jackrabbit instead of a man he could know such unclouded happiness.

GUILT FINALLY KICKED Gene's ass when he went home. He found Crispy asleep on the living room carpet and saw Stephen sitting on the couch, watching TV. He felt like telling them about the Marjorie quickie and begging their forgiveness. Only stored secrets could stir up trouble, right? But he couldn't do that to them. What do children expect of their parents? That they behave decently? That they not do things that might unravel the family? This was another test Gene had flunked.

"Hey there," he said to Stephen. "What's going on tonight?"

"Not much. How are things at the store?"

"Great. Busy."

Gene decided to be a good father and watch some TV with his son. He sat down on the couch next to Stephen and grabbed a handful of popcorn from a mixing bowl. "What are you watching?" he asked, expecting that he had walked into the middle of a vampire movie. He knew that Stephen liked the late-night Zombie Theatre features.

"Just a video," Stephen said.

Gene gazed at the TV and saw Francis in his Hollis Hurricanes cross-country team uniform, sprinting on a dirt path that runs along Coral Street. It was a video Gene had shot when he was still excited about his new camcorder. Twice he had filmed Francis's meets, and this particular time Gene followed Francis and the other runners in his car as they dashed down Coral, then he drove ahead and waited at the finish line. When the race ended, the Hurricane boys congratulated and high-fived each other for winning the meet, and Gene kept filming. He followed a winded Francis until he turned around and grinned at the camera but then shyly looked away. He kept recording even though Francis tried to wave him off. "Come on, Dad," said a red-faced Francis. He scratched his nose, stuck his tongue out at Gene, and then covered his eyes with his hands, as if that would make the camera disappear. Finally, Gene turned off the camcorder.

Damn, he shouldn't have done that, embarrassed his boy like that.

Having lost his appetite, Gene dropped the popcorn back into the bowl and dusted off his hands. He knew that next on the videotape was Crispy's eighth birthday party, which should be more tolerable since Francis only appeared in a few scenes. But instead of letting it play, Stephen rewound the tape with the remote, and there was Francis again at the starting line, waiting for the gun. It was too much for Gene to watch a second time, so he stood up and looked away from the television and asked where Helen was.

"She had a headache so she crashed early," Stephen said, his eyes trained on Francis's running legs and churning arms.

"Maybe I better check on her," he said.

"That would be nice," Stephen said.

Gene rose and stepped past Stephen, crouched to pet Crispy's head, and walked down the hall to Helen's room. It was dark in there, and he wasn't sure whether to knock or let himself in. He chose the latter approach and sighed before opening the door. There was Helen, sleeping in a white nightgown, her sheet kicked off. Her body was slack, no tension anywhere, and she was lightly snoring, which was one of the things about her that used to bug him, but right here and now, in his new life as a man who strayed, Helen's snoring was, while not endearing, quite acceptable and thus scratched off the list of complaints. He looked at her some more. Moonlight was splashed generously on Helen like some kind of balm, rebuilding damaged cells.

There was room for him to lie with his wife, but she'd surely startle awake and probably throw an elbow into his nose, another past complaint of his. She'd know that Gene being snuggly meant that something was terribly wrong, probably smell the guilt on his skin and maybe a little of the bookkeeper. No, he better start being nicer to her in much smaller increments. Perhaps tomorrow before leaving for work he'd ask her how things were going. Though that might also seem suspicious, set off alarms.

Gene was alone in his bedroom when he told Helen, in his thoughts, how sorry he was for cheating on her and for the sorrow that was due her when she found out about it.

He slept soundly, though, like a child who had been running wild all day.

EPISODE 23

Crispy's Escape

IT HAD ALL the makings of a dumb day. Her dad was at work, of course, and Mom was watching the soaps, as always, and Stephen and Nicole were having fun somewhere without her, naturally, and her pal Erin was still two hundred miles away at brainy girls camp. What to do? Crispy didn't want to read her latest *Sweet Valley Twins* book. She didn't want to watch a video. She didn't want to lie out in the sun like a bored lizard. She *did* wish that the day would pass more quickly, that time would start acting like a speedy racehorse instead of a dumb old mule you had to kick just to get it to move a few feet.

The day's dumbness would come to an abrupt halt shortly after two o'clock. Crispy was sitting at the dining table and searching through *The Ledger* for the Marmaduke and Ziggy cartoons, wondering where they hid them this time, when she saw a notice in the Entertainment Briefs section that said that Marky Mark and the Funky Bunch would be performing that Friday and Saturday night at Six Flags in St. Louis. The amusement park was only about seventy miles northwest of Hollis, and Crispy had almost been there many times. Just about every year around Christmas Gene would promise that the next summer they'd hit Six Flags. But when summer came he would be too busy at work to take time off, or so he said.

Marky is coming! Excitement started to build in Crispy, a freight train gathering steam, its conductor saying, "Next stop Six Flags." Now all she had to do was figure out a way to get there. Plane tickets were probably too expensive, and weren't all buses filled with creepy people? She decided to try her father, even though the odds against his agreeing to drive her to St. Louis were about a zillion to one.

She ran to the phone in her mother's room and dialed the number at the store, her happy fingers almost hitting the wrong buttons. "You know how you've been promising to take us to Six Flags since forever?" she said, after Gene picked up the phone.

"Hi, sunshine," he said. "I might have mentioned something about Six Flags once or twice."

"Since forever, Dad. And now's the time. We can go tomorrow, or Saturday, or both days, your choice. I can even pay for my own snacks." Crispy smiled big and showed her teeth, even though her father couldn't see her.

"That's thoughtful of you. But here's the deal: for something like this we really need to plan ahead. I can't just close up shop."

"It's only for one day. Or two."

"True enough, but still . . . How's next June sound? We'll go for a few days, have a grand old time. See the Arch, ride one of those steamboats on the Mississippi, make a family vacation out of it. I'll even put it in writing this time: 'Six Flags, June 1994, or bust.'"

"Pleeeeeeease," she said, in what sounded to her like the most pleading kid's voice ever.

"Sorry, sugar bear," Gene said. "Besides, maybe by next summer everyone will be ready to have some fun."

I'm ready right now, Crispy thought, hanging up on her father.

WITH GENE WEASELING out on her, again, Crispy determined that she had no other choice but to run away to St. Louis and join the band. Her smiling, shirtless prince was waiting.

In her bedroom she changed her clothes, putting on her spangled majorette's top and a new pair of Levis, then roamed through the house and filled her backpack with two Marky Mark and the Funky

Bunch cassettes, a Walkman, eye shadow and lipstick pilfered from Helen's rarely used makeup kit, her baton, four packs of sour apple Hubba Bubba bubble gum, three Hi-C juice boxes, six sticks of string cheese, $46 and some odd cents from her Marky Mark merchandise fund, an emergency whistle that Gene had given her, and a picture of Francis, the one from his junior year of high school where he was grinning and looking to the side, his hair parted in the middle like he was giving his brain room to do its thinking.

Crispy found her mother in the living room, watching some soap opera people argue, and told her she was going to Erin's house.

"Be home by dinner," Helen said.

"I will," Crispy said, smiling and then almost collapsing. Who knows when Marky and the band will be performing in Springfield or Carbondale, someplace close enough where she could stop by the old house for a visit? It could be months, years.

She strapped on her backpack and left through the front door, and as she strode toward the garage Crispy told herself that even though Marky hadn't come for her in his red Ferrari, this was still a pretty good plan, his traveling thousands of miles from Hollywood and expecting Crispy to go the final seventy miles. That sounded more than fair. It was already Thursday, but she figured she could bike forty miles today and thirty miles tomorrow, no sweat, and arrive at Six Flags in time for the Friday show. She wasn't exactly sure yet how she'd get Marky to notice her. She might try twirling her baton in the crowd and see if he invited her onto the stage, but what if dozens of girls were twirling their batons for the same reason?

She went into the garage and pulled the pink streamers off her bicycle handlebars and tossed them into a garbage can, then hopped onto her bike, aimed it south, and started down the road. "It's such a good vibration, come on come on come on," Crispy sang, testing her voice in case Marky asked her to sing a duet. There was still a little bit of frog in her voice and a little bit of boy, but it would have to do.

Pedaling away from 1178 Briarwood, she began crying hard. At first she thought that happiness tears were greatly outnumbering sadness tears, but then knew that the opposite was true. Imagining Francis and Stephen riding behind her, protecting her from cars like they used to do, made her feel a little better.

When she reached Groveland she took a right, rode for about a quarter mile, then hooked a left on Walnut and glided down the freshly paved street, passing by Lincoln Elementary. Some of her best days had been spent there, climbing the monkey bars, playing Four Square on the playground, and singing songs in the auditorium. Fifth graders were the queens and kings of the school but she was going to miss it.

She turned right onto Tennyson and headed west. She hadn't mapped out a route, but west was west, she'd get to St. Louis eventually. Crossing into Middleton, the houses gave way to shops, churches, and parking lots. Crispy needed a pit stop so she pedaled to First Community Church where she planned to use the bathroom and ask God and Jesus to keep a close eye on her while she was traveling. But the church was locked, so she went next door to the reverend's house and tapped on the front door.

Mrs. Gladstone greeted her with a "Hello, young lady." Crispy smiled and asked to use the facilities, and Mrs. Gladstone ushered her into the house. Crispy set her backpack down on the carpet, said hey to the Gladstones' one kid, Luke—he was playing a video game—and then ran down the hall, trying to remember which door was the bathroom. She hadn't been in the house since a church potluck a year earlier.

When she came out of the bathroom, Mrs. Gladstone had some "good news" for her. "I called your mother and we both think you should stay out here with us for a few days—a change of environment might be the best thing for you. We'll have camp outs, barbecues, a whole bunch of fun. So, what do you say? You ready to become an honorary member of the Gladstone clan for a few days?"

Crispy realized she had screwed up by staying in the bathroom too long, smelling the various soaps and shampoos and checking the cabinet for weird ointments and pills. "Sorry, I have other plans." She picked up her backpack and headed for the door.

"This is a democracy we are living in," Mrs. Gladstone said, "but it looks like the final vote is two to one for you staying here. Your mother and I are in agreement on this. Plus Luke would like it if you stayed. Right, Luke?"

"Yeah, stay," said Luke, halfheartedly, his eyes on the game.

"Thanks for letting me use the bathroom," Crispy said, pulling open the front door. "Where'd my bike go?"

"It's in the garage for now," Mrs. Gladstone said. "We have plenty of bikes here for you to use. Even a bicycle built for two!"

"Great," Crispy said, resigning. The adult world had lassoed her again. *I'm sorry for letting you down, Marky,* she said to him in her thoughts.

DINNER CONSISTED OF cheeseburgers cooked on the grill by a cheerful Reverend Gladstone and Mrs. Gladstone's famous home-made potato salad with peas in it. Before eating, they all joined hands at the picnic table. Crispy was stuck between the Gladstone males so she had to hold Luke's clammy paw and the reverend's hairy hand. "Perhaps our guest would like to say grace," Reverend Gladstone said. Crispy, who had already closed her eyes, opened one of them. "Me?" she asked.

"Sure, just tell God whatever's on your mind," the reverend said. "Thank him for the bounty."

"Oh, that kind of grace." She cleared her throat. "Dear God. Hi, it's me, Crispy Harrelson. Thanks for the cow we are about to eat and for the potato salad with peas in it, and please watch over Marky Mark and the Funky Bunch. Thanks. I mean, amen."

"Amen," everyone said.

"Who are Marky Mark and the Funky Bunch?" asked Reverend Gladstone.

"The greatest rock-and-roll band of all time," Crispy said, reaching for the ketchup.

"Devil worshippers," Luke said.

"No, but Madonna might be," Crispy said. "She sings like five songs I'm not allowed to listen to."

Halfway through the meal, Crispy said she had to use the bathroom and would be right back. Once inside the house she found a phone and called home. Helen answered.

"Come and get me," Crispy said.

"You just got there," Helen said. "Give it some time. The week will pass before you know it."

"Week? I thought it was for a few days."

"A week is just a few days done twice. It will zip by."

"These people are really weird, Mom."

"They're good people. They love you."

"So if a murderer loved me you'd make me stay with him for a week?"

"Give it another day and then we'll talk. How's that sound?"

Crispy was about to say that it sounded awful, but she could hear her parents arguing. Gene was saying if Crispy wanted to come home let her, she's old enough to make her own choices, and Helen was saying that Crispy needed to learn to get along with people she didn't like.

"What were we talking about?" Helen asked, returning to the phone.

"Nothing. I have to go eat potato salad with peas in it."

"Be strong."

"What if I promise to be good?" Crispy asked.

"Give it some time," Helen said.

Crispy spent the night with Mrs. Gladstone in her bedroom. Dressed in an oversized Mickey Mouse T-shirt that Mrs. Gladstone lent her, she sat at the edge of the bed, her hands folded together. "I think I should say my prayers," she said.

"Only if you want to. It's just us girls in here."

"I never know what to pray about anymore."

"I'll say mine later as well. I don't think God needs to hear from us every single night, do you?"

"I guess not."

Mrs. Gladstone sat down next to Crispy on the bed and asked if she could brush her hair, and Crispy nodded. The woman grabbed a hairbrush from the nightstand and ran her fingers through Crispy's hair and followed with the brush. "It's awful what happened to your brother. He was a great guy. One of the best."

"I know. I loved him a whole lot."

"Things probably aren't going to seem normal for a long time yet. Death always rattles us."

"What if I go far away? Will it hurt less?"

"Probably not. It will feel the same, but you'll just be feeling it in a new place. Are you mad at Francis?"

"No."

"When my mother died when I was about your age, I was angry with her. I thought she had chosen to abandon me, which of course she didn't, but we believe what we believe."

"Why did your mom die?"

"She had cancer. It took her pretty quickly."

"Oh. Sorry."

"Thanks."

"I'm a little mad that it lasts so long."

"Death?"

"It just keeps going on and on. I wish it was like a vacation, that it ended and people came back to life."

"That's a big wish," Mrs. Gladstone said.

CRISPY AWOKE A little after two and glanced at the digital clock on the bedside table, watching the seven in 2:07 morph into an eight. If she got up right now, got dressed, found her backpack, broke into the garage, and claimed her bike and started pedaling like a crazy girl, she could probably still catch Marky's Friday show, or at least the Saturday performance. But it was dark out, and she didn't have a bike light, and the night is very scary when you don't have a light to shine on things that are hooting or howling at you. Plus, wasn't the prince supposed to come all of the way to the castle to rescue the princess, not stop short by seventy miles?

She sighed, then flipped over and went back to sleep.

THE NEXT MORNING, Crispy and Luke were sitting on the couch and watching TV when Crispy asked him if he had any board games they could play, like Life. "Of course we have Life," he said, inviting her into his bedroom. She followed him cautiously, knowing that any boy over the age of three couldn't be trusted.

She sat down on the carpet and cracked her knuckles, ready to spin the dial and drive a car full of little pink and blue children to Millionaire Acres.

Luke dropped a game on the floor called "After Life."

"What the heck is that?" she asked.

"It's Life for people who aren't devil worshippers," he said.

Luke sat across from Crispy, opened the box, and started setting up the game. No, there was no money, he said, you collected and read Bible passages along the way. No, there was no stock market, he said, but there would be temptations, and if you couldn't resist them you'd get sent to hell. To get out of hell you had to roll a ten for the Ten Commandments.

"But the first one to Millionaire Acres still wins, right?" she asked.

"Can't you read? It's called Heavenly Acres. The object is for both of us to get there at the same time. Near the end of the game you can move either backward or forward."

"So no one wins?"

"You win by helping other people get to heaven along with you."

"As long as I get there first," she said.

There was no fun whirring plastic spinner, so Crispy rolled the dice and got a six and decided on the business route. She jumped over a yellow temptation square—you find a lost wallet on the street with $100 in it, what do you do?—and landed on the "start a Christian bookstore" square. The square was green so she had to pick up an Old Testament card.

"You have to read it out loud," Luke said.

"Okay. It says *Job* 1:12 . . ."

"It's pronounced *Jobe.*"

"Just seeing if you knew. It says, 'The Lord giveth and the Lord taketh away, blessed be the name of the Lord.' "

Luke picked up the dice and rolled an eight. He chose the missionary route and landed on the "you are sent to the African jungle" square. It was a blue square, so he grabbed a New Testament card. "Listen closely," he said, "Romans 10:9. 'If thou shalt confess with thy mouth the Lord Jesus, and shalt believe in thine heart that God hath raised him from the dead, thou shalt be saved.' "

"My turn," Crispy said.

"Wait, you know what Romans 10:9 means, don't you? It means that your brother is in hell."

"Shut up!"

"That's what my dad said and he's been studying the Bible his whole life."

"I said shut up!"

"Unless your brother said those words . . ."

"You're stupid and your dad is stupid and this game is stupid, so shut up."

"You should also read John 3:3. 'Except a man be born again. . . ."

Crispy flipped over the game board, sending the plastic cars, little people, and the dice flying, then picked up a stack of Bible passage cards and tossed them into the air.

"I'm telling Mom," Luke said. "I was just trying to save you. Dumb heathen."

"I told you to shut up!"

"Francis Harrelson is in hell, Francis Harrelson is in hell," he sang.

She launched herself at Luke and pinned him to the carpet. "Say you're sorry or I'll whack you."

Luke thought it over. "I'm sorry Francis Harrelson is in hell!"

Crispy couldn't decide whether to punch his teeth out, twist his nose, gouge an eyeball, or scratch his ugly face. But before she could do any of those things she was lifted into the air by Mrs. Gladstone, who had ahold of her by the shirt and shorts.

"What in God's name is going on here?" she asked, easing Crispy into a standing position.

"She attacked me for no reason," Luke said, "and before that she swore."

"He's lying!" Crispy said, stomping the carpet.

"Luke, go into the living room, I'll deal with you later," his mother said.

"Wait till Dad hears about this." Luke stood up, gave Crispy the evil eye, and tramped away.

"What happened here?" Mrs. Gladstone asked.

Crispy fell into the woman and started sobbing. "He said . . . he said that Francis was in hell, because . . . because he didn't say some words."

Mrs. Gladstone petted Crispy's hair. "You have to understand one thing. Luke's father can be rather conservative in these areas, and he's indoctrinated his son quite well."

"What's *indoctrinated* mean?"

"It means you make people believe certain things."

"You don't think my brother is in hell, do you?"

Mrs. Gladstone went to her knees and peered into Crispy's wet eyes, then dragged a thumb below each one. "If there's a heaven, and I'm pretty sure there is, Francis is there. I think it's all about how we lived, or what was in our hearts, that matters. It seems kind of silly to me that you'd need a password to get into heaven. Doesn't that seem silly to you?"

Crispy smiled. "When I had a girls-only clubhouse the password was 'I hate boys.' "

"That's a good one."

"I want to go home. Can I go home?"

"It might be for the best. I'll call your dad. Maybe we can try this again in a month or two. You okay?"

"Almost," Crispy said, going for a quick hug.

WHEN GENE ARRIVED at the house, Mrs. Gladstone told him that he and Crispy were welcome to stay for lunch, but Gene said that he was having such a busy day at the store that they better scoot. While he loaded Crispy's bike and backpack in the Chevy's trunk, Mrs. Gladstone and Luke waved to them from their porch, Luke sticking out his tongue when his mother wasn't watching.

"I don't much like those people, the Gladstones," Gene said, once they were on their way. "Too high and mighty for my tastes."

"The mom is nice but the rest of them are crazy," Crispy said. "They smile all of the time and they are like 'we know God better than you do,' and they're so happy and thankful."

"Weirdos," he said.

Gene glanced at Crispy's reflection in the rearview mirror. She was too damn delicate, too unarmored. What was God thinking, making something so beautiful and then not giving her much of a shield? He had been driving at the 35 mph speed limit but slowed the Chevy down to 30 mph. Screw the other drivers—let them pass him. He was going to protect his little girl.

Crispy peered out the window, at a cornfield next to a farmhouse. "Francis is in heaven, right?" she said.

"Of course he is," Gene said, not sure if he was passing on the old fable, a Tooth Fairy story that even intelligent adults were eating up, or if there really was such a place. "The good end up in heaven. And Francis was good to his bones."

She nodded. "I liked it when he used to walk me to school."

* * *

BACK HOME, Crispy had climbed out of the car and was shuffling to the garage when she noticed that across the street Cameron Dunfee was kicking a soccer ball by himself. Poor kid never had anyone to play with because most of the boys thought Cam was nerdish and weird, which he was, and all of the girls were certain he had cooties, which he probably did.

She thanked her dad for rescuing her, then ran to Cam's house and started kicking the ball with him. It was just a lazy game, though Crispy was certain she could score on Cameron at will if they ever played one-on-one. When Cam grew tired they took a break and sat in tall grass by an oak tree that was half alive and half dead. Crispy wondered how that worked for trees, how part of them could be dead while other parts were still putting out leaves. People didn't seem to have that option: half dead was all of the way dead.

She gazed at Cam through squinted eyes, so he wouldn't notice. His face was sweating and his hair was greasy—it hadn't been shampooed in about a week or two, she guessed. Cam's green eyes were pretty, but his lips looked too much like a fish's lips, and his big ears made her think of monkeys. Not exactly a Marky Mark or even a member of the Funky Bunch.

"Do you still want to go out with me?" she asked.

"For real? Or is this a joke?"

"It's for real."

"Yes!" Cam said excitedly.

Crispy then told Cam the rules of their dating: there'd be no kissing or hand-holding or any of that silly stuff, and he couldn't tell a soul they were going out. What's more, he had to start shampooing his hair on a daily basis and clip his fingernails once weekly. Additional rules would be forthcoming.

"You've made me the happiest man in the world," he said.

"I know I have," she said.

Before leaving him, Crispy informed Cam of a new rule she had just thought of, that he had to start believing and saying that Jesus died for our sins and was born again. That way, if she and Cam were killed tomorrow they could meet up in heaven and kick a soccer ball to each other.

"But we aren't going to die tomorrow for real," Cam said. "We're only ten."

"You never know," she said.

"CRYSTAL GROWS FANGS"

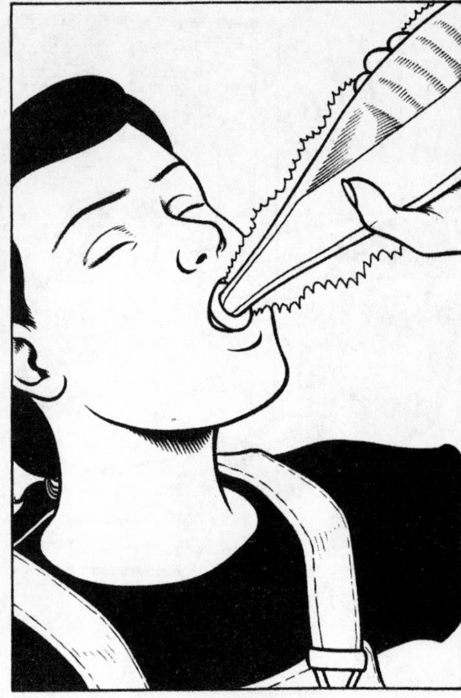

WOLF GIRL!
WG

EPISODE 24

The Shrunken Father

NICOLE WAS LYING floppily on her living room couch and reading a book about human oddities when the kitchen phone rang. Entranced by the story of a sideshow freak from the early 1900s named Myrtle Corbin, "The Four-Legged Girl from Texas," she decided to let the answering machine take the call.

Like any child, all Myrtle Corbin wanted was a normal life, but with a malformed parasitic twin attached to her, a normal life wasn't in the cards. Having control over all four of her legs, Myrtle would entertain circus crowds by galloping across the stage like a horse. Later, she married and gave birth to five children, three from her own womb and two from the womb of her half-twin.

"Hello, this is James Strussman, calling for Nicole," said a voice on the answering machine.

Why the fuck is he using his full name? Nicole set the book down and ran to the phone, picked it up, and heard the answering machine squeal in response to her violating the order of things. "Daddy?" she said, smacking the power button on the machine.

"Hey, kid," said her father. "How are you?"

"What? I don't know. How am I supposed to be?"

"Sorry I missed calling on your birthday, I—"

"And every other day for the past year."

"That, too. You know how I am with dates. I really thought your birthday was in August."

"Maybe it used to be. When are you coming to Hollis?"

"Uh, I don't know yet. So how was your birthday?"

"Dumb. Mom bought a cake."

"That sounds nice."

"Did you hear me? I said she bought a cake, didn't make one. It was probably the fat lady in the bakery at the Kroger who made it. It didn't even have my name on it, just 'happy birthday' in blue lettering. They forgot to dot the *i.*"

"Your mother was never much of a baker or a cooker."

"It's just cook, no *er.*"

"Oh, that's right. You always were smarter than your dumb old dad."

The soft, boyish way her father said "dumb old dad" caused Nicole to lose some of her anger. James Strussman was even handsome again, with his dark eyes and greased-back hair and smile-made dimples: an Elvis without the talent or money. She was about to try saying "Dad" as softly as he did, but then she heard a woman tell her father to get off the damn phone, that it was time to eat. There was also some kid sounds, two boys arguing about something. "Who's over there?" she asked.

"That's Veronica making all of that noise. I've been seeing her for nearly a year, I guess."

"Mom's been dating goofballs."

"Really? Well, everyone gets lonely. At least us old farts."

"Young farts, too. Is she French? I think Veronica is a French name."

James asked the woman if she was French. "What the hell kind of question is that?" the woman said.

"I guess she's not French," James said. "I have to go here, in a second."

"Are you in the kitchen right now?" Nicole asked.

"Yeah, why?"

"No reason. I'm in a kitchen, too, is all."

"Great. Look, I—"

"If you can't drive up here I could take the bus down to Memphis. I have enough money to buy my own ticket." Five seconds of silence followed, telling Nicole the answer.

"That could be a bit of a hornet's nest. I mean, I'd love to see you, but we don't have much space here, and Veronica isn't much into kids. Maybe something will work out around the holidays."

"Aren't there kids there?"

"Yes, two boys, hers," he said in a quieter voice. "But having kids and liking kids are two different things. There's also a baby, three months. A boy. It's a madhouse, most of the time. You can't even hear yourself think."

"Is the baby yours?"

"Good question. One in three chance."

"So I might have a little brother?"

"Same odds, one in three."

"Does the baby have anything wrong with him? Extra fingers, a balloon head, anything like that?"

"No. Why?"

"He's probably not yours."

"Hard to say. Look, I better go, before hell rains down."

Nicole said nothing, was ready for her father to be gone for another year or two or twenty.

"Kid?" he said.

"What?"

"This whole thing is breaking my heart, never seeing you. You know that, right?"

"You have a heart?" she asked.

"Of course I do. What kind of question is that?"

"Just checking."

"I really have to go," he said. "I love you."

"I'll take that into consideration," she said, hanging up.

Mudderfucker. Nicole felt tears coming on—soldiers arriving too late, the war had been lost—so she stomped the linoleum with her right foot. Now her foot hurt, but at least the tears had given up, had gone back to their camp. She turned the answering machine back on and hit the play button and heard her father's message again, and her weak "Daddy?"

"Pathetic, very pathetic," she said. Nicole pressed the machine's erase button, then played the incoming messages to make sure James Strussman was gone, gone, gone. After that, she snagged her book about human oddities from the living room and ran upstairs, turned on her Smith-Corona word processor, and got to work on an educational brochure that would soon be available to museum visitors.

NICOLE'S MUSEUM OF FUCKED-UP THINGS OFFICIAL GUIDE TO HUMAN DEFORMITIES, ODDITIES, AND OTHER THINGS THAT WILL GIVE YOU THE HEEBIE-JEEBIES

If you're a freak like I am, you might be upset that God, or whoever is up there, has seen fit to limit the range of possible human oddities. For example, while we know of no cases of humans being born with extra eyeballs, sometimes they are born without eyes, or with an extra set of eyelashes. Three ears? Unheard of, but teeth have been found growing in noses and out of eyelids, and in the foot of a thirteen-year-old boy from North Carolina named Doug Pritchard.

So don't despair, there are still many human deformities and weirdnesses out there. In fact, as you will soon find out, it is quite possible that one of these malformed freaks is living in your house. You better run and hide!

A partial list of human fuck-ups:

Gigantism: The tallest human being on record was Robert Wadlow (1918–1940), who was eight feet eleven inches and wore size 37 shoes. There are thought to be about two hundred people on earth at least eight feet tall. We should look up to them!

Dwarfism: The shortest human being ever is a man in India who is 22.5 inches tall. One of the most famous dwarfs was Geoffrey Hudson of England. At age eight he was one foot tall and was presented to the queen in a pie. No, she didn't eat him.

Fatism: The chubbiest person of all time was Jon Brower Minnoch, who weighed 1,400 pounds. Please, no fat jokes—obesity is a serious medical condition, as my mother will tell you.

Furry Women: Ever seen a bearded lady at a circus? I haven't! But my grandmother Rita in Tennessee has a pretty serious mustache.

Lobster People: In some families, the kids are born with their fingers fused together, forming lobsterlike pincers. One of them was Grady Stiles, who was murdered in Florida last year after his wife got tired of him smacking her with his claws. Those with fused toes instead of fingers are called "Ostrich People." This occurs mostly in one African tribe. They say that the deformity helps them to climb trees.

Seal People: Sealo the Seal Boy (real name Stanley Berent) and other seal people have hands growing out of their shoulders and no arms. Not to be confused with turtle people (like the famous Alzona the Turtle Girl) and penguin people (such as Dickie the Penguin Boy).

Fathers with Shrunken Hearts: Very common, perhaps one in four. These men are born with normal hearts, but they slowly shrink over the years. It is believed that James Strussman of Huntington, Tennessee, now has a heart the size of a pea. This condition may be irreversible. Strangely, the children of men with shrunken hearts often have oversized hearts. My boyfriend Stephen and his brother Francis (now dead) are/were the sweetest boys you will ever meet, even though their dad's heart is the size of a ginger snap. ALERT!!! Shrunken hearts may be infectious. If your father suffers from this condition try to avoid him, but if that is impossible please wash your hands thoroughly after each time he touches you, which won't be very often.

Siamese Twins: The most famous Siamese twins ever were brothers Chang and Eng. They both got married and between them they fathered twenty-one kids! This also happens to animals and fruits and vegetables (see museum exhibit #0000001).

Parasitic Twins: Even freakier than Siamese twins are parasitic twins, where part of a twin grows out of his/her fully developed brother or sister. Examples include the Two-Headed Boy of Bengal, whose second head was attached upside down to the top of his regular head. When he smiled his second head also smiled (the poor kid died from a snakebite at age four). Betty Lou Williams of Georgia had two extra legs and an extra arm growing out of her, and a second head in her abdomen, while Frank Lentini, known as the Three-Legged Soccer Player, had a third leg, a partial third foot growing out of its knee, and a second ding-dong. Note: no giggling on museum grounds!

The Elephant Man: His real name was Joseph Carey Merrick, and he was deformed all over, except for his left arm (his head was thirty-six inches in diameter). He believed that his condition was caused by his mother being frightened by an elephant when she was pregnant with him. Scientists now say he suffered from extremely rare "Proteus Syndrome." I think it was due to the elephant.

Tails and Horns: Yep, human beings are sometimes born with tails and horns, or the horns develop years later. While the tails are normally little nubs, there are reports of children in Paraguay with tails twelve inches long. Horns as long as thirteen inches (such as with Wang the Human Unicorn) have been found growing out people's heads, trunks, legs, feet, and penises. What did I say about giggling?

Note to the deformed: if you have any of the above oddities, including a shrunken heart, you have found a home at Nicole's Museum of Fucked-up Things. Please send a photograph and a testimonial to the address below, and a list of hours you are available to be displayed. Note: you MUST be wearing clothes in the picture.*

Sincerely fucked up,
Nicole Strussman, Curator
Nicole's Museum of Fucked-up Things
1176 Briarwood Ave.
Hollis, IL 62945

**We are planning a special "Fathers with Shrunken Hearts" exhibit for Father's Day, 1994. Don't miss it!*

EPISODE 25

The Photograph

"IT WAS A BEAUTIFUL DAY," Gene began, "and our Francis was headed to a mushroom conference in Chicago . . ."

Stephen knew this was coming: his father could never resist performing his little song and dance whenever he had any kind of an audience. It was Helen and Gene's twenty-first wedding anniversary, and although no party had been planned, Mrs. Borden brought over a cake, Don and Carla Alton came by with a bottle of scotch, and Suresh, who had intended only to drop off some paperwork for Gene to sign, saw that a party was brewing and decided to join in.

The first hour or so went reasonably well, with the adults encouraging Helen and Gene to tell stories about their early days together, and when it was time for cake they reenacted their wedding day cake-stuffing ceremony to please the crowd, though Stephen could tell, as his parents cleaned pink frosting off each other with napkins, that it was all for show. Neither of them was still in love.

As the night progressed, Gene kept drinking, and Crispy and Stephen kept glancing at each other with worried expressions.

It was Don Alton who prompted Gene this time, calling for a toast for Francis, to which everyone said "here, here" including Crispy and Stephen, who were drinking grape juice. "It's a crying shame your boy's not with us," Don said. Stephen wanted to punch Don Alton, really kick the tar out of him, because it was obvious that he was intentionally pushing Gene's buttons so he could watch him self-combust. Gene wouldn't disappoint. After breathing in and out heavily a few times, his body preparing for the coming explosion, Gene started yapping about what a beautiful day January 9 was, at least the beginning of it.

Stephen hung his head and covered his ears. The story that should never be told was being told. The story that never ended happy always started happy: "It was a beautiful day." He did not understand why his father had to engage in such a sad, public drama so frequently. Perhaps he was waiting for someone to say, "No, Gene, you have it all wrong, Francis survived that crash."

About a minute into the show Stephen stood up and went into the kitchen. He was hoping to put an end to his father's performance by leading an exodus of the audience, but it didn't work. Everyone else stayed seated.

"I had this strange feeling after he drove off that I should have said something more, or done something more," Gene continued, "but it quickly passed, perhaps because the day was still beautiful. But a storm we knew nothing of was headed our way."

Stephen paced the kitchen, trying to figure out what to do. It was dark out so he couldn't ride his bike or shoot baskets, and if he went outside and sat on the stoop his father would simply crank up the volume, making sure the sorrowful sentences found him.

"The ice storm hit suddenly," Gene said. "It went from sunny to dreary in no time at all. There were a dozen minor accidents on that mile of highway according to *The Ledger*, but our Francis was the only one killed."

Upon hearing his father say "*The Ledger,*" Stephen remembered the photo of Francis holding a gigantic mushroom that he had lent to the fat reporter, Clifford Harper. The picture was never returned, even though the man had crossed his heart and promised.

He went into the living room and glanced at his father, standing and trembling and singing his song of misery. Helen sat catatonically on the uncomfortable chair, while Crispy was on the floor, her knees drawn to her sad face. Mrs. Borden sat on the couch and watched

Gene with a look of regret. Suresh, Don, and Carla were perched on oak chairs that had been brought in from the kitchen, Don looking at Gene and nodding, encouraging him to keep spewing words. Gene, nearing the crucial part of the story where Francis was thrown from the car and about to land on the snowy roadside, did not stop the story to acknowledge Stephen's reappearance.

"There are mysteries still," Gene said. "A hundred unanswered questions. Like why wasn't he wearing his seat belt? Perhaps because it had been such a beautiful day."

Stephen marched past his father, feeling that he could barely squeeze by the shaking man who seemed to fill the whole room, and bolted to his mother's bedroom where he phoned Nicole.

"Hi, it's me," he said, when she answered.

"Are you sure you are me? I thought I was me," she said.

"Wait. I need you to meet me at midnight in my backyard. We have a very important mission."

"What kind of mission?"

"Part of Francis is being held hostage. We need to free him."

"I don't get it."

"I'll explain everything later."

"This sounds like something that is going to get us into a whole lot of trouble. Will midgets and the police be involved?"

"Hard to say. Maybe."

"Goody! See you at midnight."

"Bye."

"Capital bye with ten exclamation points," she said.

"The byest bye ever," he said.

Stephen hung up the receiver, leaned back on Helen's bed, and listened to his father's words. "On that day that started so pleasantly," Gene said, "I did not tell my son that I loved him . . ."

"You had two sons," Stephen said in a quiet voice.

* * *

NICOLE DIDN'T SHOW until 12:30, having to wait until her mother went to bed. She yawned, stretched, and asked what their mission was.

"We must travel to the headquarters of *The Ledger*, downtown," Stephen said. "They have Francis's picture. The one where he's holding a giant mushroom."

"Can't this wait until morning? They're probably closed."

"Nothing can wait for morning. We'll break in if we have to. Or I will."

"Hey, include me in any felonies. You're usually not so nuts! I love it."

"I am a man possessed," he said, not exactly sure what those words meant.

They began hiking down Briarwood. Glancing at the many dark houses, Stephen commented that so many people robotically lived similar lives, awake during the day and asleep at night, so they missed the nighttime beauty of the moon, stars, owls, and bats.

"Bats?" she said. "I'm not sure we like bats."

"I'll keep them away from you," he promised.

Nicole looped her right pinky around his left pinky. "So what's new with you?"

"My family is falling apart."

"Go on."

"Well, before my brother . . ."

"Died?"

"Yeah, that. Before that happened my parents didn't get along, but at least they pretended to sometimes. Now they both act like the other one has the plague. And my dad spends all of his time at work so I hardly ever see him anymore. I'm afraid they're headed to divorce court or something."

"First of all, if they separate and that means you and your sister are moving away, I'll slit their throats. Second, parents do whatever the hell they want to do without caring how it affects their kids.

Look at the primates my mom has been going out with. I don't get a vote."

A car came by so they dropped pinkies. The driver, some young guy with a thin orange beard, wolf-whistled at Nicole and yelled, "Nice legs!"

"Pig," Stephen said, after the man was gone.

"I wish I didn't have legs sometimes," she said. "If I cut them off, will you push me around in a wagon?"

"No, but I'll pull you around."

"Oh, that's right. Pulling would work better."

When they reached Main Street they headed west, past the stately houses in the Historical District and into the downtown area where they strolled by several vacant storefronts and closed shops, including Gene's furniture store.

"Over there," Stephen said, pointing to the *Ledger* building and its giant clock falsely telling the world that it was forever 5:08, the time of its most recent death.

They crossed the street in a playful jog, then glanced up at the curtained windows of the building: the second and third floors were still lit. "We should probably come back in the morning," she said.

"Nah." He tried the front door. It was locked but was soon opened by an exiting employee. They cautiously entered the building and looked around, then crept up a carpeted stairway and found themselves in the newsroom. There were no signs of life until Stephen spotted Clifford Harper sitting at a desk in the far corner of the office, listening to a police scanner.

Clifford turned down the scanner as Nicole and Stephen approached his desk and gave them a confused look, like he wasn't sure if they were dangerous.

"Where's my picture?" Stephen asked.

"Pardon me?"

"You came to my house last January and stole a picture of my brother. The mushroom guy. Francis Harrelson. Remember? Hello?"

"Oh, that's right. How have you been?"

"Great. So where's the picture?"

"Aren't you the kid who said his parents were dead?"

"Yeah, but they really aren't."

"I figured."

"Plus, you were supposed to write that he was the best brother ever."

"There probably wasn't room. We don't sell many ads in January so the page count is tighter."

The portly writer stood up and tucked in his shirt, stroking the fabric over his stomach in gentle motions like he was petting a beloved house cat. *What a slob,* Stephen thought. No way would *The Daily Uh-Oh* hire this guy. Clifford then ploddingly led Nicole and Stephen up the stairway and to the third-floor library.

"We call this place the morgue," Clifford said, starting to weed through a tall stack of files.

"Cool," said Nicole, looking around the messy room. "Where are the bodies?"

"Oh, they are certainly here," said the journalist.

Nicole and Stephen each took on a stack. Stephen, opening file after file, hadn't realized that tragedies happened so frequently in Hollis and Caswell County: "Woman killed in Hollis accident"; "Century Twp. man shot at laundry"; "Caswell plane crash claims two." All of this sorrow, just in this one little corner of Illinois.

"Voilà," Clifford said after ten minutes of searching. He handed the file to Stephen, who quickly opened the folder and snatched the mushroom photo and placed it in his shirt pocket.

"Sorry about your brother," Clifford said. "I always hate to write about these kinds of things."

"Then why do you?" Stephen asked.

"Someone has to."

"No they don't. You could just write about people being good brothers or sisters or parents, and what they liked to do for fun."

"I'd never get away with it."

Stephen glanced at the rest of the file: an article about the crash, the obituary, an old clip about his brother winning a high school science competition, and a short piece on Francis being named to the Dean's List at Southern Illinois University. He folded the articles carefully and placed them in his pocket. Clifford said nothing.

Nicole had fallen asleep while resting her head on a pile of yellowing newspapers, so Stephen woke her by tapping her nose, and the three of them returned to the newsroom. Stephen and Nicole started down the stairs, then Stephen stopped and looked back at the reporter. "You shouldn't lie to kids," he said. Clifford nodded, accepting the reprimand, and watched the children walk down the stairs and out into the night.

ON THE WAY HOME they stopped at a city park that had closed at dusk and sat down on a bench that lovers and other crazies had carved their initials into. It was a cloudless night and a three-quarter moon dangled above them. Stephen saw a police car coming up the street and told Nicole to freeze. "Bats?" she asked. "Cops," he answered.

When the cruiser was gone, Nicole informed Stephen that several hours earlier she had come up with a new comic book character named Lila Butterfly. She'd have drawings for him to see in a day or two.

"She's a girl, huh?" he said. "I guess that's okay. What are her powers?"

"I haven't figured everything out yet, but I know that if she moves her wings really fast she can start a hurricane or put out fires."

"Pretty cool. Are her boobs big?"

"What? Freak!"

"I'm just saying that if they are big they could launch missiles."

"Sorry, but I'm pretty sure they are going to be normal sized. Freak!"

"Wonder Woman has big boobs," he pointed out.

Nicole shook her head, then slid closer to Stephen, so that their legs touched. "I didn't like that newspaper library," she said. "All of those awful articles."

"I know. It's like you get killed and someone writes a story about it and that's all there is. It doesn't seem enough—a whole big life and all you get is one little story."

"When I die, write a ten-thousand-page book about me and call it *Nicole Was Here and Then She Wasn't.* Or even better, make it a comic book."

Stephen looked sad, didn't say anything.

"I meant like a hundred years from now," she said. "I'm not going anywhere." But Stephen didn't cheer up until Nicole announced that Lila Butterfly's boobs would be big after all, though not so gargantuan as to be able to launch missiles.

"I got it!" he said. "They could shoot out white netting, like the threads of a cocoon. She could cocoon the bad guys, tie them up."

Nicole punched his arm. "I'll cocoon you, Wolfy!"

"Owwww-oooh," Stephen howled, rubbing at his arm, which, since he was a wolf right now, was really a leg.

LILA BUTTERFLY IN- "METAMORPHOSIS"

NOBODY LOVES US ORPHANAGE

IT LOOKS LIKE FLAME-O IS BACK IN TOWN. I WAS HOPING THAT HE HAD STOPPED PLAYING WITH MATCHES. TIME TO DOUSE HIS FLAMES.
I'M COMING, TOO.

SAVE US!
HELP!
SAVE US! COUGH COUGH!
ADMIRING YOUR HANDIWORK, FLAME-O?
OH IT'S YOU, MY FURRY ARCH-ENEMY.
WHO'S THE SKINNY CHICK WITH WINGS?

SHE'S A FRIEND.
LILA BUTTERFLY!

ANY FRIEND OF WOLF BOY IS AN ENEMY OF MINE.
I'M GONNA BURN YOU UP, WOLF BUTT!
I'LL GET HIM!
YOU NEED TO COOL YOUR JETS, MISTER!
WHAT THE--?!

OWIE OWIE OWIE -- OOPS...
WHAT DIDJA EXPECT? I'M HOT STUFF, BABE!

COME TO PAPA.

POW!

SPLOOOOSSSHH!

THANKS FOR THE HELP.
YOU CAN THANK ME LATER. FIRST I HAVE TO RESCUE THE ORPHANS!
LET ME SEE IF I CAN BE OF ASSISTANCE.
FASTER...
FASTER...
WHHISSSSH!
I DIDN'T KNOW YOU COULD DO THAT.
ME NEITHER...

LATER, INSIDE THE LIFE SURE STINKS SALOON...
SO... TELL ME YOUR LIFE STORY.
WELL, I GREW UP IN THE CATERPILLAR GHETTO...
THE BUTTERFLY IN YOU
ONE DAY I FOUND A BROCHURE ON METAMORPHOSIS PUBLISHED BY THE BUTTERFLY UNDER-GROUND.
I WAS BORED AND THOUGHT I'D GIVE IT A TRY.
SLAM
I LOVED HAVING WINGS AND COULDN'T WAIT TO SHOW MY PARENTS...
BUT THEY KICKED ME OUT OF THE TREE HOUSE AS SOON AS THEY SAW MY WINGS.
IF YOU COULD UNDO IT, BECOME A CATERPILLAR AGAIN, WOULD YOU?
I DON'T KNOW...
NOT THAT SUCH THINGS ARE POSSIBLE...
THEY MIGHT BE.

I'VE HEARD THERE'S A DOCTOR IN EDENVILLE WHO CAN REVERSE METAMORPHOSIS. FOR BUTTERFLY PEOPLE AND MOTH-HEADS IT'S THE LATEST CRAZE.
REALLY?

THE GHETTO WAS A SAFE, QUIET PLACE...

NO. I NEED TO BE WHO I AM, NOT WHO I WAS.

YOU'RE RIGHT. SOME-TIMES THERE'S JUST NO GOING BACK.

I...
I USED TO BE PART OF A CRIME-FIGHTING TEAM WITH MY FATHER, NOW RETIRED, AND MY BROTHER, JOHNNY, NOW DEAD. THAT MAKES ME A LONE WOLF.
A VERY LONELY WOLF.

WILL THIS NEW CRIME-FIGHTING DUO BE ABLE TO SAVE FORGOTTEN CITY? FIND OUT IN OUR NEXT EXCITING ISSUE OF "LILA BUTTERFLY," AVAILABLE SOON AT FORGOTTEN CITY'S FINEST UNDERGROUND COMIC BOOK STORES, AND AT NICOLE'S MUSEUM OF FUCKED-UP THINGS (SEE AD IN THIS ISSUE).

EPISODE 26

August Afternoon

WHILE WAITING IN LINE at the Fayette County Clerk's Office, Helen was reconstructing, in her mind, how she got here. She had been running a few errands in Hollis—dropping off Gene's work clothes at the dry cleaners and picking up stamps at the post office—before deciding to go for a little drive. It was a warm, sunny day, and with the weather change coming in a month or so there weren't going to be too many of these golden days left, so why not head out? Or did she intend all along to travel to Fayette County? Helen wondered. The subconscious can be funny that way, she thought. Make you think you're just going for a sightseeing drive when really it's sending you someplace.

She did have a bit of unfinished business with Dotty and the Fayette County Clerk's Office. No more death certificates had appeared in the Harrelsons' mailbox since the day Gene phoned the county clerk—a man named Sheldon Teasely—and threatened a lawsuit if they didn't stop, but Helen did feel that she was owed apologies from Dotty and Sheldon. They had attacked Helen when she was at her weakest point, sent her over the edge.

Ahead of Helen a wrinkled old man was slowly filling out some kind of form, like he was hoping for a gold star for perfect penmanship. He was being waited on by an obese woman, about fifty-two or fifty-three, with permed red hair—or a wig—and painted-on eyebrows. Her fingernails were obviously Lee press-on nails, and the broach on her black dress looked like something you could buy at Wal-Mart, not a family heirloom. Was anything real about this woman?

Helen suspected that the clerk was Dotty but wasn't sure until she heard her say to the man, in a diluted Southern drawl, that she'd need to see his driver's license to make sure he was who he claimed to be. *That's the bitch.*

"If I was going to pretend to be another person, I think I could come up with someone more interesting," the man said. Dotty smiled, but Helen figured that it was fake, too. Was Dotty even human, or some sort of automaton? Helen had the urge to scratch her, to see if she'd bleed.

While waiting, Helen looked around the office. Four ladies, three old bats and one young chick in a short skirt, were sitting at desks and typing away at computers and writing in ledger books. In a back office, Sheldon—that must be him—was sitting at a desk and reading a newspaper, earning his outrageous taxpayer-funded salary. He didn't look at all like Henry Fonda but could have been a cousin to Bob Newhart. As she gazed at Sheldon and then at each of the workers, Helen's anger moved from simmer to boil, wondering if they were a bunch of sick sadists who got their thrills from sending out extra death certificates to strangers, reminding them that the most beautiful person in their life was gone for good.

Her eyes drifted to the counter in front of her. There were three different forms that could be filled out, a tray holding paper clips, rubber bands, and a few cheap pens, a laminated sign saying "$15 fee for returned checks," and a gray Swingline stapler. The stapler looked heavy and hard, Helen observed, capable of inflicting a fair amount of damage should it fall into the hands of a madman. Or a madwoman.

The oldster had finished his business so Helen scooted up to the counter. One "sorry" from Dotty and at least a regretful look from Sheldon and then she'll go.

"May I help you?" Dotty asked.

Helen looked at the woman, noticing her pearly teeth. Were they fake, too? "I'm Helen Harrelson, from Hollis. Remember me?"

"That's three H's," Dotty said cheerfully. "Helen, Harrelson, and Hollis."

"So you don't remember me?"

"Don't think so. Should I?"

"You should," said Helen, grabbing the stapler and whacking Dotty in the side of the head with its base. *Did I really just do that?*

"Ah!" squawked the clerk, covering her head with her arms, but there were still some decent openings. "What's wrong with you?"

Helen struck Dotty on the crown of her head with the stapler. *Have a little blunt force trauma, deary.* "I'm the woman whose life you tried to ruin. But it didn't work, did it? I'm doing just fine, thank you."

The automaton squeaked a protest and was still trying to avert any further blows, but dumbly stayed put instead of retreating.

"And you might also remember my son Francis," said Helen, smacking Dotty on her nose with the Swingline, the stapler nervously spitting out a staple. "He's the one whose death you kept telling me about. But he only died once. He only died once!"

In rapid succession Helen hit Dotty on a flabby, Jell-O-packed arm, her plastic chin, and the side of her robot head again. *How do you like being a victim?* The clerk dropped to the counter, stayed covered up, and started whimpering.

Helen was planning to continue the attack until Dotty said she was sorry, but someone had yanked the stapler from her hand and was pinning her arms behind her back. It couldn't be Sheldon or any of the worker ladies—they were all watching the show from a safe distance. A deputy was the one restraining her, Helen soon realized, as metal bracelets were clamped around her wrists. She figured that an officer was kept nearby due to the large number of attacks on employees of the Fayette County Clerk's Office. People can only take so much abuse before they snap.

As she was being pulled out of the office Helen gazed at Dotty.

The wounded clerk was rubbing her skull as Sheldon patted her on the back and offered her a Kleenex, as if that would help. They both gave Helen cold looks.

"You can only die once," Helen calmly said. "It's a known fact."

AT HIS SHOP, Gene locked the front door, then stuck a sign in the window that said "Will Return in a Half Hour." He didn't do much business in the early afternoon so probably no one will care that the store is closed. Gene dimmed the salesroom lights to save a few pennies on the electric bill, then went into the office, where Marjorie was sitting on his desk, not exactly spread-eagle but close to it: spread-seagull, maybe. She was wearing her tight jeans, the ones that made Gene feel like a junkyard dog ready to mount anything and everything, and a thin white blouse that allowed him to see her lacy bra.

Easy as pie, he thought, closing the office door. No resistance from Marjorie at all, no chase. Oh well, if someone was offering free dessert wasn't it his obligation to lap it up?

"I wonder what's on your mind," she said, puckering her lips and then swishing them back and forth.

"I get the feeling I won't be needing my mind for a little while," he said.

As Marjorie was unbuttoning her blouse in the maddeningly slow way that drove Gene bonkers, the phone rang, startling her—she was sitting right next to it. Gene let the machine take the call. Shortly, they were hearing Helen say, "Gene? You there? This is Helen, your wife. I screwed up again."

Gene slumped, picked up the receiver. "Yes, Helen, I'm here," he said, then listened to his wife tell him about attacking Dotty and that she had been arrested and charged with misdemeanor assault. Bail had been set at $2,000, but if Gene was able to get to the clerk's office before four o'clock and pay the bail, she wouldn't have to spend the night in jail. Marjorie, ignoring the serious tone of the conversation, had continued to undress, and by the time Gene was reassuring Helen that he would be there by four, no problem, he was wearing Marjorie's black satin panties as a hat. "Hurry," Helen said. "I don't want to stay the night here." "I'm leaving now," he said. "Be right there."

After hanging up the phone Gene looked at Marjorie, naked except for white ankle socks. "Helen isn't well," he said, removing her panties from his head and setting it on the desk. "I have to go fetch her."

"I understand," Marjorie said, scooting closer to Gene and reaching for his belt. "We'll have to make this a quick one."

"You *don't* understand," he said, pushing her hands away. "My wife needs me. My kids need me. But here I am, screwing around like none of that matters." He frowned, disgusted with himself, and roughly raked a hand through his hair. "We really need to end this, today. Start behaving like responsible adults again."

"Sure," she said, looking up at Gene, lust still owning her eyes. "You're right, we have to stop. But why not go out with a bang?"

Gene knew what he should have said—"forget it, that's like a junkie saying one last fix couldn't hurt"—but what he ended up saying was, "All right, one more roll and then we're done." *I am a weak, pitiful man.*

GENE ARRIVED at the Fayette County Clerk's Office five minutes before they closed. As he was signing the bail paperwork and writing the check, Gene was aware that the entire staff was giving him funny looks, but he wasn't sure if it was because his wife had taken down one of their own or because he had showed up at the last second and now they might have to stay a little longer.

When he was done at the clerk's office, he went to the Sheriff's Department down the hall and showed a deputy his copy of the bail agreement and receipt. The cop told Gene to have a seat, that it would take a little while to "process Ms. Harrelson." Gene wondered what exactly was involved in processing a Ms. Harrelson—it sounded rather clinical and dehumanizing—but he didn't ask for clarification.

Helen was brought out a half hour later. *My God, what have they done to you?* Gene almost said after seeing his wife. She looked pale and feeble, like she hadn't slept in a week and might be battling some kind of virus, but not battling it very well. Gene quickly realized, though, that this was his first good look at her in some time.

He met Helen at the desk, where she had to sign release paperwork and another form to claim her purse. They then left the building and walked to the Chevy, parked two blocks from the courthouse. So far, Helen had only said, "Thanks for coming," and Gene had just managed, "Sure."

At the car, Gene asked Helen if she was up for driving, and Helen answered that as a matter of fact she wasn't, so could they come back tomorrow for the car? Absolutely, said Gene, checking to make sure the doors were locked. And if Helen wasn't yet ready to claim the Chevy tomorrow, Gene said, he could always drive Suresh up here.

They marched three blocks in the opposite direction to Gene's delivery van. After they climbed into the van and pulled out of the lot, Gene thought about the fact that they were only ten minutes south of where Francis's accident occurred. Would visiting that patch of road help heal his wife, or could it make things worse? Seeing it with Stephen wasn't quite as horrific as he had thought it would be, and Gene was also curious if the little marker they had put up was still standing. But he figured he better not risk upsetting Helen any further.

Not much was said during the hour drive home, though they did talk about hiring an attorney and if Helen should plead guilty to the assault charge. "You might take your chance with a jury," Gene suggested. "Some of them will have kids. They'll understand why you did what you did."

"If only I could understand it," Helen said, looking out at the world, passing by.

* * *

When they were just outside of Hollis, Gene glanced at his wife and said, "There's something I really need to know."

"Yes?" said Helen, a worried "what now?" look on her face.

"Did it feel good, wailing on the clerk?"

"It felt great," she said, trading in her troubled expression for a smile. "Like I was finally doing something for Francis, sticking up for him. If the deputy hadn't stopped me I probably could have kept smashing Dotty for another ten minutes."

"Damn. I wish I had gotten in a few good licks. Was it big, the stapler?"

"Pretty big. And heavy, too. I think it was made of steel."

"Sweet," he said, nodding approvingly. "Real sweet."

Gene dropped Helen off at home but promised to return within an hour. There were a few things he had to take care of at the shop, he told her, not mentioning that one of them was to make sure that Marjorie hadn't left her panties in the office. Suresh was opening the store tomorrow and he didn't want him finding them.

As Helen trudged to the house Stephen and Crispy bounded out of the door and gave their mother big hugs and quick kisses. (Gene had left a message for them on the answering machine saying that Helen had had some car trouble and would be back soon.) Crispy then waved and smiled at Gene while he was backing out of the driveway.

Gene felt suddenly heartsick. That was his brittle and beautiful family over there, the woman he had married and promised to love forever and two of the three children he had helped to make and shape, all of them, like Gene, still recovering from the accident that took Francis. *They need me,* he thought, almost disbelieving that there were people in this world who needed more of Gene, not less. "I'll try harder," he said to his family, though not loud enough for them to hear.

Driving north on Briarwood, Gene sobbed and made vow after

vow that he would be a better father and husband, that he'd start living the kind of life that if someone was secretly videotaping him, he wouldn't be horrified watching those tapes. *Gene's a good guy now, and here's the proof.*

Yes, it was time to live more decently, Gene declared, his eyes so misty he was having trouble seeing the road. "Starting . . . now."

EPISODE 27

Secrets of Immortality

It was Labor Day, summer's executioner, and school was starting up in Hollis tomorrow. Eighth grade for Stephen, meaning more boys with mustaches, and some girls who went into summer flat and boyish were now wearing bras and makeup. Everyone a freak or a jock or a prep or a nerd or a retard or a none of the above, your category nonnegotiable, no appealing it. Stephen, not quite smart enough to be a nerd and not athletic enough to be a jock, was a none of the above, the ignored kids, the walking invisible. Tougher math tests were waiting for him, and a health class that was really a sex class. He'll probably have to say *vagina* out loud in class every day. No recesses, not a terrible loss, the last great schoolyard kickball game happened in fifth grade anyway, at Lincoln. Study hall instead. Sunshine and green life existing only on the other side of the windows, unless gym class was spent outdoors playing softball or running on the track. But even then there'd be expectations, like hit the ball or run faster than the chubby kid. During recess you could sit by a tree and watch pretty girls skip rope, if you wanted to. He should have never left Lincoln, should have kept failing so he could stay in elementary school forever. Stephen was somewhat popular there, had served as president of the entire third grade (there weren't any actual duties), and then as a safety patrol guard in fourth and fifth. Wore an orange belt and carried a "stop!" flag and kept first and second graders from getting flattened by cars going 20 mph. All gone. Stephen's goals this year: B's and to not be teased by girls; to not say anything dumb in sex class; to not get beat up by one of those boys with mustaches.

Stephen woke with the sun and spent most of the morning outside. It was a scorcher, summer burning up, burning out, eighty-four degrees in the morning, ninety-two by noon. "It will be a good day for sipping lemonade on the porch with your uncle Harry and aunt Ethel," Arty Gifford had said on the previous night's weathercast. It was too hot to shoot baskets or to go for a walk, so when Nicole stopped over, wilted and pink from the heat, she and Stephen sat in a shaded spot in his backyard between the privet hedges and the plum tree that could manage only inedible grape-sized fruit. They drank cherry Kool-Aid and lamented the loss of summer: perhaps if they had goofed off more they could have extended summer's stay by a week or two. Stephen gazed often at Nicole's legs and arms, recording her flesh, soon to be hidden beneath jeans, sweaters, and jackets, her T-shirts and jerseys and shorts tucked away for the winter.

While Nicole was talking about the low points of the summer—such as her failure to acquire any major items for her museum—Stephen could feel summer slipping away from him in a whoosh. Acorns were falling from the oak in the front yard. Bees were making final rounds before calling it quits. Dandelions, the second batch, were going to seed. Birds were forming V's somewhere, feeling that tug to head south.

"We have to play catch right now," Stephen pleaded, wanting to max out this last holy day of 1993, run through every second of it, push summer into extra innings.

Nicole ran home to get her baseball glove and a ball, and he fetched his mitt. They tossed the baseball to each other on Briarwood, gentle lobs at first, a few pop-ups and grounders, and then he pitched to her, Nicole calling strikes and balls and "yer outs." It seemed to be working, summer slowing down a little, leaning against the oak tree and watching the boy and girl play catch, in no hurry to leave. But then Nicole complained that she was turning into a stink factory from her sweat and Stephen's right arm was aching from pitching five sidearm twisters in a row, so they decided to go back to being lazy kids who hang out in the shade, at least until the next inspiration hit.

LABOR DAY WAS also when the city pool closed for the year, so after lunch Stephen, Nicole, and Crispy tied colorful beach towels around their waists and rode their bicycles to the pool for one last hurrah.

They paid the one-dollar fee, took showers in the "Gulls" or "Buoys" room, and padded to the less-crowded area near the deep section where they set down their towels. Smells of chlorine, beading sweat, and cocoa butter overtook Stephen as he listened to the chorus of kid noises, hearing a "Marco" but no "Polo." Where did Polo go? Did he drown? Finally the "Polo." Two towels away a plump but pretty girl was telling two thin ones about a creepy older guy who had just hit on her at the snack bar, the man telling her that she had both finesse and moxie, "Whatever the hell those things are." The thin ones didn't know.

Nicole and Crispy coated themselves in sunscreen. Nicole wore an orange bikini, which meant that every boy at the pool, most of them with more muscles and athletic ability than Stephen, could see 86.8 percent of her body, according to his calculations. How many of those better boys were checking her out right now, planning their moves? Stephen decided he better double his daily push-ups (from ten to twenty), and start lifting weights, so if a boy challenged him to a fight over Nicole, he'd stand a chance.

His eyes moved to the pool where he watched a freckled-all-over boy walk to the end of the low board, tighten the tie of his trunks, pinch his nose, and jump in. A few seconds later the kid surfaced and swam to a ladder.

Stephen had cannonballed off the low board several times, but any kid could do that. He lost interest in trying the high board the day Francis slipped and smacked his head. He and Crispy sat helpless as their brother fell to the water, his hands desperately trying to grab hold of something but only getting air. Before the lifeguard had even clambered down from her perch, Francis shot out of the water, newborn, and climbed out of the pool. "Ouch," Francis said, rubbing his skull and shaking off water. Crispy wrapped a towel around Francis and Stephen petted his wet hair. He wanted to kiss his shining brother just for being alive, but before Stephen could do that two lifeguards peeled Francis away and shuttled him to the office, where he was taken by ambulance to the hospital and examined and x-rayed. "Tomorrow I'm going to go back to the pool and kick that diving board's butt," Francis said at the hospital. But Stephen doubted that his brother ever returned to the pool, ever dove again.

"I'm going for a dive," he announced.

"Don't hurt your thing," Nicole said, rubbing sunscreen on her face. Crispy giggled.

Funny, so very funny. Stephen stood up and walked slowly to the high board, hoping a long line would form ahead of him, but when he arrived at the board it was just him: the smarter kids were using the low board or were flying down the slide. He glanced at the slippery metal steps and counted them: there were eleven. Why not a nice even number like ten or twelve? Eleven was a shaky, unsure number, two ones standing weakly next to each other like hungry orphans. Maybe he should put this off for another year, he thought, plan it out all winter long. *No.* It was time to be a man.

"You have the heart of a champion," Stephen said, and when that wasn't quite enough he promised himself an Astro-pop and a soft pretzel from the snack bar as a reward for diving, or at least jumping, from the defective (eleven steps!) board. When that still wasn't quite enough he told himself that Nicole would consider his dive heroic, which might help him keep her as a girlfriend. Those boys with bigger muscles could probably dive from the high board without even thinking about it.

He grabbed hold of the metal bars and stepped up on the first rung and kept climbing, expecting the faulty steps to collapse one by one and return him to ground level, but they somehow held, and before long he was standing on the top step, the platform. He stepped out onto the sandpapery, wet board.

"Boy on the diving board," a lifeguard bullhorned. "You need to be wearing a bathing cap." Stephen smiled and waved at the guard: it was Amanda Pierce, a pretty high school girl from his neighborhood. But what was Amanda going to do, climb up and force a cap on him?

He peered out at the narrow diving board: it was a monster's tongue, a gangplank, a bridge to nowhere. What were his odds of surviving a dive, he wondered. Probably a million kids jumped from high boards in the United States each year, and three or four of them drowned or died of fright on the way down. He hoped to not be among the casualties, but you launch yourself into the world and anything goes.

He looked over at Nicole and Crispy. They were lying on their towels, not watching him. Didn't they realize what a huge deal this was? He glanced back at the board, somehow narrower now, and was debating whether to dive or just jump when a commotion in the water drew his attention. There was a man, dressed in white and blue, floating at the bottom of the pool. He was about to call for help when he realized that it was Francis down there, in his Hurricanes cross-country uniform. Tears sprang from Stephen's eyes as his brother wriggled to life and started to crabwalk along the pool floor, as if saying, "Look what I can do now."

"Boy on the board, get down from there," Amanda tried again.

Francis rose to the surface, dog-paddled, mouthed, "Catch me if you can," and sank into the water.

"Be right there," Stephen said. *Okay, okay, okay, I have to do this. Astro-pop! Giant pretzel! Nicole!* He walked to the edge of the safe world, curled his toes and reached his arms out into the last day of summer, pressed his hands together in a gesture of prayer though he did not pray, breathed in and out, then catapulted himself into air he couldn't grab hold of and rocketed into the water headfirst.

For a few seconds he was face-to-face with his brother, at the bottom of the pool. Stephen exhaled, causing bubbles to rise to the surface. His brother had no air, made no bubbles. Francis winked a dead eye at him, then started swimming toward the five-foot section of the pool, thick with children. Out of air, Stephen swam upward, gulped oxygen, then curled back into the water and went chasing after Francis.

They swam past girls and boys at play, Francis in the lead, achingly just out of reach. *Slow down*, Stephen telepathically told his brother, but Francis started to swim even faster. Stephen was kicking and clawing at the water with all of his might, but he had to ease up when a lanky boy, swimming along the bottom of the pool like a catfish, started to surface and almost collided with him. He cursed the boy and swam around him, but could now see only Francis's kicking legs, far ahead. "Go faster!" he told his body, but then he started to choke on water, chlorine, and probably pee—he knew what boys did in pools—as he saw his brother disappear into a forest of children. He cried Francis's name and kept swimming, and finally when no air was left inside of him he stood up. Stephen was now in the three-foot deep section, surrounded by bouncy nine-year-olds. He anxiously looked around for his brother and spotted him about thirty feet away, sitting atop a cyclone fence that kept out freeloaders. He sloshed through the water, climbed out of the pool, and sprinted toward Francis, but before he could get to his brother Francis stood on the top bar of the fence, steadied himself, mouthed the words "find me," and flew into the sky, doing a loop-de-loop at the tree line. He climbed higher, past the clouds, and higher still through the troposphere, stratospheres, and mesosphere, tearing through Earth's protective gel and out into space. Stephen lost sight of his brother as Francis passed the sleeping day moon.

"Get back here," Stephen demanded, but Francis didn't return.

* * *

LATER THAT DAY, Stephen was in the basement, sitting on Francis's bed and going through some of his brother's belongings, when he found an essay Francis had written on fairy ring mushrooms. He guessed it was the paper his brother was planning to present at the mycology conference.

Francis Harrelson

BOT 352

Dr. Morris Cravens

Southern Illinois University-Carbondale

December 8, 1992

HOW DRY I AM: FAIRY RINGS AND THE BIOLOGY OF RESURRECTION

As can be evidenced by the popularity of antiaging books, potions, and diet programs, as well as the cryogenics movement, the hope for immortality or resurrection is commonplace. Yet, as far as we know, no one has either lived forever or come back to life after having died. In fact, most of us can only hope for seventy-some years of life, assuming that an accident or disease doesn't claim us much earlier. And once we are gone, we are gone.

But the "curse of mortality" is not universal. Several lower animals and plants have amazingly exhibited the ability both to survive harsh conditions and to "resurrect" after periods of metabolic dormancy exceeding one hundred years. The scientific term is *cryptobiosis,* the shutting down of life processes due to a harsh or unfavorable environment. A more lay term would be "suspended animation," a phrase frequently found in science fiction books and movies, yet for some organisms suspended animation is a scientific reality.

The cryptobiotic state causes a bit of a problem for scientists. If an organism looks dead, acts dead, and according to various measures is dead, yet can be revived, is it really dead? Many scientists would say no, if you can restore life to an organism, then it was never actually dead. For these scientists, structural integrity (plus the potential for metabolic activity) is key. Plants and animals in a cryptobiotic state tend not to degrade, and when better conditions return they'll be ready to go. To these scientists cellular degradation is one of the proofs that an organism is truly dead.

Other scientists, however, freely use the word *resurrection* when referring to the awakening of a plant or animal from a cryptobiotic state. To them, metabolic *continuity* appears to be a defining quality of a living being, and its absence proof that the organism has died. While the stopping of measurable metabolic activity for minutes or hours, perhaps even days, does not necessarily mean that death has occurred, what if that organism has been metabolically inactive for decades? Scientists have been able to revive both resurrection plants *(Selaginella lepidophylla)* and water bears (also known as tardigrades, a microscopic animal) after they've been "dead" for over a hundred years. There are many other miraculous tales of animals and plants thought to be dead suddenly showing signs of life, such as the coccid that woke up after more than seventeen years in a museum, or the larva of a wood-boring beetle *(Margarodes vitium)* that resumed development after a forty-year delay. The ability of cryptobiotic organisms to maintain structural integrity may only mean that select plants and animals have the ability to endure multiple lives and multiple deaths.

Fairy ring mushrooms *(Marasmius oreades)* are one of a small number of organisms known to be capable of resurrection. Specifically, fairy rings are anhydrobionts, organisms that can completely (or nearly completely) dry themselves out and "live" without water. The survival advantages of anhydrobiosis are obvious: the organism can withstand long periods of drought and predators may leave dead-looking plants uneaten.

In their cryptobiotic state fairy rings cease the normal metabolic functions of mushrooms such as respiration, exuding of digestive enzymes and absorption of predigested food, and mycelial growth, but it only takes a rainstorm or a glass of water poured on them by a sympathetic mycologist to restore life and function. This process of death and rebirth, or hibernation and reactivation if you prefer, has paid off for some fairy rings: a fairy ring in France is known to be over seven hundred years old, and other rings elsewhere may be much older.

While the mechanics of cryptobiosis and resurrection are not completely known, fairy rings and most (if not all) organisms capable of this process appear to rely heavily on trehalose, a common sugar that protects proteins and helps maintain lipids in the absence of water. While other chemicals may be involved in cryptobiosis, the importance of trehalose should not be understated. Yeast variants that do not contain trehalose cannot resurrect, while their cousins that do have trehalose as part of their chemical makeup can resurrect. Is trehalose the stuff of miracles? Maybe. It's been postulated that a trehalose-based solution may someday be used to preserve human organs for up to several weeks, thus improving their availability for transplantation.

Despite the human fascination with longevity and immortality, fairy rings and other cryptobiotic organisms have not been extensively studied. This needs to be remedied. While science stole some of the "magic" from fairy rings by proving that they are not formed by dancing fairies or resting dragons as people once believed, further exploration of their mechanism of resurrection may restore some of this mushroom's enchantment. If a human being could survive hundreds of years by dying and resurrecting dozens of times like fairy rings can it would be big news. Sadly, the miracles that fairy rings pull off daily are little known.

Whether research on cryptobiotic plants and animals will ultimately support human longevity and immortality efforts remains to be seen. Besides benefiting the fields of cryogenics, cryobiology (preservation of seeds, eggs, blood, etc.), and human transplant surgery, unlocking the secrets of cryptobiosis might also someday benefit "suspended animation" forms of space travel. Those movie plotlines from the 1950s where astronauts are put to sleep on earth and wake up a hundred years later in a faraway galaxy the same age and in perfect health may not be so ridiculous after all. Fairy rings and other cryptobiotic organisms are thought capable of such deeds right now. Some scientists even believe that water bears may have arrived on earth tucked in meteorites.

If I were the chair of a university mycology department I'd make studying fairy rings and their noble quest for immortality a top priority. Besides the reasons already stated, such explorations may also lead to greater philosophical debate on what exactly death is. For fairy rings and a few other organisms, death may only mean that you're waiting on some water.

STEPHEN FELL BACK onto the bed and let loose his tears. Francis had wanted to save the world from death but died before he could even begin his research. And now he was swimming in the sky and in pools and in bathtubs, seeking his saving water, trying to resurrect himself like fairy rings can so he could come home and continue his important work. A drop? A gallon? An ocean? How much would it take to restore Francis?

Stephen rubbed at his eyes, blocking the ducts, then looked out the mud-specked basement window. There was life out there, grass and shrubs and lilies, and he could vaguely hear children at play somewhere and an occasional birdsong. Life, green and noisy, but also mortal and someday to disappear. Why did God bother to make all of this stuff, if it was destined to die? A squazillion deaths already, if you counted bugs and blades of grass, and surely God counted these things. God, Stephen guessed, must be totally heartbroken. Everything he has made will eventually conk out, dry up, stop.

The children kept playing and squealing, a block or two away. Robins kept singing, or maybe that was the sound of blue jays. The boards in the basement ceiling creaked from someone, probably his living mother, walking across the kitchen floor. Cars, packed with living people, passed on the road. And Stephen's heart seemed to be pounding against the rib bone bars of its cage, the beats saying I'm alive I'm alive I'm alive. "Ahhhhhhhh!" Stephen said, balling his fists and shuddering with electric life. It was just too difficult, and strange, living in a mortal world, this planet of the doomed. He wanted to save every damn thing, or at least extend stays. Let mayflies stick around for an entire summer, instead of just a day. Let people, the good ones, live for two hundred years, or longer.

It was then that Stephen decided to take over Francis's fairy ring and immortality research, at least until his brother found his resurrection water. *Or is it too late for Francis? He must be . . .* He stopped himself from imagining what kind of shape Francis's body was in eight months after his death, and whether human resurrection was even possible.

On September 6, 1993, at 5:31 P.M., Stephen Harrelson began his project to defeat death. He would continue to write comic books and someday design safer cars, and possibly study snowflakes, but discovering the longevity secrets of fairy ring mushrooms would be his top priority. If brainless fairy rings could stick around for hundreds of years, why not human beings?

He had promised Nicole that he would stop over to toss a Frisbee with her, but that was kids' stuff—he better get started on his research. Stephen sat up and started reading one of his brother's ultra-boring schoolbooks, *Principles of Microbiology*, making it to page fourteen before being called to dinner.

* * *

STEPHEN WOULD DREAM, that night, that he was flying a crop duster over Hollis, but the plane's tanks were filled with trehalose, not poison. Whole families ran out of their houses and spread their arms wide and stuck out their tongues, eager to be coated with the life-giving spray, Stephen waving and smiling at all of them from the cockpit as the trehalose mist rejuvenated the entire town. Old people danced like they were children, and cripples got out of their wheelchairs and did cartwheels. Grass burst through concrete parking lots and grew ten feet tall. Brick buildings sprouted green ivy. Sprayed maple trees suddenly bore strange, eggplant-like purple fruit—to be called resurrection fruit—bursting with every vitamin. Lazy cats became as playful as kittens. A moth found the strength to free itself from a spiderweb. Crickets cranked out Mozart. Stephen then looped back and gave Nicole and his family, and those lucky enough to live in his neighborhood, a second and a third dosing.

And then on to the next town.

EPISODE 28

Grieving

A SHEET OF PAPER taped to the door said "St. Vincent's Grief Support Meeting Today" in black lettering, a thousand dots showing from a cheap printer. Just those arranged black dots, no teddy bears or rainbows, no warnings to the weak-hearted to steer clear.

Helen exhaled, crossed herself, then pulled open the door and stepped inside. With her stomach gurgling and her fight-or-flight response readying itself (it was always flight), she looked around the room and counted the human beings: ten, two men and eight women, some of them milling or getting coffee, a few seated. No one sobbing, not yet.

She dearly wanted to turn tail and run, but couldn't. In return for a suspended sentence on the assault charge, Helen had agreed to pay Dotty's medical bills and start twice-monthly group therapy. Six months from now, as long as she hadn't attacked anyone else, the court would stop its official monitoring of Helen Harrelson's psyche.

One of the milling women—midfifties, orange hair, too much eye shadow—approached Helen.

"Helen, is that you?" the woman asked.

Helen nodded. She was indeed a Helen.

"It's Viv, Vivian Davis," said the woman.

It took a few seconds for Helen to realize that the Vivian standing before her was the one who lost a daughter and two grandchildren in an accident last May, and the woman Helen had tried to get to on the day of her "floating attack," as she now thought of it. "Nice to finally meet you," Helen said, touching Viv's elbow, squeezing the bone.

"Come on, we better grab a seat," Viv said, "Meeting's about to start."

"How did you know I was me?" Helen asked.

Viv smiled. "I just knew."

They took their seats in the circle, Helen between Viv and an older man pushing sixty with a handsome, weather-worn face and a huge beer belly—room enough for a keg in there.

"I'm Warren," the man said somberly, noticing Helen's glance.

"I'm Helen," she said. "Sorry for your loss, whoever it is."

"My wife," he said, sighing. "The big C."

The big C? Helen wondered. *Curmudgeonliness? Crisco overdose?* There were so many possibilities.

Lisa Fesko, licensed social worker, was running the meeting. During Helen's stay at the hospital, Lisa had tried to convince her that there were only five stages of grief, a ridiculously small number. Fortunately for Helen, Lisa did not appear to recognize her. She was just another faceless whacko, one of possibly thousands who had spent some time in the St. Vincent's booby hatch.

"Let's get started," Lisa said. "I'd like to welcome regulars and newcomers, or in this case our lone newcomer. If you wouldn't mind telling us your first name and why you're here."

"My name is Helen, and . . . I lost my son Francis, in a car accident," she said. "In January."

"Welcome Helen," Lisa and everyone else said, out of synch with each other, Warren's welcome sluggishly pulling up the rear.

"The way it works," said Lisa, "is everyone is free to speak their mind, or not. I usually recommend that first-timers listen to a few regulars tell their stories before sharing. Okay, who would like to start us off?"

A slouching woman with tired blond hair raised her hand, and then told the group about a volcano-sized emptiness inside of her, all due to Robert, her husband and a decent guy, a really, really decent guy, dropping dead of a heart attack three years earlier, and about her many failed attempts to fill that void with food, sex, booze, and shopping. "He was such a decent guy," Blondie said again. "Oh, Robert!"

More sad people told their stories: a son lost to AIDS, a husband and a sister dying in a span of seven weeks, a fiancé murdered in Boston. Some of the storytellers were stone-faced, others wept openly. Two women wanted answers from God, while a man sitting next to Warren had stopped believing altogether: no God would allow his son Vincent to suffer as he did. Only humans and animals were capable of such cruelty.

Helen's heart wasn't touched until it was Vivian's turn to speak.

"I've decided I need to pay Ryan Mills a visit," Viv said, bobbing her head and shaking free tears. "I have to make sure he's damaged, that killing two kids and their mother really fucked him up. If he's not damaged, if he is still tearing up and down the country roads like nothing ever happened, I'll fuck him up myself." Viv's hands were trembling. Helen took hold of one of them, steadying it.

"It's best to leave justice to the courts or, ultimately, to a higher power," Lisa said. "But that doesn't mean you can't symbolically attack Ryan. When you go home, grab a pillow and imagine Ryan's face on it, and punch it and kick it and just go crazy until you feel better. But do leave the real Ryan alone."

"Thanks," Viv said. "But a pillow didn't obliterate most of my family, Ryan Mills did."

Warren spoke next, taking up a good twenty minutes of the allotted ninety, detailing his wife's ten-year struggle with cancer. "You fight and fight and try all of the medicines and treatments that only made her feel worse," he said, "and spend thousands of dollars, just about lose the house, and for what? That day you've been trying to avoid comes anyway." He said that he was all talked out, then covered his face with his hands and started weeping.

"Thanks again, Warren," said Lisa Fesko. "It looks like we're just about out of time. But I do want to give our newcomer a chance to share, if she wishes to."

A grapefruit had become lodged in Helen's throat, no way to push any words past it. She shook her head no.

Some of the women started to grab their belongings—purses, jackets, bibles, a white teddy bear.

"I'm not sure how hard he tried," Helen said urgently, grapefruit gone. The commotion stopped, and all eyes fell upon her. Looks of encouragement, expectation. *Tell us your sorrow*, those eyes said. *Join us.* "My Francis, I'm talking about," she went on. "I just don't know if he fought with all of his might to . . . to not die. His most important task ever, you might say."

Helen's tears fell freely. "I know Francis didn't throw in the towel," she continued, "but what if he only gave it a 95 percent effort, or even 99.9 percent? What if, at some point, he closed his eyes and said 'enough' when he still had some fight left in him? If it was anything less than a 100 percent effort I'm just not sure I could ever forgive him. His death has ruined me." Viv, still holding Helen's hand, pumped it like she was feeding her oxygen, and Warren gave her a Kleenex, which Helen balled in her left hand, the tissue serving as some sort of counterbalance. Two women excused themselves and left. The man sitting next to Warren rose to his feet but stayed standing next to his chair.

"This is all my fault," Helen said. "I talked Francis into moving back home from college, for selfish reasons. I wanted to see him more, spend more time with him. I guess every mother wants this, but the good ones, the good mothers, know when to let their children have their own lives. If I had just kept my mouth shut and let Francis stay living at college, none of this would have happened. God, I just can't believe it. I killed Francis sure as putting a gun to his head. I killed my own son." She dabbed at her tears with the Kleenex, and when she set her hand back on her leg Warren took hold of it and pressed it between his two cold paws. *Even his hands are sad.* Helen felt defenseless now, her arms held to the side by strangers, no way for her to block any daggers that might be slung at her by Lisa Fesko or the others. A woman stood up and left.

"And what about the paramedics and doctors?" Helen asked. "Do they fight as hard to save a young man as they would, say, a beautiful woman or a child? Where did my Francis fit on the scale of lives, the calculations of worth they must run in their heads? Maybe a college kid gets 90 percent effort . . . I'm just trying to work this out in my mind. And then there's Jasmine, Francis's fiancée. She tried heart pumps and mouth-to-mouth, she told us, but did she do those things the right way? I need to know, I really do. Maybe everyone fucked up that day, everyone fell short, everyone failed Francis. And get this. A man named Michael Haynes just sat in his truck and did nothing. Didn't go for help, didn't try to save Francis. That bastard was in MY HOUSE, begging my forgiveness, so I gave it to him, but now I take it back. I do not forgive Michael Haynes for sitting on his ass while my boy was busy dying."

The room fell silent for a few seconds, except for some sobs and sniffles. "Thanks for sharing, Helen," Lisa Fesko said. "You are in the second stage of grief, anger, a difficult stage but we'll help you get through it."

Helen smiled at Lisa, though inside she was fuming. *Five stages, my ass!* But she couldn't let Lisa know her true feelings since she needed her to sign a slip for the court saying that Helen Harrelson had attended today's meeting.

Helen stood up, momentarily not sure how to move or operate her body. Warren then hugged her, his embrace like a bear hug, Helen feeling like she was in danger of being squeezed out of her shell.

"Sorry about Carol," she said, after he had let her go. "That must have been awful for both of you."

"It's over now." Warren nodded at Helen and Viv, then walked away and out of the room, returning, Helen imagined, to a life that was nothing but lonely.

Viv then embraced Helen. It was a hearty "yes I give a fuck about you even though you stopped answering my phone calls and letters" kind of hug, which caused Helen to drop a few more tears.

"Let's get a cup of coffee, on me," Viv said.

IN THE HOSPITAL cafeteria, Helen gazed sheepishly at the line of self-serve food displays and beverage machines, and at a cashier, an elderly woman, arranging cracker packets in a metal tray. It was almost too much to process, the bright colors and many odors—baked chicken and cake frosting and Mr. Clean and coffee and canned peaches and chocolate pudding and cooked corn and someone's hair spray. "I'm not sure I can do this," she said shakily.

"Got it covered," Viv said, telling Helen to grab a table and she'd fetch whatever she wanted. Just a decaf and a bun or a donut, something sugary, Helen said.

Sitting in a booth in the nearly empty cafeteria, Helen began nibbling her fingernails. She had wanted to do this during the meeting, but consuming oneself was probably not considered an acceptable form of grief. She bit off a chunk of a nail and let it rest on her tongue a few seconds, Helen considering its animalistic texture before swallowing it.

Vivian arrived and set down two coffees and a basket with four muffins in it, two blueberry and two banana walnut. "Do you feel better or worse?" she asked, taking a seat. "My first few meetings I felt worse, wondered why I was doing this to myself. Then in time it started to get better."

"Worse," Helen said, tearing off a piece of a blueberry muffin and dipping it in decaf. "I should have just talked about how beautiful and wonderful Francis was. Nobody is saying those things, and that's a terrible crime."

"Keep coming, it will get better," Viv said.

"I'm not sure it's supposed to." Helen dropped the coffee-soaked muffin piece into her mouth. *Too sweet,* her tongue let her know, but she ate it anyway.

Viv took a sip of her coffee, then fished four photographs out of her purse and showed them to Helen. "That was my Lynn, twenty-eight when it happened, and this was Jordan and Emily, seven and six in that order, and this here is Brandon Jr., eleven months now. It's truly a miracle, a bona fide miracle that he survived the crash. His being so small is probably what saved him."

"Beautiful people," Helen said. The photos of Jordan and Emily were school pictures, and Helen imagined the girls excitedly getting dressed up for picture day, taking a seat in front of a screen of blue sky and white clouds and smiling awkwardly for the photographer, Jordan showing just about all of her teeth and Emily keeping her lips pressed together like there was something winged in her mouth that would fly away if she opened up, neither girl thinking, as no child should ever have to think, that this would be the photograph that made it into the paper if she died young. Same with Francis when he posed holding that giant mushroom.

Helen then gazed at the baby's picture, a big-eyed boy in a blue sleeper, no hair to speak of. "At least Brandon Jr. is too young to remember the accident," she said. "One blessing."

"But also too young to remember his sisters and mother. I'll tell him stories, show him pictures and a few videos that we took. But it won't be the same." Viv scooped up the photographs and returned them to her purse. "Got any pictures I can see?" she asked.

Helen shook her head. She never felt the need to keep snapshots of loved ones with her—she knew what they looked like. "Do you think Francis and your daughter and the girls are in the same place now? Heaven, I mean. You said something like that when we spoke on the phone. It was a nice image."

"I'm sure I did say that, but now I'm not sure. I'd rather have Lynn and the kids returned to this messed-up planet than in a heaven. Who wants eternal happiness anyway?"

"You're right. You are talking crazy."

Viv tried a piece of a banana walnut muffin, then washed it down with coffee. "What do you think about reincarnation? I've been reading a book called *The Tibetan Book of Living and Dying.* You might try and find a copy, or I'll lend you mine."

"I don't know what to think," Helen said. "I guess I wouldn't mind coming back as a tree."

"An oak? An elm?"

"A willow, on a riverbank."

"That sounds peaceful. It might be wishful thinking, but if there is reincarnation, then Lynn and Jordan and Em are back living here, their souls, in new bodies. Francis, too, and everyone we've lost. We'll never find them but at least they're here."

Helen imagined Francis reincarnated: he'd be about eight months now if it happened right away, a fetus still, unless he was a preemie. But what if his mother was crack addicted or he was about to be born in some war-torn country? He could be starving to death, just a few weeks from now, or crying for his mommy but not getting any love from her. Heaven had to be the better place.

"So how are you going to mess up Ryan Mills?" Helen asked.

Viv chortled. "I don't know, slash the tires on his car? Chop off his bite-sized penis with my hedge clippers? I'm what you call resourceful, I'll think of something. So who do you want to disfigure?"

"I have a long list," Helen said, but her mind was wandering, seeing highways, houses for rent in small towns, and a backyard with a view of a prairie or a meadow. "I've been thinking of leaving Gene, moving far away," she said, surprised that she was admitting this to Vivian. "Been looking at maps and atlases, wondering where I could be happy. Greenland sounds pretty."

"I think it's cold up there," Viv said. "There's an old saying that goes 'bloom where you are planted.' "

"And another one that goes 'run, run, run, as fast as you can.' "

"I like that one better. So if you do run away you'll take the kids with you and then divorce Gene? Is that your mad plan?"

Helen had never more than flirted with the idea of divorcing

Gene—a separation should be enough—but now, coming from functioning Viv, it sounded like a fabulous idea. Gene was trying a little bit harder these days, not spending quite as many hours at work and sometimes saying a few kind words, but he still served as a daily reminder to Helen that she was far less attractive than she once had been. If she walked into his bedroom one night wearing something slinky he'd probably throw a blanket over her so she wouldn't catch cold.

"I'd take the kids and move out of state," Helen said, imagining her new life as she spoke the words, Helen living with Crispy and Stephen in a freshly painted white two-story house in a small town somewhere, one with brick streets and a bandstand and frequent parades. "And then I'd find a teaching job. I used to love to teach. Should never have given that up."

Viv smiled big, signing off on the scheme. "Teaching is one way to invest in the future."

"We have to do something with our lives, right?" Helen said.

THE WOUNDED FRIENDS finished their coffee and the muffins and said their good-byes, hugging more lightly this time, but the embrace caused tears to brim in Helen's eyes: Viv still gave a damn, an hour later.

"So you say it gets better?" Helen asked.

"It gets better," Viv said. "Keep coming back."

Helen walked away from Vivian and left the hospital. The doors didn't try to crush her, nor did the Chevy start floating, which she was grateful for, but something wasn't right about the sun: it was doubly bright and making her squint, just so she could see the world out there. Putting on dark sunglasses helped a little.

Driving on the highway, Helen, caught up in the solar brightness and wondering why no one was talking about this major astronomical event on the radio shows, missed the exit to Hollis, and when the next exit arrived she drove past that one, too. *This is it,* something said inside of her, the day Helen Harrelson's life changed dramatically and started to make sense again, had some beauty and light put back into it. *It's about fucking time.* North, Helen was driving north, but where to? Maybe she'd stay in Chicago for a day or two, hit a few museums and pricey restaurants, then head east to Toledo, visit her childhood home on Poe Street, convince whoever was living there now to let her stay for a few hours. Bathe in sunlight streaming in through hundred-year-old windows, maybe take a nap in her old bedroom. And then she could check out some of the little towns east of there, Genoa and Woodville and Elmore, for a freshly painted house for rent, a few blocks from a bandstand.

Helen kept driving, the sun winking light at her, and her mind running through the nuts and bolts of her new life. She'd stay at the freshly painted house for a week, furnishing it and enjoying the quiet and the absence of Francis memories, and then head back to Hollis for the kids and some of her belongings. What will she say to Gene? Will it be civil or ugly? Probably ugly. He won't want to give up the kids, at least Crispy, but they shouldn't be split up. What if she let Gene keep them both, she wondered, just for a year, until she was working as a teacher again? She could visit them in Hollis every month or two. It was only a day's drive.

Excitement about having her own life was arising in Helen, a feeling like she had experienced many years ago when she drove away from Toledo for Kalamazoo, her future so wide open it was almost scary. How she had wept that first night in her dorm room at Western Michigan, but after a few days she started to enjoy classes, and meeting people from all over the world, her mind rarely slipping back to the house on Poe Street, Mom and Dad standing in the yard and waving to her as she left them behind. But in the second semester of her senior year Gene swept in and talked her into buying his dreams instead of her own dreams, payments to be spread out over many years. What were Helen's dreams? To be a great teacher and thinker and maybe an artist, a friend to a few good people. She'd take a lover now and then, nothing for keeps. The world was making enough babies, too many of them. There ought to be room for Helen to sidestep all of that, to do her own thing.

And now life was wide open again, but only for another minute. Helen suddenly remembered that later that day she was supposed to drive Crispy to the library to return videos and to get some new ones. Strangely, taking Crispy safely to the library seemed like the most important job in the world, a task almost too demanding for Helen, a mortal. Perhaps these little moments of life, returning the videos on a September day, are the ones most dappled with holiness, she thought, imagining Crispy in pigtails, though she didn't wear her hair like that anymore, sitting on the living room couch, a stack of videos beside her as she waited for her mother to return. Helen wanted to be the kind of mother who comes home, not the kind who runs away.

"I'm a goddamn mother," Helen said, not sure if she was talking about something godly, or if motherhood was on the level of servant or slave. She took the next exit and turned around and headed south, back to Hollis. Before long her mind started working on a scaled-down plan, one where she got a house or an apartment in Caswell or Middleton in a few months. A trial separation from Gene, and then probably a divorce and shared custody of the kids. And a teaching job, next fall.

The sun lowered its wattage. Helen removed her sunglasses.

EPISODE 29

Corruption Day

STEPHEN PEDALED his bicycle through the open iron gates at Elmwood Grove Cemetery and quickly spotted Jasmine's Honda parked on the blacktopped road not far from Francis's gravesite. He went to her and tried to skid, but that was difficult to do on a twelve-speed. She smiled and cranked open her window and said, "Crawl inside, get out of the burning sun." He slid off the bike and climbed into her car.

"I feel like a spy, meeting secretly like this," she said, glancing at him. "Call me Natasha. You must be Boris."

"You could have come to the house," he said, gazing at her silky black running shorts, which looked to be see-through in better light. "Everyone would love to see you."

"No, not yet I couldn't. So what was so important that we had to talk face-to-face? Not that I mind driving out to see you."

Stephen shuddered. The future itself seemed ready to burst out of his body and come to life. His and Francis's fairy ring research may one day lead to human beings claiming mastery over death and populating distant planets. He took his brother's essay from the back pocket of his shorts and showed it to her. "Have you seen this? Have you read it?"

Jasmine gazed at the paper, scratched her nose. "Yeah, I read it. I thought it was a bit flaky, like your brother was. But fun to read."

"Don't you see, this is the reason Francis is still swimming. He's trying to resurrect himself with water, like a fairy ring, so he can come home and continue his research."

Jasmine smiled again, but more sadly. "Interesting deduction, Professor. Not to rain on your parade, but I think we're just imagining similar things when we've seen his ghost. Let's call it 'wishful hallucinations.' "

"He's really out there. He couldn't go on to heaven yet because the work he wants to do is way too important. Immortality, space travel to other universes, that's all giant stuff. And don't forget transplant surgery."

"Okay, but I'm not sure studying fairy rings is going to benefit us clunky human beings much. Insects and plants can do things that no human being can do. Try walking on the ceiling like a spider and let me know how it goes. Just because a mushroom can live hundreds of years doesn't mean that we can do the same if we figure out its secrets. It's doesn't seem fair, a damn mushroom outliving us. They say that cockroaches will survive the nuclear winter that will kill everyone. Maybe your fairy rings will, too."

"I think you and I should carry on with Francis's work. Then maybe he can go on to heaven and take a rest."

"I don't have the mind for science. Do you?"

"I do okay in science."

"Good for you, but more than finding the cure for mortality I think Francis would want us to be happy. Though finding a cure for mortality might be the easier of the two."

"This is what I have to do. And write comic books when I have some free time, and maybe design safer cars."

"I vote for the last two," she said. "If you really want to carry on with your brother's work, become an anthropologist. Francis was more interested in the religious and cultural uses of mushrooms than anything else. He was hoping to spend the summer traveling through South America, hanging out with shamans and folk healers. And I was going to tag along and liberate the women and save the indigenous peoples. The best laid plans . . ."

"I didn't know about any of this."

"It was still in the thinking-about stage. But I know that your brother didn't want to be stuck in a lab somewhere studying microbes. I hope that's also true with you, but do what you need to do."

"I'm not done thinking about this yet." He carefully folded his brother's essay and put it in his shorts pocket.

Jasmine pulled open the car's ashtray and grabbed a hand-rolled cigarette and lit it. She puffed on it twice, exhaled the smoke slowly, and handed it to Stephen. The smoke didn't smell quite right, too sweet, but he took a toke and harshly coughed out the smoke. "Is this a normal cigarette?" he asked after he had recovered.

"They're a little special. I roll them myself. It's about 30 percent tobacco and 70 percent weed. Sorry, I probably should have told you this earlier. I just assume that anyone under thirty is a doper."

"Was my brother?"

"Hell yes. In fact, that's how I met Francis. Bought a bag of weed off him at a party, then we smoked it together. That night was the first time we . . . Let's just say the dope burned away our inhibitions."

"He sold drugs? He was a dealer?"

"Sure, but he didn't hang out in front of elementary schools or anything like that. Just sold to some students and profs who knew what they wanted." She gazed at Stephen, at his pinched, worried face. "Hope I didn't burst any bubbles. Francis wasn't perfect, but he was better than most. Far better."

"Did he do a lot of drugs? Like crack and stuff?"

"Not really, just pot and mushrooms, and not that often." Jasmine laughed a little. "One time when your brother was on mushrooms I caught him talking to a plant, a Boston fern, but the weird thing was that it seemed to be a two-way conversation, Francis saying things like, 'Uh-huh, good point.' I won't lie, we loved getting stoned. We were like children again, all of those blocks and doubts and accumulated crap just gone. Poof."

"I'm happy he was happy," Stephen said, wondering what it would be like to be high as a kite with Francis.

"Listen to me!" Jasmine said. "You should just say no and all of that Nancy Reagan stuff. Seriously, stay off drugs. They'll turn your brain into toaster pastry." She took a quick puff of the cigarette then rubbed it out in the ashtray. "Let's go see him," she said.

They got out of the car, ascended a slight hill, and walked toward Francis's grave, Stephen leading the way. When they arrived there, Jasmine knelt on recently mowed grass, then Stephen did the same. Gazing at the gravesite, he felt suddenly sad that it was now indistinguishable from the other graves. The overturned dirt had settled, the earth healing the cut and growing grass over it.

"How often do you and your family come out here?" she asked, gazing at Francis's simple marker: *Francis Carl Harrelson, November 17, 1973–January 9, 1993.*

"We used to come out every Sunday but now it's just once in a while," he said. "One time I rode my bike out here and I saw my dad crying and talking to Francis. I waited behind some trees for him to leave, but it took almost an hour."

"Damn. I can't imagine what it's like losing a child. Or a brother."

"Trust me, it's the worst possible thing in the whole world. What's it like losing a boyfriend? I mean a fiancé."

She frowned. "It's like watching your future get blown to smithereens."

As Jasmine whisked cut grass from the marker with her hands, Stephen's eyes roamed the cemetery, to a statue of Jesus with open, welcoming arms, to a grove of pine trees to the west, and to a freshly dug grave, about fifty feet away, the grave splattered with wilted white and yellow mums. Someday his trehalose-based resurrection serum might put places like this out of business. It will be too late for Francis, but at least other kids, kids from the future, will have their brothers returned to them.

"I have a confession," Jasmine said, rubbing her hands together. "I've seen Francis again. Imagined him, I mean."

"In your bathtub?"

"No, on my parents' TV, a couple months ago. No matter what station I turned to there he was, swimming in some kind of ocean or lake. I couldn't get rid of him. It was a hallucination, though, I'll swear to it."

"Could you tell what ocean or lake it was? Were there any ships or whales or icebergs?"

"None of that. It was just smooth water. I could see that he was making progress, but I wanted him to get where he was going to already. It's been eight months, right? Has he been swimming all this time?"

"Maybe. I saw him a couple weeks ago, at the pool." Stephen then told her about swimming after his brother and watching him rocket past the moon. "I had never dove from the high board before or swum that far, but it wasn't enough, I couldn't catch him." He decided to leave out the part about his brother crab-walking at the bottom of the pool. He didn't want to creep her out.

"So your brother helped you to face a fear, right?" Jasmine said. "Your fear of diving from the high board?"

"I guess he did."

"Good, but that also proves my point that we've been hallucinating, creating a ghost with our minds for selfish reasons. If Francis was really at the pool, or swimming above this cemetery, anyone could see him. Swimming in a bathtub or inside someone's TV is another story."

"Unless only we can see him because we are the ones who loved him the most."

Jasmine grinned. "I think you just might be on to something, Professor."

"Or because he's trying to convince you and me to continue with his research."

"Let's go with the first one."

Stephen felt the midafternoon sun baking his skin and had the urge to be as open to it as a flower, so he lay back on the grass and clover, his hands cupping his head and his arms forming wings. He looked at the sky, cloudless but with crisscrossing jet trails, then he blinked rapidly, the sun blasting him with cannonballs of light.

"Tell me what you saw, the day we buried him," she said.

He sat up to speak and then remembered he could talk while lying down, so he stretched out on the grass again, and thought *it's all about sides.* At the cemetery he and Jasmine were on the winning side, the free side, where they could catch some sun and then walk away. Francis, or at least his body, and hundreds of others here were on the losing side, six feet under and trapped. No sun, no walking to the store for a soda.

She asked him again what he saw the day of the funeral.

"I looked up and saw Francis swimming from cloud to cloud, sort of like how a turtle swims. Then he'd do a somersault, swim some more, and then another somersault. He seemed really happy."

"That's sweet. But are you sure about the somersaults? He could barely tie his shoes without causing some kind of calamity."

"I'm sure. It was the slow motion kind of somersault, like astronauts do in space."

"Too freaking weird. Why can't he just be a normal ghost? You know, rattling chains, levitating forks, that kind of thing."

"He's on a mission to save the world."

"Perhaps, but my guess is that you have to be in the world to save it." She reached into her shirt pocket and retrieved a lighter and a fresh joint, then lit it and took a deep hit. "Want some of this, Professor?" she asked.

Stephen sat up and took the cigarette from her and puffed it three times quickly. He held in the smoke as long as possible and then coughed it out, his lungs saying *what the fuck, Chuck?* He handed the joint back to her. She took a hit, blew the smoke toward Stephen, then announced that today was their one and only Corruption Day, and she made him vow that he would never do drugs again. In return she promised to never again smoke dope with minors on Saturdays in Septembers that fell in odd-numbered years.

"I tell you, your brother was one fuck of a great guy," she said, holding the joint close to her nose and letting smoke curl up her nostrils. "I loved that son of a bitch."

He was studying her eyes. They looked to be made of the same material as crystals or geodes, and he wondered if they took a billion years to construct. Her brown geodes then sparkled, and the gates inside of him swung wide open. "I love you," he said.

"I know," she said, peering at the cemetery grounds.

THEY STAYED AT Elmwood Grove for another half hour, finishing the joint and giving Francis time to appear and dazzle them with his sky-swimming skills.

"He isn't coming," she said, standing up and stretching. "Let's vamoose."

Sunlight was slipping through the fabric of Jasmine's shorts, revealing that she was wearing light-colored panties, white or yellow. A giant magnet, like the kind seen in cartoons, was pulling Stephen to her, and he could imagine being happily smooshed against Jasmine for a week. "Francis must be swimming somewhere else today," he said automatically, his eyes trained on her body, which seemed to have its own pulse, a fantastic *thum thum, thum thum.* But then Jasmine turned a little to the side, and the magnetic force dissipated. The way she rubbed her elbow and sighed reminded Stephen that she was not his, that Jasmine had a life that he was only a very small part of. She could rub her elbow and sigh a hundred times each day but he'd never know it because he wouldn't be there with her.

Stephen rose to his feet, remembered he had legs, could run away from this place.

"It's time to go," she said.

They ambled to her car, the sun pouring so much love onto them that Stephen had to fight weeping. Jasmine occasionally looked back at Francis's gravesite, like she was taking mental snapshots of it from ten feet away, from twenty feet away, from forty feet away.

After he threw his bike into the trunk of the Honda they drove out to the Dairy Queen in Caswell. She ordered a banana split and Stephen chose a Peanut Buster Parfait, mostly because he wanted to say "I'll take a Peanut Buster Parfait" to the cutie girl clerk. They took their treats outside and sat at a picnic table and started munching. The sugar in the ice cream and syrup went straight into Stephen's veins, electrifying them, and he had little doubt that he could run up and down the Rocky Mountains, each one of them, if he had a reason to do that. He was also enjoying watching Jasmine eat her banana split, how she would push a spoonful of ice cream, nuts, and syrup and a little piece of banana past her lips and onto her tongue, chew on the mess, then lick those lips free of any leftover cream and syrup.

When they had finished snacking, Jasmine wiped her mouth with a napkin. Stephen decided that he would very much like to own that napkin, but then she wadded it up and tossed it into a garbage can that was being patrolled by honeybees.

"I think I'm happy today," he said, surprised by the ease at which those words said themselves.

"That's good to know," she said. "I think I'm also a little bit happy today."

They jumped into the Honda and headed back to Hollis, Stephen noticing along the way that all the cars and trucks on the road were shinier than normal, and that some of the pedestrians and joggers looked like they had a little duck or pelican DNA mixed into their chromosomes, like their noses were just itching to be bills and their shoulder blades were on the verge of pushing out wings.

"I still talk to your brother," she said as they drove past Hollis Middle School, weekend dead. "Almost every day. I guess that sounds stupid."

"No, I talk to him, too. And that time I saw my dad at the cemetery he was saying things to Francis almost the entire time."

"What do you say to your brother?"

"Me? I tell him what's going on with Nicole, family junk, stuff about school, that I miss him and wish he'd come home, how the Sox are doing. What do you talk about, with Francis?"

"Everything. I tell him about what's happening in the world he left, or, this is the sick part, sometimes I make believe that nothing happened, that we are still engaged and are planning our wedding, how many kids we'll have, those kinds of things. Sick, huh?"

"Not really. I pretend a happier life all of the time."

Jasmine rubbed at her right kneecap, and somehow that set off sparks within Stephen as he watched her rub. *I'm an electric kid,* he thought, feeling the parfait sugar surge through his wires and hearing a faint, motorlike hum. Or that might have been the car engine.

She stopped the Honda one street over from Briarwood, on Forest.

"You sure you don't want to come over for a minute?" he asked. "Or stay for a couple days or a week or two?"

"Sorry. I'm just not ready to see your folks again." She leaned back a little, causing her shorts to edge up and reveal more of her leg flesh. "But it was great to see you, Professor."

Those sparks inside Stephen were now more like fireworks, giant gold and silver flowers blooming one after another as the crowd *ooh*ed and *aah*ed. *Let's get married in five years,* he wanted to say to Jasmine, but that horse ran away before he could get ahold of it, so what he actually said was, "Your eyes are like diamonds."

"Great," she said. "Maybe I'll try and pawn one of them."

He slid out the car and retrieved his bicycle from the trunk, wondered for a dumb second where the safety wheels had gone to, then got on it and rode up to her window.

"Write me a letter," she said, "and send along some of those *Wolf Dog* comic books."

"The score is two to two," he said.

"What's that?"

"You've seen Francis, adult Francis, twice and I've seen him twice. It's a tie, two to two."

"Oh. I don't mind if you win this one." She wrinkled her nose at him, then said, "Don't be so far away."

Stephen nodded, said no words. Jasmine honked the Honda horn and drove off, motoring down Forest. When she hooked a left on Groveland he gave chase on his twelve-speed, intending to follow her all of the way to Naperville. But despite his exceptional efforts and encouragement from the whispering trees and buzzing power lines, he was unable to catch up to her.

EPISODE 30

Stargazing

HOW BAD OF A week was Stephen having? First, his birthday had come and gone without his brother showing up or at least doing a swim by. When alive, Francis made a big deal of birthdays, often, when he was younger, spending his entire savings on gifts and always being on his best behavior, an exemplary son and brother. And Francis got the fact that birthdays lasted all day, not just the hour it took to open presents and eat cake and ice cream, saying to Stephen last year, "It's your day, kid, let's make it the best one ever," so after the festivities at home had ended he took Stephen for a drive through the rural part of the county, just to see the beautiful red barns and dying cornfields, and then to a show at the Cinema 4 in Caswell, the brothers celebrating the fact that Stephen would turn thirteen only once. On the way home they hit Sweet Surrender for ice cream cones, though by then Stephen was burned out on sweets. But now that he was dead, Francis had missed all of the birthdays so far, Stephen's, Helen's, and Gene's, as well as major holidays like Easter and the Fourth of July. He might even be a no-show for Christmas. Death, Stephen guessed, must really mess up your sense of time and dates.

Then the White Sox lost the American League championship to the lowly Blue Jays, four games to two. Stephen had just wanted the Sox to make it to the World Series, even if they got clobbered by the Phillies. And why did they even let Canadian teams into the *American* League, he wanted to know. It didn't seem right. How many American teams were playing in Canadian leagues?

Worst of all, probably, it was now autumn. While the weather was generally still pleasant and some of the trees weren't showing their Day-Glo death colors yet, early frosts had wiped out the annuals that Helen and Crispy had planted, and all but one of Sally Strussman's tomato plants. And Stephen knew that winter, tucked away in an ice cave somewhere, was conjuring up plans for gray skies, piles of snow, and killer ice storms.

But this night was a generously warm one for October, about sixty-five degrees. Stephen was sitting with Nicole on her back stoop, their legs touching as they gazed at each other, or at the ocean of stars and planets and a sliver of moon. It was a school night, about 10:30, but Nicole's mom was out somewhere with her boyfriend and Stephen's parents had apparently lost track of him.

She was in pajamas, white with tiny American flags, and red socks. Stephen wore jeans that were thin at the knees and a gray T-shirt that said "Property of the Chicago Bears." His sneakers, cheapies from Kmart, were starting to come apart, but he hated to trash a comfortable pair of shoes just because they were letting in air.

"There's the Big Dipper," Nicole said, pointing at the sky. "And the Little Dipper over there and the Medium Dipper, the Double-dipper. Why does God need so many dippers? What's there to dip?"

Stephen didn't know why God required two or more dippers, and needed a million stars: surely a smaller universe would be easier to manage. Nervously, he placed a hand on the stoop behind Nicole, feeling the cool concrete, its many pocks and pimples. That was Phase 1, the easy part. In Phase 2 he might put that hand on her shoulder, and if courage reserves were finally sufficient, squeeze a boob. A good boob feel, he was certain, could turn this week around.

"Tell me a secret," Nicole said, looking at Stephen, her eyes dewy.

"What?"

"New game, same rules. Whoever has the best secret gets a kiss."

Wanting her kiss, Stephen went inside of himself and opened his chest full of secrets, and just about every one of them sprung out. In a flurry of words he told Nicole about his brother swimming at the cemetery and the city pool, about the day thirteen-year-old Francis came for a visit, the two reported sightings in Naperville, and his brother's research ideas and how he was carrying on with the work.

When he was done talking she smacked him on his leg. "Holy moly," she said. "Why didn't you tell me this stuff earlier?"

"I thought if I told anybody Francis might stop showing up, like only me knowing about it was making it possible. Dumb?"

"No dumber than usual. But it does make sense, your brother sticking around. He did get ripped off by about sixty years."

"So you believe in ghosts?"

"Sure. Ghosts, aliens, Big Foot. I told you about Randle? He was my best friend when I was little even though he was sometimes a very bad kid. Like that time he talked me into burning the house down."

"Was he an imaginary friend or a ghost?"

"Probably imaginary. But I can't prove that he wasn't a ghost or something even freakier." Nicole grinned. "Hah! You know what this means, don't you? It means that heaven is at least a little fucked up. They have a runaway, your brother. Too cool."

They both looked at the sky, as if expecting to see Francis blazing by, sparks shooting out of his feet like a twin-tailed comet.

"You really think you can find a way to make people live forever?" Nicole asked. "Not to be a pain, but no one else has figured it out yet. Not even Einstein or Bill Nye the Science Guy."

"It's worth a try. And I'm aiming for two hundred years, not eternal life."

"Could you make it a hundred and eighty years of being a kid and twenty years of being an adult?"

"I'll see what I can do," he said.

While Stephen was plotting the possible mechanics of Phase 2, whether to reach for the boob over her shoulder or under her arm, he heard the strangest thing: his father was calling to him. "Stephen, come home," Gene bellowed, his words flying over the privet hedge that separated the Harrelson and Strussman properties. It had been many months since Stephen's father had called him home.

"I better go." He rose and started walking away, but then turned around and gazed at Nicole. "What was your secret?"

"No bra," she said, pointing to her chest and grinning like a lunatic.

"Oh man!"

"Come home, Stephen," Gene tried again.

Stephen kicked at the damp grass, wishing he had gone for Phase 2, then squirreled through an opening in the hedge. Once in his yard he saw his dad hanging halfway out of the little used side door.

"There you are," Gene said, as Stephen marched to him.

"Is everything okay?" Stephen asked. *Has someone else died?*

"Everything's fine. But it's dark and it's a school night and you should be home."

Stephen wasn't sure what to say. His father was acting like a father tonight. What's next, world peace?

He stepped past his dad and into the house, catching a whiff of Gene, his aftershave and a hint of peanut butter toast, and somehow those odors were as comforting to Stephen as the smell of an apple crumb pie baking in the oven on a Saturday night or of lilacs blooming in the Bordens' front yard every spring. "Thanks for remembering me," he whispered, before scooting away.

THAT SUNDAY, Nicole and Stephen used their savings and all of the *Wolf Boy* profits and bought a refractor telescope at the science and rock store at the Fairchild Mall in Caswell. On clear and partly cloudy nights they'd set up the telescope in her backyard and search the sky for Francis. Soon they let Crispy in on the secret, and she eagerly joined Francis Watch. They'd take turns peering through the telescope or through Helen's little-used birding binoculars. It was just a matter of time before they found Francis, they told each other. In the meantime there were UFOs to track and neighbors to spy on, such as Carla Alton, who, when Don wasn't home, liked to dance around the house in only her underwear, and Joe Koperdak, who had found a way to play Ping-Pong by himself by tilting half of the table upward.

After a week and a half had passed and they hadn't found Francis, Stephen's frustration was growing. "We need more power, more magnification," he said, after peering through the telescope at Venus. They had spent a hundred and fifty dollars on the telescope, but it couldn't show with any detail what the surface of Venus looked like.

"I hate to say this, but if he's farther away than the moon we might be screwed," Nicole said.

"Maybe not," said Crispy, telling them that there was a "gigantoid" telescope at Baldwin College, about a half hour east of Hollis. When she was a Brownie her troop took a field trip to the observatory, but the clouds never parted so the girls just looked at dumb star charts.

Stephen phoned the college the next day and learned that they offered public star-watching nights once monthly, the next one scheduled for Friday, two days away. That night at the dinner table he told his parents about the incredible star watching opportunity, and that it would be a good thing for the family to do, if not every month then at least this one.

"That's the greatest idea I ever heard," said Crispy, his coconspirator, while she twirled spaghetti noodles around her fork.

"And it's not like we are asking to go to a stupid movie or a baseball game or something," Stephen said. "It's astronomy. It will be good for our brains."

"I'd love to do something for my brain," Crispy said.

Helen and Gene smiled at each other, then Gene said, "I'll probably be busy at the shop. Maybe next month, if the weather holds."

"I might be able to take them," said Helen. "I've always liked looking at the stars."

"Yeah, why don't you do that," Gene said, using a steak knife to stab at a cherry tomato in his salad. "You know how these brilliant kids of ours love to do things for their brains."

Stephen winked at Crispy, and she double-winked back. Operation Find Francis was on track.

EPISODE 31

Small Steps

GENE HAD GONE into City News, eager to surreptitiously gaze at the covers of porn and bikini magazines, when he noticed a stack of *Adventures of Wolf Boy #4* comic books on the counter near the register. The amusing drawing of Clock Man was what first drew his eyes, but then he saw Stephen and Nicole's names on the cover, as the credited writer and artist. *What the hell?*

He tracked down the old guy who ran the store and asked him where he had gotten the comic books. "They're made by two local kids," the man said. "They've been bugging me for months to sell them and finally I gave in."

"Months? This has been going on for months?"

"Yeah, and they're actually starting to sell pretty good—we're all out of that one they made about the butterfly. Lilly. No, Lila. They're supposed to be bringing me the next *Wolf Boy* in a week or two."

"Holy damn, my kid's got a secret life," said Gene. "Give me one of these *Wolf Boy*'s here."

AT THE SHOP, Gene sat in his office and read the comic book, working his way through "Time, Thy Enemy," the profile of The Interrupter, and "Crystal Grows Fangs." Gene enjoyed the stories and drawings and shared Wolf Boy's desire to go back in time and change things, and he was happy to see Michael Haynes banished to a faraway planet. But when he was done reading he felt a little sick in his gut. Why hadn't Stephen told him about the comic books? Was Gene that lousy of a father that Stephen didn't want to share with him what was going on in his life?

He set the comic aside and slumped in his chair. Somehow, he had become less of a dad than his own father, Marvin, had been. At least Gene had felt comfortable showing his dad things he had made—art projects or essays he had written in school. How the hell did this happen? Couldn't blame it on Francis dying, Gene had just been putting in time for years. *Goddamn it, wake the fuck up. How many times do I have to say this, WAKE THE FUCK UP!* Stephen, who used to harass his old man with unanswerable questions about life and the universe, who liked to make him cards and drawings even when it wasn't a holiday, now wanted little to do with Gene. Crispy, his princess, had tried to run away, and who knew if she wasn't planning to take wing again. Helen, who he was supposed to be loving and caring for, had been hospitalized and had pummeled a government employee. How many more clues did he need that he wasn't doing his job as father or husband? That his family had dissolved into something that wasn't very familylike at all: just four individuals doing whatever the hell they wanted.

"Goddamn it, wake up," Gene said, thinking of his vow two months earlier to be a better man, and the small, inconsistent efforts he had made since that day. Was he just spitting out words, or did he have it in him to be more of a father and husband? It was time to find out.

"I'M NOT A BAD PERSON, I'm pretty sure, and I don't think I've ever hit anyone before," Helen said. "But something felt so right about it, whacking away at the clerk. It didn't bring back my Francis, of course, but if he was watching the whole thing I'm sure he was cheering, 'Go Mom!' "

Helen took a few seconds to breathe and to gauge the reaction of her fellow grievers. Did they think her foolish or heroic? Viv was giving her the thumbs-up, but that's how she was: a supportive friend, no matter what crazy things Helen did.

She was about to continue with the story when the door opened. It was Gene in his blue work overalls and white denim shirt, his "I'm a craftsman" look. Helen's heart sank, worried that one of the kids had been hurt, until she saw his slight, nervous smile.

"Is this where you can cry for free?" Gene asked, all eyes upon him. A few of the group members smiled or nodded at Gene, but no one said anything until Lisa offered, "Come in. Join us."

Gene moved toward the group tentatively, like the floor was made of ice and he feared that it might crack if he just clomped away, and he'd fall through. He pulled a folding chair from a stack of chairs and set it behind Helen, then settled into it. "I'm Gene, Helen's wife," he said to the group. Helen grinned at the verbal blunder, and one of the sad ladies giggled. Gene guffawed. "I mean husband. She's my husband. Oh Lordy, I did it again!" More laughter, including from Viv, who was crying as she chuckled, both valves wide open. "Maybe I should go out of the room and come back in and try this again," Gene said. "Gawd. I'm not normally a comedian. At least not a funny one."

Lisa was the only one who had remained stern-faced through Gene's buffoonery. "Welcome, Gene," she said. "We don't often have couples in group together. This is a nice change."

"That's because most of us have lost a spouse," said Patty, the woman with the perpetually tired blond hair. Those few words had the effect of wiping out any residual smiles among the grievers.

Lisa asked Helen to continue with her story.

"Not much more to it," Helen said. "If I could always be attacking an incompetent clerk, say one a day, I think I'd be in much better shape."

Gene took hold of Helen's left hand and held it high in the air, like she had just won a prizefight. "This is why we call her 'Rocky,' " he said. "Look out, world." Helen grinned but was actually a little sad. The feel of Gene's hand on her hand was strange, unfamiliar. *Was his hand always that bony and cool?* It had been so long since they had touched. He dropped her hand.

Lisa tapped a finger against her chin, a sign that she was about to pass judgment. "The anger stage can be a volatile one," she said, "but it's important to channel that energy in healthy ways and not hurt any innocent people, even if they are a powerful symbol of one's frustration. And, like the saying goes, don't kill the messenger just because you don't like the message."

"True," said Gene. "But this messenger wouldn't shut up. She's probably not talking much now."

Helen smiled again, happy that someone was finally in her corner. But who would have guessed it would be Gene? She looked back at her husband and he smiled at her, and eight years of loneliness and sadness and anger with Gene was suddenly gone, cut out of her. It was like a remission, just when you had concluded that there was no hope for recovery.

When the meeting ended, Helen invited Gene to join her and Viv for coffee, but he said he had to get back to work. Helen told Viv she'd meet her in the cafeteria, after she walked Gene to his van.

"Take your sweet time," said Viv, wiggling her eyebrows at Helen, like she was giving her okay for some monkey business. That wasn't going to happen, Helen knew, but she appreciated the thought.

Gene and Helen walked quietly through the hospital, Helen sometimes glancing at her husband and wondering about his motives for showing up at the meeting, if they were all pure and good or if he was setting her up for something. Gene was even walking aside her like he was enjoying her company instead of a few steps ahead.

"This was quite a shock, seeing you here," she said, as they left the hospital and began marching toward the visitors' lot.

"I bet," he said, sticking his hands in the pockets of his overalls.

"I guess I've been thinking that maybe we don't need to do everything alone so much."

"That would be nice. I have been lonely." Helen was hoping for a "me, too" from Gene, but she wasn't expecting it. The usual way Gene would admit that he was feeling a certain way was to stay silent, not deny it.

"Now don't expect me to be a regular or anything," he said. "But I might show up now and then, if they let me back. I didn't mean to be such an idiot."

"I think everyone was happy for a chance to smile. There hasn't been a lot of that, with any of us."

The sun was at their backs as they walked and cast short shadows in front of them. Helen noticed how close the shadows were to each other and that they matched each other's stride. It was nice having someone to walk with.

"Hey, do you know anything about Stephen and his little girlfriend making comic books?" Gene asked. "I just saw the fourth issue, at the newsstand."

"Fourth issue? I knew about the one. I guess if he wanted us to read it he'd give us a copy. Right?"

"Maybe yes, maybe no . . . The comic book is all about Francis, really."

"Oh dear."

They kept walking, though Helen felt a strange urge to leap onto Gene and be carried by him, at least for a few minutes. Or years. Had he ever carried her places? Probably many years ago. But if she tried that now, jumping onto Gene, he'd surely drop her or throw out his back.

"There's one thing I don't get," Gene said, as they neared the van. "How do you just go and spill your guts to strangers? It seems unnatural. Like telling an enemy your vulnerabilities so he can exploit them."

"But they aren't enemies, not really. It's like all of us in group are survivors of the same war. We just have different versions of the same story. The bomb fell, close by." Helen wiped a few tears away and looked at her husband, wondering if there was a weepy little boy somewhere inside that forty-three-year-old man, wanting to be heard. "Maybe you'll even feel like opening up to the group, one of these times."

"Stranger things have happened in heaven and on earth," he said.

At the van they stood across from each other for a few seconds, then Gene gave Helen a quick kiss on her cheek. Nothing to write home about, she thought, but, like the song says, a kiss is still a kiss.

"Try to make it home for dinner, if you can," she said. "I'm fixing chicken stir-fry. One of your favorites."

"Yum, yum," he said, climbing inside the van.

GENE DIDN'T SHOW for dinner, so Helen scooped the leftovers into a CorningWare dish and set it on the back burner of the stove on low. "Don't be too late," she said to her missing husband.

AT HIS STORE GENE was in the woodshop, pounding nails into a block of wood as a way of relieving "I'd sure like to call Marjorie" stress before heading home. He hadn't cheated on Helen since her day in jail, but the temptation was still there, every day.

He pounded a few more nails, then set down the hammer and glanced at the dust-coated table saw. He hadn't run it since January. Gene had always loved the sound of its motor kicking in and the blade turning, and even better the shriek of the saw cutting through wood. He grabbed a cloth from the worktable and wiped away the dust, then flipped the power switch and watched the blade turn so fast it almost looked like it wasn't moving. Next he put on safety goggles, then picked up a two-by-four and ran it across the saw, Gene happily inhaling the odor of freshly made sawdust. One of the halved boards had a big eye in it, so he firmly took hold of it by the ends and ran the eye straight into the saw, to see how he'd do when the blade caught and the wood jumped. He braced himself and handled it fine, still had all of his fingers and thumbs.

"Well, hell, maybe I'll try and build something," he said.

A LITTLE AFTER NINE Helen moved the CorningWare dish to the refrigerator so the stir-fry wouldn't completely dry out. Gene could heat it up when he got home. *Same old shit,* she thought.

THE FIRST DESK DRAWER he made didn't fit quite right, so Gene scrapped it and built a second drawer and this one fit perfectly, no wiggle or gaps. He then constructed another drawer and it too was perfect. The desk was ready for staining but he'd leave that for tomorrow, calling Stephen into work after school and letting him do most of it. That would give them a couple more hours together. Fatherhood, Gene had concluded, was mostly about putting in the time.

He knew that he should get going home, but it had been so long since he had done any work in the woodshop that he wanted to build one more thing, something quick and easy. Maybe a toy box or a footrest.

AT ABOUT ELEVEN Helen took the dish out of the fridge, walked it outside to the backyard, and tossed the stir-fry onto the lawn, for the birds and ants and muskrats to enjoy.

"Small steps," she said, going back inside. "Small fucking steps."

GENE CAME HOME at eleven thirty. By then Helen was in her room, reading the book *Eric* by Doris Lund. She listened to Gene walk through the house and into the kitchen, and then fish through the refrigerator in search of his dinner. It gave her some satisfaction knowing that his meal was out on the lawn, and that she had power to deny him the things he wanted, just as Gene had the power to deny her what she wanted. On this night, it had been companionship and conversation. And love. Just a little.

"Good night in there," Gene said a few minutes later, walking past her room.

"Nighty," Helen said, wondering if he'd try the door.

EPISODE 32

Saying Good-bye to a Ghost

At a neighborhood tavern called Ace's Hideaway, Jasmine sat on a bar stool, sipping her third Molson. She had been here less than an hour but had already been hit on twice: her "don't screw with me" shield was malfunctioning, she figured. The first would-be Casanova was Gary, a real estate agent with a sweaty bald spot, and the second one, Tucker, was a muscular firefighter who seemed to be dripping testosterone. Both men met the same fate: Jasmine let them spit out a few lines, then she said sorry, but she had given up on love, sex, everything messy, that there was only one man right for her and he was dead and buried. Gary retreated to the far end of the bar and Tucker rejoined several firefighter buddies at a booth.

There wasn't much for her to do, other than watch an old *All in the Family* episode playing on a TV perched above the bar. The sound was turned down so Jasmine studied Archie's lips, trying to figure out what he was saying to the meathead. If she had practiced lipreading before she saw Francis's ghost for the first time she might have understood him. What was he trying to tell her, she still wondered. Francis's lips were puckered as if in an "oh" sound, then they fell back, like he was forming an "aaa" sound. *Oh-aaa? Do-aaa, fo-aaa, go-aaa. Go back? Go back to start?* Was Francis trying to tell her that life was some kind of board game and that she needed to start over?

"Oh-*aaa,*" she said out loud, trying to think of other possibilities besides "go back to start."

"That just happens to be my favorite female noise," said Tucker, standing next to her again. "Ooooh, aaaah!"

She glowered at the firefighter. "Didn't I send you away?"

"Yes, but now I'm back. Look, I know your heart has been broken, but I'm not planning to mess with your heart, exactly. I just want to have a little fun. You remember fun, don't you?"

She sized him up. He had a small brain, a tiny heart, a ruined liver, and hyperactive sex glands. A caveman in jeans and an NFD T-shirt. Most of the world's ills, from pollution to war to domestic violence were due to men like Tucker strutting around while children starved and the planet shriveled. "I remember fun," she said.

"Good, let's go have some."

Jasmine took a swig of beer, considered spitting it in his face, then swallowed it and said, "All right. Let's have fun."

"Hot damn." Tucker smacked the bar, then gave the thumbs-up to his friends. His pals whooped and applauded.

She stood up and left with Tucker. "I suppose I should know your name," he said, holding open the door for her and placing a meaty hand on the small of her back.

"It's Daisy, like the flower," she said.

Outside, Jasmine pushed Tucker against the tavern's white brick wall and kissed him hard and bit at his lower lip until she tasted blood. "You want to do it right here?" she asked.

"A tigress!" he said, laughing. "Hell yes I do, but there are laws against that kind of thing. How about we go to your place?"

"I can't wait that long," she said, grinding into the fireman. "You have a car here? What kind of car do you drive?"

"An Escort. Not very roomy. Let's hit a motel. We'll be there in ten minutes."

"Nah, I'd feel like a slut. We better head to your place."

"There's a bit of a problem with my house."

"Oh?" she said, backing away.

"It's being fumigated as we speak. Damn dog brought home fleas. I have to get a motel room anyway."

She smacked his face. "Liar. You have a wife and twelve kiddies. Admit it. I can handle anything but lies."

He rubbed at his cheek and smiled, like he was used to getting hit by women, even enjoyed it. "Okay. Wife, one child. A girl, seven weeks old. Happy?"

"You should be ashamed of yourself."

"I am, but that hasn't stopped me."

"Go home to them."

"Don't be that way. How about just a quickie in my car? You're so beautiful. Please? Five minutes and then we'll go our separate ways. I'll pay you whatever you want."

"Twenty thousand dollars?"

"Not that much."

"Then go screw yourself."

As the fireman headed back inside Ace's, Jasmine sat on the bar's steps and started to weep. It was the kind of cry that was attached to her bladder so she had to clench down to keep from pissing her jeans. "What the hell are you doing?" she asked. Was she really about to sleep with someone who was the polar opposite of Francis?

After she was done sobbing, Jasmine stood up and marched to the parking lot, where she retrieved a tire iron from her car and went hunting for Tucker's Escort. When she found it she almost felt bad for him. The Escort was old, ugly, and dented all over from an accident or three, the kind of vehicle a family man without any money for a flashy sports car was forced to drive. *Poor baby.*

She bent the Ford's antenna into an upside-down U, then smashed out the rear window on the passenger's side, imagining Tucker vacuuming up the tiny shards with a car vac while cursing that feisty bitch he met at the bar. She moved to the rear of the Escort and was about to wind up and smash the windshield when she saw a sticker for Washington University stuck to the glass.

Jasmine dropped the tire iron. Francis wasn't saying, "Go back to start" that night in the bathtub, but "Go back to school." That's why he was still out there swimming; he was trying to save her life by sending her back to college. And that whole TV thing was a message to Jasmine that she must swim on, keep going, no matter how big the ocean, how mean the sharks, how far away the shore. She glanced at her reflection in the windshield and mouthed the words "go back to school." Yes, that was it, his exact words. Heeding Francis's ghostly advice, Jasmine decided to move back to Carbondale first thing in the morning. She'd spend these next weeks reading and healing, and then enroll for winter term.

She looked for a sign that Francis was nearby and found it a minute later when a breeze stirred some crimson leaves that had fallen onto the parking lot gravel. "Go on now," she said to her boyfriend's ghost. "I finally get it."

Driving to her parents' house, where she'd begin packing her bags, Jasmine kept telling herself that it was definitely Francis rustling those leaves and saying good-bye. From this point forward she was free to walk into a bathroom or turn on the television without having to worry about encountering some rotting, mute, swimming thing trying to talk to her. *Please?*

But then she saw Francis, in tattered black slacks, attempting to swim alongside the highway in a ditch that held maybe five inches of rainwater. She honked the car horn and wished him peace, but decided not to stop.

EPISODE 33

Somewhere on Jupiter

FRIDAY PASSED SLOWLY, as if worried what the night might bring, but finally it was time to leave for the observatory. Helen, Stephen, Nicole, and Crispy loaded into the Chevy, then Helen started the car and was about to back down the driveway when Gene came hurriedly out of the house and flagged her down.

"What's wrong?" she asked Gene as he neared the car.

"Nothing. I just decided that looking at a few stars won't kill me," he said, smiling in such a goofy way that Helen wondered if he was drunk.

"Hurray," said Crispy, undoing her seat belt then climbing in back, between Nicole and Stephen. Gene gazed at Helen to see if she was going to slide over and let him drive, and when she failed to budge he frowned and took the vacated front seat. Gene had many times let it be known that he always preferred to drive, hated to be a passenger. There was nothing important to do with his hands and feet.

"This is a surprise," Helen said, taking a quick look at her husband. "I thought you'd be excited about finally having the house to yourself."

"It's only a house," Gene said.

The sky was mostly clear, so on the way to the college Crispy took out the binoculars and leaned over Nicole, trying to get a glimpse of the first stars.

"Why all of the sudden interest in astronomy?" Gene asked.

"We're searching for Francis," Crispy let slip, covering her mouth too late.

"Shut up, dummy," Stephen said to his sister.

"Dad!" Crispy complained, still looking at the stars.

"That's more than enough," Gene said. "Don't make me make your mother stop this car."

Helen glanced at Stephen's reflection in the rearview mirror. "You're hoping to find Francis in the sky? Like in heaven? You're looking for heaven?"

"In a way," Stephen said.

"That's rather ambitious," Helen said. "But I suppose heaven has to be somewhere."

"Now I've heard everything," Gene grumbled.

As they pulled into a parking lot at Baldwin College, Stephen gazed at the observatory. It was designed like a turret, like it could spin suddenly and blow them to bits. Stepping out of the car he locked pinkies with Nicole, while Crispy, with the binoculars, tracked a spaceship that turned out to be an airplane. Stephen looked up: dozens of stars and planets glimmered and waited. If his brother was up there he was going to find him.

"Tonight's the night," he said confidently, as they walked to the observatory. Nicole kicked his sneakers and made him stumble, a code that translated "true love always." Crispy found the next UFO: it turned out to be a red warning light atop a faraway radio tower.

INSIDE THE STONE turret Nicole, Crispy, and Stephen ran up the steps to the observatory while Helen scouted out emergency exits, in case disaster was about to pounce on the Harrelsons once again. When finished, she found Gene standing in the doorway, gazing at the sky. "Coming upstairs?" she asked.

"I don't need any help seeing the stars," he said.

"It's a close-up view."

"That would ruin it, don't you think?" He stepped outside and

Helen joined him. A few gauzy clouds floated above them and a fresh handful of stars emerged every few minutes.

"It's all so beautiful," she said.

"Beautiful, yeah, but I don't trust any of it," he said.

She took hold of his hand. Strangely, he didn't pull it back.

"I'm messed up," he said, starting to shake.

"We're all messed up."

"Okay, but deep down I must have thought there was more to Francis than just his body. Hell, we changed a thousand diapers, nursed him through fevers."

"We?"

"All right, you did most of that stuff. Thank you. But my point was all of that happened, and we got excited when he walked for the first time and learned to catch a ball and ride a tricycle. And we, you, patched up all of his cuts and made sure he had three meals, and yet, despite all of the evidence, at some point I decided, subconsciously I suppose, that he was something greater than the sum of his physical parts, that Francis would survive any accident, or virus, or whatever the threat was, because no bullet or car or bug could get to *Francis*, no matter what happened to his body. That's why I can't accept this mess. He has to be out there. I can live my whole life not seeing him again if that's my lot, but not because he doesn't exist in this world. He has to be in Georgia, or Australia, or Timbuktu. Someplace I can get to."

Helen squeezed Gene's hand: it felt cold and malleable, like refrigerated cookie dough. She slunk a finger toward his wrist and found a pulse. It was drumming quickly. Life, we have life here, she wanted to say, but Gene would take it the wrong way, as a joke about his sexual vitality instead of what should be stunning news: the continuing miracle of a beating heart.

Gene wiped his wet eyes with a shirtsleeve, then looked at Helen and smiled. "Well, what do you know," he said. "Here we are on a college campus, acting like two love idiots again."

"That's the best kind of idiot to be," she said.

Helen let a minute pass, then announced that she was going back to teaching. "Next year at the latest. I need a bigger life, Gene. I have to do some good, while I still can."

"Great, fine," he said.

She was also still planning on leaving him, but she couldn't tell Gene, not yet. The first holiday season without Francis was going to be hell enough to get through, even without a big "I'm divorcing you" scene. But the divorce, or at least a separation, was a near certainty. This moment of closeness with Gene was just an aberration, Helen believed. Quite soon his defenses will regroup and call in reinforcements. She squeezed his hand again, forcing more blood into it.

STEPHEN, ALONG WITH Crispy and Nicole and ten or twelve others, listened to an astronomy professor with bushy salt-and-pepper eyebrows talk about the constellations and planets prominent in October. Stephen had positioned himself next to the professor, hoping to be the first to look through the giant telescope. Nicole and Crispy periodically jockeyed for the number two spot. "Enough of my words," said the astronomer. "I'm just a mammal in a suit pointing to the sky and saying 'looky looky.' Let's let the sky do its own talking. We'll start with the planets, if there aren't any violent objections."

The professor punched a red button on the wall beside him and the dome's window scraped open, slowly revealing a swath of stars. He bellied up to the telescope and looked through its eyepiece, turned a small wheel attached to the scope, checked the view, cranked a second wheel a half revolution, and said, "Got ya!" He turned and nodded at Stephen. The boy anxiously approached the telescope and put an eye to the eyepiece. *Be there*, he demanded of his brother.

OUTSIDE, BIRDS STARTLED by the window's opening began to resettle in the trees. The night was suddenly colder, so Helen leaned into Gene and placed her head on his shoulder. It used to be a safe place.

"There was more to our Francis than the physical," she said. "They broke his shell. That's all."

"I hope to hell you're right," he said. "I wish I could just believe, be a more normal kind of man. But when I try to hold on to ideas like the afterlife, or any of it, they slip away from me."

Gene was shaking again and some of his trembles went into Helen. *So much for iron fortresses,* she thought. Okay, she'd give him one last chance. In a week or two she'll abduct Gene and drive to the Michigan dunes, lead him to the spot where Francis was conceived and see how he acts. That's where it all began, in the space between two dunes. Not just Francis's life, but all of the days that followed: marrying Gene, the honeymoon in rainy Toronto, Francis's strangely easy birth, the day Francis said "moo" for "mama," his first day at preschool, safety town, half-day kindergarten, and then regular school. Homemade Valentine's Day cards, the piano lessons that didn't take, and then Stephen was born, and a second cycle of big and little days began. Three years later Crispy arrived, an unplanned pregnancy, and she must have been pissed about it because her birth was like trying to squeeze out a porcupine, and so Crispy's cycle of big and little days started. It was almost too much, managing these three overlapping and forward-moving lives, knowing better how it would be with the little ones, yet still surprised that things *worked*, that all of her children grew strong and beautiful, capable of thought, language, learning, locomotion, kindness, and art: all those finger paintings full of smiling people, sunshine and rainbows—more art than they could fit on the fridge. Yes, it was almost too much. But Gene did what he could, playing with the kids and occasionally changing their diapers, even though it made him gasp and lose the color in his skin. And Francis seemed to always be there, too, wiping jelly stains off Stephen's face or feeding Crispy her Gerber's, while Helen was doing the laundry or taking a teensy-weensy little rest. It was almost too much happiness.

In a way, she realized, Francis's death also began that night at the dunes. And Stephen's and Crispy's eventual deaths, for they are also children of that night. *God, do not take them before at least a hundred years have passed. They are my babies, not yours. Got it? DO NOT TAKE THEM.* "You cannot have them," she said out loud, her voice breaking.

"Have who?" Gene asked.

"Sorry, that came out wrong. I meant to say that I better go check on the kids, see if they've found heaven yet." She started to pull away, but Gene wouldn't let go of her hand.

"The kids are fine," he said.

She leaned into his shoulder again and started to shiver. "Must be a storm moving in," Helen said.

STEPHEN WAS ABOUT to let Crispy and Nicole take their turns, when the telescope, even though he had followed the professor's instructions and had not touched any of the knobs or wheels, started zooming in on Jupiter's red spot, then provided a view like a spaceship traveling through the planet's magnetosphere might, speeding through miles of orange and violet clouds packed with blue lightning, past a V of giant silver birds flapping in unison over white, glittering mountains, and following blood-red tributaries that led to an ocean where a man, Francis, was swimming in place, the cobalt sky above him offering a view of four moons and a million stars. Francis, still in his cross-country uniform, flipped onto his back and started lazily floating. The telescope zoomed in on Francis's ashen face as he smiled, then mouthed the words, "You found me." "I found you," Stephen mouthed back, while watching his brother back float through Eternity. Francis smiled, silently said, "Love each other," and turned over and started to swim away, across a vast ocean free of waves, and when he finally reached the horizon he shot out of the water and disappeared into the night sky, as if passing through a doorway.

Snowflakes began to fall through the observatory's window and landed on Stephen. He trembled, realizing that the telescope was a two-way, that he used it to see his brother and that Francis used it to see him. He turned in the chair and watched Crispy and Nicole catch snowflakes on their hands. He wanted to say something about the miracle he had just witnessed, but the professor spoke first. "Looks like the show is over, folks. We'll try again next month." He smacked the red button and the observatory's window started to noisily close. "I found you," Stephen mouthed again to his dead brother, before the sky was lost.

"DID YOU SEE Francis?" Crispy asked. Stephen shook his head and said there wasn't enough time. Nicole raised a skeptical eyebrow and took hold of his hand. Crispy grabbed Nicole's free hand and the three children snaked their way through the slow-moving crowd exiting the observatory.

Helen and Gene were nowhere in sight so they marched toward the parking lot, Crispy dragging her feet, making lines in the newly fallen snow. When they neared the Chevy they suddenly stopped. Gene and Helen were standing outside the car, holding each other as snowflakes tried to bury them. *They are hugging each other to death,* Stephen thought. Crispy started to break away, but he told her to wait, give them another minute. Stephen had a strange feeling that when they left the observatory they had stepped into a radically different world, one that not only didn't exist twenty minutes earlier but also couldn't have existed, a freakish world of snowstorms in October and hugging parents. They had better be careful not to disturb this newborn universe before it was sure of its footing. "One more minute," he said.

"I'm freezing my ass off," Nicole said, letting go of Stephen's hand and running to the Chevy, Crispy in tow. Helen and Gene saw them coming and separated and climbed inside the car. Gene, whistling, "It's beginning to look a lot like Christmas," fired up the Chevy and started the windshield wipers and rear-window defroster. Crispy and Nicole hopped in back, leaving the door open for Stephen, who was plodding to the car, letting the snowflakes attach themselves to him like cockleburs, wanting that free ride. He shook off some of the snow and crawled inside the Chevy, fastened his seat belt, and glanced at his parents and at Nicole and Crispy, all of their faces flushed due to the cold. They looked so temporary. Why would God favor ugly fairy rings, letting them resurrect and stick around for hundreds of years, over his reasonably attractive parents or a peppy Crispy or a freckled and sporty Nicole or a smart and kind Francis? He better start doubling his immortality research, Stephen thought, and begin some experiments like sneaking trehalose into the Harrelson and Strussman food supply, if he could find the stuff.

Helen turned toward the children and asked if they saw anything interesting with the college telescope.

Crispy aimed a thumb at her brother. "Ask the telescope hogger," she said.

Stephen was peering at the milky sky, imagining God furiously cranking out snow in limited but spectacular designs. "Just Jupiter," he said. "And some really strange birds."

GENE BACKED the Chevy out of the parking space and fell into a line of cars leaving the college. As they drove through town the snow thickened, the flakes oversized and clustered, as if teaming up. Stephen was almost embarrassed for God, spitting out these giant snowflakes, showing off. God playing with his snowmaking machine while cities burned, while kids' brothers flew out of wrecked cars.

Despite the near whiteout conditions Gene kept driving. When the Chevy fishtailed then slid on the snow-dusted road he corrected the slide by turning the wheel and then cutting it back the opposite way. "The key is not to panic when you run into trouble," he told his very captive audience. "My dad taught me that."

Stephen gazed at his father and wondered what was pushing him to face the blizzard head-on instead of waiting it out on the side of the road. Was he attacking the storm with his car, and God, too, maker of storms? *You stopped Francis but you're not stopping me, you're not stopping us, you son of a bitch.* Probably waited all year for this chance to even the score. Stephen understood his father's anger, would even root for him in any Gene versus God boxing match, but ultimately his old man didn't stand a chance.

"Pull over, the snow's too thick," Stephen said, in a voice more confident than he was used to. He suspected that those few words weren't born in his own throat but were borrowed from a stronger, wiser Future Stephen, that designer of safer cars and immortality researcher who lived in the wonder world of the next century. That man needed this kid to survive the blizzard.

"Good idea," said Helen. "Let's stop somewhere."

"I vote to pull over, too," said Crispy.

"Me three," said Nicole.

"I'm being ganged up on," Gene complained, but at the next intersection he pulled over at a closed Shell station, set the Chevy in park, and cut the engine. They'd stay there, he promised, until the snow let up and a salt truck scraped by.

Helen bought five sodas at a station vending machine, and they drank Cokes and root beers while listening to folk and bluegrass music on the car radio. Nicole belched the opening to "Rudolph the Red-nosed Reindeer." Crispy mumbled a prayer and then fell asleep, her head resting against the window and her mouth hanging open. Gene and Helen interlaced hands, two kids on a date. And the world vanished, the snow a white cloak surrounding the Chevy. No interstices, no proof that life existed outside of the car save a signal reaching them from a radio station in Carbondale and a muted flashing yellow caution light at the intersection.

Snowflakes kept tumbling down. A silent assault, like being attacked by feathers or flower petals. Were they all going to die tonight? Stephen wondered. Not impossible on a stormy planet prone to periodic ice ages.

Come back here, life, please. Stephen wanted the entire snow-stolen world returned. He wanted to see houses with lights burning inside of them, cars parked in driveways, and, down the road, a cornfield and a stand where a farmer sold pumpkins and gourds. Children making snow angels, and an old man shoveling his driveway while his dog, a black terrier, yipped at the falling snowflakes. A 7-Eleven after that, more lit houses, and then an elementary school with kid-made Halloween decorations in the windows. But the world stayed hidden.

Nicole set her head on Stephen's shoulder, said, "I promise not to fall sleep," but then was quickly asleep, her body jolting against his body as she crossed over.

In time the snow started to ease up a little, God's cranking arm tiring. Stephen could see the gas pumps and station, and a few frosted trees and power lines. The flashing yellow caution light had gained strength, though no one appeared to be on the road yet, except for a boy about Stephen's age in a parka and scarf, tramping down the middle of the street, kicking through the slush. A radio announcer then interrupted a song and said that the freak storm, already being called the Blizzard of '93, was passing quickly and should be out of the area within the hour.

"Thank God," Gene said. "We'll be home soon."

"It's been kind of nice here, all of us together," Helen said. "Almost all of us."

"A night we'll long remember," said Gene, rubbing Helen's hand with a thumb.

Hallelujah, Stephen thought, watching the snow thin out even further. It wasn't the start of a new ice age and they weren't going to die at this dumb gas station. He kissed Nicole on the forehead, wondered if that caused her to dream of being kissed, then shut his eyelids, thinking he might rest his eyeballs for a little while and try to come up with some *Wolf Boy* stories he could write.

"Bleep bleep bleep, bleep bleep bleep. Attention citizens of Forgotten City, Edenville, and the eastern colonies. The Intergalactic Weather Service has issued a blizzard alert for this region. All citizens should refrain from driving and space travel until the threat has passed. Due to the possibility of Level 3 toxic snow capable of eating

through flesh and metal, children and pets, both organic and robotic, should be brought indoors immediately . . ."

He opened his eyes and quickly realized that something wasn't right: that a million things weren't right. The car was moving, but it wasn't the Chevy but some kind of futuristic vehicle being piloted by Buddy Laredo. The radio had become a blipping radar screen, and a hologram newscast, the robot anchor warning of blizzard conditions, hung in the air. Helen was now a titanium android named Sarro, Crispy was Crystal, and Nicole had grown blue and orange wings and transformed into Lila Butterfly. Outside, refugee camps had replaced housing developments, strip mines had supplanted strip malls, orphanages were burning, and warplanes and spaceships patrolled the sky. A roadside sign aerated by a hundred bullet holes said, "Welcome to Forgotten City. We Hope You Survive Your Stay."

"THE GREAT BATTLE OF HEAVEN"

MINUTES LATER, ON A LANDING STRIP IN HEAVEN...
SEEMS AWFULLY QUIET...
KA-BLOOOM!
THUD!
HOLD ON!
THANKS FOR SAVING MY LIFE. EVER SINCE THE GREAT BATTLE OF HEAVEN BEGAN...
THE GREAT BATTLE OF HEAVEN?

"LED BY SATAN, THE ANGELS WHO WENT TO WORK IN HELL HAVE RETURNED AND ARE TRYING TO TAKE CONTROL OF HEAVEN AND BANISH GOD."
WE CAN'T LET THAT HAPPEN. TAKE ME TO THE DEVIL, IT'S TIME TO KICK SOME TAIL.
SATAN WAS LAST SEEN SOMEWHERE IN THIS PRIMITIVE FOREST.
I'M OUT OF HERE!
WATCH THOSE WINGS.
A LITTLE FLAME RETARDANT CAN GO A LONG WAY.
JEEPERS...

AH-HA!
ARGH! WHY CAN'T I FIND GOD'S MANSION?

SURPRISE!
OWY! OWY!
CRUNCH!

OH, IT'S YOU, WOLF BOOB. YOU ARE SAVING WAY TOO MANY LIVES IN FUDGESICLE CITY. CUT IT OUT, FELLA.

IT'S FORGOTTEN CITY. NOW GO HOME AND TAKE YOUR FALLEN ANGELS WITH YOU.
NAH. WHY DON'T YOU GO BACK TO FIDDLESTICKS CITY INSTEAD, WOLF BORE?

I SAID GO TO HELL!
AMATEUR!!

HAVE YOU FORGOTTEN WHO I AM?! I'M THE BADDEST DUDE IN TOWN!
I TRIP OLD LADIES! I EAT LOST DOGS! AND I STOLE YOUR BIKE IN THE THIRD GRADE!
I AIN'T GOIN' ANYWHERE, BOY.
I HAVEN'T FORGOTTEN...
NOW I'VE GOT SOMETHING FOR YOU TO REMEMBER.
EH?
I CALL UPON THE COLLECTIVE POWER OF THE LATE WOLF BROTHER AND OF ALL OUR WOLF SUPERHERO ANCESTORS! HELP ME!

POW!
GET OUT OF HEAVEN AND STAY OUT!!
YAAAARRRGH!!!

MINUTES LATER...
TH-THANKS S-SO MUCH FOR SAVING HEAVEN.

I'M HAPPY TO HELP OUT. AND IT'S GOOD TO SEE THAT YOU ARE GETTING WELL.

AS A SMALL TOKEN OF OUR APPRECIATION YOU CAN TAKE ONE RESIDENT OF HEAVEN TO EARTH WITH YOU FOR TWELVE HOURS.
12 HOUR EARTH PASS

MY BROTHER!
WHERE CAN I FIND JOHNNY LAREDO!?

HMMM... LET'S SEE...
TRY THE RIVER OF SOULS ON JUPITER.

G-GOOD LUCK, MY F-FRIEND.
KEEP HEALING...
YOU'RE OUR ONLY HOPE.

AT THE RIVER OF SOULS...
THIS MUST BE THE PLACE.

JOHNNY!

IS THAT YOU, DINGUS? WHAT ARE YOU DOING ON JUPITER?
I'M HERE TO TAKE YOU HOME! I HAVE A DAY PASS FROM HEAVEN!

OH BOY! LET'S GO!

SOON, ABOUT TWENTY KILOMETERS AWAY FROM FORGOTTEN CITY...
WAIT.

STOP.
WE CAN'T DO THIS.
WHAT'S WRONG?

I DON'T BELONG HERE ANYMORE.
THIS IS YOUR WORLD, NOT MINE. TAKE ME HOME. PLEASE.

COME ON, IT'S ONLY FOR THE DAY. WE'LL PLAY CATCH, WHISTLE AT GIRLS, STAY UP LATE TELLING EACH OTHER SCARY STORIES.
I'M SORRY.

I NEED TO SAY GOOD-BYE TO YOU, AND YOU NEED TO SAY GOOD-BYE TO ME.
IT'S TIME.

I'LL TAKE YOU BACK.
BUT FIRST I WANT TO SHOW YOU SOME-THING.

A SHORT TIME LATER...
CLOAKING DEVICE ON.
RATTLESNAKE AVENUE
WE HAD LOTS OF FUN HERE, DIDN'T WE?
AS MUCH AS THE WORLD WOULD ALLOW US, KIP.
LIFE IS A PRECIOUS THING.
WHICH IS WHY WE CAN'T WASTE ANY MORE OF YOURS.
HOME, DING-A-LING!
HOWL...
HONK HONK

LATER, BACK IN FORGOTTEN CITY...

WELCOME HOME, HONEY.

SO HOW IS YOUR GOOD FRIEND GOD DOING?
BETTER. HE'S ALMOST HIS OLD SELF.
AND I FOUND JOHNNY.

I WAS HOPING TO BRING HIM HOME WITH ME BUT IT DIDN'T WORK OUT.
I'M SO SORRY, DEAR.

COME INSIDE. I'LL FIX YOU SOME TASTY MARIGOLD BURGERS!

STAY TUNED, READERS!

OUR NEXT ISSUE WILL FEATURE A TEN-ROUND KICK-BOXING MATCH BETWEEN WOLF BOY AND THAT OLD RASCAL, THE ANGEL OF DEATH, WINNER TAKES ALL!

ACKNOWLEDGMENTS

I'd like to thank the following writers, artists, and professors for their generous help and encouragement: Michelle Boyajian, Deborah Kennedy, Jason Skipper, Bethalee Jones, Ann Stewart, Eric Goodman, Peter Orner, David Schloss, James Reiss, Keith Banner, Constance Pierce, Valerie Sayers, Steve Tomasula, William O'Rourke, M. E. Barnard, Kevin Ducey, Paul Ducey, Theodore Harakas, Daniel Kirk, and David Prok.

I am forever grateful to my agent, Daniel Lazar, for believing in *Wolf Boy*, and to my editor, Sally Kim, and the staff at Shaye Areheart Books for adopting and grooming the manuscript.

And thanks to my family and to my friends for love, support, short-term loans, and food.

CREATING THE *WOLF BOY* COMIC BOOK STORIES

By Evan Kuhlman with Brendon and Brian Fraim

EVAN KUHLMAN:

When I wrote the comic book sections of *Wolf Boy*, I was primarily thinking of them as guides for whatever artist the publisher and I would find to illustrate the novel, not finished stories that would work just as well without accompanying art. Comics are primarily a visual medium. There is little need for narrative, the pictures tell the story, and dialogue and character thoughts, when they occur, are normally quite brief. I had no illusions, then, that my descriptions of what was happening in the comic book stories, or for that matter much of the dialogue, would make it into the actual comics. What my editor Sally Kim and I needed were artists who could convert the stories into comics, while staying true to both the *Wolf Boy* story and the traditional comic book form, where art and words maintain a delicate balance. Fortunately we found Brendon and Brian Fraim, who transformed the stories into comics that, as some reviewers and readers have noted, are as good or better than anything you can find at your local comic book shop.

BRENDON FRAIM AND BRIAN FRAIM:

That was probably the biggest challenge with *Wolf Boy*, working from a "non–comic book writer's" script. Scripts for comic books are written very differently than novels. A twenty-two-page comic book is written with each specific action described for every panel on every page. Depending on the writer and the details, the panel descriptions can be a sentence long to more than a paragraph. The simple descriptions for the comic book sections in *Wolf Boy* could be liberating for some, allowing for the freedom of unrestrained creativity, or confining, not knowing what to do or how to pace the story flow. We seem to always work from comic scripts with less descriptions and details, so we were accustomed to letting our imaginations run wild. And that's what we did with Evan's *Wolf Boy* scripts, but there was a lot to figure out, such as determining the number of pages for each story, the number of panels on a page, et cetera.

This all comes from what comic book creators call storytelling. In comic books, storytelling can be defined in its most simplistic form as narration with illustrated images in sequence. At what pace does the story or scene need to flow? What emotion is the character in the scene feeling? Which is the best camera angle to show the action? These are just a fraction of all the considerations one must think about when drawing comic books. One of the rules for comic book artists is that the reader should be able to understand the story without the dialogue or word balloons. Imagine the scenes of Wolf Boy thinking about his departed brother Johnny. They wouldn't have the same impact if Wolf Boy was smiling, would they? There is too much to go into here about the art of storytelling, but if you're interested, check out *Understanding Comics* by Scott McCloud and *Comics and Sequential Art* and *Graphic Storytelling* by Will Eisner.

One of the challenges we did find with working on *Wolf Boy* was that a thirteen-year-old girl, Nicole Strussman, draws the comics in the novel. So, how do we approach this? Should we "dumb down" our style to make it look like a thirteen-year-old's, because we can obviously draw better than Nicole, or do we just draw the comics how we normally would and ignore Nicole's skill level? We decided that we would simplify our style a bit but keep it at our normal high level of quality for two reasons. The first reason was that we thought by keeping the level of quality of our art, it became an idealized version of what Stephen and Nicole wanted to achieve or even how Stephen saw the stories in his head. The second reason was that we knew this was going to be a publication with a huge amount of exposure for us, and we wanted to show off our skills.

EK:

Before they picked up their pens and pencils, the Fraim brothers, in order to better understand how the comics fit with the text portions of the novel, read the entire book. If Kip Laredo of Forgotten City was going to be a true mirror of Stephen Harrelson of Hollis, Illinois, they needed to know Stephen as well as possible. The first panels they drew were the opening panel in comic book one, where Wolf Boy is speaking with the angel as God watches the many monitors, and the opening panel in comic book three, where the Laredos are gathered around the television set and Mom is about to blow a fuse, literally. These were their audition drawings, and once Sally and I saw them they were offered the job.

BF & BF:

From out of the blue we received an e-mail from Evan asking if we would be interested in working on his Random House novel. Our careers were in a bit of a slump at the time, and we were on the lookout for the next big project. The strange thing about it was they only wanted to see two non-sequential panels. Usually in comics, the editors want to see three to five pages in sequence to make sure your storytelling abilities are up to par. But we did as they asked and were hired for the job.

EK:

Creating the comic stories was essentially a four-step process. I wrote the stories (step 1), then Sally and I decided which ones worked best in the novel and where. Yes, parts of some comic book stories ended up on the scrap heap, primarily to move the stories along, lest readers lose track of or interest in what was happening back in Hollis, Illinois. Story lines that never made it into the final novel included most of Lila Butterfly's early days in the caterpillar ghetto (cut for story flow reasons) and Buddy Laredo owning Forgotten City's last disco accessories shop (cut for excess silliness reasons).

BF & BF:

In case you're curious, there are no unused comic book pages. Everything we drew was used for the book. No deleted scenes!

EK:

When the Fraims were ready to start on the comics, they first drew rough storyboard style sketches (step 2), so we had a sense of how each comic would look on the page and how much space they would need. Brendon then drew the comics in pencil (step 3), and it was here where Sally and I often made suggestions for minor changes, such as making Lila Butterfly's expression fiercer in the panel where she is about to battle evil Flame-o, or adding humans to a bar scene dominated by aliens. Once the pencil versions were completed, Brian inked all of the panels (step 4), creating the final version of the comic books. Going from storyboard sketches to complete comics took about three months. The comics make up forty-six of the book pages in *Wolf Boy*.

To give you a better idea of the process, here is the evolution of three panels from the "Time Thy Enemy" comic, in copy, storyboard, penciled, and inked forms. When I first wrote the following lines in the manuscript I had no idea how the artist would chose to illustrate Wolf Boy essentially giving up, then his sudden empowerment by moonlight.

> Sick with sadness, Wolf Boy decided to stop his struggle to free himself. He hung his head and waited for the end to come.
>
> Just then . . .
>
> A blade of moonlight shined through a window on Wolf Boy, quadrupling his powers.

When the Fraims first sent us their storyboard sketches, it was thrilling to see my words slowly gel into comic book form, and I was pleased by the Fraim's often unexpected choices in layout and design. For example, I didn't anticipate that the moon would appear twice in side-by-side panels, but that ended up working quite well.

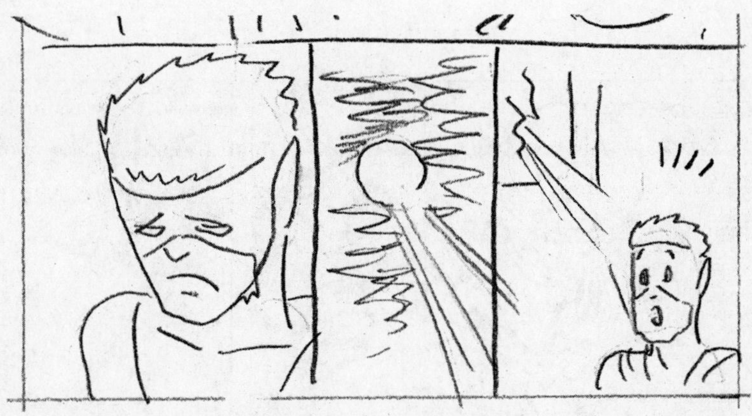

BF & BF:

Step 2: The storyboards, or the layouts, as we call them, are usually drawn very small, but we did them in a much tighter style for *Wolf Boy* than what we do for our other comics. Since Evan and Sally needed to see and understand them, they needed to be drawn better. But usually, no one other than us sees them, so the layouts are very simple and crudely drawn figures just to get the storytelling down and the poses of the characters in the story. One of us then takes them to our local copy place and enlarges them to 11 × 17, the standard comic book page size, and moves on to step 3.

EK:

Then Brendon drew the panels in pencil and did the lettering. As you can see, the Fraims ad-libbed the line from Clock Man and showed Wolf Boy's sadness through a simple thought cloud. Notice how the X marks indicate black shading, which was an interesting "penciling secret" for Sally and me to learn.

BF & BF:
The X marks are more of a comic book shorthand that tells the inker where to fill in the black areas—a time saver so the penciler doesn't have to shade every black area in with the pencil.

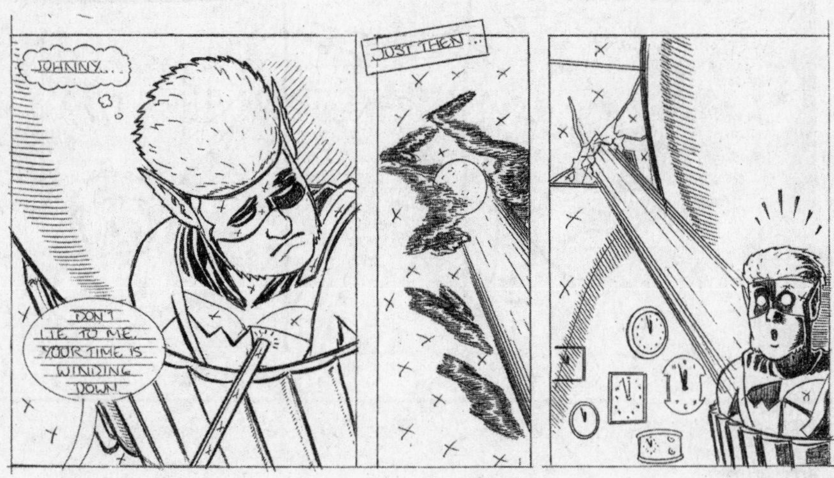

Step 3: Taking the enlarged layouts, Brendon uses his light box to trace the layouts onto the final page, a piece of 11 × 17 bristol board. This is the standard board for drawing comics. While tracing the layouts onto the bristol, he also does the lettering in pencil. That's right, in this computer age Brendon still does the lettering by hand, the old-fashioned way. Once the layouts and lettering are finished, he finishes drawing the page in his usual tight style. The page was then scanned into the computer and e-mailed to Evan and Sally for approval. We made any changes that were suggested and then readied the page for step 4. A change you may notice is that, originally, Wolf Boy didn't have eyeballs. It was decided that Wolf Boy should have eyeballs so the reader could see his emotional state better.

EK:
And then it was Brian's job to ink the final drawings.

BF & BF:
Step 4: When we refer to inking, what we mean is taking the pencil art and redrawing it in ink. This is done on the same board as the pencil art and is necessary to make the final art reproducible. There are a variety of tools one can use to be an inker, but Brian prefers to use a Raphael 8404 Kolinsky Sable brush size 3 and Koh-I-Noor Rapidograph technical pens. Brian uses the brush for almost everything on the page and then uses the Rapidograph pens for all the straight lines, long curves, and other technical drawings like cars, buildings, machinery, et cetera. He also incorporates a variety of french curves and oval templates to get all the shapes and curves needed in the drawing.

The inking stage is also when the lettering in the word balloons is done. Brendon does all the dialogue in the balloons by hand. The sound effects, all the "BOOM!" "CRASH!" "WHAM!" and the like, were also done by hand, though we have done them using computer fonts in the past. We decided to do all the sound effects by hand for *Wolf Boy* to keep the "handmade" feel of the comics. The cover to the second issue of the *Wolf Boy* comic is an excellent example of several different styles of typography that were hand drawn.

EK:

So there you have it, the nuts and bolts of the comic book creation process as it applied to *Wolf Boy*. A year later I am still amazed by the overall beauty of the Fraim's work and the archetypal "beyond the page" qualities of several of the panels: the broken Laredo family sitting and watching TV in the third comic, for instance, could be any family wounded by sudden loss. At times the Fraim brothers seemed to possess an intuitive sense of my intentions and hopes for the comic book stories, which is a bit odd since I didn't know Brian or Brendon before they were hired to do the illustrations. Finding the Fraims, and their availability and interest in the project, turned out to be an enormous piece of good luck.

BF & BF:

The pleasure in this project was all ours. The comic book sections were written with such imagination and potential that we really enjoyed this different process of creating comics. We both had more of a hand in developing the comics about Wolf Boy than we normally do with other writers, and both Sally and Evan were very receptive to our ideas. They affectionately referred to us as "the experts"—a title we enjoyed but still don't think we deserve. If it weren't for the brilliant story written by Evan, we wouldn't have had the opportunity to bring Wolf Boy's comic adventures to you, and for that, we are forever grateful. Collaboration is the key!

WOLF BOY

A NOVEL

EVAN KUHLMAN

READING GROUP GUIDE

ABOUT THIS GUIDE

On a frosty winter's day, Francis—the sweet, generous, responsible eldest child of the Harrelson family—dies in a car accident on an ice-covered highway, and Wolf Boy is born.

The earth doesn't rumble, no angels descend, and the sun doesn't weep. Nothing, in short, to signify the deep change that each member of the Harrelson household will undergo. Parents Gene and Helen turn away from each other and look inward, losing themselves in private fantasies. Ten-year-old Crispy devises elaborate strategies for her escape from the suffocating clutch of the Harrelson home and into the waiting arms of pop star Marky Mark.

But the heart of this family portrait is younger brother Stephen, who, along with his quirky and creative friend Nicole, crafts an alternative reality in which their comic book hero, Wolf Boy, battles the forces of evil, champions the powers of good, and fights to keep his family intact. Through Wolf Boy, Stephen finds an outlet for his grief and a concrete expression for his place in a family spiraling out of control and for all the natural yearnings and hopes of a typical thirteen-year-old. Wolf Boy's adventures are featured throughout the book, introducing a graphic-novel subplot that adds humor and visual interest and stretches the limits of the conventional novel.

The questions in this guide are intended as a framework for your group's discussion of *Wolf Boy*.

QUESTIONS FOR DISCUSSION

1. Throughout the novel, all of the members of the family express the belief that, had they done one small thing differently the day Francis died, the accident would not have happened. What did you think of each person's fears that they are to blame? Did you fault any of them for their actions (or lack of action)? Why or why not? Why do you think these thoughts occur to everyone? Have you ever felt similarly?

2. In the throes of loss, a couple of the characters have encounters with Francis in their dreams. Discuss these dreams and what you think the subconscious message of them is. Specifically, look at the first dream Stephen has, on page 15. What feelings do you see manifesting themselves?

3. Why is it that even after the loss of one son, Gene remains so distant from Stephen? Do you think it's a function of the difference in his relationships with each of them, as Stephen suspects? Or that he's simply too wrapped up in his own grief to see and help his children? Do you think that parents really do love one child more than the others?

4. Discuss the character of Nicole. What does she gain from her relationship with Stephen? What do they have in common, and what needs do they fill for each other? What kind of woman do you think she will grow up to be? Why does she collect "fucked-up things"?

5. Why does Francis keep appearing to Jasmine and Stephen either actually in water or in motion as if he's swimming? What is the significance of the water imagery to the novel?

6. In *Wolf Boy*, the reader is party to the thoughts and perspective of almost every character. Whose story resonated the most with you, and why? Who were you really rooting for?

7. Jasmine's reaction to her visions of Francis are different than Stephen's. Why is it that she is afraid, despite her love and the fact that she misses him? Several times, she sees the ghost, runs

away, then tries to return to it, only to find it gone. Why is Stephen never similarly fearful?

8. Consider the relationship between Helen and Gene. What is your opinion of their marriage, throughout the course of the novel? Did you ever think it was over? Did you think it should have been over? What holds them together in the end, and do you think it will last?

9. Discuss the cycle of Helen's grief. For one who seems to be dealing so well with her loss at the outset, she has the most dramatic breakdown of anyone in the family, culminating in the attack on Dotty at the County Clerk's office. What did you make of her? Did you see her angry outburst coming? What were your feelings about her while you were reading? What would you have liked to see her do that she didn't, or vice versa?

10. How did the comic book sequences add to your reading experience? What additional insights did you gain from seeing Stephen and Nicole's creation as it unfolds? What did you make of their vision of God?

11. Who or what do you think is to blame for Francis's death? Of the many players who blame themselves and the seemingly random events that led to the accident, which, if any, do you think directly led to his losing his life that day on the highway? Who or what would you hold accountable and in what ways?

12. On page 257, Helen and Viv talk about the concept of reincarnation as compared to the idea of Heaven and ask the question: Would you rather have your departed loved ones away from this world and someplace eternally peaceful and happy, or would you prefer to have them here, reincarnated somewhere, despite all the things that could go wrong in their new lives? They disagree on the answer. What do you think? What would you want for your loved ones who have passed away? Are you more comfortable with them being in this world, despite the fact that they could end up with a bad life, or do you prefer the idea that they have moved on to a better place, even if it is far away and unknown to you?

13. Discuss the moments of realization that all the characters have that snap them out of the haze of grief and back onto the path of their own lives. What similarities do you see between them?

14. Do you think that Stephen will see Francis again after the last encounter through the telescope? Why or why not?

ABOUT THE AUTHOR

EVAN KUHLMAN's stories have appeared in *Glimmer Train*, *Salt Hill*, *The Madison Review*, *Third Coast*, and *The Vincent Brothers Review*. He is the winner of the Short-Story Award for New Writers and several journalism prizes. This is his first novel. He lives in Ohio.